"TAKE OUT A DEATHWISH POLICY. THAT WILL GIVE THE MOVEMENT ALL THE PUBLICITY IT NEEDS."

For the first time in years, Roy Cos felt the itch of intrigue. "What's a Deathwish Policy?"

"You have your life insured in return for having an international drawing account for a million pseudo-dollars continually at your disposal—for as long as you live," said Forrest Brown. "If and when you die, the beneficiary collects the benefits."

Roy looked at him blankly. "But suppose you lived for years?"

Forry Brown laughed shortly. "Don't be a dizzard. From the moment that policy goes into effect, you're on the run. Some of the insured don't live the first day out. The Graf's hit men are the best-trained pros in the world."

He paused, then went on softly, "Just think of it—a million pseudo-dollars. You'd have plenty to buy yourself premium Tri-Di time. Every day, until they got you. And you'd be top news. Everybody and his cousin would listen in. You'd have your chance to put your message across such as no one has ever had . . ."

DEATHWISH WORLD

MACK REYNOLDS with DEAN ING

BAEN
SCIENCE FICTION
BOOKS

DEATHWISH WORLD

Copyright © 1986 by The Literary Estate of Mack Reynolds

A Baen Books Original

Baen Publishing Enterprises
260 Fifth Avenue
New York, N.Y. 10001

First printing, February 1986

ISBN: 0-671-65552-3

Cover art by Wayne Barlowe

Printed in the United States of America

Distributed by
SIMON & SCHUSTER
TRADE PUBLISHING GROUP
1230 Avenue of the Americas
New York, N.Y. 10020

Foreword

The greatest land acquisitions by any power in the history of the world took place without even the faintest threat of arms. Not a shot was fired by the conqueror in this unprecedented colonization program. Alexander, Caesar, Genghis Khan, and Tamerlane were tyros, by comparison, for none of them ruled a whole continent, much less two, with scores of neighboring islands.

And it was possibly the softest sell of all time. The United States Government simply issued a declaration that it welcomed any countries in North, Central, or South America, or the Caribbean, to join it, conferring all rights pertaining to American citizens, including the Guaranteed Annual Stipend, or GAS—sometimes called Negative Income Tax. Our English friends called it "the dole." They had seen it before. The English had seen everything before—including permanent decline.

Though the United States of America became the United States of the Americas without force, all was not simplicity. Military dictatorships, particularly in the banana republics, did all in their power to remain separate. Armies were ordered to fire upon mobs demanding admission to the new United States. But the soldiers laughed. One had to reach the rank of major to attain an income equal to that of a citizen of the United States on GAS.

So, with little strain on the Yankees, the Western Hemisphere assimilated into the United States of the Americas.

And, in the eyes of some, that was only the beginning . . .

Chapter One:
Horace Hampton

A battered hovercar pulled up in the parking lot behind the aged apartment building. There were few other vehicles there.

Three men got out and headed across the parking area for the back door. The one in the middle carried a cane and affected a slight limp. The other two carried tired-looking attaché cases. All three were dressed neatly, though their clothing was only a thin cut better than prole level.

The one in the middle looked up at the paint-flaked wooden building which was their destination. "You could sell it for an antique," he said.

One of the others grunted and told him, "You could sell all New Salem as an antique. Restore it—something like colonial Williamsburg over in Virginia. You could put up a big sign for the tourists: *'New Salem, Bible Belt Town, Circa 1900.'* "

They ascended the stairs to the second floor. Thus far they had seen nobody at all, which was understandable. They had counted on the total population being down at the park for the political rally. Aside from Tri-Di, there was precious little in the way of local entertainment.

On the second floor, the largest of the three men looked up and down the hall, dipped a hand into his side pocket, and brought forth a pair of thin black gloves. His right hand went back into the pocket of his shorts and came forth with a key. He unlocked the door and all three filed through quickly. He locked the door behind him.

The other two put their attaché cases and the cane on the room's center table and also donned gloves. They seemed in no hurry. They took out handkerchiefs and carefully wiped the cane and case with professional care.

Their leader, a black, went through the small apartment, which consisted of bedroom, bath, and kitchen, besides the living room into which they had entered, and checked it out carefully. He, too, had left his attaché case on the table after wiping it clean.

His companions looked about at the nondescript furniture, which included a broken couch and an old-fashioned rocking chair.

The two were of dark complexion, but there the resemblance ended. One was tall, wiry, and cougarlike of movement, black of hair and eye. The other was below average height, stocky, muscular. He tended to smile, while his companion was stoic of expression in keeping with his Amerind tradition. The smaller man was Latino.

The stocky one said, "Look, civilization." He pointed at the sole representative of modern furnishing, a small Tri-Di set.

The black, who had checked out the other rooms, returned and said, "Wizard, let's get the show roadbound."

Jose Zavalla took up the walking stick and began to unscrew the handle. His limp was gone. The handle came away and he upended the cane to let its contents slide gently into his right hand. It was a metallic tube about three feet long, threaded on one end externally, internally on the other. He laid it back on the table.

"Jesus, it's light," he said.

Tom Horse, the Indian, who was opening the two attaché cases, said, "Titanium alloy."

The sole contents of the hand luggage consisted of seven items, all carefully wrapped in foam rubber. Tom took them out gingerly, one by one, and laid them in a row on the table.

He said, "How's it look up the road, Hamp?"

Hamp was the black, a well-built, dark-chocolate man with features more caucasian than Bantu. He went over to the middle of the three curtained windows that lined the street side of the room. He pulled one curtain aside a bit and peered out, looking toward the north. From a jacket pocket he brought forth a small monoscope, twisted it open, and took off both lens shields. He put the eyepiece to his right eye, adjusted the focus.

He said, "Quite a turnout. Must be triple the population of the town."

"You don't hear the governor sound off every day in New

Salem and environs," Tom told him, unwrapping his packages with love care.

"Nice big banner above the speaker's stand," Hamp said. "Says, *America for the Americans*. Very sentimental. American flags at both ends. They look a little out of date. How many stars in the flag these days?"

"Who keeps track? About a hundred," Tom said. He had taken up the tube Joe had extracted from the hollow cane and was carefully screwing one of the other objects—a stubby rectangular affair—into the threads of its interior.

He said bitterly, "America for the Americans. You can be an Englishman or German whose parents came over twenty years ago and took out citizenship papers and you're an American. But you can have ancestors going back twenty thousand years on this continent and you're on the shit list."

Hamp said, still surveying with his monoscope, "You damn redskins are always complaining. Wait a minute, I think they've erected that speaker's stand thirty meters farther up than we figured on."

"Hell," the Indian said, taking up an aluminum rod from the table. One end of it was threaded. "I had it all zeroed, sighted-in, calibrated."

Joe, watching the assembly job, said, "That's the smallest breech I've ever seen."

"Uh huh," Tom said, winding the aluminum rod into a hole at the end of the deadly device. "This is a single-shot bolt action. But the bolt doesn't stick out to the side, it's this little knob on the top."

"What's that?" Joe said of the steel rod the other was manipulating. He had obviously never seen the thing before, assembled or otherwise.

"Part of the skeleton stock," Tom told him, tightening it firmly. The rod canted downward from the breech at an angle.

Hamp came back to the table where Tom Horse and Jose Zavalla were assembling the gun.

Tom was saying to Joe, "Hand me that other rod."

Hamp brought a quarter-liter bottle from an inner pocket. He studied its label for a moment, then unscrewed the top. He held it to his lips and took a long pull.

"What's that?" Tom said, not looking particularly happy as he twirled the new rod into its place.

"Cognac," Hamp told him. "Brandy. Have a slug. Listen, what effect is it going to have, their erecting that stand in the wrong place?"

"No thanks," the Indian said, still not happy about the liquor. "I'm driving. Besides, didn't you know we savages can't handle firewater?"

Joe said, "Brandy?" reaching for the bottle. "You mean aguardiente? Man, you blacks really live it up. I haven't had anything but syntho-gin for as long as I can remember." He took a hearty pull, brought the bottle down, and stared at the label admiringly. "V.S.O.P. What the hell's that mean?"

"It means it's worth its weight in diamonds," Hamp said. "Cloddies like us can't afford it. It's forced on me by admiring women who lust for my body. I brought it along as medicine—never know when I might get sick. How about the range, Tom?"

Tom had finished screwing the shorter aluminum rod into the back of the breech. It stuck out at a shallower angle, so that the two rods looked like two sides of a narrow triangle. Joe handed him the short, curved base, padded with holes drilled into it near both ends. There was no threading now. Tom simply inserted the aluminum rods in the holes and gave the base a whack with the heel of his right hand, driving it tightly home.

He said to the black, "It's not important. This scope we've got is an Auto-Range. Latest thing. Combines a range finder with a regular telescopic sight. No sweat. Hand me that silencer, Joe."

"You're sure?" Hamp said, pushing the back of his left hand over his mouth.

"Sure I'm sure," the other told him. "Take a minute or so to get it all sighted in again." He took the long tube Joe handed over and began screwing it into the barrel. It projected about a foot and a half when he had it tightly fitted. The silencer was about two and a half times the diameter of the barrel.

Tom said, "Where'd you get this sweetheart, Hamp? It's a handmade work of art."

"News reporter I used to know. Used to collect offbeat guns. He picked it up in one of the bush wars over in Africa. Assassin gun. For all I know, it's the only one ever made."

"He was crazy, giving this away," Tom said. "It's a real collector's item."

Joe handed him the telescopic sight. There were grooves gouged into the metal top of the barrel. The Indian carefully eased the sights into them. On the top and right-hand side of the instrument were small vernier screws for adjusting the crossed hairs inside the scope.

"Where's the fuckin' trigger?" Tom said, holding out his hand.

"Mind your fuckin' language," the Chicano told him. "I'm a lady on my mother's side." He brought forth from one of the attaché cases a twirl of tissue paper, unwrapped it, and handed the contents over.

The sliver of a trigger was slightly curved and there were threads on one end. Tom Horse began screwing it into place below the breech.

"Why couldn't that have been built in?" Joe said.

The Indian took up the assembled gun and handled it admiringly. "Same reason there's no protruding bolt. This whole thing is constructed to disassemble into parts that any man could carry around while wearing an overcoat. Most of it would go into deep pockets. The barrel would be the only thing that's clumsy. You'd have to suspend it from your belt, or maybe by a strap under your shoulder."

Hamp took another slug of the cognac and looked at his watch. He said, "The governor and his committee ought to be showing up any time. Let's move this table over to the window."

While the others were doing that, Tom went to one side of the room and selected a straight chair. He put the chair next to the end of the table, which now stood against the middle window, and took from one of the attaché cases a very light, bipod rifle support. It was of aluminum, held in place by an elastic strap. He slipped it over the end of the rifle and its attached silencer.

He said to the black, "How does it look now, Hamp?"

Hamp had his monoscope to his eye again. "Wizard. They're filing onto the speaker's stand, everybody shaking hands and smiling at each other. Very jolly. They've really got a turnout. The crowd must have come from all over the county."

"The more the merrier," Joe growled. "Bastards will have something to see this time."

Hamp said, "Now here's the setup, one last time, Tom, just to be sure. The speaker's stand is about twenty-five feet high. Old Drive 'Em Out Teeter stands way above the assembled mob so that they have to throw their heads back to gawk at him. He likes to speak with a rail before him so he can lean on it and thump it from time to time. Somewhere along the line he must have seen some of the old historic films of Mussolini hassling the wops from his balcony."

"All right, all right," Tom said impatiently, bringing forth from one of the attaché cases a black rubber block in which were stuck three long, pointed cartridges. They were of small caliber but necked down from a large casing. He pulled one round out and put it on the table next to him. The brass casing gleamed softly in subdued light.

Hamp was saying, "Teeter doesn't like to speak directly into a mike. Instead, he has two of them hooked into the railing to each side of him, about two meters apart."

"Right," Tom muttered, brushing the window curtain slightly to one side so that he could see up the street. "So I focus a meter beyond the mike nearest us."

Hamp pushed his left hand over his mouth again. "Wizard."

Joe had stationed himself at the window behind where the Indian was setting up his assassin rifle. He said, "You better get your ass in a hustle. Here comes the chairman."

"Plenty of time," Tom said evenly.

Hamp took up the small bottle of brandy, now nearly empty, and took a quick swig before setting it down on the table. Tom shot him a disapproving glance but said nothing.

The Indian glued his right eye to the telescopic sight. It had already been sighted in, but he reached out delicately and adjusted the focus. The chairman's face leapt into clarity before him.

The marksman took the nub of the bolt in his thumb and index finger and gave it a counterclockwise twist, pulling the bolt back in its groove to reveal the trough for the long bullet. He took up the cartridge and inserted it, thumbed the bolt back home and flicked it clockwise, smoothly locking it into place.

He settled comfortably into his chair, pushed the curtain of the window back a little more.

"Open it," he said softly.

Hamp pushed the window up sufficiently to make room for firing.

The Indian snuggled into position behind the scope eye-piece. "All right, Governor Teeter, last of the racist rabble-rousers," he murmured softly. "You've sounded off once too often."

On the outskirts of the teeming crowd which had gathered to hear Teeter, two blacks stood inconspicuously in the shade of an ancient live oak, near the trunk. From their distance, the white-clad speaker was hardly distinguishable, but the loud-speaker system brought his words clearly enough and his fist-shaking gestures of emphasis could not be misunderstood.

One of the blacks said softly, "Old Drive 'Em Out is in full voice today. I'm beginning to suspect he doesn't like bloods."

Without warning, the figure on the speaker's stand came to a shocked stiffening; red blossomed out in a large blot on his white shirt. He staggered for a moment and then slowly crumbled, falling out of sight.

One of the blacks shook his head. "Drunk as a lord," he said.

The other surreptitiously brought a transceiver from his pocket, activated it, and said softly, "Bullseye." He put the communication device back into his pocket and said urgently, "Let's get the hell out of here, Jackie."

In the run-down apartment, Hamp picked up the assassin rifle by its fore end, its bipod still hanging free, and took it into the bedroom. He pulled the bipod off, held up the aged mattress with one hand, and stuck the gun and stand under it. He smoothed out the bed neatly and returned to the other two.

Joe said, in deprecation, "It won't take them long to find that."

"Who cares?" Hamp said. "It's untraceable."

He picked up the rubber container holding the two unspent rounds and dropped it into a side pocket, then took the small flask of brandy. After offering it to both Tom and Joe Zavalla, who shook their heads, he finished it. "Let's drag ass," he said.

He unlocked the door, let them precede him, and then

relocked it. They headed for the stairs, unhurried as before. They'd left the cane and attaché cases behind.

Down in the parking lot, they stopped before a waste receptacle, stripped the gloves from their hands, and dropped them in. Hamp also discarded the empty bottle and the unused ammunition after wiping them.

They got into their hovercar, all three in front, the black driving, and unhurriedly left the parking area.

They emerged onto the main street and headed away from the park where the rally had been taking place. Even at this distance, they could hear the swell of shouts and screams, though almost drowned by police sirens.

"Couldn't have happened to a nicer guy," said Joe, who was sitting by the window, his vague smile on his lips. "I wonder how many men, women, and children have been killed as a result of his racist rantings?"

They left the environs of New Salem and headed, at a moderate speed, out into the countryside. They passed a sign welcoming all to New Salem.

"Salem," Tom said, musing. "Wasn't that where they burned all the witches?"

"Yes," Hamp told him softly. "This time we reversed it and clobbered a witch hunter. Joe, there's a bottle in that glove compartment."

But the Indian beside him shot the black one of his looks from the side of his eyes and said quickly, "Take it easy, Hamp. The day's not over. We wouldn't want them to hang a drunk driving romp on you."

"Wizard," Hamp said. "But I'm not drunk."

"You don't have to be. They'd book you anyway, if you showed any indication at all of drinking. Joe, throw that bottle out."

Joe took the half-liter of booze from the dash compartment and looked at the label sadly before tossing the bottle far off the road into a field of sweet corn.

For a while, they drove along silently, each absorbed in his own thoughts in the anticlimax of what they'd just been through.

Joe said finally, "That was a good spot to pot him from. How'd you locate it?"

Hamp said, "Not much trouble. Teeter always starts off

his campaigns in New Salem. It's the oldest town of any size in the state. That apartment was ideal. The renter lives alone and goes up to Chicago six months of the year to work on some part-time job. He hates the big city, so he returns here for the rest of the year. As it turned out, we needed the place just when he didn't.''

Tom looked over at him. ''How'd we find out about it?''

''One of our whitey members came to town and hung around for a while in bars in the neighborhoods we were interested in. He finally got to talking to this fellow.''

They held silence for a while. There was a certain tenseness in waiting for what they knew was to come, the inevitable.

Hamp said, ''Oh, oh. Here it is. Road block.''

Up ahead were two State Police vehicles barring the way. There were also two police hovercycles. Of the seven officers, two carried automatic Gyrojet carbines; the others, holstered side arms. There were red lights flashing above the cars.

Hamp said, ''Play it cool. No temper, Joe, and no wisecracks.'' They came to a halt some thirty feet from the barricade.

Two of the police troopers strolled toward them. About twenty feet off, one of them stopped and stood there, his legs parted, his holster unsnapped. The second trooper came up to the driver's window and looked in at them.

Hamp said, his voice modulated, ''What's the difficulty, officer?''

The state trooper said, ''I'll ask the questions, boy. Now, you three get out of there and line up against the side of this here car. Spread your legs and lean your hands up against it.''

Hamp said, his voice still quietly even, ''What's the charge, officer?''

Joe had brought a pocket transceiver out, flicked back the cover, activated it, and said, ''We have been stopped by police and ordered from our vehicle, evidently to be searched. The police officer's badge number is 358.''

The trooper looked at him coldly. He was a rawboned, lanky type, probably in his late twenties. His uniform boasted all the glory of a Hungarian brigadier. He said, ''Who you talking to?''

Joe smiled. ''A friend.''

Hamp repeated, "What is the charge, officer? Isn't a warrant required to search a citizen?"

"Don't smartass me, boy," the trooper said grimly. He dropped his hand to his Gyrojet pistol.

The black said, still mildly, "My name isn't Boy. It's Horace Greeley Hampton. And I consider myself acting under duress."

He opened the door of the hovercar and got out, followed by Tom and Joe, but not until Joe had said into his transceiver, "The police officer called Mr. Hampton 'boy' contemptuously and made a gesture toward his sidearm, reinforcing his demand that we be searched."

The three lined up against the car, as ordered, and the second trooper came up to help in frisking them. They were thorough.

The second state policeman said, as though disappointed, "They're clean, Rance."

Rance said, "Go through the car." While the other was obeying, he said to Hamp, Tom, and Joe, "Okay, you three. Let's see your ID."

They handed over their Universal Credit Cards, which performed the functions of identity cards, driver's licenses, and everything else a prole needed for identification.

He looked at them carefully, brought forth a police transceiver, and read off names and identity numbers into it, then asked for a police dossier check of the data banks.

He turned his pale eyes to them. "Horace Greeley Hampton, Tom Horse, Jose Angel Mario Zavalla. Born in Ohio, Colorado, and Texas. All on Guaranteed Annual Stipend." He sneered at that—an overly done, artificial sneer. "What're you doing in this state?"

"We are on our way through," Hamp said, his accent still that of an educated man.

"Where'd you just come from?"

"New Salem."

"Oh, you did, eh? What were you doing there?"

"We went over to see the rally, listen to the governor's opening campaign speech."

"Then what're you doing here?"

"The crowd was so large that we couldn't get anywhere near the speaker's stand. Besides, there had been quite a bit of drinking. Some of the, ah, gentlemen in the crowd didn't seem to like our complexions. At any rate, we decided to return to where we're staying.''

"Where's that?"

Joe said into his transceiver, "We're being questioned, although thus far no charge has been made and we have not even been told whether or not we're under arrest. Our vehicle is being searched without our permission and without a warrant.''

Rance glared at him but forced his eyes back to Hamp, who seemed to be the spokesman of this unorthodox trio.

Hamp said, "We're staying at the We Shall Overcome Motel, near Leesville.''

The washed out, grayish eyes of the trooper tightened infinitesimally. He looked at Joe and said, "And that's who you're talking to?''

Joe smiled his constant smile. "That's right, Mr. Policeman, sir.''

Hamp looked over at him and slightly shook his head.

The second trooper emerged from the vehicle. He said, grudgingly, "It's clean, Rance.''

Rance's police transceiver buzzed and he listened to the report on the police dossiers of the three, his face less than pleased.

Joe said, in his communication device, "We have been checked out in the police data banks and have obviously been cleared; however, we are still being held without charge, without warrant, and . . .''

Rance began to go red around his neck. "Take that damned thing away from him," he snapped to the other trooper, who was leaning back against the car, arms folded. He came erect gladly and started in the Mexican-American's direction.

Joe began to retreat backward, saying quickly into his transceiver, "State Police officer Number 358 has ordered my transceiver taken. One of us is a black; notify the nearest Nat Turner Team. One of us is an Amerind; notify the Sons of Wounded Knee. I am a Chicano; get in touch with the Foes of the Alamo. Notify our legal department! Notify Civil Liberties. Alert the Reunited Nations Human Relations . . .''

The trooper was on him, grabbing the transceiver away. Joe smiled and winked at him.

Hamp, his face very serious, turned to Rance and said, "You're in the dill now, officer."

The trooper's face was suddenly wan and he was breathing deeply. He looked from Hamp to Tom and Joe, then back again. His tongue came out and licked dry lips.

"All right," he said. "Okay. You can go. We have nothing to hold you on. The governor was shot in New Salem an hour or so ago." He took in a deep breath. "It's our job. No hard feelings, fellas."

Joe smiled, "In that case, fuzzy, how about a donation for the Anti-Racist League?"

"Get the hell out of here," Rance snarled. He turned to the other trooper, who was looking at him in surprise. "Give them back that transceiver and their IDs."

When the three had left, the second trooper looked at his companion. He said, "What the hell, Rance. You practically kissed their asses and they were driving right from New Salem."

The other glowered at him. "How'd you like somebody to toss a grenade into your living room? Those bastards never quit, once you're on their list. They don't care if it takes years. Sooner or later they hit you."

Hamp, Tom, and Joe drove along in silence for a time, letting the tension drain away, until Hamp turned to Joe and said, "What in the hell's a Nat Turner Team?"

And Tom Horse added, "Or the Sons of Wounded Knee?"

"Damned if I know," Joe said, grinning. "I made them up as I went along. Same with the Foes of the Alamo. What's the old gag? If there'd been a back door to the Alamo there would never have been a Texas."

The We Shall Overcome Motel was well done. Extending over quite a few acres, it was completely surrounded by a high, heavy, barbed-wire fence. A strong steel gate spanned the dressed stone entrance and, behind it, several public buildings, including a large store, a recreation hall, and a restaurant. An auto-bar clubroom stood off to one side of these, near a good-sized swimming pool, which was crowded with swimmers and sunbathers, mostly of dark complexion but with a scattering of whites.

In the center of the compound was a sizable grove of trees,

largely pines. A person could wander into the pine grove, find a bit of a clearing, and spread out on his back, to stare up at clouds or stars and feel, so temporarily, free.

The area around the little forest was devoted to mobile homes and campers of all varieties. At present, a small mobile town with an art colony theme—some forty homes in all—was temporarily parked en route to Mexico and parts south. Not all proles on GAS crammed themselves into mini-apartments in high-rise buildings in the cities.

Hamp pulled up before the administration building, dropped the vehicle's lift lever, and switched off the engine.

Maximillian Finklestein issued from the office and strolled over toward them. He was a tallish, sparse, stoop-shouldered man of about forty-five. As they emerged from the hovercar he came up and said, "How was the rally, chum-pals?"

Tom shrugged and said, "We didn't stay. Too big a crowd. We heard there was a lot of excitement after we left. Somebody took a shot at the governor."

Finklestein clucked his tongue. "Imagine that. Was he hurt?"

Joe said, "We got the impression he was hit. Didn't you see it on Tri-Di?"

"I was working," Max told him. "Come on in and have a drink; we'll check the news."

Hamp said, "Your invitation appeals to me strangely, especially the drink part, but I want to stretch my legs a little first."

"Me, too," Tom said. "A little stroll before the firewater."

The three of them, accompanied by Max, set out leisurely for the wooded area.

They entered the trees, for the time holding silence. After a couple of hundred feet they reached a small clearing, the ground well covered by pine needles and leaves. Then, in silent agreement, they all stretched out on their faces in a starlike arrangement, their heads close together. Their faces were to the ground, partially into the needles and leaves. Even the best shotgun mike would play hell listening to them now.

Max said softly, "What happened?"

"Plumb center," Tom whispered. "The capslug shattered

right on his chest and splattered red goo all over his shirt. I could see his face go pale and his eyes pop. He fainted.''

The motel manager growled, ''The loudmouth bastard'll know it could have been the real thing. Might even rethink his racist campaigning if he's smarter than he is bigoted. How tough were the fuzzies?''

Hamp took over the report, also whispering into the leaves. ''About as expected. They hated it, every minute of it, and they hated us and our uppity ways, but they weren't about to stick their necks out. They'll toss it all into the laps of the IABI. They've heard all the silly rumors about how tough we are. They had no intention of becoming martyrs for a state cop's pay.''

Finklestein said, ''I've already got instructions for you. You three will be under special observation. The IABI isn't completely dull. They might not dig up proof but they'll strongly suspect you of the burlesque assassination. Your dossiers will tell them you're members of the Anti-Racist League. You were admittedly present in New Salem and Governor Teeter was an anachronism, the last of the really all-out rabid politician racists. They know it was just a matter of time before we zeroed in on him. They'll probably be surprised we didn't actually bump him off.''

''Swell,'' Tom said into the leaves, a note of extreme weariness in his voice. ''So what do we do now?''

''You break up as a team. None of you will continue to operate in this section.'' Max fished in a jacket pocket. ''Tom, you go to southern Illinois. You're an unknown there. Go to a town named Zeigler and report to the section leader. Here's the address.'' He handed the paper over.

Tom looked at it and said, ''What do I do there?''

Max seemed surprised at the question. ''I haven't the vaguest idea,'' he told the Indian. ''I understand that it's a pretty backward part of the country: fundamentalists, high illiteracy rate—you've seen it all before. But I don't know what they'll have you doing. You might as well take off. No need for you to know where Hamp and Joe are assigned.''

''Yeah,'' Tom said, scrambling to his feet and stuffing the address into his shorts pocket. He looked down at the other two, hesitated for a moment, then said gruffly, ''Hang loose, chum-pals.''

They both looked up from the leaves and nodded. The team hadn't operated together for very long, but they'd been more than unusually compatible.

"So long, Redskin," Joe said softly.

When the other was gone, the remaining three returned their lips to the pine needles and leaves.

Max said, "Joe, you head south for Mexico City. Here's your contact." He handed another note to the Chicano.

"Mexico?" Joe said. "I've never been down there. What do I do?"

"No need for me to know. But the way I understand it, there seems to be an unlikely situation, particularly in the big centers like Mexico City and Monterrey, where all the best positions wind up in the hands of whites of Spanish descent. Next in the highest job and power echelons are those with a high percentage of Spanish blood. Mestizos, they call them. And, surprise, surprise! Guess who's the low man on the totem pole?"

"The full-blooded Indian," Hamp growled. "How do they get around the computers supposedly selecting the best citizens for whatever job comes up?"

Max grunted at that. "Undoubtedly, the same way they do here. The rumors continue that sometimes the data banks are jimmied, rigged. But the programmers know angles. And that will probably be one of Joe's tasks."

Joe sighed. "Same old story," he said. "Fuck the colored races. What's my cover?"

"The obvious one, most nearly the truth. You're on GAS and can't find a job up north. So, since you're bilingual, you head south hoping to use your two languages to advantage in getting work." Max hesitated a moment before adding, "You'd better get underway, too. You never know. The IABI could show at any time to pick you three up."

Joe came to his feet. He smiled at Hamp, warmer than his usual humorless smile. "Nice knowing you, Blood."

Hamp said, "Feeling's mutual, compañero. Luck."

Joe left.

The two remaining readdressed themselves to the ground.

Hamp said, "What about me?"

Max said, "Your request for a leave of absence has been okayed." He looked over at the black from the side of his eyes. "How come, Hamp? There's a hell of a shortage of top men and, from what I understand, you're continually taking leaves."

"Wizard," Hamp said in deprecation. "But we'll have fewer field men than ever if you wear us down to the point where we lose efficiency. I've been in the trenches too often in the past couple of months. I need a breather. I think I'll spend some time in New York. Where do I report when I'm unwound?"

Max handed him a note. "To me. As usual, I haven't the vaguest idea of what your next assignment will be. However, there's one item of business on your way back east, a new contact. A Lee Garrett, who lives in Greenpoint, Pennsylvania."

"A new contact?" Hamp said, moderately indignant. "Have I sunk to the level where you're using me for elementary propaganda?"

"Headquarters seems to think that this one is a better prospect than usual. A whitey. Not on GAS. Better than usual education. Our local section isn't too top-level, so they want a good agent to make the initial contact with Garrett." Max handed the black another note.

"Wizard," Hamp said, coming to his feet and brushing pine needles from his shorts and jacket. "Do I leave now, like Tom and Joe?"

Max stood, too. "Why don't you come over to my place and we'll talk some shop and have a couple of quick ones. Tom and Joe never did get that drink I promised them."

"They're dedicated," the other snorted. "Both of them hardly touch the stuff. Lead me to it. As a matter of fact, I've got some good French brandy in my luggage. We can crack that."

Max Finklestein wondered vaguely how the other could afford a bottle of imported brandy. It would take a month of GAS credits to buy such a potable.

Chapter Two:
Franklin Pinell

When the two corrections officers from the prison handed
Franklin Pinell over to the court bailiffs in the Justice Department Building, he was still handcuffed to the heavier-set,
tougher-looking guard. While the second officer was getting a
bailiff to sign the receipt for their charge, the prisoner was
freed of his cuffs. The guard dialed the appropriate number
on the shackles and then put his thumbprint on the tiny
screen. The titanium alloy handcuffs came away.

"There he is," he said, obviously bored. "Frank Pinell.
Supposed to be tough. Haven't you got cuffs for him?"

"No," the bailiff said. "We don't usually use them."

The prison guard looked the two court officers up and
down. The older one was pushing sixty, much overweight,
and the second didn't look much more competent.

"He's supposed to be tough," the guard repeated. "A
killer. You fellas heeled?"

"We don't usually carry guns," the other said.

Frank Pinell stood there rubbing the wrist that had been
confined. He looked at the prison guards emptily as they
turned to leave. "Be seeing you," he said.

The one to whom he had been handcuffed snorted back
over his shoulder. "Not where you're going, chum-pal."

When they were gone, Pinell looked at the bailiffs.

"This way, son," the older one said, and then added
gruffly, "Tough luck. I've got a son your age."

The three of them ascended marble stairs to the second
floor and then proceeded to the left down the wide corridor.

The younger bailiff said, "Those types see too many crime
Tri-Di shows. What good do they think it would do you to
escape? Without a credit card you couldn't buy a stick of
chewing gum, or a ride on the metro, not to speak of a meal.

You have no home and it's a felony for any friend to take you in.''

"Stop it, stop it," Pinell said without tone. "You're breaking my heart."

He was twenty-five years of age, looked surprisingly athletic as proles went, was medium tall, clean and neat even in less than top quality garb, and his bearing would have passed muster in any upper class gathering. His dark brown hair was worn full and combed directly back. His eyes were a dark green and his rather long face had a Scottish cast. In less plebeian dress he might have been typed as a graduate student or a junior executive.

"Okay, son," the older one said. "Here we are." He opened half of a heavy double door and the bailiffs led their charge through before them.

The judge looked up from his desk. He was dressed in his traditional black robes and resembled the older and kindlier of his two court officers. That is, he was about sixty, overweight, his face lined not with an immediate weariness but with one that had accumulated down through the years.

"Franklin Pinell, Your Honor," the younger bailiff said.

"Yes, of course, James." The judge looked at the prisoner. "Be seated, Pinell." Then back at the guards. "Please wait outside. I believe you already have your instructions."

"Yes, Your Honor." The younger bailiff hesitated, then said, "Judge, the corrections officers from the prison said Pinell is reputed to be dangerous."

"Indeed?" John Worthington looked at the youthful prisoner. "Are you?"

Frank Pinell hesitated, then let air out of his lungs and said, "Under the circumstances, no." He took the chair across from the judge's desk.

"Very well, that will be all, James, Bertram."

The bailiffs left and the judge sighed, studying the prisoner for a moment. Pinell returned the scrutiny, his expression saying, *it's your ball, start bouncing it.*

The judge sighed again and took up a report from before him. He said, "I am afraid we have bad news for you, Franklin."

"I expected it."

The judge ignored that, looked at the report, and said,

"The legal computers have found you guilty and recommend deportation."

Frank Pinell's face went blank. "Deportation? But I've got only one major . . ."

The other was shaking his head. "Your criminal dossier lists four felonies. As a four-time loser, your sentence becomes deportation for life."

"But Your Honor, those first two romps were kid stuff. I was only in my early teens."

"But you served time for your offenses, no matter how short, as you did for your third, ah, romp. The fact that your first felony amounted to no more than taking an unguarded hovercar for a joyride is beside the point. You served several months in a youth detention camp. And your second offense and third . . ."

"All right. Who can argue with a damned computer? Isn't there any way I can appeal?"

"Not at this point," the judge told him. "If you can claim new evidence later and it is made available to the data banks, you can then appeal. Appeals are seldom successful. The computers don't make mistakes, Franklin. Judges and juries used to, perhaps, but computers don't."

"It's a hell of a thing to call justice," the younger man said bitterly. "Being thrown out of your own country."

The judge looked at him in weariness and said, "What was it the old cynic asked? 'Come now, the truth; who among us would be satisfied with justice?' The fact is, your fourth crime was the only really reprehensible one. But it was homicide, and under rather strange circumstances. Had that been your only felony, you would not have been deported. Our penal system allows for rehabilitation even of murderers. But with three other felonies on your record, the computers opted for deportation."

"I don't want to live anywhere except in the States," Pinell said.

"Unfortunately, that is now out of your hands, Franklin. You should have considered it sooner. Deportation makes sense, from the viewpoint of the government. Some decades ago, when the penal laws were revamped, they found that it cost more to keep a criminal in prison than to send him to Harvard. As it is now, the government will no longer be put to the expense of keeping you in prison, or even on GAS. Nor will you be free to commit new felonies upon serving your time or being paroled.''

The older man put that part of it behind him and said, ''You will be issued one thousand pseudo-dollars in the form of Swiss gold francs. You will be deprived of your Universal Credit Card, and you are forbidden ever again to enter this country.''

''What happens when the thousand runs out?'' the other said, his voice still low.

''That is not the concern of the United States of the Americas. You make what arrangements you can in your host country.''

Frank Pinell squared his shoulders. ''All right. What country are you sending me to?''

''To a certain point, that is your decision. Obviously, the advanced nations will not accept you. However, some Third-World nations will take you under certain circumstances. Their situation is something like Australia and the American colony of Georgia when they were first colonized. They needed population desperately, so England allowed convicts to decide whether to spend their sentences in jail or to be hanged, as the case might be, or to become colonists.''

''What's that got to do with here and now?'' Pinell said, impatient at the older man's ramblings.

''In some nations, particularly in Africa and Indonesia, even partially educated persons are in very short supply. Some of them, upon gaining independence from the former colonial powers, had no university graduates whatsoever. No doctors, no engineers, no lawyers—no one really competent to hold high government office. Later, with the support of the Reunited Nations and the assistance of the more advanced countries, they were able to send students to America and Europe, in hopes of alleviating this problem. Unfortunately, the majority of such students chose to remain in the advanced countries or, at least, to emigrate to nations less backward than their own. A facet of the brain drain, in short.''

''So I've got to choose a country so desperate for even semi-educated manpower that they'll admit killers as immigrants.''

''I'm afraid that's it, Franklin. Mozambique, for instance,

or the Seychelles, where the climate is said to be excellent, though the islands are rather small and isolated.''

''Any place where there'd be more whites? More people I could speak the language with?'' The prisoner's voice had grown sullen.

The judge took up a sheaf of papers from his desk. He perused it a few minutes before saying, ''According to your dossier, your schooling was far above average for these days. And while you were never chosen for regular employment by the National Data Banks, you have on several occasions held down minor, short-term positions. This would undoubtedly make you eligible for residence in Morocco, or at least Tangier.''

''Tangier?''

The judge, his tone unhappy, said, ''A disreputable city immediately across from Gibraltar on the North African coast. Although nominally part of the Sherifian Empire, and subject to the Sultan, it's an International Zone where few laws seem to apply. There is no extradition, for instance, and few taxes. With the possible exceptions of Nassau and Malta, it is usually considered to be the, ah, most wide-open city in the world.''

''Many Americans there?''

''The population is international. You'd find many English-speaking residents. However, anyone seeking to rehabilitate himself would find Tangier an unhealthy atmosphere, I should think. Its reputation is rank indeed.''

Frank Pinell grunted, impatient again. ''Who said anything about rehabilitation? All right, I'll take Tangier.''

Pinell was kept in a detention cell in a high-security prison in New Jersey only two nights before the plainclothes agents came for him. They were typical of the breed, lower echelon operatives of the largest police organization in the world—unless the Soviet Complex held that honor. The Inter-American Bureau of Investigation was a product of its times, which led to amalgamation of just about all areas of the productive or governmental systems. In this case, it applied to the police. The all-embracing IABI included what had once been the FBI, the CIA, all military espionage and counterespionage services, the Secret Service, all state police, and all local police forces. Each former group had a certain amount of autonomy, but ultimately they were all a part of the great law enforcement octopus which was the IABI, presided over by Director John Warfield Moyer. For more than two decades Moyer had dominated the American police system like a colossus.

The two were inconspicuous young men of averages, deliberately chosen to blend into a group—average of height, weight, coloring, facial characteristics, and dressed to conform. Frank Pinell had come in contact with them before, particularly in the past two months since his latest and most serious fall. They could all have been clones from one source.

When the cell door opened, one of them said, "Okay, Pinell, get your things. You're on your way."

He had two suitcases. They were packed with all of his earthly belongings, save the suit he wore. It was a conservative suit, government issue, just slightly above usual prole standards. Even so, it was as good as Franklin Pinell had ever worn. They were also to issue him a thousand pseudo-dollars in the form of Swiss gold coinage, the judge had told him. He had never had, at one time, such a sum. There was something ironic about the fact that as a criminal deportee, the State was sending him off in better shape than he had ever enjoyed as a free citizen.

He took up the bags and went out into the corridor saying, "You mean everything has already been cleared for me to emigrate to Morocco?"

"Tangier," one of them said. "It's not exactly Morocco. And as far as allowing you to immigrate, they'd take Jack the Ripper in that town. Come on, Pinell. I'm MacDonald and this is Roskin. We're your escort. Just for the record, we're under orders to shoot if you try to escape between here and the Tangier airport."

"My chum-pals," Frank muttered.

"And just for the record," Roskin added, "if you crack smart you'll wind up with dentures."

MacDonald brought forth handcuffs and joined his left wrist to Frank's right.

Frank said, "For Christ's sake, how can I carry my bags, shackled like this?"

"You carry one of them under your left arm and the other by its handle," Roskin told him. "You didn't expect us to act

as your porters, did you? If it's too much, you can leave one
of them. They probably don't contain anything worth having
anyway. Whoever heard of a prole with anything worth own-
ing? He'd flog it to buy syntho-beer."

Frank looked at him coldly, even as he fumbled the smaller
of the two suitcases up under his left arm and took the other
in his left hand. The weight of the two put him somewhat off
balance. He said, "I have a few family mementos. My father
wasn't exactly a prole."

MacDonald grunted disinterest. "Oh? Well, he didn't seem
to pass anything great along to you. What happened to him?"

"He was shot to death," Frank said flatly. "Are we or
aren't we getting out of this stinkhole?"

"Don't press your luck, smartass," Roskin told him, leading the way down the prison corridor toward freedom.

At the Long Island shuttleport they were lobbed over to the
International Supersonic Port, which floated some twenty
miles off the coast, and from there took the next laserboost to
a similar jetport stationed off Lisbon. A shuttlecraft lobbed
them over to Madrid. Next stop: Tangier.

While Roskin was checking out their reservations, Mac-
Donald and Frank Pinell waited in the terminal.

The IABI man said, "Too bad you can't take time out to
see Madrid, Pinell. Great town for a fling. Prettiest mopsies
in Common Europe. You pick them up at Chicote's bar,
where they've got the biggest collection of guzzle in the
world. Oh, you'd love Chicote's. They've got a jog of Chinese brandy going back to the Ming Dynasty. Something like
a thousand years old."

"Maybe I'll see that guzzle museum someday."

The other laughed nastily. "Not you, chum-pal. You'll
spend the rest of your life in Taniger, knocking back rotgut
absinthe—when you can afford it. The asshole of creation,
Tangier."

"How big is it?"

"A few square miles. Before you can get up a good dog
trot, you're over the International Zone boundary, which is
taboo. Then the Moroccan police throw you in the slammer.
The dungeons in Morocco go back to the days of Harun-al-
Rashid. Not that you've ever heard of him."

"Calif of Baghdad in the *Arabian Nights*," Frank replied. "He never got to Morocco."

Roskin came back with their reservations and hurried them up. "Royal Air Maroc," he said. "This airline you've got to see to believe."

"Flying carpets?" Pinell muttered.

The flying equipment of Royal Air Maroc was obviously secondhand from more prosperous lines, but the old-fashioned jet got them there. They landed at the shabby airport on the outskirts of Tangier in the afternoon.

The three had been the only passengers from Madrid, save for two swarthy-looking types, both wearing red fezzes but garbed in European dress, and wearing it as though it was a penance. On the way down Frank had heard them talking in some language he had never heard before.

He asked Roskin about it. "What do they speak in Tangier?"

"Just about everything," the other had told him, begrudging the information. "Mostly a Rifian version of Arabic. But any native you're apt to have anything to do with usually speaks either French or Spanish." He snorted with contempt at his prisoner. "Do you speak either?"

"I took some French," Frank said. He didn't add that it hadn't been much. To hell with these guys.

Roskin removed the handcuffs at the foot of the aircraft's ladder and the three waited for a few minutes until the plane's crew had brought their luggage.

Only one customs examiner stood in the administration building. Frank put his bags on the long, low table and, at the other's gesture, opened them. The Moroccan official was two days unshaven, had a stub of a cigarette in his mouth, and though he wore a uniform, it looked as though it had never been laundered since leaving the factory. His shirt was unbuttoned two buttons.

He dug roughly into Frank Pinell's things with dirty hands, making no attempt at neatness. He came upon a sub-miniature Leica-Polaroid camera which had once belonged to Frank's father and pocketed it.

"Hey, for Christ's sake," Frank exclaimed.

"Take it easy," Roskin told him. "And just hope he doesn't see anything else he thinks is worth flogging."

Seething inwardly, Frank held his peace. His cursory examinations completed, the customs officer took up a piece of blue chalk and marked each bag with an Arabic scribble, then made a contemptuous gesture of dismissal. He looked at the overnight bags that Roskin and MacDonald were carrying, but the latter said something in French which Frank didn't get, and the Moroccan shrugged and moved off.

"This way," MacDonald said, gesturing with his head toward an office door.

There was no identity screen on the office door. The IABI men didn't bother to knock, but simply pushed the door open and ushered their prisoner in. The office beyond was as filthy as the large hall outside and the fat official behind the sole desk was almost as disreputable in appearance as the customs man. He had a warm bottle of some orange-colored drink sitting to his left and from time to time took a swallow of it. The day wasn't particularly hot, but his round, lardy face was oozing oily sweat.

The three came up to the desk and MacDonald spoke in French, then brought forth several papers and put them before the other. The Mokkadem took them up and looked expressionlessly at Frank Pinell for a long moment, then down at the papers. MacDonald took from his pocket a small gold coin and put it on the desk. The Moroccan swept it with a fat hand into his top desk drawer and grunted.

"That came from you," the IABI man told his charge. "We'll settle later."

Frank sucked in breath but said nothing. It was their top, all he could do was let them keep spinning it.

The Moroccan official took up a rubber stamp and banged it on several of the papers, handed two of them to Frank, and put the rest in his desk. He looked up at MacDonald, then over to Frank, then returned to scanning the tattered pornographic magazine he had been perusing when they entered.

Frank said, "You mean that's all? That's all that's involved in my entering this country for good?"

They turned and left. As they went, Roskin said to him, "Not quite. Tomorrow morning you go to police headquarters on the Place de Mohammed Fifth and register. They'll want to see your papers, photograph and fingerprint you, find out where you're staying. Every time you move, you have to report your new address."

"That brings us to my money," Frank said.

MacDonald brought forth a booklet, opened it, and took a stylo from the pocket of his shirt. "Sign this receipt," he said.

Frank scanned it quickly. One thousand pseudo-dollars in gold Swiss francs.

As he signed, he said, "What do they use as a means of exchange in Tangier?"

"They use currency," Roskin said. "In Morocco, it's the dirham. Five dirham are approximately one pseudo-dollar."

MacDonald returned his receipt booklet to his pocket, brought forth some small gold coins, and counted them out into Frank's outstretched hand. "There's your severance pay," he said.

Frank said, "I owe you one for that bribe you gave the official."

"Never mind," the IABI man said, amused. "Let's say it's on me."

That set Frank back. He looked down at the small number of Swiss coins in his hand and looked at one to check its denomination.

"How many francs to the pseudo-dollar?" he said, scowling.

"Two," Roskin told him.

Frank calculated quickly and looked up. "This comes to only two hundred pseudo-dollars."

MacDonald said to his fellow agent, "He's not only an intellectual but a mathematician."

"I'm supposed to get a thousand," Frank said, his voice tight.

MacDonald scoffed at him. "What'd you do with a thousand pseudo-dollars? Probably waste it. Go through it in a week. As it is, Roskin and I will lay over in Madrid on our way home, and we'll hoist a couple of drinks to you in Chicote's."

Frank stared from one of them to the other. "You miserable bastards," he said, his lips going white. He took a step forward.

The other two stepped back warily, and Roskin's hand slipped inside his jacket.

MacDonald said, his voice low, "You know what the Moroccan police would do if we shot you, here and now?

Exactly nothing; they couldn't care less. Your type is a dime a dozen in Tangier.''

As Frank glared, Roskin smiled. "Over there's the exit to the taxi stand. The fare into town is five dirhams. Don't pay more. You can't trust these gooks.''

The two IABI men turned and left him standing there. Frank Pinell glared after them for a long moment. There was nothing he could do. Sure, once he got organized, he could write a letter of protest to Judge John Worthington. And a fat pile of crap that'd get him. He'd been silly enough to sign the receipt for one thousand pseudo-dollars, hadn't he? Signed it before getting the funds in his hands.

He picked up his bags, made his way to the *cambio* booth, and exchanged fifty Swiss francs into dirhams. The Moroccan money came in coins rather than paper currency.

From the money exchange booth he went on through the door to the taxi stand. The driver was a small, evil-looking type with a dirty rag of an orange turban wrapped carelessly around his head. The garment he wore looked like a seamless bathrobe made of brown homespun and there were yellow, backless leather slippers on his feet.

Frank looked in the window of the ancient cab, even as he sharply slapped the hand of an urchin who was trying to pick his pocket. He said, "Do you speak English?''

The cabby's shifty eyes took him in, evidently deciding his potential fare was American, rather than British. He said, "I talk everything, Jack.''

Frank put his bags in the back of the small cab and sat up front next to the driver. The cabby evidently wasn't accustomed to bathing. Frank rolled down the window and said, "Take me to the cheapest hotel in Tangier.''

The other grinned at him, displaying teeth like a broken-down picket fence. "The cheapest European type hotel, eh, Jack?''

"The cheapest hotel, period,'' Frank said definitely.

"You ever slept in a caravansary, Jack? Very cheap. One dirham a night. You sleep on a pile of straw, eh? Twenty other people in the same room, eh? Donkeys and goats, sometimes maybe even a camel. Other people are Rifs, down from the mountains to bring their things to the *souk* to sell, eh? Very bad people, some of these Rifs. Stick a knife in you if they figure you got ten, maybe twenty dirhams in your pockets."

Frank sighed. "All right, take me to the cheapest European hotel," he said in surrender.

The cabby dropped the lift lever of the prehistoric cab and, when they were aircushion borne, tromped on the accelerator, at first without result. He kicked it viciously and they started up. The American realized that the vehicle must be battery powered, rather than using power packs or picking up juice from the highway. Obviously, the gravel road wasn't auto-mated. However, from what he had read, Morocco wasn't energy-poor. At least a third of the southern stretches of the country were in the Sahara and, in common with neighboring Algeria, the Sherifian Empire of Morocco had been among the first to use major solar power stations with Reunited Nations assistance. Endless square miles of them had been built before the satellite solar power stations began microwaving energy down from orbit.

He had thought himself prepared for poverty of the North African variety, but he wasn't. He couldn't imagine any American being so prepared. The thought came to him: could parts of Latin America have been like this, before joining the United States of the Americas?

From time to time, they passed small communities consist-ing of single-room dwellings made of wood scraps, card-board, tin cans beaten flat, small boulders, and mud. There was no pretense of streets, or even alleys, obviously no running water, and garbage and refuse lay heaped in filthy piles, often with naked children playing on their summits. Flies and other insects droned in such swarms that Frank rolled up the window again, despite the stench of his driver.

The cabby grinned evilly over at him. "Not so good, eh, Jack?"

Frank didn't answer.

After suburbs of such appalling filth, Tangier itself came as a surprise. The part of it they entered was European in appearance, rather than Moslem. That figured. The French had once owned this town on the Straits of Hercules, even before the International Zone. And the French might have loony logic, but they didn't live in midden heaps.

The driver assumed the role of travel guide. "This is Route

de Tetouan, eh, Jack? And this here we come into is Place d'Europe.''

They proceeded to the right and merged into what street signs proclaimed to be the Avenue de Madrid. At least, that's what the French proclaimed. Frank couldn't decipher the Arabic scrawl.

They turned left on the Boulevard Mohammed Fifth. The city continued to improve, and now there was considerably more traffic. Tangier had no restrictions on surface traffic. From time to time they were even held up by minor traffic jams. Most of the cars and trucks seemed as elderly as the hovercab.

"Pasteur Boulevard, she the center of European town, eh? She just two streets up. You like, I think. Cheap hotel.''

They turned down Rue Moussai Ben Moussair, barely wide enough for two vehicles to pass, and two blocks later pulled up before a sadly decrepit four-story structure.

"Hotel Rome,'' the driver said expansively. "Very cheap. Almost clean. Not much bugs, eh, Jack?''

Frank looked out blankly. "Where?'' he said.

"She's on second floor, third floor, fourth floor. You don't pay more than ten dirhams, eh? Luigi, he's a crook. He try to charge you more, eh? You can't trust Italianos. Okay, Jack. That'll be fifteen dirhams, Jack. Cheap. All the way from the airport.''

Frank got out of his side of the cab, brought forth his Moroccan coins, and handed six dirhams through the window. "The rate's five dirhams and here's one more for a tip,'' he said.

The other was furious. "Fifteen, you cheap Yankee,'' he yelled.

"Five,'' Frank said flatly and reached for the door to the back of the hovercab to recover his bags.

Before he could get it open, the vehicle surged ahead, wrenching his hand from the doorknob and nearly knocking him sprawling.

His eyes bulging, Frank stared aghast at the hovercab careening up the street with his luggage. He searched desperately for its license plate, and could see none. His eyes darted around to other vehicles parked in the street. None of them had license plates. Evidently, there was no such thing in the International Zone of Tangier.

He groaned audibly. He knew nothing about the layout of this town. He didn't know where he could find the police. He didn't know the cabby's name. And the taxi looked like every other one he had seen in this—this ripoff Mecca.

He stood there, staring after it, until the vehicle swerved around a corner and was gone from sight.

Less than two hundred pseudo-dollars to his name and his every belonging stolen.

He finally took a deep breath and turned. Now he could make out the faded sign for the Hotel Rome. It was over a drab wooden stairway. The ground floor of the building was taken up by two stores which seemed almost identical. They resembled, in their window contents, the general stores in American small towns of long ago, selling everything from groceries to textiles, and toys, liquor, non-prescription drugs, shaving supplies, and what not.

The lobby of the Hotel Rome was on the second floor. Only one window overlooked the street. It was furnished with an aged reception desk, keys openly displayed on a rack behind it, and several thoroughly defeated chairs, their upholstery looking as though wild animals had savaged it. In one of the chairs snored an obese man, as disreputable as the furniture.

"Hey!"

The other opened first one eye, then the other. He brushed a fly from the top of his almost bald head and looked accusingly at the man who had awakened him. What do bald, fat Italians dream of, Frank wondered.

"Who do I see about getting a room here?"

"Me," the other grunted, somehow getting his bulk erect. "I'm Luigi. This place, it's mine."

Frank said, "I want the cheapest room you've got."

Luigi took him in, his plump face expressionless. "You got no luggage? You pay right now. Twenty dirhams."

"Ten," Frank said wearily, fishing in his pocket for two five-dirham coins.

"This way," Luigi said, shrugging.

The room was on the same floor as the lobby. It had one primitive electric bulb hanging from the ceiling, one sagging bed, one straight chair, one chipped dresser with a drawer missing. No bath, nor running water. Not even a window. There was a toilet down the hall, but no bath there, either. Seemingly, the tenants of the Hotel Rome didn't bathe, unless they managed a sponge bath out of the filthy lavatory, crammed next to the toilet bowl.

When Luigi was gone, Frank Pinell looked about his room.

"Home at last," he said acidly, running a hand down over his long face.

In another part of town, a stranger to Frank Pinell was speaking into his pocket transceiver. He was saying, "He pulled in on the three o'clock from Madrid. At the airport, those sons of bitches, MacDonald and Roskin, pulled their usual little romp. He got into Hamari's cab and Hamari took him to Luigi's and was able to take off with his luggage. He must be running scared by now. It looks as though we've found our patsy."

Chapter Three:
Roy Cos

Roy Cos looked out over the small, shabby hall in Baltimore with its pitiful group, members of the Industrial Workers of the World—"Wobblies," in their own jargon. Inwardly, he felt depressed and weary. It was the same old story: there were sixteen in the audience. At least ten of these were either Wobblies or sympathizers who had heard or read all that he had to say a hundred times. They were there not to learn but to give him support. Another two or three, looking bored, had drifted in from the street out of mild curiosity, or because they had nothing else to do. Another trio, seated together at the rear with identical condescending sneers, were hecklers come to give him a bad time. Only one stranger, who sat in the last row on one of the rickety folding chairs, looked at all like promising material. He was a small man, better dressed than the prole audience, and he had a notepad on his lap. From time to time he took notes. But for all Roy Cos knew, the man could be an IABI agent checking out just how subversive the speaker might be.

Roy took in the tattered banners which the committee members had hung about the walls. SOLIDARITY! UNITE! And, the longest of them all, PEOPLES OF THE WORLD UNITE. YOU HAVE NOTHING TO LOSE BUT YOUR CHAINS. Roy Cos knew that such signs had once read, WORKERS OF THE WORLD UNITE. But there were no workers any more, for all practical purposes. Over ninety percent of the population was on GAS. Two percent were affluent members of the upper class, who did not worry about employment. And five percent were actually all that were needed to produce an abundance of goods and supply the services of this automated, computerized society. And they, the professional technicians, engineers, scientists, doctors, and teachers, seldom thought of themselves as workers. Their pay was such that they identified with the upper class, rather than the proles on GAS.

Roy Cos, a second-generation radical, was in his early forties. He was an outwardly average, unprepossessing man, faded brown of hair, hazel of eye, earnest of expression, but projecting a hint that somehow he realized that life had passed him by and that his efforts were meaningless in the long run. He was some ten pounds overweight. Too many hours studying, too many hours sitting around tables, arguing dialectics, too many hours talking, talking, talking, largely to people not really interested in blueprints of Utopia.

He was saying: "And is this the final destiny of man? The overwhelming majority living on the verge of poverty? The history of the human race has been a hard and proud one. Since first our ancestors emerged from the caves, we have fought upward. And from the beginning we have been the thinking animals, the tool users. Who first utilized fire, we cannot know. What early men first developed the hand ax, the knife, the spear, the bow and arrow is unknown to us. But each generation that came along added its contribution to human knowledge and we slowly acquired agriculture, the domestication of animals, the wheel, the hoe, the plow. And as each generation emerged, its geniuses now forgotten, our knowledge grew. The arts and the sciences began to emerge."

"Great!" one of the three cynical listeners called out. "So what? Get to the point."

Roy nodded and went on. "The point is that all of these developments, this accumulated knowledge down through the centuries, is the common heritage of all mankind. They are not the property of a few, but of the race as a whole. A modern, automated factory is possible only because these tools were handed down to us over the centuries. The products of modern society should be the common property of the race, not of a mere fraction of it. And if this is true, where is justice today when a few live idle, in luxury, while the rest of us are forgotten? As John Ball, centuries ago, put it in a sermon to English poorer class rebels:

" 'When Adam dalfe and Eve span Who was thanne a gentil man?' "

The stranger made a note on his pad. He was thin, gray-faced, probably in his mid-forties, and Roy largely directed his talk toward the man. If you could make one convert at a typical Wobbly meeting you were doing fine. One valid convert, potentially an activist, would more than pay for an otherwise depressing evening.

He went on to explain the Wobbly program: organizing all presently employed workers so that they could use the only clout that really counted—the control of production, distribution, communications.

When the question period came, the chairman took over again. No one seemed prepared to ask an initial question of the speaker. As usual, in such a case, one of the Wobbly members stood up and started the ball rolling.

He said, "Since so few people support the Wobbly program, won't it take one hell of a long time for it to ever come about?"

Roy took over the podium again, nodded, and said, "Good question. And the answer is, no . . . not necessarily. What counts is the correctness of the program, the extent to which it solves our common problems. Our support can grow very quickly, given a breakdown in the current system and an obvious need for change. Take the American Revolution of 1776, for instance. Had you suggested to the average colonist in 1774 that he needed to throw off the rule of King George in favor of an independent union, he probably would have taken a patriotic swing at you. But the need was there and, overnight, a handful of farseeing men like Tom Paine, Sam Adams, Jefferson, pointed out the way. The revolution wasn't long in coming."

One of the hecklers held up his hand. When Roy Cos recognized him, he came to his feet and yelled, louder than was called for, "Aren't you people just a bunch of soreheads? There's only so many jobs around these days. The computers select the best men and women to hold them. Those that get jobs, deserve the extra money. The rest of us are lucky to get GAS. It's a pretty good system when everybody eats regular and is taken care of, even if he's not chosen for a job. What the hell are you beefing about?"

Roy nodded, and paused a moment before answering. "In the first place, let's not give those computers more credit than *they* deserve. Science is great but it mustn't be a sacred cow. Computers can be programmed into shortcomings.''

"Like what!" one of the hecklers called out. His friends laughed, backing him. Several of the Wobblies, seated down front, turned and glared at them.

Roy said, "Well, let's take a couple of scientists that the computers would have passed by. Two of their big requirements are a good education and a top-notch Ability Quotient. Thomas Edison had only a couple of years of formal education—he never got through grammar school. The computers wouldn't have picked him for a job. Steinmetz was a hunchback cripple, in spite of his I.Q., and would never have gotten a high Ability Quotient, much of which depends on physical attributes.

"But science isn't the only thing. Lincoln had practically no formal schooling and wouldn't have been chosen. Winston Churchill was a rotten student. Among writers, Jack London had very little schooling and was an alcoholic from his teens onward. O. Henry, poorly educated, also had a prison record. Scott Fitzgerald was a dropout at Princeton and never did learn much grammar, spelling, or punctuation. Hemingway finished high school but certainly took no honors there. Let's face it: few outstanding artists, musicians, or actors would stand up to the scrutiny of the computers. No, I'm afraid the computers are not yet programmed for judging the arts. And we Wobblies look forward to going further into the arts as well as the sciences. Millions of citizens could be employed in the arts.''

There were few questions. Roy had been hoping for one or more from the note-taker in the back row. You could usually tell the extent of a newcomer's real interest by his questions.

Following the meeting, while the balance of the small audience drifted from the hall, the membership gathered around to shake his hand and congratulate him. As a National Organizer, he was used to the plaudits of his fellows who were unable to express themselves in public speaking. So far as he was concerned, the meeting was a flop and he could see that the chairman felt the same way. Not even the little stranger in the rear had remained.

When the other members had gone their way, the chairman asked Roy if he'd like to come home with him for pseudo-coffee and talk. He was the local Group Organizer, a good man, but Roy was aware of the fact that the man's wife was rabidly against the Wobblies, in fact was a militant member of the United Church who considered all radicals slated for hell. Besides, Roy Cos was emotionally exhausted. His depression had been growing over a period of weeks.

"No thanks, Jim," he said. "I think I'll get on to bed. I have to take the vac tube to Newark tomorrow for another meeting. And you know Newark. The membership there is so apathetic they probably haven't gotten around to hiring a hall. I'll wind up on a soapbox in the park and damned few people are out in the parks anymore."

"Yeah," Jim said. "Only those who have no place else to go and screw. Well, see you on your next trip around, Comrade."

Roy said wearily, "Jim, for God's sake: please, *please*, don't call me comrade. I hate the word. If you use it, ninety-nine people out of a hundred think you're a Eurocommunist, or some other reactionary bastard."

They separated at the door and Roy Cos headed for his third-class hotel. His mind was empty.

The streets were deserted as usual at this time of night, especially of the few vehicles that were allowed surface traffic. He was surprised when two figures materialized to either side of him and he could hear the footsteps of a third close behind him. His first inclination was to think it was three of the organization members who happened to be going in his direction.

The voice of the one to his right disillusioned him on that score. It snarled, "We didn't like what you had to say, chum-pal."

Roy's mind raced for options, but found none. He continued to stroll at the same speed. "Sorry," he said. "It was what I believe." He had been through this sort of thing before. He expected a beating. Probably not bad enough to hospitalize him, this time, since they didn't seem particularly heated up, but probably enough of a working over to keep him from the Newark meeting.

The other said, "We reckon you need a little lesson in Americanism."

"Your version of . . ." Roy began, but was interrupted by

a heavy blow from the man on his left, then another in his back, even as he reeled sideways.

Neither blow was crippling, but between them, they threw him against the wall of the decrepit building, so that he banged his head against the bricks. Stars flashed before his eyes, red heat bloomed in his brain, and he began to fall. The pain was such that he hardly felt the kick in his side. The three were surging in, babbling incoherently about their anger, their frustrations, their hate of the nonconformist. All three were younger and in all probability in better shape than he. His chances of meaningful resistance were all but nil. He struggled to bring his arms up over his head, unable to restrain a groan of pain—though he tried.

More kicks came. They weren't pros and the beating was less damaging than it might have been. His best bet was to wait it out, curling into a fetal crouch to guard his head and groin.

But then came a shout and a pounding of feet. "Halt! Get away from that man! Halt or I'll fire!"

Cursing in surprise, the three were off in as many directions.

Panting, he staggered erect and tried to assess the damages. Except for bruises, there weren't any. His three assailants hadn't had the time for a complete mauling. He brushed at his street-grimed clothing with shaking hands.

He looked around. Down the avenue he heard another order to halt but, unless his rescuer was actually willing to shoot, he wasn't going to have much luck.

Only a few doors down was the entrance to a prole autobar. He staggered toward it, still brushing his jacket. Just before he entered, he straightened up as best he could, but the attempt was needless. The sorry little bistro was empty of customers.

He fumbled himself into a chair at the first table he could get to and for a time sat there, catching his breath. For all he knew, the police officer would return and pick him up on general principles, and before he could make adequate explanations, he might wind up in the banger. He might even louse up his schedule and miss the Newark meeting.

He brought forth his Universal Credit Card, put it into the table payment slot, and dialed a syntho-beer. He knew that his monthly GAS credits were low and there were several days to go before next month's deposit was credited to his account, but he needed that drink. Largely, national organizers of the Wobblies had to be self-supporting. The membership made minor contributions to the National Fund, but since they were all on GAS themselves and needed their credits for their own survival, it couldn't be much.

The beer had come and he had taken his initial swallow before the newcomer entered the autobar, looked around, and then descended on his table.

Roy Cos brought his gaze up. He had expected a uniform, but the other was in ordinary garb. Then Roy recognized him. He was the note-taking stranger.

The gray-faced man couldn't have weighed more than fifty kilos. He wore a wispy mustache, in a day when facial hair was long out of style, and his faded eyes had a perpetual squint. He slid into the chair opposite Roy.

Roy said, in resignation, "I thought you were an IABI man. But thanks, anyway. You came up like the Seventh cavalry rescuing the wagon train."

"Who, me?" the other said in false innocence, dialing for a drink. He looked at Roy's beer. "You look as though you could use something stronger than that. How about a whiskey?"

"Can't afford it. You mean you're not a cop?"

"No, I'm a reporter. And I *can* afford it." He dialed for the whiskey, his own credit card in the table slot.

Roy eyed him. "What was all that about, 'Halt, or I fire'?"

The other grunted sour amusement and fished a package of cigarettes from a side pocket. "If I'd shouted, 'Halt or I'll write,' they'd be kicking my butt right now. I figured they'd hardly hang around demanding to see my badge."

He stuck a smoke into his thin pale mouth and lit it with a lighter. To Roy's surprise, it wasn't marijuana, but tobacco. You couldn't mistake the odor of this forbidden narcotic.

Roy said, "Well, thanks again. You think you ought to be smoking like that in a public place?"

"There's nobody here but us. What happened?"

"You know as much about it as I do. I suppose it was those three hecklers. Who in the hell are you?"

The other extended a scrawny hand. "Forrest Brown. Call me Forry. I'm from the local area Tri-Di news—stuff that you don't get on the national networks."

As they shook hands, Roy said, "You're a news commentator?"

Brown shook his head. The smoke drifted up his face from the cigarette that drooped in his mouth, making him squint still more.

"Just a leg man. Oh, I go on video occasionally, when one of the regular men is off. But I never reached commentator level. I suppose I wasn't pretty enough. You've got to project personality to hit commentator level."

The center of the table had sunk and returned with the whiskey. Roy took a glass, still shaky, and said in defiance, "Here's to the revolution," and knocked it all back.

The gray little man nodded and swallowed a third of his own booze. "You think it'll ever come—at this rate?"

Roy ignored that and focused on his job again with professional ease. "You were going to do a story on the Wobbly movement?"

The other shook his head. "No, actually I just stopped by your meeting from sheer boredom. I had nothing else to do."

Roy was bitter. "The conspiracy of silence, eh? It's like pulling teeth to get any of our meetings or demands into the news. But what should I expect? The news media are owned by the enemy."

But Forry Brown shook his head again. "You people overemphasize that. Oh, it applies to a certain extent. Word from above is to not give too much coverage to any minority organizations. Not just your Wobblies, but the Neo-Nihilists, the Libertarians, the Luddites, the Gay Libbers, and all the rest. But there's no taboo, no conspiracy of total silence. The thing is, you people aren't news. Nobody cares about your programs. They want something exciting. You're not exciting. A good murder, some scandal about the latest Tri-Di sex symbol, government corruption, one of the bush wars in Africa or Asia, even a hurricane or earthquake, bring in more viewers than some yawner about a Wobbly meeting attended by fifteen people. But that isn't the big reason I'm not filing a story on you, even after you were attacked by members of your audience. If they'd killed you, maybe somebody would have a story." He took another cigarette and lit it from the butt of his last.

Roy Cos forgot his bruises temporarily and said, "Damn it,

I'd almost be willing. How can we present our program to the people if we can't get any media coverage?''

The little man's grimace was sour. "Wish I could help you, but just this morning the computers spelled me down. I'm surprised that I was able to hang on this long, even as a second-rate legman in a backwater Tri-Di area. It's not enough being selected by the damned computers for a job. Each year a new batch of journalism graduates apply for positions. As you said in your talk, over ninety percent of the population is unemployed. We who have jobs try desperately to hang onto them, and sometimes the experience we've accumulated helps out. But sooner or later some new kid with a higher Ability Quotient steps into your boots.'' He shrugged. "I've been expecting the axe for a long time.''

Roy Cos had never held a job in his life—not that he hadn't religiously applied each year. He said, in compassion, "I'm sorry. What happens now? Do you get a pension or something from your Tri-Di network?''

The other snorted and finished his drink. "Hell, no. I go back on GAS. Theoretically, I should've saved a portion of the pseudo-dollar credits I earned while I was working and invested them in Variable Basic government stock, or one of the private corporations. The dividends would supplement my GAS.'' He snorted again, took his cigarette from his mouth and looked at it. "I'm afraid I developed some expensive habits. Lady Nicotine doesn't come cheap these days.''

The Wobbly organizer took him in. He had never met anyone before who was actually hooked on tobacco. He didn't move in the circles that could afford it. He also had the usual prejudice against the use of the poisonous weed.

Roy said, "Why didn't you ever take the cure?''

Brown laughed dryly. "Because, once you take it, you're allergic to nicotine for the rest of your life. I guess I didn't really want to be cured. I like to eat better than you proles can afford, like to drink better, travel better. I even took a trip around the world once and I've been in Europe a couple of times. Free rocket shuttle fare as a newsman, but the other expenses were largely on me. You ought to see some of the bordellos they have in the East.'' He sighed. "That's one thing they'll never automate. Knock on wood.''

As a Wobbly, Roy Cos didn't approve of prostitution any

more than he did of the deadly nicotine, so underneath was a certain smug satisfaction when he said, "So now you're in the same position as all the rest of us. You should join the Wobbly movement."

Brown ground out his cigarette and brought forth another. "Not me," he said. "What I've got to do is dream up some other manner of supporting my vices."

Roy switched subjects, knowing the unlikelihood of the ex-newsman ever accomplishing that. "Any idea how we could get more media coverage? It's a sore point with us. When those old American revolutionists wrote the Constitution and the Bill of Rights, it never occurred to them that freedom of speech and of press and assembly would one day become meaningless. In those days you got up in the village square, or the town meeting, and stated your beliefs. If your program had merit, it was probably accepted. Starting a newspaper was in the range of almost any individual, or certainly of any small group. But today, unless you can get on Tri-Di, you simply aren't heard. Freedom of the press is fine; sure, you're perfectly free to get out a little magazine and circulate it as best you can. But who reads it? A few hundred people, most of whom already have the same beliefs you do. Freedom of speech is meaningless if all you can do is stand on the beach and shout your message to the wind."

Forrest Brown thought about it, squinting through curls of smoke. He said finally, "You've got to have enough money to buy Tri-Di time, but above all, you've got to be newsworthy. You've got to have something that makes people want to listen to you, watch you."

"Great," Roy said sarcastically. "And how do I accomplish that?"

The newsman, half joking, said, "Start a religion. Become a Tri-Di star. Take out a Deathwish Policy."

The Wobbly organizer scowled at him. "What for?"

"You'd have the credits to buy Tri-Di time. Deathwishers are news. Everybody'd be in a tizzy wondering how long it'd be before you got hit. There'd be standing room only at your hall lectures. You'd be out in the open and they'd come in hopes that they'd be there when the Graf's boys, or whoever, got to you. Something like in the old days in Spain and Latin

America, where they'd pony up for bullfight tickets in hopes they'd see the matador gored to death.''

"What the hell are you talking about?" Roy said. "What's a Deathwish Policy?"

Forry grunted and dialed another two whiskeys before lighting a new smoke off the old. "Oh," he said, "just a jargon term we use in the news game. You've probably never heard it. You have your life insured in return for having an international drawing account for a million pseudo-dollar credits continually at your disposal—for as long as you live.''

"Never heard of . . . oh, wait a minute. I guess I did. Something in the news about six months ago. Somebody was blown up with a grenade or something. His life had been insured for something like five million pseudo-dollars only a few days before. I forget the details. I don't usually follow crime news."

"It's crime, all right," Forry said, putting his thumbprint on the table's payment screen to pay for the new drinks. His credit card was still in the slot. "The thing is, so far, the law hasn't been able to get at them. It's too complicated. Most of the insured are Americans. But you never sign the policy with an American company. The outfit that's going to collect the benefits is usually based in the Bahamas, or Malta, or Tangier, or somewhere else where practically anything goes. They shop out the deal to Lloyd's of London, where they'll insure anything—dancer's legs, a violinist's fingers. Hell, they'll insure an outdoor entertainment against loss due to rain. So you've got four countries involved: the insured is usually a citizen of the States, the beneficiary is in the Bahamas or wherever, Lloyds of London is in England, and your credits come from Switzerland. For that matter, you might say five different countries are involved, since it's said that the Graf has his headquarters in Liechtenstein.''

"Now, wait a minute," Roy Cos said, taking up his new drink and swallowing part of it. For the first time in years, he felt the itch of intrigue. "Start at the beginning."

Forry shrugged thin shoulders. "You sign a contract that grants you what amounts to an unlimited credit account for as long as you live. If and when you die, the beneficiary collects the benefits. The company you've signed with pays huge daily premiums. It's a gamble, as all insurance has always been since the days when Phoenician ships set sail from Tyre to Cadiz for a cargo of tin. The insurer was gambling that the ship would get back safely and the insuree was gambling that the ship would sink. Well, in this case, the insuree is gambling that you'll die before the premiums paid mount up to more than the benefits he'll collect when you kick off. Lloyd's is gambling the other way: that you'll live so long that the premiums accumulated are higher than the life insurance benefits.''

Roy looked at him blankly. ''But suppose you lived for years? And you have a million pseudo-dollar account to draw on to any extent you wish? Hell, the company that's the beneficiary would go broke paying the premiums plus your expenditures.''

Forry Brown laughed shortly. ''Don't be a dizzard. From the moment that policy goes into effect, you're on the run. Some of the insured don't live the first day out.''

Roy stared, then tried a tenative smile. ''You're kidding, of course.''

''Yeah? The Graf's hit men are the best-trained pros in the world. He usually gets the contract, I understand.''

Roy slumped down into his chair. ''Jesus,'' he said. ''Who'd be silly enough to sign up for that?''

The newsman let smoke dribble from his nostrils. ''Somebody who had already decided to commit suicide but couldn't bring himself to do it and decided he might as well go out in a burst of glory, living in one of the biggest hotels in one of the swankest resorts in the world, drinking champagne and gorging himself with caviar.''

''I can see that, but nobody else would sign.''

Forry finished his second drink and said slowly, ''You underestimate human desperation. Take some prole who's fed up with living right at the edge of poverty on GAS. He figures he might as well live it up for a few weeks, or hopefully months. Frankly, this guy's a dreamer. His chances of lasting for any length of time at all are just about nil. Most of them think they've figured out some dodge to beat the odds, some special gimmick. They haven't. They can't.''

''Now wait a minute,'' Roy said, increasingly intrigued by one more example of the degeneracy of the present system. ''What you're saying is that an assassin . . .''

"More than one, I'd think," Forry put in.

". . . is immediately sent after the person who's signed this contract. All right, what happens if the killer's caught?"

"He's arrested, of course, and they throw the book at him. But they can't prove anything except his own guilt. None of the advanced countries have capital punishment any more. If he's caught in America, he's subject to deportation. If they nail him in, say, Common Europe, he's thrown into the banger for, say, twenty years. But the Graf takes care of his own. Who ever heard of one of the Graf's boys spending much time in jail? One way or the other, he's soon out, usually legally, since the Graf keeps the best criminal lawyers in the world. But if not legally, then illegally. His escape is greased and he drops out of sight, possibly to Tangier, where there are no extradition laws. He remains on pension for the rest of his life, unless they get him some local job. One of the Graf's big centers is Tangier."

"Who the hell's this Graf?" Roy Cos said.

"It's a German title, something like a British earl. He's the boss of Mercenaries, Incorporated," the little man told him. "Haven't you ever heard of the Graf?"

"No, I told you I didn't bother with crime news. But this thing fascinates me. What are some of the tricks the victims try to pull to remain alive?"

"Oh, I've heard of various scams. Often they'll try to hole up in some manner so that the hit men can't get at them. They'll rent the whole top floor of some luxury hotel and try to seal themselves in, like Howard Hughes in the old days. Bodyguards and all. But in those cases, the assassin usually bribes one of the poor bastard's hirelings to slip a cyanide mickey into one of his drinks, or whatever. Once or twice, it turned out that one of the bodyguards was a Graf man. Curtains."

Roy Cos shook his head in amazement. "A million pseudo-dollars, always available. But suppose he spent that much in one day, and then the next day spent that much again, and so on?"

"It'd be damned hard to do," the newsman told him. "There are clauses in the contract. He's not allowed to buy presents that cost more than two hundred pseudo-dollars. He's not allowed to donate to any cause. Once a crackpot religious fanatic decided to sign up and donate hundreds of thousands to the United Church, but that wasn't allowed. On top of that, the company becomes your heir. Everything you buy reverts to them, after your death. You buy something expensive, like a luxury car, or a big house, or jewelry, and they take it over when you die.''

Roy shook his head. "I'd think the Lloyd's underwriters would get leery.''

Forry shrugged again. "Like I said, it's a gamble. To keep it that way, the daily premium is sky high. If the insured lives more than a few days, Lloyd's wins. As usual, the computers of both the policyholders and the insurers have figured it out down to a hairline.''

Roy finished his drink, thought about it some more, shook his head again. Then he scowled and looked over at the other. He said, "What was that you mentioned about my taking out one of these Deathwish Policies?''

And Forry Brown said softly, "A million pseudo-dollars. Like I said, you'd have plenty to buy yourself premium Tri-Di time. Every day, until they got you. And you'd also be top news. Everybody and his cousin would listen in. You'd have your chance to put your Wobbly message across such as no minority organization has ever had.''

There was a prolonged blank silence until Roy Cos said finally, "Where do you come in on this, Forry Brown?''

Forry looked him straight in the eye, squinting through his cigarette smoke. "Somebody's got to run interference for you, keep you alive long enough to do your thing. And I need a job—one that doesn't have to match the computers of the National Data Banks.''

"You must think I'm drivel-happy," Roy said in disgust.

"No, I think you're a dedicated Wobbly and as things stand now you'll spend your life trying to put over a message that no one hears. Have you ever read of Sacco and Vanzetti?''

Roy frowned. "Vaguely. A couple of early 20th century radicals.''

"That's right. They were railroaded, charged with a payroll robbery where two men were killed. Because they were philosophical anarchists, they were sentenced to death. You wouldn't believe the reaction that went up all over the world. American consulates and embassies in a dozen countries were marched upon. There were riots and demonstrations everywhere. Tens of thousands of letters of protest, ranging from students to world-famous intellectuals; hundreds of petitions, signed by hundreds of thousands. American officials were astonished. The President, getting reports from his ambassadors, is reported to have asked, 'Who in the hell are Sacco and Vanzetti?' But in spite of it all, after going through all possible appeals, they were executed.'' A pause. "I'll put it more strongly: they were martyred.''

"I guess I have read something about it,'' Roy said vaguely, still scowling.

The newsman brought forth his wallet and fished in it. "This is one of the final things Bartolomeo Vanzetti wrote. He was self-educated.''

Forry Brown read softly from the tattered clipping: *"If it had not been for this thing, I might have lived out my life talking at street corners to scorning men. I might have died unmarked, unknown, a failure. Now we are not a failure. This is our career and our triumph. Never in all our full life could we hope to do such work for tolerance, for justice, for man's understanding of man, as now we do by accident.*

"Our words—our lives—our pains: nothing! The taking of our lives—lives of a good shoemaker and a poor fish peddler— all! That last moment belongs to us. That agony is our triumph."

Forry Brown looked up from the clipping. "Their deaths weren't the end. Hundreds of articles about them were published for years. Best-selling books were written about the Sacco-Vanzetti case. There was even a long-running play on Broadway, and a hit movie film. In becoming martyrs, Bartolomeo Vanzetti and Nicola Sacco at long last put over their message. Decades later, they were vindicated by the State of Massachussetts. They hadn't even been guilty.''

Across the table, the eyes of Roy Cos were shining.

Chapter Four:
Horace Hampton

Horace Greeley Hampton looked about appreciatively at the Mini-city of Greenpoint when he emerged from the vacuum tube metro station. He had been in similar towns before, but never this one. Located scenically in the rolling hills of Eastern Pennsylvania, it was composed of four ultra-modern high-rise apartment buildings, the condominiums of the 21st century. Each seemed approximately fifty stories in height, twin-towered and sheathed in aluminum and glass. Not as imposing as the hundred-floor apartment buildings of the big cities, yet large enough to contain all the amenities—an ultra-market, automated kitchens, parking areas, theatres, auditoriums, sports arenas. Much of it lay in the several basement levels below ground. The restaurants throughout each of the buildings would be in wide variety, ranging from Malay and Polynesian to vegetarian, by the way of every well-known cuisine the world offered. Greenpoint offered all of the amenities, far beyond those available to the high-rises devoted to proles.

In the early days of the mini-cities, there had been comparatively little class discrimination. An ultra-condo would house five thousand or more families, ranging from proles on GAS in apartments on the lower levels, to the extremely wealthy in the rarefied heights, in swank penthouses and terrace apartments. The higher you ascended in the towering buildings, the larger and more expensive became the apartments. Needless to say, the more posh became the restaurants, nightclubs, and theatres.

Around each of the four apartment towers of Greenpoint lay a square mile of gardens, lakes, small streams, carefully tended woods. It was complete with bridle and bike paths,

48

sports and picnic grounds, playgrounds, sidewalk cafes, and skating areas. Very attractive indeed.

Greenpoint was a new development in the progress of the mini-city. Hamp doubted that a single prole family was in residence, not even in the lowest levels. The only proles in Greenpoint would be service workers commuting from other nearby towns. Private cars and even hovercabs were, of course, prohibited on the surface; small electric buses wound slowly around the narrow roads that connected all points, all buildings.

Hamp looked again at his note, checked a bus schedule on a bulletin board next to the entry to the metro terminal, and waited to be taken to the William Penn Building.

It was late afternoon and he hoped to be in Manhattan by evening. This line of League work was strange to him. In the years that he had been active in the organization, he had never been utilized for making initial contacts with possible recruits. He was aware of the continuing necessity of the work and the League system. Someone would attend a lecture and sign the card handed around at its end. Or someone would hear a League Tri-Di broadcast and write in for more information. Or someone would read a League pamphlet or book and be moved to request a visit from a member for discussion. But Hamp had quickly risen from the ranks, had been sent to the training school for field operatives, and had participated in trouble-shooting ever since.

But it would seem that Lee Garrett was a possible recruit worthy of special attention. Max Finklestein had said the new contact was white, which was easy to believe. Hamp doubted that there were many blacks or other racial minorities residing in Greenpoint. Not that there would be any restriction, *theoretically*. The nation's laws wouldn't stand for that, but non-whites would be made to feel less than welcome.

He entered the sumptuous lobby of the William Penn Building, very well done in marble, beautifully furnished and decorated in an early Pennsylvania motif, and approached one of the small bank of reception desks. He sat across from the reception screen and said, "I wish to visit Lee Garrett. I believe that I am expected."

"Your identity, please, sir," the screen said.

Hamp brought forth his card, put it in the slot with his right thumb on the appropriate square.

"Thank you," the mechanical voice said.

He retrieved the credit card and relaxed in the chair.

After only a couple of minutes, the screen said, "You are expected, sir. Apartment 1012. Please take elevator seven, eight, or nine."

Hamp stood, looked about, and located the elevators. A few people in the lobby looked at him with mild surprise. Not only was he black, but his clothes, though a bit above the usual prole level, were hardly of the quality most often seen in Greenpoint. He had expected such interest and ignored it.

Elevator eight was empty. He stepped in and said, "Apartment 1012, please."

The elevator's screen said, "Your identity card, please."

He put it in the slot, pressed his thumb on the identity square of the screen.

"Thank you, sir." The door closed and the elevator smoothly began to rise.

He emerged on the tenth floor and arrived shortly at Apartment 1012. Its identity screen picked him up as he stood before it and the door opened. He entered and found himself in a small entrada.

A feminine voice called out, "In here. You'll have to forgive me, but I'm busy."

Hamp shifted his shoulders in a shrug and walked into a living room. He blinked slightly at its opulence. The Anti-Racist League had its wealthy members, but there must have been few who lived on a higher scale than this. One whole wall, facing a terrace with a superb view beyond, was glass. The furnishings were a little on the ultra-modern side, and Hamp was somewhat taken aback by its feminity. It was hardly a man's room. Could this Lee Garrett be gay?

At the far side, a young woman was busily stirring the contents of a crystal mixing glass. She concentrated as though counting the exact number of turns of the long green swizzle stick in her hand.

She looked over at him as he entered and offered a dazzling smile. "I guessed that a martini would be in order, right?"

It wasn't an autobar, and sitting on its top were an Imperial quart of British gin, whose label Hamp recognized, and a fifth of French vermouth. Excellent guzzle!

"It sounds wizard," he admitted. "Uh, my name is Horace Hampton. I had an appointment with Mr. Garrett."

"Ms. Garrett," she said, smiling again as she poured drinks into two cocktail glasses. "I'm Lee Garrett."

Hamp stared. He'd had no indication from Max Finklestein that this new contact was a youthful blonde, startlingly blue of eye, immaculately turned out and, frankly, implausibly beautiful. She wore a gold and red afternoon frock that would have cost half a year's credit to a prole on GAS. Her hairdo and her cosmetics were such that surely she had just emerged from a beauty salon, or a dressing room of an advertising agency.

She strode over gracefully, handed him one of the martinis, and smiled again, devastating him. "Shall we toast the end of all conflict?"

"I can't fight that," Hamp told her.

They sipped, Hamp taking her in all over again, not quite believing it. In real life, they just didn't come so downright pretty.

She said, "Please be seated, Mr. Hampton. I'll have to confess that this is all new to me. I've never joined any sort of organization before."

Hamp sat on a couch and took another sip of the cocktail. "About eight to one," he judged.

"Seven," she told him. "My father's formula. He was a fanatic. A perfect martini had to be made just so. I believe he actually dropped one friend because the man insisted on putting in an olive rather than a twist of lime rind."

Hamp said, "Well, I can't fault him on this formula."

Lee Garrett had seated herself on the couch with him. Now she leaned forward and put her half empty glass on the cocktail table before them.

She said, "Tell me all about the Anti-Racist League, Mr. Hampton. I've read quite a bit of the standard literature this past month or so and I'm in complete agreement with your stated goals. But it occurred to me that there must be restrictions on what you can openly publish."

"How do you mean, Ms. Garrett?" He put his own glass down, empty. It had been a lifesaver. He had put away too much brandy the night before and was now wondering if she'd offer another.

She said, "Oh, call me Lee. After all, if we're to be comrades in arms, we shouldn't stand on formality."

Hamp said, "Comrades in arms call me Hamp."

"What I mean is, the League is no namby-pamby organization. But it certainly can't come right out and advocate force and violence. That's illegal. So it doesn't say that in so many words in the public literature. Is there other written material, meant only for members?"

"Not that I know of. Just what did you want to know about the League that you couldn't find in our books?"

"Well . . ." She frowned prettily. "Just about everything, I suppose. I mean, tell me all about it."

"You know, I'm surprised at your interest. Why should you be concerned with racism?" He smiled to take the edge off his words. "Back in Adolf the Aryan's day, you would have been considered the Nordic ideal."

She thought about it, finally coming up with, "Well, I suppose I'm a do-gooder, at heart. And I'm developing a bit of guilt over all this," she waved at the elegant furnishings, "when so many, especially among minorities—or in some countries where the colored are actually the majority—have so little and suffer so much. My father left me more than I need for the rest of my life. But . . . well, I do nothing. I'm fed up with my friends and relatives all in the same position. I want to do something worthwhile."

Hamp nodded. "It's not an unknown reaction. Engels, the collaborator of Karl Marx, was a wealthy manufacturer. The Russian anarchist Kropotkin was a prince. Norman Thomas, the American socialist, was married to a very wealthy woman." He grinned suddenly. "But they rose above it."

"So tell me more about racism and how you . . . we . . . can go about ending it."

Hamp took a breath and said, "You must realize that racism is one of our oldest American traditions. The United States declared its independence, utilizing some of the most noble language in the history of the fight for man's freedom, in 1776. One hundred years later marked the last major battle between the whites and American Indians. The Sioux won the battle but lost the war. One century. In that short span whole tribes disappeared. Many tens of thousands were killed outright; many more died of starvation. Some went down before the white man's diseases: measles, smallpox, and so on. At any rate, here was racism at its naked worst."

Lee nodded, her eyes serious, then glanced at his drink. "Good heavens, I'm a terrible hostess. Could I give you a refill?"

He handed his glass to her and she went over to the ornate little bar. She brought the new ones in champagne glasses, so that they were at least doubles. Hamp made no complaint.

She told him, her voice very sincere, "I couldn't agree with you more in regard to the Indians. Most white Americans will concede the Amerind got a raw deal."

"Now that it's too late," Hamp said.

"Well, but we actually *invited* Chinese labor." Perhaps, he thought, she was testing him.

"Sure—coolie labor, back in the 19th century, to do manual work on the railroads. The discrimination was pretty tough. Among other things, they weren't allowed to bring over their wives and families, under the Oriental Exclusion Laws. *No women at all*. They resorted to all sorts of tricks to get around that. The smuggling of Chinese women into the United States from Mexico was very common. Even Jack London, in his yacht, *The Snark*, participated in that." He saw the blank look on her face and added, "Jack London was an American writer of the rough and tough school. Quite a radical. Damn' good man."

"Those, I like," she replied, and took more of her martini. "Go on."

"The Chinese and later Japanese were hard workers. The whites in the Western states, especially California, could see the handwriting on the wall. Soon Orientals, even when born American citizens, were forbidden to own land. The Japs, who were wonderful farmers, got around that by leasing land for ninety-nine years. They become real competition to the United Farmers, multi-millionaire whites living as far off as New York, who were the first in the world to invent so-called factories-in-the-field. These were farms of hundreds of thousands of acres, tilled by wage workers using the latest agricultural machinery and fertilizer. At any rate, the Japanese, with their driving industry, had just about achieved a monopoly in truck farming, involving a great deal of hand labor. When the Second World War came along, the whites solved this by having all Japanese on the west coast rounded up and shipped to concentration camps. Their property went for sacrifice prices. Even after the war, they never really recovered.''

He took a sizable swallow of his drink and she got up to replenish his glass, bringing what remained with her to the cocktail table.

"In actuality," she told him, "I've become most interested in you blacks and what you're doing to fight back. I want to know what I can do to help."

Hamp was feeling the soothing qualities of the drink now, and stretched his legs before him in comfort. "Well," he said, "you've undoubtedly read most of it in our literature. Blacks were brought over as slaves. At least a slave had comparative security. As valuable property, he was clothed, fed, sheltered, and given some medical care. After the Civil War freed him, he worked for pay and if he became ill, injured, or old, he was fired and had no way of maintaining himself."

"Weren't lots of whites treated the same way?"

"Some," he admitted. "But blacks could take it for granted. By the 1950s they began to revolt nationwide. They held parades and rallies, fought segregation in the courts, the whole bit. It helped, but not enough. By the 1970s, more teenage blacks were unemployed than ever, to the point of fifty percent in some cities. Twice as many blacks as whites dropped out of school in their early teens."

She leaned forward. "So how do you expect to change that now?"

Hamp nodded, took another swallow, then leaned forward and poured more from the mixing glass. He said, "The trouble was, they were too polite, too easygoing about their fight for equality. They paraded and protested and petitioned and tried to vote for politicians, sometimes blacks, who supposedly supported their cause. The politicians must have had many a private laugh, including the black ones, who were just as crooked as their white colleagues. In short, our people turned the other cheek, rather than really fighting. When such outfits as the Ku Klux Klan came into their segregated areas to burn their homes, schools, and churches, they most often ran in terror. When some militant blacks were killed, they did no more than protest to the police and the Civil Liberties Union, which gave them some support."

There was a shine in Lee Garrett's eyes. "So how have you changed your program now?"

He moved over, slightly closer to her, and looked into her face, his own very serious. "Now we fight back—a tooth for a tooth, as the Good Book says. We no longer run in terror when the Klan dons its silly white sheets and begins burning crosses. Today the Klan hardly exists as an active organization. They're the ones who are afraid now. We've combined with Chicanos, Puerto Ricans, Amerinds, Jews, and so on. And we fight on every level, from the streets to the senate floor, and we never give an inch in any field. We return, blow for blow, every intrusion on our rights as American citizens . . . and members in good standing of the human race."

"You accept conflict," she said.

He moved still closer to her, his face slightly slack, as though from the drink, and put an arm around her shoulders. At that she stiffened slightly.

"Yes," he said. "We fight. No longer do we bob apologetically and call all white men, 'Captain,' or say, 'Yes, suh.' No longer do we step down off the curb when a white comes along. We'll fight that to the death."

"You mean, you've actually participated in . . . killing people who stand in the way of minority rights?"

He moved still closer and scowled his surprise. "Oh, of course not. A few extreme cases have taken place—blacks who have returned gunfire, that sort of thing. But not League members. We don't condone violence. That would just give the enemy an opening, a wedge to get at us." He moved closer still.

She tried to maneuver away from him, without being too obvious about it, but his arm was a restraint around her shoulders.

She got out, "Yes . . . but, you just said that now you fought back."

His dark eyes were hotly on her own blue ones now. There was a slur in his voice. "That was, uh, figuratively speaking, not literally meant."

She was breathing in short gasps as his left hand came forward and rested on her belly.

Suddenly, her eyes widened in fear and she pushed back

violently. "Don't . . . don't!" she shrilled. "Let me loose, you nigger!"

Hamp stood up and looked down at her, shrinking against the far end of the couch. He laughed. Gone were all signs of his drinking.

She panted, "What are you laughing at, you black bastard?"

He rubbed the knuckles of his left hand over his mouth and, laughing still, said, "You make a hell of an *agent provocateur*, Ms. Garrett. I'm afraid you're the victim of your own prejudiced beliefs. You see, one of the oldest wive's tales is the one about blacks lusting for the fair white bodies of Caucasians. On the face of it, it's nonsense. Didn't it ever occur to you that possibly you're not attractive to blacks? Your fine blonde hair might lack appeal. Didn't it ever occur to you that blacks might prefer brunette beauty, that perhaps your nose might be much too thin, your complexion—forgive me—washed out, perhaps all but repulsive? If I had to pick the most attractive whites, it would be the girls of southern Italy and Sicily, of Andalusian Spain, or Greece. Brunettes with dark complexions. But Scandinavians? No thank you, I don't screw blondes."

"You're disgusting," she said contemptuously. "Every word of this is being taped, of course."

He laughed again, preparatory to leaving. "I suspected it. I *always* suspect it. But you see, Ms. Garrett, I have said nothing to you that isn't to be found in our literature—our leaflets, pamphlets, and books."

"You said that these days you're fighting back. An eye for an eye and so forth."

He smiled at her. "All figurative, Ms. Garrett, as I pointed out to you. The League does not condone violence. And now, thank you for the excellent martinis, and good day."

He turned and left.

On his way down to the ground floor he wondered who had sent her. Possibly the IABI? Or, just possibly, she might have been working on her own. He had been poorly managed, whoever had set it up. Undoubtedly, they had thought that her obvious wealth and position would immediately gain her access to the higher echelons of the Anti-Racist League, where she could infiltrate and secure inside information. He shook his head again. They simply couldn't realize that the

League, although it had a scattering of white members, wasn't particularly impressed by either their whiteness or money. The usual militant in the League was better educated than most, though often self-educated, and was dedicated, disciplined, and competent.

He retraced his way to the transportation terminal and retrieved the suitcase he had checked earlier. He took the first twenty-seater scheduled for Manhattan's Grand Central Terminal. On his way, he brought forth his transceiver and reported to the National Activities Committee the results of his contact with Lee Garrett.

He hailed an automated hovercab, the only vehicle allowed on the surface in the city, and dialed a renowned men's store. Manhattan was still a center for those who ignored the ultra-markets and resorted to privately owned swank shops.

There, he quickly disillusioned the clerk, who eyed his color, shabby suit, and battered suitcase, saying, "I'm just in from the Coast where I've been roughing it, gathering material for my latest novel. I want a complete outfit in which I can walk out of here. The very best, of course."

"Oh, yes, sir," the other said. "I'm sure we can accommodate you."

When Hamp left, an hour or so later, he not only wore the latest in expensive men's wear, but also had two new pieces of imported British luggage. He had paid with an International Credit Card issued on a Berne, Switzerland bank.

The boys carrying his luggage took everything out to the curb and summoned another hovercab for him. He dialed and settled back. His destination turned out to be one of the taller, more impressive office buildings the island boasted. The cab had been directed to a minor entrance on a side street. He entered alone. There was no doorman nor any other building employee nor resident to be seen. He brought a key ring from his pocket, selected a small silver key, and opened the door of an elevator.

The elevator compartment, without a command as to his destination, accelerated not too quickly but for a lengthy period before reaching its ultimate speed. He was able to adjust without bending his knees.

He emerged finally into a large office reception room which was unoccupied and strolled across it to a heavy door.

Though metallic, it was attractively well done to disguise its strength. He opened it with another key.

Beyond was a roomy office with four desks and beyond that, a still more ample one with a single large desk. He passed through both of the silent rooms and on into an extensive terrace apartment.

Obviously at ease, he made his way to a master bedroom, where he put down his bags and stripped, then entered the bath, which had a connecting dressing room. In the bath, he used still another small key to open a medical cabinet, from which he brought forth a hypodermic needle, a small bottle, and a jar.

Expertly, he loaded the syringe and injected himself. He then sat before the dressing-room mirror and removed the contact lenses from his eyes, revealing their natural dark blue. He put the fingernails of his two little fingers into his nostrils and brought forth two ring-like metal spreaders which altered the shape of his nose. He returned to the bathroom, took up the jar he had taken from the medical cabinet, and entered the shower stall. When he had adjusted the spray to his satisfaction he began vigorously to shampoo his hair with dabs of the contents of the jar. He entered the shower with black wiry hair and left it with darkish red hair, considerably straighter and looking like a young athlete's crew cut.

He checked in a mirror, found that the injection hadn't begun to work. In a white silk kimono and matching slippers, he shuffled back into the living room and the extensive study.

He sat at the desk and flicked on the TV phone, activating the stud which would prevent his own face from being transmitted, punched two numbers, and waited until the screen lit up. He said to the subservient face there, "Simmons, I shall be in residence, here in Manhattan, for an indefinite period. Please summon the staff immediately. I wish to dine here this evening. Inform Henri that I expect him to surpass himself. I have been subjected to atrocious food for longer than I care to think about."

"Very good, sir."

The face of Simmons faded and Horace Hampton punched two more numbers. The new face was that of an efficient businessman somewhere in his early middle years.

Hamp said, "Barry, I'm back in the States, here in Manhattan. Have one of the office teams assembled. Include yourself and, let me see, Ted, and, ah, Lester. Among other things, we'll have to do some immediate work on the investments in Lagrange Five and the Asteroid Islands.''

"Yes, sir," Barry said. "Sir, something has come up. I tried to contact you by every means but . . . well, with the usual results. It seems we have a situation fraught with . . ."

"Tell me about it when you get here," Hamp said brusquely. "What's the enjoyment in being a recluse if every senior member of your staff can get in touch with you every time he thinks an emergency has surfaced?"

"Yes, sir." There was resigned disapproval in the other's face.

Hamp faded him off, arose from his chair, and stretched his shoulder muscles. In spite of the time of day, he went over to the bar and brought forth a bottle of stone age Armagnac and a snifter glass. He poured a sizable jolt, then went over to the bookshelves, searching for a moment before selecting a copy of Cheikh Anta Diop's *The African Origin of Civilization* in the original French, and returned with it to his chair.

In the next half hour he went through a good quarter of the brandy, several times checking with the mirror. At the end of that period he was satisfied with what he saw. The face that looked back at him was that of, say, a well-tanned Frenchman.

He went back into the study and again sat at his restricted phone screen. He punched for a foreign call and then twice again.

The face that appeared was a twin of his own, including dark blue eyes, crew-cut reddish hair, and the well-tanned face of a European playboy.

Hamp said briskly, "Jim, I'm taking over for an indefinite time, probably a month or so. Go to ground. Assume your usual identity. I'll get in touch when I need you."

The other grinned. "Any suggestions?"

"You might try the Malta retreat. But be on immediate call."

"You're the boss," Jim told him. "You slave driver."

The face of his stand-in faded.

Chapter Five:
Franklin Pinell

Frank Pinell looked about the shabby, windowless room of the Hotel Rome in the International Zone of Tangier. Ten dirhams a day. Two pseudo-dollars. Cheap, perhaps, for any shelter at all, but with the cost of food, his bankroll would melt away in short order.

It was late afternoon, but he'd had lunch on the jet with his two escorts and wasn't yet hungry. The thing to do was to get out and start to make contacts. If there were jobs to be had, he was going to have to find one soonest. He had only been here for a couple of hours but he had seen what poverty was like in the old, old town of Tangier and wanted no part of it. Seemingly, there was no sort of government relief whatever for the poor; certainly nothing like GAS.

It was orientation time; he must contact his fellow English-speaking residents. He went into the hall, taking the key that Luigi had given him, locking the door behind. Why, he couldn't say. He had left nothing in the room. He had nothing to leave. On his way out, he hung the key on the rack behind the desk. On the face of it, anyone coming along could have taken it down, or any of the others, and stripped the place. But strip it of what? He doubted that any of the other tenants of the fleabag had much more in the way of possessions than he had.

He walked down the rickety stairs to the ground level and looked up and down Rue Moussa Ben Moussair, as drab a street as he had ever seen. The cab driver who had stolen his luggage had told him that Pasteur Boulevard, the town center, was two blocks up. He headed left, reached Rue Goya, turned left again. He carefully checked his route, having no desire to get lost.

Two blocks up, Rue Goya came into Pasteur Boulevard

and the immediate change couldn't have been more definite.
Its two or three blocks could have been directly out of a
swank Florida or Southern California resort. The cars, many
chauffeur driven, were the latest from Common Europe, the
Americas, and the Asiatic League. The pedestrians were largely
Europeans with a sprinkling of Orientals and a few North
Africans. All seemed prosperous—the suits of the men had
been cut in London, Rome, Manhattan; the clothes of the
women in Paris, Budapest, Copenhagen, or Los Angeles. The
women were strictly Tri-Di shows. Most of them could have
passed as the latest sex symbols of the entertainment world,
or as fashion models. Every hair seemed to be in place. Quite
a few tripped along behind poodles and Pomeranians.

Surprised by the opulence, Frank turned left on the boulevard and walked along slowly, staring into the shop windows.
Save for such centers as Manhattan in his own country, in an
age when cities were crumbling, Frank Pinell had seldom
seen privately owned shops before. His was an era of automated ultra-markets, through which credit could purchase
anything from a safety pin to a yacht. But these that lined the
main boulevard of European Tangier were the purveyors of
ultimate luxury—clothing and shoe stores, art galleries, jewelry stores, gourmet food shops, liquor stores. Mingled among
them were small, intimate restaurants, offering the outstanding cuisines of the world, and even more intimate cocktail
lounges. On the face of it, not all of Tangier was poverty-
stricken.

He stood to one side for a moment and watched the pass-
ersby. An Indian woman, a red caste mark on her forehead,
went past in a golden sari. He had never witnessed a more
graceful female in his life. A Parisian—by the looks of
her—went by, complete with arrogant champagne poodle.
What had MacDonald said about the Madrid mopsies being
the most beautiful in the world? Frank doubted it. Perhaps
this girl wasn't a prostitute, or even a mistress, but if she was
he wondered vaguely what she charged for a night's entertainment. Two men passed briskly, attaché cases in hand, in
business suits that looked as though they'd come from the
tailor's less than half an hour previously. They had the healthy,
tanned, barbered, massaged look of the ultimately successful.
Then an Oriental girl tripped along in an off-white silken

cheongsam, the slits at the outer thighs mesmerizing him. He had thought the Indian in her sari the epitome of grace, but this lovely little creature looked like a Chinese doll.

He looked up and down the boulevard, wondering where to go and what to do. All his impulses were to enter one of the bars and have the drink he needed. His present finances didn't allow for alcoholic beverages, certainly not at the prices that would prevail here.

A voice from behind him said, "Cooee, mate. You look like a flashing lost soul. Dinkum you do. Could a bloke give you a steer?"

Frank turned sharply. Grinning down at him from a height of at least six foot four was a long, cheerfully rugged type, a spanking new Australian bush hat pushed back on his head, but otherwise as nattily dressed as the other males on the street. Somehow, he looked slightly uncomfortable in his tailored afternoon suit. Indeed, he was on the gawky side, and obviously meant for the ranch, rather than a city's sidewalks.

Frank said, "What?"

"You look like a Yank, strewth, a Yank or maybe a Canuck, new in this barstid town. Don't want to be cheeky, but you don't look like you know your way around, what-o?"

Frank said, "Oh. Thanks. Fact is, I just pulled in and don't know the ropes. Is there some place, a neighborhood, where Americans hang out? Not just Americans, but anybody who speaks English." He hesitated, then stuck out his hand and said, "Frank Pinell. And, yeah, American. You're Australian?"

"Too right. Nat Fraser. Bonzer to meet you, Frank." His hand was huge, dry as the outback, and strong. "Not as many Yanks, Aussies, or even Limeys in town as you'd bloody well wish. You go crazy as a kookaburra for a fresh face or two."

"You're permanent here?" Frank said, regaining his well-squeezed and -pumped hand.

"Too true, oh my word. And don't think I wouldn't do a bunk if I could. Crikey, I haven't had a contract for donkey's years. Now, let's see. A bar where the English speaking coves hang out. Well, mate, actually there's three. There's the Parade, where the toffs take on their plonk." He took in Frank's suit. "Probably too rich for your blood, what-o?"

Frank said, after letting air out of his lungs ruefully, "Sounds like it. I'm on a limited budget and I need a job."

The Australian cocked his head at him. "Going to be in this googly town for a spell, eh?"

Frank could think of no reason for disguising his status. "I'm a deportee," he said, watching the other's face to get his reaction.

There wasn't any. Nat Fraser was going on as though he hadn't heard the confession. "Then there's the Carousel, over on Rue Rubens. Not your cup of tea, cobber. What do you Yanks call them? Gays. I doubt you get your lollies that way."

"No," Frank said. "What's this third one?"

"Paul Rund's, down on the Grand Socco. That's the biggest *souk* in town. And Paul sells the cheapest plonk in Tangier. Drink it and you wake up with the jumping Joe Blakes in the moring, fair dinkum. As a matter of fact, cobber, I was off in that direction meself when I bagged you looking lost."

"If you don't mind, I'll tag along," Frank said.

"Bloody well told. Let's go."

They started up the boulevard.

Frank looked up at his elongated companion and said, "Do you think I might make a contact at this Paul's bar?"

Nat Fraser considered it. "With the two thousand Swiss francs I suppose you've got in your kick from your flashing government, I'd think you could wait it out until you're able to cobber up somebody who could give you a steer."

Frank inwardly winced but said nothing about the fact that his thousand pseudo-dollars had melted down to less than two hundred.

At the end of Pasteur Boulevard they entered an attractive square, largely lined with sidewalk cafes.

"Place de France," the Aussie told Frank.

The sidewalk tables were well patronized, largely by prosperous European types, most of whom were reading newspapers. Moroccan waiters, in red fezzes and baggy black pants like bloomers, scurried around taking and delivering orders. There was a superfluity of shoeshine boys.

They turned right, down a winding street considerably narrower than Pasteur Boulevard had been. The composition of the pedestrians began to change radically. As they progressed, they saw fewer people in European clothing and more in the dress of Africa, the Near East, and the Orient.

"The Rue de la Liberte," Nat Fraser told him. "Where the bloody twain meets. You know, East is East and West is West." He gave running comment on races and costume.

There were growing numbers of Rifs, Arabs, Berbers—even an occasional Blue Man down from the mountains. The name of the latter, Nat explained, sprang from the indigo dye of their robes which, when they sweated, came off on their skins, giving them an eerie look. At least half of the women still wore the *djellaba* or *haik* with veil; half the men wore the brown camel's-hair *burnoose*. Africa, evidently, changed slowly even in the 21st Century.

"And this is the Grand Socco, mate. Cooee, a fair cow, eh? Ever see so many wogs in your life?"

It was a large square, packed with humanity and with a hundred different varieties of stalls—flower booths, food stands, and herb stands, hashish being among the other so-called herbs. There were displays of vegetables, fruits, hand-woven textiles, yellow or white *babouche* slippers, and a multitude of other commodities, some seemingly desirable in the eyes of Moroccans and some aimed deliberately to attract tourists. There were still more of the Arabs and Rifs, plus sailors up from the port and European riffraff from a score of countries. Donkeys seemed to be the means of transport; no car could have gotten through the press of bodies. Odors of mint, saffron, and *kif*, the North African cannabis, mingled in the air.

Rather than press into the *souk*, the teeming native market, they turned left and did their best to get through the crowded way, the Australian in front, running interference. It seemed one hell of a strange location for an English-speaking bar.

Nat was explaining over his shoulder, "Paul's been here for donkey's years," he said. "He's so warm in half a dozen countries, he'll never be able to leave. Owes something like a hundred and fifteen years in Italy alone for smuggling, and with his TB he wouldn't last six months in one of those cold, damp, wop nicks. No extradition from Tangier. He'll never leave, oh my word. Interpol would grab him in ten minutes if he put a toe down in Gibraltar."

They arrived at Paul's Bar—there was a small faded sign hanging out in front.

Inside, it was dark and cool but hardly prepossessing. There were six or seven stools at the bar, three tables with chairs. On the walls were pasted aged clippings about the proprietor's exploits in the old days when he was allegedly a ranking lockpicker, screwsman, grifter, and smuggler. They were alternated with pinups from aged pornographic magazines. From the ceiling hung a fisherman's net and a ship's wheel which doubled as a chandelier, a vain attempt to give Paul's Bar a nautical decor.

There were only three people present—one slumped at a table, head on arms, one seated dejectedly on a stool at the bar with a bottle of beer before him, and the bartender himself. Automated bars seemed to be unknown in Tangier, at least in this part of town—the *medina*, as Nat had named it.

The bartender had once been a larger man. Now he was emaciated. His sallow face had a sardonic quality and he wore a moth-eaten Vandyke beard tinged with gray. He looked up when the newcomers entered and wiped the well-worn bar with a dirty bar rag, uselessly.

He said, "Cheers, Nat," then looked at Frank. It seemed that in Paul's Bar one was introduced before being served.

Nat and Frank crawled onto stools and the Austalian said, "Paul, meet Frank Pinell, a new cobber in town from the States. He's looking for a contact."

Paul put a thin hand over the bar and shook hands.

However, his eyes were narrow. "What kind of a contact?" he said. It was the tone that bothered Frank. He said, "Well, I don't know. Just about anything, I guess."

"You warm?" Paul Rund said. Frank thought he understood what the other meant. "Only in the States," he said. And then, not particularly liking this, added, "Why?"

Paul leaned on the bar and said, "Because this is a poxy town, Frank. There's no extradition laws, there's practically no laws at all, but what there are get pretty well obeyed, get it? This is the end of the line for a lot of grifters. There's no place else to go if they kick you out. So we're poxy careful not to foul our own nest, get it? We lay doggo, that's the word, lay doggo. We don't take no scores here in Tangier.

Absolutely. And the boys take a dim view if anybody tries it. We don't want the present easygoing laws to be no way changed.''

"That's the dinkum oil," Nat said, nodding. "But you've got it wrong, Paul. Gawd strewth. Pull your head in. Frank didn't come here to do a romp. Deported from the States, he was. The poor cove's got to cobber up with somebody and get an angle.''

Paul evidently took the tall Australian's word for it. He said, "Good show. Just wanted to tell you the drill here, Frank. You look like the type of sod who'd pinch something here in Tangier and put all our bloody arses in a sling. What'll it be, lads? First drink's on the bloody house, Frank.''

Nat said, "Make it a couple of Storks, Paul." He looked at Frank as the bartender turned to serve them. "Not up to Aussie brew, strike me blind. But, from what I hear, better than you Yanks are turning out these days.''

"It wouldn't have to be very good," Frank told him. "They make syntho-beer from sawdust or something.''

The two took their bottles of beer and glasses and went to the remotest of the three tables and sat down. The beer glass wasn't clean but Frank didn't give a damn. He poured appreciatively. It was the first drink he'd had for several months and a lot of guff had been thrown at him in the past couple of days in particular.

"Not bad suds considering it's made by ragheads," his companion said, downing his whole glass in one vast draught. "The cheeky barstids don't suppose to ever enjoy a shivoo in their whole narky lives. Oh my word, no. Against Allah's buggering rules.''

Frank didn't take much longer to finish his. The Aussie was right. It wasn't bad beer at all. Probably still made from malt and hops, he assumed, instead of the crap being turned out at home these days for the prole palate.

Nat said, "How about another, cobber?" He came to his feet. Frank said, "All right, but I ought to pay for this.''

"Don't be a zany. You can't afford to play the toff until you get yourself settled in. Been down on the bone meself in me time. Settle down, cobber." The Aussie went over to the bar and secured another couple of bottles from the thin-faced bartender. Frank looked after him thoughtfully.

When he had returned and they had refilled their glasses, Frank held his up and said, "Thanks, Nat. Mud in your eye."

Nat said, holding up his glass in toast, "Fuck Ireland."

They both drank and then Frank said, "What did you say?"

"Oh. Fuck Ireland."

Frank looked at him. "Why?"

The Australian's easygoing face took an expression of being put upon. "Cooee, cobber, I don't know. That's what we say in Melbourne, strewth."

Frank said, "Look here, Nat. Do you always talk this way? I miss about half of what you mean."

Nat Fraser grinned, a ruefulness there. "A bit thick, eh? Always sets you Yanks back. I wasn't trying to cozen you."

Frank chuckled, the first occasion he could remember having done so for some time. He said, "All right, no harm done, but let's keep it on a level where we communicate."

"Fair dinkum."

The American looked about the room, then brought his eyes back to his newfound friend. "Nat," he said. "This doesn't exactly look like an employment agency. In fact, it's obviously a low-class bar where the town's less prosperous, uh, grifters, I believe is the term Paul used, hang out."

Nat looked around too, taking in the other customers, both on the seedy side. "Too right," he admitted. "Shall we do a bunk?"

"You mean get out? No," Frank told him. "Why'd you bring me here, Nat? "

The over-lengthy Aussie let his sun-faded eyebrows go up. "What-o, cobber? You think I was trying to cozen you?"

"Look," Frank said patiently, "I'm game, but not everybody's. I was walking along the street, minding my own business. Suddenly you're there, winsome as a pimp, but you sure as hell don't act like one. Fifteen minutes later, we're in this dump. Why?"

The Australian went over and got two more bottles of Stork beer and returned with them. He was grinning. "You said you were a deportee," he told Frank as he put the bottles down.

"So?"

"I'm the local recruiting sergeant, cobber."

*   *   *

Frank stared at him, even while upending the bottle over his glass. "What is that supposed to mean?"

"Had any military training at all?"

"No."

Nat Fraser looked disappointed. "Don't twig anything about a shooter, eh? What did they nail you for, cobber?"

"I didn't say that. My old man was a gun crank. Had quite a collection. I didn't see much of him but he used to get a kick out of showing me the workings of everything from cap-and-ball revolvers to new Gyrojets. What was I nailed for? Homicide."

The easygoing Aussie took him in for a long moment.

Frank said, "Recruiting sergeant for what?"

"Mercenaries, Incorporated."

Frank scowled. "Never heard of it."

"The Graf's outfit."

"Never heard of him, either. You mean professional soldiers of fortune?"

"That's the dinkum oil. This is one of the big staging areas for many a contract. The Graf gets a contract and we put the operation together here in Tangier."

"I thought Paul said you pulled nothing off here. That Tangier was sort of neutral ground. The boys, as he called them, didn't want to foul their own nest."

"Fair dinkum. We don't *do* anything here in Tangier. Just recruit blokes who want to earn a little money, and put the operation together. The Graf's sometimes got other operations going. We crew some of them, too. Aren't as many bloody contracts these days as there used to be, but some. Bush wars down south between all the dictators, presidents for life, and that whole mucking lot. Some in the Far East, too. But we don't handle those operations. They're based in Singapore and Penang. The Graf's got his representatives there as well."

Frank said, "Soldiers of fortune, eh? Hiring yourself out to kill for money." There was disgust in his voice.

The ordinarily amiable Aussie looked at him coldly. "What other reason is there to fight, cobber? A soldier's job is to win wars. If you pick that pro-bloody-fession, you wind up killing people, usually other soldiers who've picked the same trade."

Some of his exaggerated Aussie slang seemed to have dropped away.

Frank said, "The theory is that the usual soldier is fighting for his country. He's doing his duty, defending it."

"Too right. That's the theory, but it's not the reality. I'm not talking about blokes drafted during wartime. They can't get out of it, even if they want to. But your professional soldiers are a bunch of hypocrites. At least a mercenary can choose what side he fights on. But your career soldier fights whoever the politicians tell him to. Look at the Germans in the Nazi war. Were they fighting for their country? Fucking well not. They were fighting for that dingo barstid Hitler and his gang."

Frank was irritated by the other's strong opinions. He said, "Even granting that doesn't excuse a mercenary, fighting for whoever will pay him."

"Half a mo, cobber. I've never taken a contract for some fucking barstid like Hitler or any other politician I thought was buggering up his country. Sometimes I've been offered contracts where I wouldn't fight on either side."

Frank stood and said, "I'll get another, ah, buggering beer."

Nat said, reaching into a pocket, "You ought to let me shout the suds."

"Why?" Frank said. "I'm not a potential recruit. No reason I should be freeloading on you."

At the bar, while Paul Rund was getting the fresh bottles of Stork, the wizened bartender said, "Signing up with the Graf, Frank?"

Frank eyed him. "I don't think so. Do you know of any other jobs kicking around?"

The other popped off the two beer caps, then ran his thin fingers through his bedraggled Vandyke. "You might get a berth on one of the boats. Not as many of them as there used to be, but I heard Sam McQueen needed a couple of men."

"What kind of boats?"

Paul Rund looked at him as though he had hardly expected that question. "Smugglers."

Frank said, "For Christ's sake, I thought you said there was nothing illegal pulled off in Tangier!"

The bartender said patiently, "Smuggling ain't illegal. You

buy a cargo of hashish or tobacco here, perfectly legit, and run it to one of the countries where it's taboo, get it? And you sell it there, so you haven't broken any law in Tangier. Smugglers are reputable citizens here, get it?''

The American shook his head and took up the two beers. To his relief, they cost only two dirhams apiece in Paul's. Back at the table, after they had both poured, Nat Fraser said, "So you're not interested?"

"I suppose not. Look, I'm not holier than thou. In fact, I suspect my father was some sort of mercenary; possibly in espionage, I don't know. He and my mother were separated when I was a kid; I didn't see him much. He was usually out of the country, I think. At any rate, he was finally shot on one of his trips. I haven't any desire to end the same way."

The other shurgged broad shoulders. "The Graf's got other operations, like I said. Maybe he could find a place in the organization for a nice presentable cove like yourself."

"From what you've said so far about his operations, I doubt it," Frank said, finishing his beer. He stood. Somewhat to his surprise, he could feel the drink. Possibly, Stork was stronger than the gassy anemic American brew he was used to.

He said, "Thanks anyway, Nat. I'll see you around."

"Too right, cobber. If you change your mind, I'm usually here this time of night."

Frank sent his glance out of one of the dirty windows. It was dark out on the Grand Socco. He hadn't realized they'd been talking for so long.

He left after waving to Paul Rund and stood for a moment before the door. Not a fraction of the teeming Moroccans were still on the streets or in the *souk*. Evidently, everything folded in the medina with the coming of night. He made his way past shuttered stalls, past steel-barred store fronts, retracing his route as best he could.

He shook his head over the experiences of the past few hours. No crime in Tangier, eh? Uh-huh. Aside from the IABI men ripping off eight hundred of his thousand pseudo-dollars, the customs officer had lifted his camera, his cab driver had stolen his luggage, he had been offered a job as a mercenary despite his lack of experience, and had been told he might land a berth on a boat smuggling narcotics.

He came to a street that might be Rue de la Liberte and headed up it. It was too dark to make out the signs. He thought the street should have had more pedestrian traffic and more lights than this.

The blow that struck him on the back of the neck took him completely unawares. He felt his mouth sag open even as he crumbled.

At first, he wasn't completely out but agonizingly paralyzed. He could feel hands hastily going through his pockets, turning them inside out. Two more shadowy figures came hurriedly to his side. He tried to last but could feel no power in his limbs. One of his assailants thoughtfully kicked him in the side of the head and then the fog rolled over him.

Chapter Six:
Roy Cos

From Greater Miami they were lobbed over to the island of New Providence by laser boost in approximately ten minutes.

Roy Cos, strapped into his enveloping seat, took a deep breath as acceleration loads mounted and said, "Never been in one of these things before."

"I wish I could say the same," Forry Brown told him, in his usual sour voice. "I hate the damn things."

Roy looked out the small, thick glass porthole at the unbelievable blue sea with its occasional frothed ripples of waves. "That's the Gulf Stream, eh?"

"Yeah," Forry told him. "It keeps the Bahamas at a constant year-round temperature of between seventy and eighty in the shade. George Washington was one of the first tourists here. He called them 'The Isles of Perpetual June.' "

Below, the Wobbly organizer could already see small islands. He said, "How many of them are there?"

They had reached the peak of their arc now, and for a few seconds were in free fall before their shuttle began the deceleration.

The little ex-newsman said, "Most people think of the Bahamas as only the town of Nassau, but actually, there are about 700 islands and nearly 2,000 cays and rocks." His tone took on a cynical singsong parody of a tour guide. "Scattered like a fistful of pearls in turquoise waters extending over an area of 70,000 square miles."

Roy looked over at him. "You've been here before, eh?"

"That's right. Actually, it's one of the most beautiful resort areas in the world. Ah, we're coming in."

The shuttle landed at the Windsor International Airport and Forry Brown had a cigarette in his mouth before they started down the gangway, jostling along with their fellow passengers.

Roy Cos hadn't experienced much in the way of nature's charms in his forty-some years. It cost money to seek nature out on the mainland and he'd never had more than GAS. Now, his first impression as they walked in bright sunlight toward customs was one of flower-scented breezes. Even here at the shuttleport, there were gaudy Bahamian flowers—purple and red bougainvillea, yellow and red hibiscus, pink, white, and red oleander, royal purple passionflowers. Their mingling perfumes gave a subtle fragrance to the southeast trade winds. Not that Roy Cos knew their names. Beyond roses, daisies, and tulips he was lost in the world of flowers, as his parents before him. He was a prole born, and proles seldom had gardens.

Customs was the merest of formalities. Forry Brown's attaché case and Roy Cos's battered briefcase weren't even opened. However, Roy's credit card, which doubled as his passport, brought up the eyes of the black man in the Bahama immigrations uniform.

He said politely, "Suh, GAS credits are not valid in the islands."

Forry said, "Mr. Cos is my guest." He handed over his own Universal Card.

"Jolly well, suh," the other told him, returning the ex-newsman's credit card and then touching the brim of his cap in an easygoing salute.

They passed on toward the metro station, where everyone seemed to be heading.

Roy looked over at the other from the side of his eyes and said, "I didn't know that immigrations men could tell what type of pseudo-dollar credits were accredited to a Universal Credit Card by just looking at it. And what was that about GAS credits not being valid?"

"You can't spend your GAS outside the limits of the United States of the Americas," Forry told him. "The government wants you to spend it at home. Why subsidize foreign countries by spending unearned credits in them? The Bahamas, along with Cuba, are the only Caribbean islands that don't belong to the United States. The Bahamas won't join because it's more profitable to stand on the sidelines and offer gambling and offbeat banking practices, such as numbered accounts, and multinational commercial deals like

Deathwish Policies. Anything goes in the Bahamas; they
haven't got the restrictive laws we rejoice in at home. They
figure any adult should be allowed to go to hell in his own
way, just so that doesn't interfere with anyone else.''

"I'll be damned. You mean you can even buy heroin here,
openly—and things like tobacco?''

"Yes," the other told him ironically, flicking his cigarette
butt into a waste receptacle.

The metro system had probably been imported from the
United States, Roy realized. The vacuum cars had them into
downtown Nassau within minutes.

They emerged from the central metro station onto an avenue teeming with pedestrians and bicycles but even more
devoid of cars than an American city would have been. This
was the downtown area, the harbor immediately before them.
Roy's first impression was that the whole place was a museum. Only in historical films had he seen buildings which
seemed to go back to at least Victorian days.

Forry looked around too, a warmth in his squinting eyes.
He obviously liked the town. He said, continuing his tour
guide lecturing, "This is Bay Street, the main tourist shopping center. It's a free port, no taxes, so the tourists go hog
wild. Over there is Rawson Square, with the government
administration buildings. Over there's the post office, and
that statue's Queen Victoria. The garden behind contains the
Public Library and museum, which dates back to 1799 and
was originally built as a jail.''

They turned left on Bay Street, walking along as rapidly as
the shopping traffic would allow. The buildings seemed completely devoted to tourist stores, bars, and restaurants.

Roy said, "I wouldn't think they'd have much need for
jails in a place like this.''

His small gray companion laughed. "In its earliest days,
this island was a pirate center. Blackbeard himself built a
lookout tower down the beach a ways. After the pirates were
kicked out, the Bahamas went into a depression until the
American revolution, when they became prosperous smuggling military supplies to the colonists. Then they went into
the doldrums again until our Civil War, when they became
the clearinghouse for sneaking cotton out to England and
France and smuggling guns in to the Confederates. Then

another depression until Prohibition, when they all got rich running rum. Eventually they hit on becoming an all-out, anything-goes resort area. Now they've parlayed that up to include international banking—and other criminal activities. Oh, never fear, they've always been able to use a good jail here in Nassau.''

They turned down Parliament Street, and shortly the shops gave way to small business buildings and private homes. Even business was housed in ancient structures. The private homes were largely built of island limestone with upper porches that hung over the streets. To protect them from the sun, wide verandas had been built in graceful wooden construction with louvers to admit cooling breezes.

The Wobbly organizer stared at something coming down the street. He said, ''I don't think I've ever seen a horse-drawn carriage before.''

''That's a surrey,'' the other told him. ''They hate cars out here. You seldom see one, except those used by government.'' The newsman looked at a card he drew from his jacket pocket. ''This seems to be the address.''

It was a prosperous-looking business establishment, in the Victorian tradition. There was a small bronze plaque which Roy couldn't make out above the entry, and a uniformed black standing before it. The man touched his cap at their approach and held open the door. They seemed to use more manpower here than in the automated States.

The interior continued the Victorian motif, with a few concessions to the tropics. There was a pervasive Britishness about it all. Roy had expected the company would be American, with some affiliation to a sinister background such as the Mafia.

Forry Brown seemed to sense what his companion was thinking and said, ''This outfit is a subsidiary of one of the big insurance companies in Hartford. It's multinational, of course, specializing in Deathwish Policies, though it has some other far-out bits of business going.''

There was a sterile reception office presided over by a live receptionist, plain of face, her dull hair done up in an unfashionable bun. She wore a washed out, shapeless light dress.

Forry said, "Good morning. Mr. Roy Cos on appointment to see Mr. Oliver Brett-James."

"Very good, sir," she clipped, checking a notepad. "You are expected. Mr. Brett-James will see you immediately." She did the things receptionists do, speaking into a comm set, saying, "Yes, sir," a couple of times, and then pressing a button.

She came to her feet saying, "This way, please," and led them down a short hallway.

She held open a door and bestowed on them what she probably thought was a smile.

Roy and Forry entered a moderately large office, once again with a Londonish feel—stolid, spotless, cold. Mr. Oliver Brett-James was standing behind an old-fashioned wooden desk. He was tubby, almost naked of scalp, red rather than tanned, his complexion more from bottles than the Bahamian sun. His smile was conservatively polite, though he seemed surprised to see two of them. "Mr. Cos?" he said.

"That's right," Roy told him. Neither of them made a motion toward shaking hands. Under the circumstances, it didn't seem exactly called for.

"And you, sir?" the Englishman said to Forry.

"Forrest Brown," Forry said. "I'm Mr. Cos's business agent."

"Business agent? Well, no reason why not, I daresay. Be seated, gentlemen. Shall we get immediately to business? Here is the contract. It goes into effect tomorrow. And here is your International Credit Card, drawn on our Swiss bank in Berne. Each day, as you undoubtedly know, you will have one million pseudo-dollars at your disposal. It doesn't accumulate, of course, but each day you have that amount available."

Roy and Forry had taken chairs in front of the desk. Forry said sourly, scratching a thumbnail over his meager mustache, "Suppose we read the contract before signing."

"Certainly, old chap," the Briton said. "I merely thought that you were already cognizant of its contents, in which case there'd be no point in mucking around." He handed a three-page sheaf of paper to each of them and then leaned back patiently in his swivel chair.

His two callers read what he had given them carefully.

Forry had already dug up copies of the standard Deathwish Policy and this didn't deviate from it.

After a few minutes, while they were still reading, Brett-James cleared his throat and said, "Please take note of Clause Three. You must understand that we will not tolerate frivolous expenditures. That is, suppose you decide to purchase a diamond or a painting. If the price is over 10,000 pseudo-dollars, we will have an expert evaluate the item. We do not expect to have you spending, say, 50,000 pseudo-dollars on something which is really worth but 15,000. We expect our specialists to check out the true value, within reason. Of course the gem or painting, as the case might be, reverts to us upon your, ah, unfortunate demise."

Forry looked up finally and said, "Just how much does the policy pay off in benefits to you when Mr. Cos, ah, passes on?"

Oliver Brett-James stiffened. "I say, that isn't really a concern of yours now, is it?"

Forry took him in. "Yes," he said. "The details of this transaction will help me in supervising his interests."

The other didn't like it, but he said finally, "Our corporation will receive ten million pseudo-dollars in the way of benefits."

Forry said gently, "And how much are the daily premiums that you must pay?"

"See here, Mr., uh, Brown. This is of no interest to . . ."

"We think it is," the ex-newsman said. He brought a pack of cigarettes from his pocket and shook forth a smoke. "We either find out, or Mr. Cos doesn't sign." He put the cigarette in his colorless lips and brought forth his lighter.

Brett-James stared at him for a long moment, but finally said, "The daily premiums are one million pseudo-dollars."

The gray-faced Forry nodded as he lit up, blowing smoke through his pinched nostrils. "Clear enough. You have to do Roy in within ten days or you start losing money."

The signing of the contract was witnessed by the receptionist and another nonentity she brought in, a young man who avoided Roy's eyes as he signed.

When the two witnesses were gone, Brett-James rubbed his hands together and said, "Jolly well. I daresay you'll be returning immediately to the mainland. Where will you be staying?''

Forry looked at him flatly. "Get serious," he said. "Do you think we'd give you that much of a head start?" He put Roy's copy of the contract into his attaché case.

When they had left, the other pressed a button on his desk and four men entered, one of them the young witness. Brett-James said, "You've got the photos, the tapes and all?"

The oldest of the four nodded. "Yes, sir."

"Very well, get to work on both of them. Check out this Forrest Brown chap. We'll want to know just where he fits in." Brett-James made a motion with his hand. "All right, Maurice, tail them. Follow the instructions I gave you earlier."

As they walked back toward Bay Street, Forry looked at his wrist chronometer. "We've got over an hour before the next shuttle to Miami. We might as well eat. Blackbeard's Tavern is a good place."

"Right," Roy said, immersed deeply in bleak thoughts.

They reached the shopping center and turned left.

The little ex-newsman stopped at a shop and said, "Just a minute. I might as well stock up here."

The sign said, 'Solomon's Mines,' and they entered to find the store devoted almost exclusively to tobacco products. Roy muttered, "Jesus Christ. In the States this shop would've been raided before it opened."

His companion ordered a dozen packs of Russian Imperial Gold Tip Blacks and began stuffing them into his pockets. "A fraction of what they cost on the black market at home," he said. "Here, stick these away." He handed Roy six packs.

"Wait a minute," Roy Cos said indignantly. "Suppose they nail me with them at American customs. It's a bad policy for a member of the Wobblies. A radical can't afford to be anything else offbeat. It gives them a handle to get at you."

Forry said impatiently, "They never search your person at customs unless you're a known smuggler or have a criminal record when they check you out in the data banks."

Roy shrugged in resignation and distributed the six packages of cigarettes about his pockets.

As they left the shop, the little newsman was tearing one

pack open. He shook out a gold-tipped, black-papered cigarettee and said, "Like to try one?"

"For God's sake, do I look stupid? You think I want to wind up with my lungs eaten away and my heart pounding overtime?"

Forry grinned. "They've been denouncing alcohol for centuries, but I notice you're not particularly opposed to taking a drink."

"It's only excessive use of alcohol that's condemned," Roy told him, his tone righteous. "Moderate use of alcohol has been a blessing to man since prehistory."

"By Christ, you radicals are the most conservative cloddies going. You're worse than the United Church. Excess of *any*thing will do you in. Drink enough water and you'll drown."

They argued companionably, deliberately avoiding the subject uppermost in both their minds.

Blackbeard's Tavern turned out to be a cozy bar and restaurant, with a small calypso band playing in the background, surprisingly softly. They took a table and a white-jacketed, barefooted black was there immediately to take their order.

Forry said, with obvious anticipation, "Native Bahamians have their own food specialties that are hard to get elsewhere. Conch, for instance—a kind of shellfish. We'll have conch chowder, green turtle pie, and baked Andros crabs. And black beer to go with it."

Roy put down his menu and let the other do all of the ordering. When the waiter was gone, he said, "I think we were followed."

"Yeah, I noticed that," Forry said. "Forget about it. The contract doesn't go into effect until tomorrow. But don't forget that tomorrow starts at midnight. Meanwhile, they most certainly don't want anything to happen to you before then. That bastard tailing us is more like a bodyguard than anything else, at this stage. It'll be something else if we see him tomorrow."

The waiter brought large mugs of very dark beer and, shortly afterward, the conch chowder. They ate without joy, stolidly going through the motions while lost in their thoughts. It had been one thing, planning this coup, but getting down to the nitty-gritty in Brett-James's office had brought home

reality. The contract was signed now and there was no going
back; as of midnight, Roy would have a price on his pelt.

Again they avoided saying what was uppermost in both of
their minds. Forry skated near it with, "Funny how societies
always seem to provide for the future by accident. Ever
consider that maybe this bland food is preparing us for a dull
future?"

Roy frowned at his plate. "It *is* kind of tasteless. You
mean we're getting ourselves ready for an era of the blahs?"

The little newsman said, "A slow dissolution, maybe." He
nodded agreement with himself. "Without necessarily deliberate planning, society provides for the future. In this case, a
future in which over ninety percent of the population became
proles. The big difference between proles and slaves is that
the slaves had to work to maintain the upper classes. But now
machinery does practically all of the work and proles are real
drones, absolutely worthless."

Roy said, scowling, "How do you mean society provided
for *my* future? I didn't ask to become a complete drone. It
was foisted on me."

The newsman nodded again and put down his fork, giving
up the food for which neither of them had found enthusiasm.
"You're an exception. But over a century ago society was
already preparing for the day of the prole. Most kids at that
time were already spending more time watching TV than they
were spending in school. Oh, there were good schools in the
United States, such as MIT, Johns Hopkins, Berkeley, Caltech,
and so on. And the good schools turned out possibly five
percent of the college graduates of the time. But the rest of
the school system was a shambles. Kids got out of grammar
school unable to read and write. Hell, many of them grad-
uated from high school unable to function as adults—couldn't
make out an application, couldn't keep up a checkbook. Their
reading was confined to comic books or strips in the
newspapers, or painfully wading through the sports pages.
They got their news, to the extent they were interested at all,
from TV commentators."

"I still don't see how that leads to society preparing for the
future," Roy said, scowling still. This wasn't gospel as laid
down by the Wobbly movement.

"Our people were being prepared for becoming proles,

unemployables. In modern society you've got to have a good education to hold down a job. Fine, the five percent needed today got a good education. It's not necessary that the ninety percent have one. In fact, it's a disadvantage. An educated man, unemployed, is a potentially dangerous man. He can think, and question, and act on the answers he comes up with. Our educational system was weaning our youth away from an aggressive approach to life, taking the guts out of them, preparing them for their future as proles.''

Roy said softly, still in rejection, "So what's *our* future? What lies ahead for *us*?''

"Probably more of the same. And the upper class will continue to get richer and smaller, as it eliminates the lower levels of its own class, who are thrown down into the ranks of the proles if their fortunes are lost by whatever means— including being pissed away.''

The Wobbly looked at him, thoughtfully. He said, his voice slow, "You're more interested in these things than you've admitted, aren't you, Forry? How come you picked a Wobbly on this project of yours? Why not a Luddite, or Neo-Nihilist, or possibly a Libertarian? And why *me*?''

Forry Brown tossed his napkin to the table and looked at his wrist chronometer. "We have to get going,'' he said, bringing his card from his pocket. "You weren't my first choice, Roy. I approached another National Organizer of the Wobblies before you. He evidently wasn't cut out to be a martyr. He turned me down.''

Chapter Seven:
Lee Garrett

Cary McBride entered the *Nuits St. Georges* restaurant, his eyes on his wrist chronometer. He looked around hurriedly, frowned, and then went into the bar lounge.

Lee Garrett sat at a small table, a glass before her. She seemed not at all impatient.

He came up to her, his smile just slightly drawn. "Ms. Garrett, of course?" he said. He took in the glass with its light, golden contents. "By George," he said. "Not a drink before eating the specialties of Burgundy?" He took the table's second chair. "I'm Cary McBride."

She smiled brightly at him, her almost unbelievably blue eyes taking in his male fashion model appearance. Not only was Cary McBride handsome, in the best upper class tradition, but he was dressed for the part. His suit, shirt, and shoes were exactly what the youthful senior executive in Manhattan was wearing, not just this year, but probably this week.

She said, after shaking hands, "Only a sherry."

"Tio Pepe, I should hope," he said. "Anything stronger or less dry would play havoc with one's palate."

She did a little laugh, as though he were joking. "Tio Pepe is so dry it gives me heartburn."

"Then not another sip of that," he told her severely. "Andre would be desolate. Shall we go to our table?"

He took her arm and led her to the dining room. Lee was dressed in green Irish tweeds which would have denigrated any figure less superb than her own. She looked very businesslike, her simple white blouse and low heels very sincere.

The maitre d' greeted them unctuously and led them to a table tucked intimately away in a small nook. The decor was early French bistro: reproductions of Toulouse Lautrec's posters, aged advertisements of Ricard, Pernod, and a Rheims champagne. The room was moderately full of prosperous diners.

Andre put menus before them, brought forth a pad and stylo, and looked inquiringly, politely, and most earnestly at Cary McBride.

Cary McBride said to Lee, "The menu is in French. Shall I order?"

"Please do," she said, putting down her own *carte*.

Consulting with the headwaiter as he went, very seriously indeed, Cary McBride ordered as their first course *Oeufs en Cocotte Bourguignonne*, with a Meursault '48 to accompany it. When the wine arrived, Andre again presided pouring a small amount into McBride's tulip-shaped glass. He sipped it carefully, after he tested the bouquet, and thoughtfully pursed his lips.

Andre murmured, *"Le vin est a votre gout?"*

"Excellent," Cary McBride nodded, and the headwaiter filled both glasses two-thirds full.

Eggs *a la Bourguignonne* turned out to be poached in red burgundy, and for a moment, both were silent as they sampled.

Cary McBride said, "A pity to discuss business while eating, my dear, but I understand that you were contacted, as planned, by a member of the Anti-Racist League."

Lee nodded. "Yes," she said. "I'm afraid I muffed it."

"Not to worry, my dear. What went wrong?"

"I underestimated him. He was a black; well-educated. What tipped him off, I have no idea, but he saw through me. I suppose it was rather humorous. He pretended to get somewhat tipsy and, ah, pretended to make a rather crude play for me."

His eyebrows went up.

She shook her head and made a mouth in self-deprecation. "I became terrified, like a simple ninny, remembering all that I'd heard about rape, and revealed that I wasn't truly material for the Anti-Racists. He told me off very efficiently, greatly amused."

"I see. Then your cover is blown, so far as the Anti-Racist League is concerned."

"I'm afraid so."

"Not to worry," he said again. "Ah, the duck."

The *Canard a L'Orange* arrived with the Richebourg '65

he had ordered, and again went through the wine-tasting ceremony.

When the waiter had retired he said, "You were not alone. The Foundation has several, ah, agents making the same attempt to penetrate the Anti-Racist League. You were but one. Others, it is to be assured, will be more successful."

She said, "I wasn't told a great deal about the purpose of my mission. Actually, in spite of my silly scene with Horace Hampton, I am not particularly prejudiced so far as minorities are concerned. I was rather surprised that the Race Research Foundation was interested in infiltrating his organization. I thought its research would be along other lines."

"It is but one ramification of a much broader project. You see, Lee, the Anti-Racist League is a racist organization itself."

"I don't understand."

"In much the same way that the Zionists were."

She frowned slightly at him. "I'm not anti-Semitic, either."

"Nor am I, nor is the Foundation. We're far above such ridiculous postures. But there are most pertinent matters involved. The Anti-Racist League was not of particular import to us so long as it was active in the original fifty states alone. The minorities they represent numbered but some sixteen percent of the population; no great danger to our status quo. However, they are now, ah, beginning to spread into Latin America and other areas of the new United States of the Americas."

She scowled down at her plate. "I don't believe I follow you."

"These new citizens have the vote, Lee. There are enough blacks in Haiti, Jamaica, and even the Guianas to assure that their senators and representatives will be represented in Congress by blacks—if steps are not taken. It's equally true for Mexico, Central America, and the parts of South America which are chiefly Indian."

"So the purpose of the Race Research Foundation is . . ."

"Ultimately, to maintain the status quo. To see that *our* people, yours and mine, do not vanish from the positions of power they now assume. Ah, but here is the cheese. I have ordered a selection of Roquefort, Brie, and Chevre."

The cheese was accompanied by a bottle of Rose d'Anjou, following which the waiter brought *Crepes de Chapitre*.

Lee, who had been silent and thoughtful through these culinary wonders, said at one point, "But since my cover has been blown, as you put it, I am no longer of value to the Foundation."

He smiled at her condescendingly. "We'll discuss it later in my office, my dear."

When they finished the meal, Andre returned, bowing unctuously again.

He said to Cary McBride, "*Ça vous a plu, le repas, Monsieur McBride?*"

"*Il etait superb, Andre,*" the other told him grandly.

Andre looked at Lee. "*Et Madam?*"

Lee said, "*Mes felicitations au chef pour ses crepes. Ils etaient commes des diners de George Garin au Chateau du Clos de Veuheot. Il y avaient des autres nobles efforts.*"

"*Merci, Madam.*" Andre bowed deeply and was gone.

Cary McBride gaped at her. "Parisian French," he said accusingly.

"My father was in the diplomatic corps. In Paris, I attended the Lycee Janson de Sailly. I also have Spanish, Portugese, and Italian, and can get along in German. My Russian is atrocious."

"All Russian is atrocious," he smirked, then saw irritation in her face. "Or did I make a mistake?"

She said, evenly, "Several. Never order such a wine as Richebourg with such a dish as Canard a L'Orange. Nor any other wine, for that matter. The acid of the orange sauce destroys the enjoyment of any great wine. The sole exception is Bouzy, from the Champagne district. If you must order Richebourg it is worthy of a much greater dish, such as Venison Grand Veneur or Lievre a la Royale."

"I see," he said coldly. "And what else?"

"None of the cheeses were from Burgundy. A Brillat Savarin or ripe Epoisse would have been preferable. And Rose d'Anjou, a suspect wine at best, is anathema to both Burgundy food and any cheese and most certainly should never do for the crepes, which were excellent, as I told the maitre d'. By the way, his French has a horrible Brooklyn accent."

"I see," he said. "Shall we go?" He stood, tossing his napkin to the table.

She looked up at him. "Why? My one assignment for the Race Research Foundation came a cropper. I should have looked further into the whole thing before undertaking it. If I had, possibly I would have refused the job. I was too thrilled at the prospect of actually being employed when the computer selected me to work for you, Mr. McBride. Now, even if you did have some position I could hold down, I'm not sure I would choose to be associated with such a pompous superior."

He grinned suddenly, which completely altered his face. He said, "Good. We've got some things to discuss."

She shrugged in resignation, dropped her own napkin to the table, and stood. "I can't imagine what," she murmured.

At the desk, he brought forth his card and placed it in the payment slot, saying, "Please add a twenty percent tip."

"Thank you, sir," the screen said.

As he was returning his credit card to an inner pocket, he turned his eyes to Lee and smiled again. "How's my French?"

Her face was expressionless. "Only fair," she said. "You seldom acquire a proper French accent outside France or Switzerland. I suspect that most of your instructors were Americans. The French are fanatical about accent."

"I surrender," he said, taking her arm.

The Manhattan office of the Race Research Foundation was within easy walking distance and since it was located in the vicinity of New Columbia University, it made for a pleasant stroll. They maintained silence during the walk and Lee Garrett was surprised at the fact that he was still amused. This was a different Cary McBride. Gone was the affected front. What in the world was this all about? The fluffing of the job wasn't particularly important. But what she had told Horace Hampton had been partly correct. She was tired of the frivolous life and would have liked something worthwhile to do.

The Manhattan offices of the Race Research Foundation were modest. In the outer office were three desks, two women and a young man at them, equipped with the standard vocotypers, phone screens, and library boosters for consultation with the National Data Banks. All greeted Cary McBride by his first name, which surprised Lee. She had expected a stuffy atmosphere, at best.

He didn't bother to introduce her. His private office turned out to be a room of warmth and informality. He seated her in a comfortable chair before rounding the desk and taking his own place.

She still didn't know why she had come. Now that she had fluffed the Hampton contact, she couldn't see how she could possibly infiltrate the Anti-Racist League.

Cary McBride, smiling again, picked up a sheaf of papers from the desk and said, "This is your Dossier Complete. It reports that you attended the Lycee Janson de Sailly, one of the oldest private secondary schools in Paris. You were there for several years, invariably top in your class."

She glared indignantly at him. "What the devil are you doing with that? The Dossier Complete of any citizen can be consulted only by proper authorities for adequate cause. You need the highest priority in the National Data Banks to . . ."

He held up a hand and grinned his boyish grin at her. "Exactly." He watched suspicions chase across her face and then nodded. "We enjoy such a priority."

She was staring at him in sudden realization. "You knew all the time, there in the restaurant, that I spoke French."

"Guilty as charged."

"But . . . then why did you pretend to make such a fool of yourself before that . . . that Brooklyn Frenchman?"

He grinned once more. "Lee, the organization of which we are but one subsidiary makes every effort to recruit the best personnel. Practically every employment position filled in the United States goes through the National Data Banks computers. The computers select the most suitable person available for each job." He paused, then winked. "But we get to the data banks before the government computers even begin their selections. We skim the cream of the crop." He could see her confusion. He tapped the sheaf of papers before him.

"Lee, the Dossier Complete is possibly the most comprehensive tally of a citizen's life ever assembled. It begins before your birth, references going beyond your grandparents. And, from your birth, every aspect of your life is checked: health, upbringing, education, sports accomplishments, criminal record, employment record, travels, and on and on. Among other things checked is your ability quotient. Your dossier builds profiles of your verbal and numerical abilities, spatial ability, memory, speed of reflexes, dexterity, mechanical aptitude, emotional maturity, veracity, sensory limits, natural charm, persistence, neurosis, powers of observation, health, and a few others.''

She smiled. ''Depressing idea. We're all confronted with these confounded tests every few years. That is, if we have any interest in work or running for office. Maybe I should've refused to take them. But what's all this got to do with . . .''

He held up a hand. ''There are a few things, my dear, that can't be tested. Luck, for instance.''

''Luck! There is no such thing.''

''I'm afraid there is, just as there is accident-proneness, which also defies computer analysis. Even though you were given unbelievably high marks, suppose that when I entered the Nuits St. George I found you wearing two left shoes, or you were hunched up in posture, or you were dressed in khaki shorts and a man's shirt like a prole. Suppose further that when subjected to a 'pompous superior'—I believe that was your term—you were willing to accept him as your boss.''

She laughed. ''That was all put on! You were testing me.''

He grinned back and nodded. ''If you hadn't the other qualifications we were looking for, you might still have been employed—somehow. But we also wished to check your poise, grooming, physical attractiveness, and sensibilities. You passed with flying colors.''

She looked at him levelly. ''So, if I passed your exam that goes beyond the Ability Quotient tests, just what is this position you have in mind? I've already bombed out as an infiltrator of the Anti-Racist League.''

The other leaned back in his swivel chair and was silent for a few seconds. ''What do you know about the World Club?''

''Why, I suppose what everybody else knows: it's the think tank to end all think tanks—a multinational philanthropic organization which digs into socioeconomic problems confronting the world. Lagrange Five and Asteroid Belt Islands, too, for that matter.''

He nodded but said, ''It's a great deal more than that. It also keeps track of the population explosion, resources, pollution, religion, the tendencies toward the police state, terrorism, and . . . racism. For your ears only, the Race Research

Foundation is a subsidiary of the World Club. That would be a shocker even to the most diligent news media exposé experts.''

She was wide-eyed now. ''But what has this got to do with me?''

''You've been selected to work directly under the Central Committee, which likes a low profile. For the media, it doesn't exist.''

She was too flabbergasted to speak.

He took up a stylo and readied it over a paper pad. ''Before we go further into that, suppose we get the details of this interview you had with the black from the Anti-Racist League. His name?''

''Horace Hampton. Known as Hamp.''

Cary McBride flicked on a desk screen and said into it, ''Liz, check out a Horace Hampton, a.k.a. Hamp, of the Anti-Racist League, a black.''

Lee said, ''I don't know his I.D. number.''

Cary smiled at her. He was a damned sight more likeable than he had been in the restaurant. He said, ''He's black; a member of the Anti-Racist League. He'll be one of their better men if he was your contact. We'll have some record of him.''

They did. Shortly, his dossier began flashing on the screen. From time to time, he read out some extract to her. ''Seems to have some independent source of income, since seldom uses all of his GAS. No criminal record, though he is suspected of being one of the top trouble-shooters of the Anti-Racist League. Suspected in the slapstick fake assassination of Governor Teeter, though thus far there is no evidence.''

Lee was taken aback by that. ''He said that they were against violence.''

Cary chuckled as he looked mockingly at her. ''That's what he said. From what you've reported, he knew that you were a plant. What else could he say?''

''But he seemed sincere.''

''Oh, he's sincere, all right. He sincerely believes that extreme racists, such as Teeter, should be dealt with.'' Cary McBride, still scanning the black's dossier as he spoke to her, grunted his surprise.

He glanced up at Lee. ''This is strange,'' he said. ''That's possibly the thinnest dossier I've ever seen—especially when it comes to the criminal record.''

She wrinkled her forehead. ''How do you mean?''

''He has none whatsoever. Not even a traffic violation. And, as a result, he has no fingerprint record.'' He thought about it. ''I think I'll just forward the name of Horace Hampton to Rome. Perhaps they'll wish to look further into this.''

''Rome?''

''That's where the World Club is based. And that's where you're going, my dear.'' His smile was disarming. ''That is, if I can talk you into it.''

Chapter Eight:
Frank Pinell

A voice from a far distance was saying, "Cooee, wot in the flashing hell happened?"

Frank came alive to find, groggily, that he was sitting on the sidewalk, supported by an anxious Nat Fraser, who was hunkered down on one knee.

Frank got out, "Mugged. Two of them, I think."

"Barstids," the Australian growled. "Damned buggering ragheads. A bloke's not safe to walk up the street. Come on, cobber. We best get you to a sawbones. Never know, might have some broken ribs. They give you the bloody boot?" He got a long, sinewy arm around the fallen American's body and up under his armpits.

"I . . . I think so," Frank got out, trying to help himself erect.

"My car's over here. Just luck I came along. Don't usually use this street, Rue d'Angleterre, but I was heading up to Panikkar's place on Cape Spartel."

Frank half staggered, was half manhandled by his rescuer, to the small sports model hovercar which was parked, door open, at the curb.

As he was wedged into the bucket seat he got out, "I . . . I can't afford a doctor."

"Don't be a bloody fool, cobber. Let me worry about that."

The Aussie slammed the door shut and went around the front of the vehicle to the driver's side and got in, not by opening the door, but by winging a long leg over the side, slipping down into place. He said, as they took off up the wandering street, "It's bonzer I did a bunk from Paul's right after you left, cobber. A bit of luck, eh?"

"In English?" Frank said. The rush of the cool night air was bringing him around.

The Australian laughed and pushed his bush hat down more firmly on his head. "We'll be there in no time flat, cobber, and then the fur'll fly. Did you see them?"

"No, not well. Couple of Moroccans, I think. Native clothes." Frank hadn't the vaguest idea what the other was talking about. What fur would fly?

The streets weren't well lighted but they seemed to have left the medina completely and were now in the European part of town. The road climbed.

"Up here's the Marshand," Nat called over to him. "The more money a bloke's got in this bloody town, the higher up on the mountain he lives."

Frank felt the back of his head gingerly. He had no doubts he'd have a beautiful knot there in the morning. He felt his ribs. Nothing seemed broken, but you never knew. He understood you could go around with a broken rib for weeks and sometimes not know it. He searched for a handkerchief and came up with one, about the only thing that his assailants hadn't taken. He coughed and spat into it. There was no blood.

They emerged from the town proper. The houses were more widely spaced and reminiscent of the Spanish Colonial architecture of Southern California and the older towns of Mexico. Most of the villas were surrounded by pine and gum trees and now the road ran along a cliff with incomparable views of the sea and the Spanish coast beyond.

Frank said, "Where'd you say we were going?" He was feeling better by the minute.

"My boss's digs. He'll have a sawbones there." Shortly afterward, Nat said, "Cape Spartel. Farthest west a bloke can get in Africa."

Frank blinked at the group of buildings they were approaching, by far the most extensive estate they had passed. They were surrounded by a wall of dressed fieldstone, possibly six feet high. Wrought-iron uprights were planted at the top, and the spaces between were entwined with vicious barbed wire.

They came to a halt outside a small fortress of a gatehouse, also of fieldstone. Frank noticed that they had passed over a trigger plate in the road.

A guard came out. He was wearing a beret, what looked like a paratrooper's combat uniform, and heavy leather boots. He carried a small submachine gun which he handled with the ease of a professional. A bright light came on from the guardhouse and zeroed in on their faces. There was a series of audible clicks and Frank got the feeling that a TV lens was on them. Okay, it was their needle, they could thread it as they liked.

Nat Fraser said, "What—o, Hercule?"

The guard nodded at him but said nothing. The light went out, and in a moment the clicking sounds came again. The automated steel gate swung open and the little vehicle slithered through. The winding road that lay beyond must have been a full quarter of a kilometer in length.

They pulled up before an ornate entry and a young man dressed like the gate guard, but bearing no visible weapon, issued forth.

He approached, smiled at the Australian, and said, *"Willkommen, Herr Fraser."* He looked at Frank questioningly.

Nat said, "A new Yank recruit. I vouch for him, Karl. Is the colonel in?"

"He is expecting you, Herr Fraser."

Evidently, the Australian had called ahead on his transceiver on the way up. Frank hadn't noticed, but he had been in no shape to be noticing things.

Nat got out of the little hovercar the same way he had entered it—over the side—pushed his bush hat back on his head, and went around to help Frank out.

Karl assisted, seeming to find nothing strange about the appearance of the soiled and battered newcomer.

They got Frank up the four stone steps and to the door. Nat took over completely there.

Karl said, "Colonel Panikkar is in the study, Herr Fraser."

"Too right," the Aussie said, and helped Frank down the short hall that stretched ahead.

There was an identity screen on the heavy carved wooden door. Almost immediately, it clicked and opened. Beyond was the most impressive study Frank Pinell had ever seen. By the looks of it, it was a combination of library study and

office. Bookshelves lined the walls, floor to ceiling, filled
with leatherbound books of the old style. Tasteful paintings of
both East and West were represented on the walls, none of
them modern. But there were also steel files and on both of
the two desks were the usual office equipment, including a
voco-typer on the smaller one. The furniture was heavy and
functional, but in excellent taste. Only the battleship gray of
the carpeting detracted from the otherwise impressive decor.
It gave a military effect.

Behind the larger of the desks, looking up at their entry,
was a man of possibly sixty. Square of face, gray of hair and
heavy mustache, he was dark complexioned. He wore traditional Indian clothing, including a black, frock-length coat
and jodhpurs. He had a dignified military posture.

Nat said, "This is the young Yank I called you about,
Colonel. Strike me blind but he's got the luck of the Irish.
Been in this buggering town no more than hours but a couple
of the flashing ragheads set on him and leave him on the
street with a broken block."

Then he became more formal. "Colonel Ram Panikkar,
Frank Pinell."

The colonel came around his desk to shake hands, western
style. His face was indignant as he took in Frank's dirt-fouled
clothing and bruises.

He said to Nat, "Make your man comfortable, Nat. I'll be
with you in just a moment."

The Australian got his still-shaky companion into a chair.

The colonel said into a TV screen, "Doctor, could you
bring your bag and join us at once in my study?" He then
flicked a switch and commanded, "Get me Foud, immediately."

He looked up at Nat. "Where did this take place?"

"On the Rue D'Angleterre, just up from the bloody Grand
Socco."

The Indian looked at Frank. "Just what did the hooligans
get away with?"

Frank took a deep breath and said, "Most important, about
two hundred pseudo-dollars worth of Swiss gold francs and
dirhams. Also my Moroccan police papers which I got at the
airport, my pocket transceiver, and the usual odds and ends."

A face had appeared on the phone screen—a dark, evil face

crowned by an orange turban. Its owner would have had no difficulty whatsoever landing a part as a stereotype fanatic assassin on Stateside Tri-Di.

The colonel said, his voice dangerously crisp, *"As-salaam alaykum, Foud."*

The other answered, his own voice careful, *"Alaykum as-salaam, Ram Panikkar."*

The Indian spoke rapidly in what Frank assumed was Arabic. Perhaps the colonel was Pakistani, rather than Indian.

In short order, Ram Panikkar turned back to Frank and his Australian rescuer.

"Your possessions will be at your hotel in the morning, Mr. Pinell." And then to Nat, "It was Mustapha and Jabir. The dogs become bolder each month that passes." He added with satisfaction, "I let Foud know that your friend was under the protection of the Graf."

A roly-poly little man entered from a side door, the traditional black bag of the physician in his right hand. He was a fussbudget, pink of rounded face and wearing old-fashioned pince-nez glasses on a bulbous little nose.

The colonel made introductions. "Dr. Fuchs, Mr. Pinell. Mr. Pinell has been the victim of street desperadoes. We thought it best that he be checked. Do you wish to take him to the clinic?"

The doctor bobbed his head and said in accented English, "Ve vill zee."

The examination was comparatively brief. The doctor hummed importantly as he worked. He wound up very pleased with both himself and his patient. All was well. He gave Frank four pills with instructions for taking them, assured all that Frank was in good repair, then shook hands all around, said goodnight, and left.

While this had been going on, the colonel had gone to a bar along one wall and, when the doctor had gone, returned with three tall glasses containing the most excellent Scotch Frank had ever tasted.

As he handed the glasses around, the colonel said, "I prescribe this as even more effective, under the circumstances, than the good doctor's pills. Cheers, gentlemen."

"Fuck Ireland," Nat murmured.

But in spite of his light words, the Indian was frowning.

He took a small sip of his neat whiskey and said to Frank, "Two hundred pseudo-dollars? I understood from what our good Nat said that you had but landed this afternoon. Surely you have not already gone through eight hundred pseudo-dollars. Doesn't your, ah, former government issue each deportee a full thousand?"

Frank said bitterly, "My IABI escorts decided that such a sum would be wasted on me. They handed over two hundred. It seems that on their way back to the States they intended to lay over in Madrid and blow the rest of it at, uh, I think a bar named Chicote's where the whores congregate."

Nat blurted indignantly, "And wot'd you do, mate?"

Frank looked over at him in disgust. "What could I do? They were armed and I was completely out of my element and in a strange country."

"I see," the colonel said ominously. "And what other adventures did you have today?"

Frank told him about the cab driver and his stolen luggage.

The colonel's dark complexion became even blacker with fury. He said ominously again, "And what else?"

Frank shrugged it off. "The customs officer took a rather valuable camera that had been left me by my father."

"I'm not sure that even I can do anything about that," the colonel muttered.

He turned back to his elaborate TV phone, dialed, and said, after a moment, "Rafa? Ram Panikkar, in Tangier. Tonight there should be two IABI agents in Chicote's. They've shaken down one of the boys for eight hundred pseudo-dollars." He looked up from the screen and over at Frank. "What were their names?"

Frank said, "MacDonald and Roskin. I don't know their first names. Look here . . ."

But the colonel was back at his screen, where he repeated the names. He said, "I want the eight hundred back here by morning. I also want them taught a small lesson. Not to be overdone, you understand, but I want them left in no condition to travel tomorrow. You understand."

He listened for a moment, then said, "Yes, two IABI men, probably armed, but this has been going too far. I do not wish Tangier to get the reputation of being wide open for extortion. If you wish to check this out with Peter Windsor at the

Wolfschloss, go right ahead. I am sure he will agree with me."

He flicked off the screen, thought a moment, then dialed again. A face must have appeared, since he said, "Samir? I am speaking in my capacity as Tangier representative of the Graf. One of your drivers this afternoon stole two suitcases from a passenger from the airport. I make this perfectly clear, Samir. I want those two bags here, with all contents, before the night is out. No, I do not know the name of the driver. That is all, Samir."

He flicked off the screen again and turned back to Frank and Nat, grim satisfaction on his face.

Frank stammered, "I . . . I don't know how to thank you, Colonel Panikkar."

The Indian waved a hand in dismissal. "You simply presented us with an opportunity, Frank. Tangier is possibly the most extensive center of the Graf's operations. We have no intention of putting up with small-time local hoodlums bothering our people, disrupting our activities."

Frank said unhappily, "But that's the point, Colonel. I'm not one of your people. I told Nat I didn't think that I could come in with you."

The other looked from Frank to Nat and then back again. "Ah, I didn't know that. However, it is your own choice, of course. We have no intention of coercing you. Nat, would you see to refills for our glasses?"

"Too right," Nat said, heading for the bar.

The colonel said wryly, "And Nat, dear boy, where in the world do you get those hats?"

The Aussie grinned back at him over his shoulder and touched the bush hat, which it seemed he never removed, even indoors. "Me titfer?" he said. "Had it shipped from Sydney. A bloke's got to keep up appearances, that's wot I say." He returned to the others with an imperial quart of whiskey and poured for all.

The colonel snorted but turned back to Frank. "I am rather surprised. It would seem, under the circumstances, that you would welcome employment."

Frank said unhappily, "It's not that I don't appreciate your kindness, Colonel. But I heard Nat out and I don't believe I'd make a good mercenary."

The colonel shrugged and sipped lightly at his new drink. He said, "The Graf's activities are not limited to mercenary matters, Frank. Let me give you some background. In the very old days, such as when Xenophon led his 10,000 Greek mercenaries to fight for Cyrus of Persia, such matters were handled on a large and efficient scale. But of recent centuries wars have largely been conducted by national governments with citizen armies, along with such related matters as weapons procurement and so forth. Mercenary activities have been hit and miss. Professional soldiers of fortune would apply singly or in small groups for employment. Seldom were more than a few hundred involved. Often, those that were found themselves, ah, holding the bag when the war was over and their side had lost. They could only whistle for their hard-earned pay. We are changing that. For one thing, modern weapons are not easily mastered by uneducated peasants. A Congo bushman does not fly a rocket fighter plane."

Frank nodded at that.

"So today, in the occasional wars that develop, it is necessary for large numbers of professionals to be at hand in the underdeveloped countries. Would it surprise you to know that the Graf can handle a complete action without going outside his own organization? He can field a full disciplined division within a month, and arm them completely, including air cover. From espionage preceding the actual conflict, to getting money out for the officials of collapsing governments, washing it, depositing it in Nassau or Swiss banks, and then spiriting absconding officials to safety to enjoy their, ah, loot. Or, another service might be the—removal?—of other politicians. All of this is on contract, so arranged that the Graf's organization is always guaranteed its pay, bonuses, and insurance in case of death or disability. The Graf takes care of his own." He grimaced in amusement and looked about the luxurious study. "As you see, I do not live in poverty."

Frank was frowning. "It's hard to believe that this Graf can field a completely armed division. He has ten or twenty thousand men on his payroll?"

Nat chuckled and poured still more of the priceless Scotch.

The Indian smiled and shook his head. "No, of course not. He supports a permanent staff spotted about the world, such as my operation here in Tangier. Senior executives such as myself, office workers, and so on. He also has on retainer, between actual contracts, a cadre of officers who can spring to duty within hours; all experienced veterans. He then has, on call, thousands of available infantrymen, pilots, tank men, logistics specialists, and so on, ready to enlist at any time for any duration. They are not on the permanent crew. They usually exist on GAS, or its equivalent in the advanced countries, between employments.''

Frank said, ''You've suggested that you took on other contracts besides wars and revolutions.''

Panikkar nodded. ''Yes, many. Last month we conducted a commando action which involved only twenty men. One of our best officers, a Major Shannon, and nineteen veteran non-coms.It seems that there was a half-mad dictator on one of the smaller Caribbean islands. His people overwhelmingly wished to join the United States but he, understandably, refused. He and his family were vampires upon that island's population. However, funds were raised, and the commando detachment was sent to take him out.''

''Then you actually do individual assassinations.''

The Aussie chuckled again but stuck to his drink, rather than joining into the conversation.

The colonel shrugged. ''On occasion. We see little difference, morally speaking, between entering into a full-fledged war or killing an individual. But see here, you are an educated young man. You must have read of Genghis Khan, one of the great military men of all time. He rose from being a simple chieftain of a small nomadic tribe in Central Asia to conquer the largest empire the world had ever seen. He destroyed whole civilizations. He slaughtered millions of sedentary peoples so their lands could be devoted to his flocks. Only one thing stopped his hordes from engulfing Europe: he died. Now, tell me, my good Frank, what would the world have been saved had our Genghis Khan been assassinated when he was a young man?''

Frank was nonplussed.

The Indian went on. ''It goes both ways. Suppose your Abraham Lincoln had been suitably *guarded* against assassination. What would have been the difference if this good man had lived on to preside over the reconstruction of your South?

It took a hundred years for the South to fully recover from your Civil War.''

Frank said hesitantly, "Your Graf provides bodyguards, I take it.''

"Naturally. He has the most efficient bodyguards in the world.''

"I hope so. Assassination is—well, hell, it isn't civilized!''

"But it can improve civilization." Panikkar finished his second large whiskey. "Take Mahem Dhu, who recently proclaimed himself the Mahdi in Central Africa.''

"Never heard of him.''

"The Mahdi is a figure of Moslem mythology," Panikkar explained. "Something like a messiah, he is to return as the world is about to end, unite all believers, and destroy those who are evil. It is a most primitive aspect of Islam. The last major leader who proclaimed himself the Mahdi was Mohammed Ahmed in the Anglo-Egyptian Sudan in the 19th Century. He called for a holy war and in a few years his followers overwhelmed an area half the size of Europe, slaughtering hundreds of thousands. They beat the British army and killed General Gordon.''

"But this new one?" Frank said.

"Mahem Dhu. He's trying the same thing in Central and Northern Africa. He refuses to join the United Church, while many Islamic sects are joining. If he continues, millions of uneducated blacks and Arabs will die. If he should be, ah, removed, their lives will be spared and, with the help of United Church missionaries, their countries will be rapidly upgraded.''

"I see your point," Frank admitted. He pulled at his drink unhappily. "Still . . .''

Nat Fraser scoffed. "Mate," he said. "You bloody well told me that the Yanks deported you for homicide. What's the buggering difference? You knock off some cove on your own, or you do it for the Graf for mucking good pay. And you don't have to take a contract if you don't like it. Strewth, I've turned down more than one.''

Frank looked back at the colonel. "I don't see what use I'd be to you. I'm no soldier.''

Ram Panikkar shrugged it off. "It's not important, Frank. Sleep on it. We might find you a position appropriate to your abilities, seeing that you're a most personable and a reasonably educated young man." He looked at his wrist chronometer. "But you must be tired after all your troubles today. And you must be hungry." He looked at the Australian. "Nat, I suggest that you see that Frank gets a good meal and then put him up for the night in one of the dormitories. I'd suggest the non-com quarters. Tomorrow morning he can return to his hotel."

"Too right, Colonel," Nat said, coming to his feet.

Frank stood too and began his thanks but the colonel waved them aside, smiling, and returned to the papers on his desk without further words.

Next morning, driven to his hotel by Nat Fraser, Frank found not only his suitcases and the personal things that had been stolen from him by the muggers, but a pile of Swiss francs and Moroccan dirhams atop the rickety dresser. They totalled a full equivalent of a thousand pseudo-dollars, slightly more than he had been robbed of. After all, he had owed the cab driver five dirhams and had paid Luigi ten dirhams for room rent, and had bought a round of drinks at Paul's Bar. Even his camera was in one of the suitcases. The colonel had clout.

A vague thought came to him. How had Panikkar known he was staying at the Hotel Rome? He had told neither the Indian nor Nat Fraser.

Chapter Nine:
Roy Cos

The shuttle from Nassau to Greater Miami was brief and uneventful. Both men were so deep in their thoughts that Roy Cos didn't even bother to stare out the heavy glass ports at the sea and islets below. Obviously, he was having second thoughts about this whole project. How had he ever allowed the damned newsman to talk him into it?

Forry Brown squinted over at him and tried to rise to the occasion. He knew very well what was in Roy's mind; he even had a twinge of guilt about it. But, the whole thing was now irreversible. He said, "You know the trouble with you Utopians?"

Roy sighed and said, "No."

"You won't like Utopia."

Roy sighed again and said, "There is no such thing as Utopia. As soon as you get to your goal, there's a better one beckoning. No science is more in a condition of continual change than socioeconomics. Utopian? Our revolutionary forefathers in 1776 thought they were creating a Utopia. They didn't."

"Fine," Forry said. "But whatever you call it, most of you won't like it."

"Why?"

"Because you all have a different picture of it. Vegetarians will picture the future society as one in which no meat will be eaten. Prohibitionists expect the end of booze but a good Italian radical would be aghast at the idea that wine and good food, including meat, would be taboo. Nudists expect nudism, puritans expect purity—in petticoats, at that. Serious straight-laced Wobblies expect the world of the future to be very serious and very efficient, but the easygoing ones look forward to a frivolous, bang-up time for everybody. And the differences on the sex question are going to be wild! I'll bet the march toward complete promiscuity will continue but I've noted that most of the Wobblies I've met are on the conservative side.''

Roy sighed once again and shifted uncomfortably in his seat. "Wobblies don't believe that establishing our social system will solve all problems. We only contend that it will solve a good many of the most pressing problems."

Forry grunted and rubbed along his wisp of a mustache with a thumbnail. "I wish I could smoke in this flying sardine can," he said. "What the hell ever happened to socialism? I don't believe I've even heard the word for years."

"Scientific socialism stopped being scientific about a century and a half ago," Roy told him. "It got to the point where everybody was called socialist, from Roosevelt to Hitler. Sweden was socialist. So was Russia, not to speak of England, which still had a royal family left over from feudalism. It stopped making sense. The only group in the States that would have been called socialists are the Libertarians."

"What do they want, as compared to you Wobblies?"

"To reform People's Capitalism, or Meritocracy. We want to end it and establish a new system. They want more GAS for everybody, better education, better *every*thing. They're reformers, not revolutionaries." He looked out the small porthole. "Hey, we're coming in." Then, in a lower voice: "Did you notice that the man who was following us is on our shuttle?"

"I noticed."

They walked down the shuttle's ladder, their small luggage in hand, and headed for the customs hall. Customs was the merest of formalities; the twelve packs of illegal cigarettes went through unseen.

Passed by customs, they headed for the exit and were immediately accosted by two young men, one in prole garments, the other in a fairly presentable sportsman's garb. The prole was big and square and on the rugged side, the other was trimmer. Both were in their early twenties and both wore grim expressions.

Forry looked at them warily but Roy said, smiling and extending his hand, "Hi, Ron. Hi, Les. I knew you'd make it." As usual, a smile worked wonders on the face of the

Wobbly organizer. "Forry, these are the Wobblies I told you about. Ronald Ellison, Lester Bates, meet Forrest Brown."

Forry nodded as he shook. "Glad to see you fellas. We're being followed."

"I spotted him," the husky youth, Ron, said. "I thought this contract thing didn't start until tomorrow morning."

Forry said, "It starts at midnight. But meanwhile they'll be wanting to know where Roy is going, where he'll be when the contract does go into effect. Did you get a car?"

Les, the better dressed one, nodded. "Right."

They left the administrative building and started out into the large parking area.

"Where's the car?" Forry said.

"Not in the parking lot," Ron told him. "We thought there might be somebody waiting for you to land. Just follow me."

Mystified, Roy and Forry let the other two lead the way. They walked to the far end of the shuttleport's administration building, then entered a narrow alley between it and a huge hangar. The drab narrowness gave the passage a sinister quality.

The little ex-newsman said in protest, "What the hell?" He looked at their two guides suspiciously and then at Roy.

Roy said, "It's all right. If they say it's okay, then it is. Lead on, Les."

They hadn't gone fifty feet down the deserted alley before two others entered it. One of them was the unknown who had tailed them from the time they had left the offices of Oliver Brett-James in Nassau. The other was a stranger. They were pretending to be in deep discussion, as if unaware of the four ahead of them in the narrow alleyway.

Les, Ron, Roy, and Forry continued on their course, the newsman nervous about their followers.

And then two more huskies entered the alley behind those followers.

Ron said, with grim satisfaction, "Here we go." He and Les turned and watched expectantly as though ready to return.

The need didn't materialize. The action that took place was brutal and brief. One of the new arrivals had a short truncheon in his right hand; the other seemed to have something metallic over the knuckles of his right fist. With no preliminaries whatever, they attacked. In fifteen seconds, the two who had been following Roy Cos were down on the alley floor, arms over their heads in a futile attempt to protect themselves. The newcomers lashed into them with heavy shoes, kicking at ribs, stomachs, and kidneys.

"Jesus," Ron said in admiration. "If Billy doesn't look out he's going to kill those funkers."

"Couldn't happen to nicer guys," Les growled.

Forry looked over at Roy Cos. "You *are* an organizer," he said in awe.

Roy said, "I have my moments."

Leaving their unconscious victims behind, the two additional guards came up, grinning as though embarrassed.

The first one said, "If either of those bastards are out of the hospital in less than two weeks, I'll turn in my merit badge in mugging."

Roy said, "Forrest Brown, meet Richard Samuelson and Billy Tucker."

Forry said, even as he shook, "You gentlemen take your work seriously, don't you?"

Dick Samuelson and Billy Tucker were in the same age group as Ron and Les, both six-footers, both around two hundred pounds. They greeted Roy Cos warmly after they shook hands with the little newsman.

"Holy smog," Forry muttered. "If all you Wobblies are like this, why didn't you put over your damned revolution years ago? Let's get out of here before somebody else shows up."

The six of them hurried on up the alley.

"Glad I made it in time," Billy said. "I had to come all the way from Denver. Had a meet there."

Forry looked at him. "What kind of a meet?"

"Wrestling."

The alley debouched on a small parking area. For all but a few, private cars were a luxury.

They came up to the limousine Ron indicated, and Forry began to get into the driver's seat, saying, "I'm the only one who knows where we're going to ground."

But Roy shook his head. "Les is a racing driver," he said simply.

The ex-newsman looked at Les Bates thoughtfully and

then nodded. "Fine," he said, getting into the back seat instead. "Get out on the highway and turn right, Les." He said to Billy, "I saw you give those two characters in the alley a quick frisk after they passed out. Did you get anything?"

"A shooter," Billy said, satisfaction in his voice.

"Well, as soon as we get out into the countryside, you ought to ditch it. We can't afford to be found by the police with an unlicensed gun. If they coop Roy up in some banger, the Graf's men will figure out how to get to him within hours. If any of the rest of your boys are heeled, think about that."

They looked at him respectfully even as Les, obviously expert at the wheel, took them out onto the highway. Dick Samuelson said, "Yes, sir," meek as a mouse, and brought out a compact black automatic, holding it in a gloved hand to be tossed out a window.

Billy dipped his hand into the side pocket of his prole denim jacket reluctantly and came out with a Gyrojet pistol. "It's a beauty," he said with regret. "Whoever those cloddies were, they didn't skimp on equipment."

"They're probably employees of the Graf," Forry said sourly.

Dick Samuelson hissed between his teeth. "Then Roy wasn't just whistlin' Dixie when he said that most likely we'd be in thick soup, eh? I've heard about the Graf."

Ron said, "There's a car behind. I think it's a tail."

Les grinned gently and snicked his gear selector. "I picked out this pile of iron myself," he said. "Belt up, boys."

Billy said to Forry, "You still think we ought to toss these shooters out?"

"Absolutely," the newsman said. "The first time we turn a corner, so they can't see you do it. For all we know, they're police. We don't want to take on a carload of fuzzies."

"Okay," Billy said. "Get our asses out of here, Les. Graf's men or fuzzies, they're sure to be heeled."

Shaking their pursuers was child's play for Lester Bates. He was not only a racing driver but a very smooth one, powering through the apex of every turn, using every inch of the road.

It was only after there could be no doubt that they had lost their pursuers that Les turned to Forry. "Where do you want to go?"

Forry gave directions and then, after a time, said, "That tavern, there. Pull in behind it."

Roy looked at him. "You don't mean we're hiding out in a roadside bar?"

The little man grunted amusement. "Hardly. That's just where we drop this car. You know what's happened by this time? Whoever was following us has noted our license number and relayed it to either the police or some of their own organization. So we switch. I have a car stashed here; the owner's an old drinking buddy who can keep his mouth shut."

Dick Samuelson looked over at him as they pulled into the parking area. "Even if the Graf's hit men are working him over?"

"No, not then," Forry admitted, drawing deeply on his cigarette. "But Ted doesn't know enough to tell them anything. His instructions are to give them the truth. We left a hovercar here and later picked it up, leaving this one in its place."

They pulled up beside the vehicle he indicated. Les looked at it questioningly. He said, "It has no license plates. That'll make it conspicuous."

Forry nodded. "On purpose. Ted couldn't tell anybody what the numbers were, even if he wanted to. We'll put the plates on shortly, down the road a bit."

Continually checking to see whether they had picked up new pursuers, they finally made it to their destination. It was an old house on the beach to the south of Miami, fairly well isolated. Undoubtedly, it had once been the winter home of a wealthy northerner. Forry had Les Bates back the car into the garage, so that it would be hidden from view but poised for escape.

The six of them went into the rambling one-story villa. Forry led the way to the living room. Roy looked about him. "How'd you manage this?"

Forry said, "I rented it for a week, using my international credit card. I've got a few thousand saved up. We won't use your million a day until after we've made our initial play. We don't want them to zero in on us at this stage."

They all found seats in comfort chairs or on couches. Ron said, on edge, "What happens now?"

Forry said, "In a minute, one of you go up to the sundeck on the roof as a sentry. But I want to talk to you first, before the others get here."

"What others?" Roy said.

"You'll see," Forry told him. He looked around at Ron, Les, Dick, and Billy, ran his tongue thoughtfully over his gray lower lip, and said, "The question becomes, how do Roy and I know we can trust you? I think his idea of getting Wobbly members to act as his bodyguard, rather than professionals, was a good one. In the past, Deathwish Policyholders have hired professionals. Often they wound up getting hit by their own guards, who were either bribed by the Graf's men, or were already on his payroll. No offense intended, but how can we know that one of you can't be gotten to, if the bribe's big enough?"

Silence. When Roy spoke, his voice carried rock-solid confidence. "Forry," he said, "it's a thing you wouldn't know about. All of these boys are at least third-generation Wobblies. They got their ethics at grandpa's knee."

"Two of my great-grandparents, as well," Les said quietly.

Roy continued, "I've know Les, Ron, Billy, and Dick all of their lives. Their parents are personal friends. When I was Billy's age, I lived next door to his folks. I've changed his diapers. You see, Forry, being a radical becomes a way of life. Practically all of your family's friends are Wobblies. You play with the children of other Wobbly families. Your fun is mostly picnics or dances or other entertainments thrown to raise funds for the movement. You attend meetings with your parents before you're old enough to understand what the hell that sweaty, sincere guy with the microphone is talking about. When you're old enough to notice girls, the ones you can approach easiest are Wobblies themselves, probably one of the girls you grew up with. If you have children, they're raised in the same tradition, a sort of political ghetto. The radical movement in the United States started in 1877 with the socialistic Labor Party. The Wobbly movement got going in 1905, mostly with socialists. Do you know how many generations ago that was?

"Think of it! Eight generations of us. Oh, new recruits do come in; not many, I admit. And sometimes Wobblies drop out and stay out. But largely our membership consists of people raised in the radical tradition. Forry," he chuckled, "I'm beginning to suspect we're starting to breed true. Young fellows like these four are *born* Wobblies."

"There goes your credibility," Forry growled.

"Just kidding, of course. But I selected these four because they're third-or-more-generation revolutionists and all personal friends of mine, like their parents before them. If I can't trust them, I don't give a damn how soon they kill me."

"Okay, okay." Forry Brown looked around at the four, one by one. They all wore expressions of faint embarrassment, with pride shining through.

Roy said, "Now I've got a question. Back in Nassau, you asked Oliver Brett-James how big the benefits to his company were when I die, and how much the daily premiums he had to pay were. Why did you want to know?"

Forry brought a pack of his smuggled cigarettes from a pocket and took his time lighting up. He said finally, "I wanted to know how much time we had before his company started hurting. As of midnight tonight, I start earning my way. Your publicity starts tomorrow. I've already gotten in touch with my contacts in Tri-Di news. They're all going to broadcast the story of the Wobbly who took out a Deathwish Policy so that he'd acquire the credit needed to spread his message. Oh yes, tomorrow I start earning my ten thousand pseudo-dollars a day. The longer I keep you alive, the longer I keep my job. It stops the moment you do."

Les blurted, "Ten thousand a day!"

Forry spread his hands. "Why not? There's a personal risk. Suppose I get into the line of fire when somebody takes a shot at Roy? Or suppose somebody heaves a bomb that gets all of us? Besides, what is ten thousand to Roy? He has a million on tap every day. He can afford to keep his hired help happy. By the way, you four bodyguards will each get ten thousand daily."

Dick Samuelson growled, "You're one thing, but *we* didn't get into this for money. We don't want any pay."

Roy Cos shook his head at that. He said, "No. Forry's right, Dick. There's nothing in that contract that says I can't have a bodyguard and pay him as much as he's worth. I'm not allowed to make donations to organizations—political, religious, or whatever. But you can squirrel your wages away. When I've finally had it, you boys can contribute as much to the movement as you like. If I last long enough, you'll be rich. I don't believe I've ever known a rich Wobbly. You'll be in a position to make the biggest donations to the organization ever.''

An identity screen bell rang from somewhere and all stiffened.

"That's probably Mary Ann," Forry said, getting up. "But we should have posted a sentry before this. How about one of you fellows going up onto the roof? Make your own arrangements; I'd suggest a two-hour shift.''

"Okay. I'll take the first shift," Billy said, standing too.

With Ron going along, just for caution, Forry went to the front door of the villa and checked the screen. He seemed to be satisfied.

The woman who came through looked every inch the office worker. A little on the plain side, though with a comfortably nice figure, she was neatly efficient in appearance, conservatively dressed, and wore no makeup whatever. She was in her late thirties and carried an attaché case.

"Good evening, Forrest," she said.

"Forry," he told her. "We're going to be seeing a good deal of each other under rather hectic circumstances in the days to come. No need, nor time for formality. Did you bring your things?''

"They're out in the car I rented," she said. "It's automated, so we can return it to the agency without any difficulty.''

"This is Ron Ellison," he told her. "One of the team. He'll get your bags and you can pick out a room for yourself. Meanwhile, come on back and meet the rest.''

While Ron went for her luggage, Forry and the newcomer went to the living room. The men stood to be introduced and Forry did the honors.

Roy said, "Isn't there a drink around here?''

Forry had stocked a fairly good bar. While Les was making the drinks, Forry told the Wobbly organizer, "I've known Mary Ann Elwyn for years. She's a damn good secretary. Her pay will be the same as everybody else's—ten thousand a day." He smiled a small smile as she gasped. "Enough to keep her honest, we'll hope. If we last the week out, she'll have enough to retire. Seventy thousand pseudo-dollars, on top of her GAS, could equal a nice standard of living. If you last for more than a week, each day adds another ten thousand to her nest egg."

Roy Cos was frowning. He said in complaint, "Forry, what the hell do I need with a secretary?" He sent his eyes over to the young woman. "Not that I have anything against you."

"Are you kidding?" Forry said to him. "When this thing starts, you won't even be able to handle your mail. If you last the first week out, she'll be needing stenographers to help her."

"I'm highly experienced, Mr. Cos," Mary Ann said briskly. "Forry has explained the situation to me and my duties. I'm not too keen on the physical danger, but—well, ten thousand pseudo-dollars a day . . ." she hesitated for a moment, then, ". . . buys me a lot of courage."

Roy made a gesture of acceptance. "It's all right with me. Forry's the organizer of this scheme. I suppose he knows what he's doing."

Billy Tucker came hurrying into the room. His eyes swept quickly over the new secretary but then went on to Roy Cos. He said, "Roy, there's a car coming down the road. At least two men in it."

"Probably Ferd and Jet," Forry said, putting down his glass and grinding out his cigarette. "We don't really have to start worrying until after midnight, Billy. Then this guard duty becomes serious." He stood and headed for the door.

The younger man said after him, "Yeah. And I wish to hell you hadn't made us throw away those guns."

"We'll see about that soonest," the ex-newsman said over his shoulder. "As soon as the publicity starts, we'll put in a demand for gun permits through our law firm. We've got a law firm on retainer, too, Roy. If they refuse to issue gun permits for the bodyguard of the Deathwish Wobbly, a howl will go up that'll mean just that much more publicity."

He left the room to go for the front door. Billy went over to the bar, poured himself a ginger ale, and carried it with him to his post.

Roy Cos said to his brand new secretary, "Do you know anything at all about the Wobblies, Ms. Elwyn?"

"Mary Ann," she said. "I knew practically nothing, until

Forry brought up the matter of a temporary job . . ." She flushed, then quickly added ". . . or maybe not so temporary, with you. I looked your organization up in the National Data Banks but I'm afraid that it's not my cup of tea. I've never been interested in political economy."

Forry re-entered, followed by two newcomers. Both carried portable typewriters—one a late-model voco-typer and, by the looks of the case, the other an old electric.

Roy and his three bodyguards stood for introductions, and again, Forry did the honors.

Roy looked at the two blankly, not having the vaguest idea why either of them were present. But Forry took over, first sending Les for drinks for the newcomers and then for refills for the rest of them.

When all were seated again, he said, "Jet Peters is your publicity man, Roy. He used to work for one of the big cosmocorps, a multinational corporation specializing in uranium. But he was spelled down, the same as I was, by the computers. A younger guy got his position."

Roy could see that possibility. The other was somewhere in his early fifties and looked both tired and cynical. He was sloppily dressed, a bit bleary of eye, a tremor in his hands. A drinker, the Wobbly decided.

Roy said, "Publicity? I thought you were handling publicity, Forry."

"I am," the ex-newsman said, getting out his cigarettes again. "But I won't be able to handle it all. Jet's an old pro. He'll come up with dozens of ideas that wouldn't occur to me. He's got a lot of contacts, too. He'll earn his ten thousand."

All eyes went to the second of the two newcomers, who had been introduced as Ferd Feldmeyer. He was not just overweight, but almost obscenely fat. Like many fat men, he bought his clothes too small so that he bulged in them. He was pale of face, thin of dirt-blond hair, and his small mouth seemed to pout. Ferd Feldmeyer was less than handsome.

Forry said, "Ferd is your speechwriter."

"Speechwriter! Holy smog, Forry, I don't need a speechwriter. I do my own speeches, usually off the cuff. Why, this guy isn't even a Wobbly, so far as I know. How could he write my speeches, even if I wanted him to?"

Ferd Feldmeyer might not have been much for looks but

his voice was deep and had a ring of sincerity. He said, "Since Forry approached me on this, I've been reading up on your movement day and night—including your own publications, not just the material in the National Data Banks. I'll tell you something about political organizations and religions, or philosophies, for that matter. You should be able to sum yours up in two hundred words. If you can't, something's wrong with your movement. Right now, I could sit down and tear off a speech for you that would give the Wobbly position—maybe better than you've ever presented it. On top of that, I'd drop in a little humor, some good quotations, and wind it up with a blockbuster of a gimmick ending that'd have them anxious to tune in to your next broadcast."

Forry said reasonably, "You're not going to be able to give your standard talks off the cuff on Tri-Di, Roy. They've got to be written out, and you're going to have too many to write yourself. You're not only going to speak often on Tri-Di, TV, and even radio, but we're going to line you up for personal appearances, lectures, and so forth. Ferd and Jet are also going to double for you as your ghosts."

Roy stared at him. "My what? That's one thing that nobody else can do for me . . . die."

The former newsman said, "Sorry, Roy; poor choice of words. I meant ghost writers. If this publicity hits the way I think it will, there'll be calls for articles from all sorts of periodicals from all over the world. Maybe we'll even do a book." He squinted his eyes and said thoughtfully, "That reminds me of something. Do you speak Spanish?"

"No."

The little man turned his eyes to Mary Ann Elwyn, who had been sitting quietly, primly, her hands in her lap. She had refused the drink Les offered. Forry said, "Make a note, Mary Ann. We need computer translators to put Roy's speeches into Spanish, French, and Italian."

The secretary quickly opened her attaché case, brought forth a stylo and notepad, and scribbled away.

Jet said, "How about Russian and Mandarin?"

Forry thought about that but then shook his head. "Not yet. For the time being, the Wobbly movement is aimed at the West. Maybe later, if I understand the program correctly, it might spread to the Soviet Complex and China. Okay, Roy?''

"I suppose so,'' the Wobbly said. This whole thing seemed to be getting more and more out of his hands. The ineffective-looking little Forrest Brown was taking over with a vengeance. Thus far, Roy Cos had precious little to do—except to stay alive as long as possible.

Forry spoke through the smoke that dribbled from his mouth. "We'd better get down to definite plans. Like I said, we start the publicity tomorrow. We also wrap up the arrangements for the first Tri-Di talk, nationwide, beamed worldwide from satellites. When Roy's made that first speech, the publicity will really hit. He'll be big news. Everybody in the country will be on the edge of their chairs waiting for the Deathwish Wobbly . . .'' He broke off and looked at Jet Peters. "I think we ought to use that bit of business in our publicity. The Deathwish Wobbly. The revolutionist so sincere that he's willing to die for the chance of spreading it.'' He looked back to Roy and the others. "They'll be sitting on the edges of their chairs, waiting to see how long it'll take for the Graf's men to get to you.''

He ground out his current cigarette and took up the drink sitting on the cocktail table before him. "Until the first Tri-Di broadcast, we won't show. We'll not leave this house. Nobody here will use their credit cards, on the off chance that the enemy might have connected one of us with Roy. I'll pay all expenses, as I did for renting this place, with my card. It's an unnumbered account and they won't be able to trace me with it. The moment we make that broadcast, Roy will begin to use the million pseudo-dollars a day available to him on his Swiss International Credit Card. And from then on we're on the defensive. But the more this pyramids, the more publicity Roy gets, the better his chances are of avoiding the Graf's hit men. There'll be mobs wherever he goes, making it difficult for assassins to get through to him. I hope. A good many of those people are going to be on Roy's side. He's the underdog, and fighting against terrible odds. They'll be out to get any assassins who turn up. And these men of the Graf's are pros, not fanatics. They're not interested in making martyrs out of themselves. That'll be one of the biggest advantages we have.''

Les Bates looked at his wrist chronometer. He announced, ''Four hours to go until midnight.''

Chapter Ten:
Lee Garrett

Of all the major cities of the world, only Rome, the City of the Seven Hills, had not banned surface vehicles. It wouldn't, at least not in the older areas of town, originally settled by Romulus and his tribesmen, glorified by Augustus, later made the center of the world's most powerful religion. It couldn't because old Rome was a museum of three thousand years' standing. It would have been impossible to dig metros and underground highways. The archeological world would have been up in arms. Excavations would have destroyed a multitude of buried ancient temples, tombs, arenas, and fortifications going back as far as the Etruscans. These all lay ten to fifty feet below the surface, someday to be dug out with loving care. Even the pressures of modern transport could not threaten to destroy the remnants of a tiny synagogue where once, perhaps, Paul had given sermons; a governmental building where Caesar had issued his edicts; an aqueduct which once supplied the water for the baths of Diocletian.

However, private vehicles were discouraged to the point where only the most powerful, through wealth or governmental position, were allowed their personal conveyances. Otherwise, traffic was limited to emergency vehicles and to public cabs and buses. It still amounted to considerably more traffic than was to be seen elsewhere.

Thus it was that Lee Garrett found herself riding from the shuttleport to the city's center in a small taxi. It had been some years since she had been in this wondrous city, and she recognized a score of landmarks with a thrill.

"*Destinatio, Signorina?*" the admiring cabby had asked her, his eyes indicating appreciation of her fine blond hair, piled high on her head, of her very un-Italian blue eyes, not to speak of her svelte figure.

The Roman way of the male toward any girl with the least pretensions of pulchritude returned to her and she smiled, remembering. "Number 17, Via della Pilotta," she told him in impeccable Italian.

He looked over his shoulder again. "But *Signorina*, the Palazzo Colonna is no longer open to the public, not even on Saturday mornings."

"So I understand," she told him.

They were passing through the Piazza di Spagna, for centuries the center of the Bohemian artist element, with its medieval Fontana dil Barcaccia by Bernini still watered by a Roman aqueduct. And with its famed Scala di Spagna, known as the Spanish Steps by many tourists. Lee Garrett smiled.

A church here, a palace there, a monument to some long-dead emperor farther on. They sped through the Piazza di Trevi, with its baroque fountain where visitors threw coins to guarantee that one day they would return. And shortly they pulled up before the huge complex that was the Palazzo Colonna, once the most sumptuous of the patrician houses of Rome. Lee brought her International Credit Card from her handbag and put it in the payment slot of the cab.

There were two uniformed young men at the entry, looking in their red medieval garb something like the Swiss guards at the Vatican and bearing, of all things, halberds, shafted weapons of the 15th century with axlike cutting blades, beaks, and terrible spikes. Lee, amused, remembered reading somewhere that the unlikely looking devices had been designed as can openers against armored horsemen. She wondered if there was presently a horse in all Rome, not to speak of a man in armor.

One of them approached, bowed, and politely opened the cab door for her.

Lee got out, flashed him a smile, and said, "I have an appointment with Signorina Duff-Roberts. Meanwhile, I am not sure where I'll be staying tonight. Could you get my bags and hold them for me somewhere?"

He bowed again. "Signorina Garrett?"

"Why, yes."

"Your things will be taken up to your suite, Signorina."

"Thank you." Lee's eyebrows went up slightly but her poise was built in. So: she had a suite in the Palazzo Colonna!

Without doubt there would be a small plaque on the door reading *Lucretia Borgia Slept Here*, or some such.

Inside the entrance were four more young men, in outfits of pages, complete to satin berets with tassels atop. They had been lounging, idly talking among themselves, but now one advanced for a sweeping bow, very much in character. "The Palazzo is not open to the public, Signorina."

"I'm Lee Garrett," she told him. "I have an appointment ..."

"Of course, Signorina," he blurted. "If you will come this way. Signorina Duff-Roberts awaits you."

She followed him up the impressive stone stairway to the vestibule. Years ago, her father had brought her here to see the famed home of what had once been the most powerful family in Rome. Popes had been born here, and cardinals without number, and kings, queens, dukes, duchesses. In the vestibule were paintings of several schools, including Van Dyke, Murillo, and Lotto.

The way led them through the Hall of the Colonna Bellica, past the steps leading down to the Great Hall, and then up another stairway almost as magnificent as that at the entrance to the palace. The priceless treasures of the palace might have been expressed in tonnage. Then followed a series of coldly superb chambers, each a museum of murals, marbles, and tapestries. Why would anyone choose to live in such a place? But then they arrived at the spacious salon of Sheila Duff-Roberts.

There was no identity screen set into the magnificent carved door; that would have been a desecration. Her guide knocked softly and then, without waiting for a response, opened the door and closed it behind her.

On her visit as a youngster, Lee hadn't been in this part of the rambling building. In those days it had still been occupied by descendants of the Colonna family and visitors had been excluded from the private quarters. This room had obviously once been one of the minor salons, now converted into a baroque office. The furniture was of the fifteenth or sixteenth century, with all the stiffly uncomfortable appearance of that era.

Sheila Duff-Roberts arose from her chair behind the desk. She was a large woman physically, but was built in handsome proportion. She enjoyed the long limbs and proud carriage of an Olympic champion. Her face was classical and she knew how to bring out her best features. Her hairdo, cosmetics, and jewelry were the products of experts. Basically, hers was a severe face, brightly intelligent rather than friendly, and her smile was cool. A cigarette dangled from the side of her mouth, man-style. She was dressed in a slack suit which Lee recognized as the latest style in Common Europe. She approached Lee briskly, hand outstretched. It proved to be a warm, firm hand, somehow projecting a caressing quality.

Sheila Duff-Roberts said throatily, "Well, my dear, in spite of your photographs, I didn't expect you to look quite so darling."

Lee didn't quite know how to respond to that. To cover the fact, she looked at the desk and said, "Marvelous."

It was done in sandalwood and was adorned with lapis lazuli, amethysts, and other semi-precious stones. In the front it had twelve small amethyst columns, and at the top, gilt statuettes representing the Muses and Apollo seated under a laurel tree.

The other chuckled and said, "Isn't it beautiful—in a repulsive sort of way? I couldn't resist; had it moved in from the Room of the Desks. One of the others there is possibly even worse. It's done in ebony with twenty-eight ivory bas reliefs, and the central relief is a copy of Michelangelo's *Last Judgment*. A real monstrosity. We'll get it for your office, if you'd like. But do sit down, darling. You're Lee Garrett, of course. I'm Sheila Duff-Roberts."

Feeling a little overwhelmed, Lee took the sixteenth century chair the other indicated. She said, "Yes, Ms. Duff-Roberts. I was given instructions by Cary McBride to . . ."

"Yes, of course." Sheila Duff-Roberts strode briskly around her ornate desk, resumed her chair, and touched a sheaf of papers before her. "I've been going over your qualifications. Very impressive, my dear."

Lee said, "*What* qualifications? I haven't the slightest idea what my duties are. Mr. McBride only told me I was to work for the Central Committee of the World Club."

The other smiled her sparse smile and dispatched her cigarette in an elaborate ceramic work never meant, by the artist who had conceived it half a millennium ago, as an ashtray.

She said, "You were selected by our computers as my secretary, darling."

Lee let out her breath, trying to disguise exasperation. "But what is *your* position? What do you do? What are these qualifications I'm supposed to have?"

"Relax, dear. I'm the secretary." She took another cigarette from a medieval gold and ivory box and lit it with a modern gold desk lighter. "One of your qualifications is that you don't need the job. Or any other job, for that matter. You're filthy rich, dear."

Lee looked at her blankly.

The Junoesque woman said, "So are all our other upperechelon personnel. If they were not born with such resources, we make them available. In short, none of us is motivated by desire for money. We already have money. We are motivated by the dream."

"What dream?" Lee said, still far out of her depth.

The other let heavy smoke flow from her nostrils. "The dream is to create a stable world, Lee. It's been dreamed before, throughout history. For limited periods it has even been achieved, here and there—in Egypt for centuries; in Mexico by the Mayans; in China, at least to a certain degree, before the coming of the Europeans."

Lee said, "What do you mean by stability?"

"For the first time, darling, the human race finds itself in a position to achieve a stable, unchanging society on a worldwide basis. No national disorders, wars, or extreme poverty."

"It sounds like quite a dream," Lee said skeptically. "I knew the World Club was a nonprofit think-factory seeking solutions to current problems, but I had no idea its scope was so all-embracing. Frankly, I'm having second thoughts. It sounds—well, impossible. It's true that I want it to be something rational. Not a . . . forgive me . . . pipe dream."

The secretary of the World Club chuckled throatily again. "Lee, darling, do you approve of GAS in the United States of the Americas?"

"I think so. I can't think of any other manner of dealing with mass unemployment brought on by automation."

"And do you approve of the United States taking in any North or South American country that wished statehood?"

"I think it was one of the most intelligent acts my country has ever performed."

"Both were subtly engineered by the World Club."

"But that's ridiculous. I've never even heard a rumor of such a thing."

Sheila smiled. "I said 'subtly,' did I not? First steps, darling. You see, our basic desire is to maintain the status quo in society, based on what now prevails in America and Common Europe. However, we are not really a conservative organization, certainly not a reactionary one. The World Club is quite revolutionary, in the broadest sense of the word. It aims at a stable, desirable world for the overwhelming majority. It cannot be all things to all people, but it can aim at making a stable society for the average person. To do this we must align ourselves against subversive elements: nihilist terrorists, the Wobblies in the States, Eurocommunists in Common Europe, even the Anti-Racist League. But we are not reactionary."

"I see," Lee said, somewhat less doubtfully. "What are some of the other ills that the World Club thinks it can solve?"

The handsome Amazon shrugged. "Bringing all religions together under the leadership of the United Church, perhaps. A universal language based on Esperanto. We already have a committee working on this. Meanwhile, English is the nearest to a universal language that we now have. Elimination of differences in religion and language will help guarantee a world society which will last indefinitely."

"English, a universal language?" Lee said. "I thought there were a billion Chinese who spoke Mandarin."

Sheila chuckled in her humorless manner. *"Touché,"* she said. "But most all of them *are* in China. The problem of assimilating China into our world society will have to be held in abeyance for the time. By the way, are you a women's rights advocate?"

"In most ways," Lee nodded. "However, I don't claim that women are equal to men in all respects."

The other looked at her sharply. "Why not? Certainly women are equal to men in all respects."

"For one thing," Lee said wryly, "they don't have as long a penis. We can carry this chip on our shoulder to ridiculous extremes. It's like the contention that blacks are the same as whites in all respects. Nonsense. One has a darker complexion than the other. So far as women are concerned—well, there has never been a female heavyweight champion of the world. A second-rate male pro would flatten the best female fighter who ever lived; they simply have more upper-body strength! On the other hand, I've always thought the first astronauts should have been women. We're generally smaller and take up less space, use less food and oxygen, and on an average, we're more deft with our hands. We seem to have more endurance under stress. I wonder how the average man would hold up under a difficult childbirth.''

The tall Sheila eyed her. "You have one quality that doesn't come out in the computer reports—the strength to state strong opinions, darling. Do you have any other questions?''

"Yes," Lee said definitely. "I'm surprised that both you and Mr. McBride have revealed so much to me, even before I've consented to take the position. You've told me that most workers for the World Club don't even know it exists. But you've bared everything to me."

The other lit still another cigarette. "Not quite everything, dear," she said dryly. "You must realize that our computers selected you above all others. The computers seldom make mistakes in these things. We are assured that you are the best person for the position and the computers are of the opinion that you will take it. Obviously, it was required that you know what you are stepping into."

Lee took a deep breath and said in resignation, "What would my duties be?"

"This first week, to give members the chance to become acquainted with you, since in this position you will be privy to many of their innermost decisions. The committee is now in session and will be for the rest of this month. Most of them are now in residence. These regular sessions are held twice a year. They're informal, and consist largely of their sitting around, two by two or in larger groups, and discussing developments of the program. Not all are present at this session. Grace Cabot-Hudson, who is rather old and infirm, remained at her residence in North America." Sheila Duff-Roberts looked at her timepiece. "But now, my dear, you must be

tired, and will wish to see your suite and freshen up. And I
have duties, of course.'' Her eyes shifted slightly. ''By the
way, there is to be a *partous* tonight. Would you be interested?''

Lee shook her head. She wasn't shocked, not in this age,
but she was somewhat surprised. She said, ''No, I'm not
interested in group sex.''

The Amazon's brows went up. ''Lesbian?''

''No.''

''Pity,'' Sheila said. ''However, perhaps in time you'll
change your mind. Which reminds me. We have a staff of
half a dozen office girls.'' She took her lower lip in her
perfect teeth. ''Some of them are quite darling.''

There was a knock at the door and a man with the look of a
well-tanned European, somewhere in his mid-thirties saun-
tered through. He wore his red hair in a young athlete's crew
cut and his dark blue eyes seemed out of place in his dark
complexion. There was an easygoing sardonic quality in his
smile. ''Sheila,'' he said, ''you are looking particularly
Brunhildic today. Have you been butchering male chauvinists
with your broadsword again?''

The secretary of the Central Committee snorted at that and
said, ''Where the hell have you been, Jerry? I've been trying
to get in touch with you for weeks.''

''Reclusing,'' he told her easily. ''Haven't you heard? I am
currently labeled the world's wealthiest recluse and also its
most eligible bachelor. Want to get married? Oops, no, of
course not.''

Sheila snorted again and said, ''This is Lee Garrett. She's
to be my new secretary. Lee, Mr. Jeremiah Auburn. Mr.
Auburn is a member of the Central Committee; its youngest,
by the way. How he ever got into its membership is a mystery
to me.''

''Mind how you speak to your superiors, Ms. Duff-Roberts,''
he said amiably. And then, as he shook hands with Lee,
''Wizard, we meet again.''

Lee wrinkled her forehead. ''I . . . I've heard about you,
Mr. Auburn, but where did we ever meet? I'm sure that I
would recall.''

A glint of laughter came into his eyes. ''It's an old ploy of
mine. I'm terrible at remembering people and women become
so distressed when I don't recall their faces, particularly if I

once spent a long weekend with them in the Bahamas, or Hawaii, or wherever, that I say, 'Wizard, we meet again,' just to be sure.'' He headed for an elaborate Florentine cabinet, which turned out to be a disguised bar.

"How good of you, Jerry," Sheila said sarcastically. "It must be distressing to be such a ladykiller."

"A distress you'd love to share," he said over his shoulder. And then, "Hmmm, perhaps you do."

"I hope you worry about that a lot," Sheila said, obviously well used to his banter.

He called, "Anybody else up to a bit of guzzle? I just checked. It's twelve, so you won't be considered a morning lush."

Sheila asked for Scotch but Lee shook her head, still uneasy. Somehow, this man seemed familiar; possibly it was his voice, but she knew that she'd never seen him. There wasn't a woman in the world who could meet Jerry Auburn and forget about it. The leading light of the rocket set for a decade, he had suddenly reversed his engines and disappeared from sight, in the tradition of Howard Hughes. From time to time he would pop up in the news but largely he was, as he had said, a recluse. Lee couldn't imagine him being a member of the World Club, much less of its Central Committee.

He brought Sheila's drink back to her, held up his own darkish brandy and water, and said, "Cheers, Sheila, old chum-pal. A new secretary, eh? What happened to the ultra-efficient Pamela?"

"I'm sure you'll learn all about it," she said, and sipped. "Lee just came in today."

"Wizard," Jerry Auburn said, looking Lee over again. He made with a mock leer. "You certainly pick them, Sheila."

Sheila didn't disguise her impatience at that. "Attractiveness and poise are requirements of employees who must meet the public, the news media, and so forth, Mr. Auburn. As you very well know."

He finished the drink in one fell swoop and looked at his chronometer. "This is as good an opportunity as any for me to become acquainted with our beauteous Ms. Garrett. Are you available for lunch, ah, Lee?"

"Why," she said, "I haven't even seen my rooms yet, but

I'm not really tired and we didn't eat on the shuttle from Paris.''

"Wizard," he said. "Then with Sheila's permission, I'll whisk you off."

"I'll see you later this afternoon, dear," Sheila told her. "Don't forget about the, uh, party this evening, if you change your mind."

Out in the hall, as they walked toward the staircase, Jerry Auburn grinned and said, "Has Sheila already invited you to one of her versions of the *partous*?"

She looked up at him from the side of her eyes. "Yes."

"I went to one once. They're rather in the far-out line—in the Roman tradition of Nero. Not my cup of tea. I love ladies one at a time and I don't like boys at all. And I'll leave the building of horizontal pyramids to the pharaohs. Must've been unhealthy; they're all dead, I notice."

She laughed. "We seem to share similar ideas," she told him, before realizing that he might misinterpret that.

He chuckled and took her arm as they began to descend the stairs without saying anything further on the subject of sex.

The pages at the door came hurriedly to attention as Jeremiah Auburn approached, as did the guards with their halberds.

There was a beautiful sportster at the curb, one of the extreme models from Bucharest. Lee was moderately surprised when he ushered her to it and saw her seated on the passenger side. "You have permission to drive your own car in Rome?" she said.

"Ranking members of the World Club have their prerogatives, Lee. Having our central headquarters here is a feather in the caps of the city fathers. They turned over the Palazzo Colonna to us about ten years ago. Do you know Rome? Any preferences on where to eat?"

"I haven't been here for years. I'll leave it to you."

"Wizard, let's say the *Hostaria dell'Orso*. I believe it's supposed to be the oldest restaurant in town. Dante used to live in the building."

He turned the corner and sped down the Via Battisti in the direction of the looming monstrosity that was the monument to Vittorio Emanuele.

As they passed it, Lee shook her head. "Imagine leveling several acres of the Roman forum to erect that thing."

"My sentiments exactly," he said. "So, you're to be Sheila's new secretary. Did she give you her song and dance about the dream?"

Lee looked over at him in some surprise. "She made rather a moving appeal for the goals of the World Club, a stable society in which most of history's problems would be solved."

Jerry laughed softly. "Did she discuss her final solution to the women's rights problem?"

"Why, no. She asked how I stood on the question but we didn't go very far into it."

He said, "I suspect her goal is the reestablishment of a matrilineal society. Get Sheila a bit into her cups and she begins to point out that women predominate numerically in the world but for all practical purposes are ignored in its governing. For instance, we've never had a female president of the United States. I suspect that Sheila wouldn't object to taking the job." He grinned again. "I can just see a whole cabinet of lesbians."

Lee said, confused, "But what does motivate the Central Committee, if not what Sheila calls the dream?"

He shot a look over at her, even as he maneuvered through the narrow streets. "Did our good Sheila tell you anything about the composition of the Central Comitttee?"

"No, not yet. Aside from you, she mentioned Grace Cabot-Hudson."

"And what do you know about Grace?"

"Not much, really. Isn't she supposed to be the richest woman in the world?"

"Uh huh. And what do you know about me?"

"Well, aside from the news media nonsense, not much. Oh, yes, I've heard that you were possibly the richest *man* in the world."

Jerry laughed outright. "Harrington Chase would hate you for that."

"You mean that anti-semitic Texan who supports those ultra-right wing organizations. Good heavens, what has he got to do with it?"

"Harrington's a member of the Central Committee, my dear. So is Mendel Amschel, for that matter, which sometimes drives poor Harrington up the wall."

"The Viennese banker? He's another one that's sometimes

called the richest man. Why should Mr. Chase object to him?''

''If you count his whole family, Mendel may control more wealth than anyone else. The irony is that while he's a Jew, I doubt if he's religious at all. Ah, here we are.''

The *Hostaria dell'Orso* was located in a medieval palace, elegant and very expensive. Jerry Auburn asked the maitre d' for a private dining room and they were immediately escorted to the second floor.

''Sorry,'' Jerry said to Lee. ''There are still some who remember my face, especially women. Unfortunately, I'm seldom mentioned without that 'most eligible bachelor' label being hung around my neck, as though anybody bothered to get married anymore. But even in a place like this, it can be a hazard. Especially when radicals sometimes send a nut case to nice joints on the off chance that they can take a shot at some bloated aristocrat like me.''

''No wonder you're a recluse,'' she told him in a low voice. as they were shown into a luxurious private room.

The maitre d' turned them over to a captain and bowed himself out. The captain gave them menus and stood back, his face stolid.

''Are you a bloated aristocrat too?'' Jerry said as they scanned their *cartes*.

''I suppose so,'' she sighed. ''But not as bloated as you are. I'm sure I'm not bloated enough for a Nihilist to take a crack at me, as you put it.''

He looked over at her appreciatively and said, ''Bloat is not the word. *Zaftig, guapa,* sleek—those are the words.''

''Oh, hush,'' she said, laughing.

When the captain was gone, Lee looked at him accusingly. She said, ''Very well, then. If you don't have the dream, why are you a member of the Central Committee?''

He thought about that a moment. ''Probably to protect my own interests.''

''And all of the other members?''

''To protect theirs. That's what motivates almost everyone, you know—their own interests.''

She looked at him in disbelief. ''Sheila said that it was the World Club which pushed through the assimilating of the United States of the Americas. In my opinion that is *the* outstanding political development of this century. How did that protect your interests, Mr. Auburn?''

He smiled mockingly at her and said with deliberate pomposity, ''Ms. Garrett, the greater part of my investments are in multinational corporations. Almost all corporations of any size are multinationals these days, staffed by the most competent people the computers can locate. But we still have our Cubas to deal with. Americans owned practically everything in basic Cuban industry until Castro took it over. No buy-out, nothing; lady, the investors took some lumps. Why d'you think the CIA financed the Bay of Pigs invasion? To let us get 'our' Cuba back! We feared Allende, in Chile, might take the Castro route, so Allende was murdered and a military junta took over, demolishing what was left of democracy in Chile. However, we could never be sure that our properties were safe. Now, Ms. Garrett, with the establishment of the United States of the Americas, they *are* safe. And so are all the raw materials of Latin America, in return for a comparatively small amount of GAS to keep the peons pacified.''

She was inwardly upset. ''I still say it was a wonderful step of progress.''

''Wizard,'' he said. ''I didn't say that the Central Committee worked against the interests of the majority of people. It was to the personal interest of Washington, Jefferson, John Hancock, and Franklin to win independence from England. They were all rich men. But it was also a good thing for the poorer colonists as well.''

She looked confused, doubtful.

He grinned wryly and said, ''Believe me, Lee, in taking all of Latin America into the United States, the multinationals didn't exactly lose money. Oh, in some of the poorer countries and islands, we drew blanks temporarily. But how do we know what riches might lie under the jungles of, say, Paraguay? Just imagine taking over such nations as Brazil, potentially almost as rich as the original United States. Not to speak of Mexico, Venezuela, and Bolivia, with all their unexploited raw materials. We get contracts for high-rise apartments for all the new recipients of GAS. And somebody has to get richer building roads, public transportation, communications systems, power distribution systems. Believe me, Lee, the multi-nationals did not lose money when the States invited Latin America to join our union.''

She said, still arguing, ''But the expense of putting all of those millions on GAS. Your taxes have skyrocketed. It surely must have counterbalanced . . .''

He was smiling still. ''No. You'd be amazed how cheaply a prole can be maintained from the cradle to the grave. Planned obsolescence has disappeared, so far as the prole is concerned. Everything he consumes has been produced by the most advanced automated equipment. He wears textiles that last damn near forever. He lives in prefab buildings that can be erected overnight. He eats mass-produced foods manufactured largely in factories: His entertainment is canned. His medical care is computerized and automated, as is the pitiful education he wants. I repeat: it costs practically nothing to send a prole from the cradle to the grave.''

The waiter entered with Jerry Auburn's cognac, put it on the table, and stepped back.

Lee felt puzzlement but did not know why. Perhaps it was something subtle in the waiter's movements.

Suddenly, Jerry Auburn knocked back his chair and spun. His foot lashed out and upward with the grace of a ballet dancer and kicked the small automatic in the hand of the slim, now snarling, Italian waiter. The weapon struck the ceiling before falling to the side.

The waiter cursed in some dialect that neither of the two diners understood and snatched for something in his clothing.

Jerry reversed himself, his back to the other, and lashed out with his foot again, high. The shoe connected with the chin and mouth of the attacker, who was slammed back viciously against the wall behind him. In a daze, he slid down to the floor. Jerry did not see the automatic.

Lee got out in a gasp, ''Where did you ever learn Savate?''

''From the first guy who used it on *me*,'' he said. ''We bloated aristocrats learn fast, don't we?''

''Yes, we do,'' she said, and displayed the automatic in her hand.

Chapter Eleven:
The Graf

On the Eastern side of the Rhine, between the Grisons and Lake Constance, lies a tiny baroque toy of a country, Liechtenstein, the last remnant of the Holy Roman Empire and, save for Switzerland, the only nation in western Europe still aloof from the loose confederation called Common Europe. It boasts a population of some 22,000 and an area of 62 square miles, supposedly still a monarchy under His Highness Prince Johann Alois Heinrich Benediktus Gerhardus von und zu Liechtenstein und Duke von Troppau und Jaegerndorf. The prince had gone bankrupt a quarter of a century earlier and these days lived a rocket-set existence on the proceeds of the outright sale of his country. The buyer was Graf Lothar von Brandenburg, who now resided in the Wolfschloss. The schloss, once a robber-baron stronghold, had been built in the 13th century, burned in the Swabian Wars of 1499, then last overhauled in the late 20th century. The Wolfschloss was a forty-minute climb by path northeast of Vaduz, the tiny capital of Liechtenstein, or a few minutes by modern road ending in a cablecar terminal which provided access to the castle. The climb was forbidden to such tourists as still came to the country, and the road was private—unbelievably well patrolled. There were various roadblocks along it.

Liechtenstein had once owed its prosperity to tourism, the winter sport industry, and its many editions of colorful stamps. Since its acquisition by Graf Lothar von Brandenburg it was no longer prosperous, save for Vaduz, whose working population was largely employed by the Graf himself. Tourism was barely tolerated, certainly not encouraged, and the ski resorts were either closed down or sparsely patronized. The once-famous art collection of the Vaduz Museum was now largely to be found in the Wolfschloss.

The office of the Graf contained no desk, and had precious little else to resemble a business office. One whole wall was of glass and looked out on an unsurpassed view of the Rhine Valley over part of the castle's ward. There was but one article of decoration, a Franz Hals, which dominated another wall. The office presented an air of Spartan luxury, as it were: austere but very, very expensive.

This morning it was occupied by three people.

Lothar von Brandenburg, at sixty-five, was still hale and in season skied each morning, or hunted his extensive game preserves. He also made a point of swimming thirty laps of the large swimming pool he'd had installed in the courtyard of a schloss so extensive that a regiment of cavalry could have paraded there. He was only five feet four but had a lean, athletic build. His short hair, once blond, was now a platinum white. It was his eyes that were most remarkable. The irises were of flecked smoky grey and they had no expression. Whatever went on behind the smokescreen, nothing came through. With few exceptions, people newly introduced to Lothar von Brandenburg were uncomfortable about his eyes. He dressed during the day in formal business wear, complete with dark cravat, although ties had seldom been worn for half a century. His suits were invariably faultless; though it was untrue that he never wore one twice, still they gave that impression.

Peter Windsor was of a very different sort. Possibly twenty years younger than the man he served as second in command, he was fresh of face, lime green of eye, handsome in the English aristocrat manner. Over six feet tall, his lank body gave an impression of indolence if not downright laziness, he being inclined to sprawl rather than sit. From this graceful indolence, one could easily reach a wrong impression. Peter Windsor, which was not the name with which he had been christened, had come to the attention of the Graf some twenty-five years in the past when the pink-cheeked lad gained a field promotion to brigade commander in a desperately close-fought action in East Africa. Most of the senior mercenary officers were casualties. The Graf had immediately drawn Windsor under his wing, knowing a good thing when he saw one.

The third person was Margit Krebs, long-time secretary,

stenographer, girl Friday, and brain trust of the Graf. Her hair
was black, unlikely for a Dane, and her face was not Scandinavian, but broad with a wide chin and Magyar cheekbones—
the kind of face that aged slowly. Indeed, she could have
passed for anywhere between thirty and fifty. She invariably
dressed in British tweeds during the business day, which
understated her marvelous legs and figure.

The Graf lowered himself precisely into his favorite heavy
leather chair and nodded to his two underlings. "Margit,
Peter," he said, even as he pressed a button set into the side
of the chair's arm.

"Good morning, chief," Peter Windsor said.

And, "Good morning, *Herr Graf,*" Margit told him.

A side door opened and a servant entered. He was garbed
in the medieval livery of a Germanic court and bore a tray
with coffee things. All were of gold save the Dresden cups.
The servant, granite of expression, put the tray on the small
table about which the three sat.

"Thank you, Sepp," the Graf said and reached for the pot.

"Bitte," Sepp murmured, then bowed and backed from the
room.

Peter, as he watched the other pour, said, "Lothar, if the
organization ever goes broke we can flog this service of yours
and retire in comfort, I shouldn't wonder."

His superior didn't smile but said, "It was ever my boy-
hood ambition, Peter, to start the day off having one's break-
fast and morning beverage served on gold."

When all had their coffee in hand, the Graf turned his
enigmatic gaze on his second. *"Und zo,* Peter: the day's
crises?"

The tall Englishman, dressed with all-out informality in
sweatshirt, slacks, and tennis shoes, had a clipboard beside
him. He took it up saying, "No real crises this morning,
Chief." He looked at the top sheet on the clipboard. "A
contract has come through to have Senator Miles Deillon hit.
One of his business competitors."

"Ah, the American agricultural tycoon? Why bring it to
my attention? Couldn't you have handled such a routine
matter? A senator, eh, and a major landowner at that. It
would be a double-A contract, very lucrative."

Peter nodded. "But there may be complications."

The older man nodded, waiting.

Peter said, "The senator has had his wind up for some time. Afraid of being kidnapped or worse by the American Nihilists, you know. We supply his bodyguard. Three men per shift on a round-the-clock basis—nine men in all."

"Yes? And the complication?" The Graf sipped his coffee, holding the cup in a small womanish hand.

His British subordinate blinked. "I say, we can't be hired both to assassinate a man *and* guard him from assassination."

"Why not?"

Peter put down his own cup of coffee and closed his eyes for a moment. "Well . . ." he said.

The Graf waved a hand negatively. "I assume that Luca Cellini in New York is supplying the guards. If he fails in protecting the senator, it will be a mark against his reputation in the organization. I assume your hit men will come from the ranks of Jacques's Corsicans. They're the best. Very well, if they are unsuccessful in their attempt, Jacques will be shamed. Luca and Jacques are good organization men but we cannot put up with incompetence. Too many contracts inefficiently carried out would lead to a bad image and our competitors would take advantage. I would dislike seeing either of these men go, but business is business. There are many young men with us who are anxious for promotion, willing and ready to step into the shoes of either Luca or Jacques."

Peter shook his head and made a mark with his stylo on the sheet of paper, then folded it back to scan the next one. "I've still got much to learn in this field."

The Graf said, "Speaking of competitors, it has come to my attention that our Colonel Boris Rivas, in Paris, is again taking measures to undersell us and provide a mercenary group for some chief in Mali who wishes to overthrow a neighbor. Approach the colonel once more with a suggestion that he join with us."

Peter said, after making his note, "There's one small item that might be of interest. One of these so-called Deathwish Policies. We get several a day, of course, but this is an exception."

"Yes?" the older man said politely.

"A chap named Roy Cos. He took a standard contract with Brett-James in Nassau. It seemed simply routine."

"Really, Peter, this is a minor matter."

"It has its element. You see, the clod's disappeared—dropped out of sight. Hasn't used the International Credit Card Brett-James issued him nor, for that matter, his own American card. The lads assigned to hit Cos can't put the bloody crosshairs on him."

The Graf frowned. "It seems to me that we had a similar case some years ago which eventually cost us quite a bit." He looked over at Margit, who sat quietly, hands in her lap. "Refresh me on our position in this regard, my dear *Fräulein*."

Margit said, "If the subject is liquidated within the first week of the contract, we receive half a million pseudo-dollars. However, this amount is lowered to a quarter million if he is not liquidated within the following week. If three weeks elapse before he is eliminated, instead of being recompensed at all, we pay a penalty of half a million pseudo-dollars for each day he survives."

"Indeed? Yes, now it comes back to me." He looked at Peter Windsor. "I assume that you have investigated. Have you come to any conclusion?"

"I checked this Roy Cos's Dossier Complete. He is a national organizer of the Wobblies."

The Graf turned his empty eyes to Margit.

She closed her eyes and began to recite in an inflectionless voice. "A revolutionary group founded in 1903 by American unionists, anarchists, and socialists, under the name Industrial Workers of the World, or I.W.W. Their program involved organizing workers into one Big Union which would take charge of the world's economy by legal means. For a time they grew rapidly but their anarchists began to advocate sabotage and violence around 1908, and the government was able to legally crush them. By the 1930s, they had all but disappeared.

"But not quite completely. Their goals and methods have changed until now they have few similarities to the old I.W.W. They contend that the means of production, distribution, and so forth, should be democratically owned and operated by the people as a whole rather than being private property or in the hands of the State. They believe that this would give rise to full employment and a new surge of progress."

Peter snorted. "Full employment? With all the automation

available? They're heading for the bend, if they're not already around it.''

Margit opened her eyes. ''They seem to believe that the present-day proles, now on GAS, should be put to work in the arts, cleaning up ecology problems, that sort of thing.''

Von Brandenburg sighed. ''Very well, the man is a revolutionist. Does this have any connection with his taking out a Deathwish Policy? It doesn't seem consistent.''

The tall Englishman looked back at his notes. ''He's beginning to get a bit of publicity, don't you know? The news media are making quite a story of it. Before, these Wobblies were seldom heard of.''

His superior snapped to Margit, ''Get through to Luca Cellini in New York and have him put his best people on this. Cos is to be hit absolutely soonest.''

''*Ja, Herr Graf.*''

They spoke alternately in English, German, and French. One might ask a question in any of these languages and be answered in another—even occasionally in Spanish, Italian, or Russian.

Von Brandenburg looked back at Peter Windsor. ''How is that fracas in Somalia progressing?''

''Dormant. However, the Sheik has put in an order for two hundred infantrymen and six hover-tanks, the British Vickers model.''

The Graf looked at his secretary. ''Do we have them available?''

''At the Gao depot,'' Margit said. ''They can be available for shipping within twenty-four hours, with crews.''

Peter shook his head. ''Where does the beggar get the funds for a contract of this size? One would think there would be Sweet Fanny Adams in his treasury.''

''From the Arab Union,'' his chief told him. And then, ''Speaking of Africa, what is the latest on Mahem Dhu? I had an indignant call from the Prophet's man last night. This fanatic's movement is spreading like wildfire. He wants the man to be taken care of immediately.''

Peter nodded. ''It's had its complications, you know. I put Spyros Kakia on it. He's our best cover-builder and analyzer. Spyros concluded that hitting the so-called Mahdi wouldn't be overly difficult; he's out in public constantly, for all practical

purposes without guards, as befits a holy man. But Spyros
sees no possibility of a successful hit. I fancied that our only
possibility was to locate a gull—a patsy, as the Yanks call it.
One's turned up from the States. Chap named Franklin Pinell,
a deportee. Guilty of a homicide romp. He was duped into
selecting Tangier for his refuge and that Aussie Nat Fraser
took over. Pinell was stripped of everything and then con-
vincingly taken under the wing of Ram Panikkar, with his
usual efficiency. A bit of a swine, Ram, but unbeatable at this
sort of thing. Pinell is grateful to Ram and agreed to take the
Mahdi assignment. His cover will be as a media man, which
will guarantee his access to Mahem Dhu. He'll perform the
hit.'' Peter sighed. ''Unfortunately, the fast chopper which is
supposedly posted for his escape will never materialize.''

The Graf nodded acceptance. ''Those fanatical followers
will tear him to pieces.'' He frowned. ''What did you say his
name was?''

Peter looked down at his clipboard. ''Franklin Pinell.''

Von Brandenburg thought about it, his smoky eyes narrow-
ing. He said finally, ''What was the name of Buck Pinell's
son? Remember? Buck was always proudly bringing forth his
wallet and insisting we look at his snapshots.''

His right-hand man thought back. ''Frankie,'' he said.

''The name isn't that common.'' The Graf looked at Margit.
''Buck Pinell was before your time, *Fräulein*, but get me his
dossier and that of this Franklin Pinell.'' He looked back at
Peter Windsor. ''What was Buck's real first name?''

''Willard, wasn't it? He never used it. I didn't know him as
well as you did, Lothar. What was it the news chaps used to
call him? The Lee Christmas of the 21st century.''

''Yes,'' the Graf murmured. ''We were young men together in the early days of the organization. My best friend, I
suppose you would say. Who was Lee Christmas, *Fräulein*?''

Margit Krebs had already activated the communications
screen which sat next to her chair, to order the required
dossiers. Now her eyes seemed to film and she recited, ''Lee
Christmas, most notable of the pre-World War One American
mercenaries, operated in South and Central America. Almost
singlehanded he was successful in several revolutions and
military revolts, especially in Honduras. He would attain high
rank in the new administration but inevitably step on the

wrong toes and be dismissed, often to flee for his life. Later
he might return and participate in the overthrow of the government he had brought to power. A lone soldier of fortune
who owned a Maxim or Vickers machine gun, could gather a
handful of followers and defeat a Central American army. He
was considered unique among the other mercenaries because
he refused to fight on the side he thought in the wrong.''

The Graf laughed softly, which brought Peter Windsor's
eyebrows up. The other wasn't prone to displaying humor.
"That sounds like Buck," he said. "It was his one short-
coming.''

He came to his feet absently and went over to the huge
window to stare out over the Furstensteig path along the high
ridge dividing the Rhine and Samina valleys. The peaks
reached six to seven thousand feet, the highest in the
Leichtenstein Alps.

The dossiers, in printout, dropped from the slot in front of
the secretary. Margit took them up and quickly scanned them.
She said, "You were correct, *Herr Graf*. Franklin Pinell is
the son of Willard Pinell. Their photos are even remarkably
similar.''

Lothar von Brandenburg said musingly, "And why was
young Franklin deported?''

"He had four felonies on his record. The final one was
decisive. He shot a man to death.''

"Why?''

"He refused to reveal that. His victim was evidently unarmed, shot down in cold blood.'' The revelation didn't faze
Margit Krebs.

The Graf turned and faced Peter Windsor, who was already
eyeing his superior in concern. He said, "Find an alternative
gobemouche to liquidate the Mahdi.''

Peter stood, one hand out in protest. "Oh, look here,
Lothar, this is a million-dollar contract! We can't afford to
flub it, don't you know? The Prophet would be incensed.
This Pinell chap seems to be a natural, and I daresay it might
take donkey's years to find another dupe.''

The older man's expressionless, smoky eyes took him in.
"I will not condone the sacrifice of the son of Buck Pinell,
Peter.''

"I didn't expect sentiment from you, Chief.''

"Neither did I. However, I suggest that instead of the Mahdi contract, you send young Pinell to Paris. Have him remonstrate with Colonel Rivas, who seems to be getting too big for his britches, as Buck would have put it. Let him accompany Nat Fraser on the assignment. The Australian is an old hand; he can report how Franklin Pinell reacts to being blooded. I'll want a full report from him and then, possibly, we'll have Buck's son here to the Wolfschloss to gather our own impressions."

His second in command shrugged it off, clearly dissatisfied, and turned back to his clipboard. "Now: this Dave Carlton chap in New Jersey has been poaching on our military surplus enterprises. Last week he sold one hundred Skoda assault rifles to Chavez, that guerrilla in Colombia who is attempting to arouse the Colombians to throw off their affiliations with the United States of the Americas."

Chapter Twelve:
The Nihilists

Rick Flavelle looked over at his sole surviving companion, who leaned against the steel wall near one of the gunports.

Rick said, "It's damn quiet."

"Yeah," Alfredo said. "Ever since they yelled for us to surrender and you told them to get fucked. You know what they're doing? They're bringing up something to open up this tin can."

"Hell," Rick said, checking the clip in his Gyrojet automatic. "They'd need a laser rifle. How's your arm?"

"I immobilized it with a syrette. But it's sure as hell useless. How's your side?"

"Okay," Rick lied. He carefully slid back the slide of his gunport and peered out. There was nothing to be seen.

The steel pillbox in which they were making their ultimate stand was beautifully camouflaged in almost the exact center of the Dunninger Mountain resort home, in a beautiful patio garden. Beautiful, but on the shot-up and bombed-out side right now. From the exterior, as they well knew, the pillbox looked like an innocent rock garden. One had to scramble about it quite carefully to find the well-disguised door, not to speak of the gunports.

Rick said, "How's your ammo?"

"Down to the last clip. I'm too fucked up with this dead arm to throw the clip and count them."

"You better click the stud over to single fire," Rick said.

The other made a face in pain and growled, "You think I'm a dizzard? I long since did that."

Rick brought his gun up and carefully brought the barrel to the gunport. He squinted and gently, gently, squeezed the trigger.

"What the hell you shooting at?" Alfredo growled. "Did you get him?"

"I don't know. Just keeping them honest. I thought I saw something move. You think the bastards might be gone?"

The other laughed bitterly. "You think the fucking sun will rise in the west tomorrow? Why should they be gone? We've had it. Whatever they want, it's sitting in their laps now. I haven't heard any fire from the other boys for ten minutes. They've had it."

"What they want is Dunninger," Rick said emptily. "He was the only one here when they came in. All the family just left for Mexico. Have you called him?"

"Hell, no. He's down there in the bomb shelter, probably shitting his pants. Damn this arm. You know, maybe Cliff had some shells left."

Rick looked over at the body lying still where it had fallen. "He had an assault rifle," he said. "The ammo wouldn't fit either of our gyros."

Alfredo snarled, "Use your goddamned head. Get his rifle, and when you've used up your rocket shells, use his gun. I'd get it myself but you can move easier."

Rick nodded, leaned his automatic against the metal wall, and painfully made his way over to the fallen body. There was little chance of enemy fire penetrating the two small gunports but he moved in a crouch, instinctively. The wound in his side wasn't helping any. He could have taken a syrette to localize it but he wasn't sure of the effect. He couldn't afford to have his whole right side paralyzed.

The inert Cliff had no spare clips. That stupid bastard Dunninger had insisted that their uniforms be neat and presentable. He didn't want them distracting the family and visitors with bandoliers of ammunition and grenades dangling from their belts. So, aside from the clips they'd had in their weapons, the bodyguards had at most two spares. They had largely used them up in the first moments of the assault on the Dunninger home. And from then on, they'd had insufficient firepower to keep the attackers at bay. It had been a balls-up from the start. Nobody had time to make his way to the little armory for more ammo.

Rick worked his way back to his gunport, trailing the

assault rifle behind him. His side was feeling worse by the minute.

He peered through the small port again. He said, trying to keep down their mutual fear and apprehension by talk, "What the hell happened, anyway? Who are they?"

"The Holy Mother only knows. If that stupid bastard Luca Cellini hadn't pulled the other four guys off, we would've had a chance. But eight of us weren't enough, especially with one shift sacked out when the sons of bitches hit."

Rick said, "Cellini was rotating them. Another four guards were supposed to show up for replacements."

"Yeah?" the other sneered. "Bullshit. It's too much of a coincidence. Old man Dunninger's family leaves him alone here, four of his bodyguards are relieved, and next thing we know, we're all in the dill. There must be twenty of the bastards out there. They knocked off the dogs and three of the boys before we got wise. We're lucky we made it to this overgrown tin can with me covering for that fat cat Dunninger. Listen, there's not enough money in the country to pay for holding down a job like this."

Rick said wanly, "You should have thought of that during the two years we've been on this cushy assignment."

"Yeah, great, but I wish Luca Cellini was here with us right now. Or, better still, the Graf himself. You know what we oughta do, Rick? Call out and tell 'em we're willing to surrender if they won't kill us. Hell, they don't want us, they want old man Dunninger."

His companion, his side cramping up now, looked over sarcastically. "Sure, Al. And then spend the rest of our lives on the run from the Graf. He doesn't like his boys to surrender. And what happens if we do? Not only are we on the run but that's the end of any compensation, any pension, any further credits from him at all. We'd be back on GAS and, so far as I'm concerned, I've got two kids I want to get through a good school, two kids I want to leave a few shares of U.S. Variable Basic Stock so they won't wind up living on nothing but GAS the rest of their lives."

"Oh, great," the other sneered. "Two kids, eh? A regular one-man population explosion. Well, I'm not that far around the bend, Rick. I don't have any kids. I'm on my own. Those guys out there'll let us go. They want the big shot hiding down in the bomb shelter, not us. Screw the Graf. We'll worry about him when the time comes. We've both copped one, haven't we? What does he expect?''

Rick shrugged it off and peered through his gunport. He thought he could hear something going on in the house. What a sonofabitch of a pickled situation. If the attackers were smart enough to just wait it out another hour, he and Alfredo would have stiffened up to the point that they couldn't resist anyway.

There came a heavy explosion up against the door that threw him to the steel floor of the small pillbox. He landed, agonizingly, on his wounded side. He lay there, breathing deeply, not sure he could move. A thin piercing tone began a steady whistle in his ear.

He called out finally, ''You all right, Al? They've got some kind of heavy weapon out there. That was an explosive shell, not just a bomb.''

''Shit! Whad'da'ya mean, am I all right? I keep telling you, we've had it! Yell to them. Toss in the towel.''

Another ear-blasting explosion whumped against the steel door. It sagged inward.

''Oh, Jesus,'' Rick panted. ''Why can't those four new guards show up? Take 'em from the rear.'' He struggled to work his Gyrojet automatic around.

''You stupid dreamer, you,'' Alfredo got out. ''They're not coming. We've been set up. Left holding the fucking sack.''

The next explosion blew the heavy door off its hinges, sent it crashing to the floor, barely missing the fallen Rick Flavelle.

''Here they come,'' Alfredo snarled.

Two prole-garbed fighters popped through the blasted entryway and jumped immediately to each side, crouching. They carried automatic shotguns, on the ready.

Alfredo swore, brought up his gun with his one arm, pulled the trigger, widened his eyes at the weapon's failure to fire, pulled desperately again. A shotgun blast tore his stomach away.

Rick threw his weapon aside, screaming, ''I'm out of it. Don't shoot! Give me a break!''

The first of the two approached him gingerly, covered by the second. Grimed by dirt, eyes wide with excitement and exertion, he was a good-looking young fellow in his late teens, looking more like a student than a gunman. He kicked Rick's weapon even farther to one side and shot a quick look at the bodies of Alfredo and Cliff.

He stared down at Rick and said, "Why didn't you dizzards give up? We weren't after you. We want that plutocrat, Dunninger. You're just a couple of working men, doing the best you can to make some kind of decent living."

"Yeah, yeah," Rick panted. "That's it. Don't shoot."

The young gunman looked around at his companion. "Call for the medic, and Ostrander."

The second one nodded and went back to the door and shouted, "It's secure. There's only one left and he's wounded. Where's the doc?"

A newcomer entered the breached pillbox and looked about, making a face at the carnage. He was middle-aged, and toted an old-fashioned assault rifle under one arm.

He looked down at Rick and said, "Where's Dunninger? Don't make us force you to tell."

Rick was losing most of his sudden panic but was still breathing deeply. He got out, "Down in the bomb shelter. Over there; the trap door."

"He armed?"

A doctor entered, carrying a medical bag. He was older, gray of hair, and obviously tired. Rick, undoubtedly, wasn't the only combat victim he had treated in the past hour of action. He shot his eyes around, dismissed the obviously dead pair, and came over to Rick.

Rick said, "Yeah, he's armed," to the one in command.

"That trap door locked from inside?"

"I don't know. I've never been down there."

The doctor said, "Shut up. Let me look at you," and knelt down next to the fallen bodyguard.

But the commander said, "Is there any way of communicating with him from up here?"

"That phone over there, hung on the wall."

"Shut up," the doctor repeated, fishing in his bag.

The commander went over to the phone, examined it briefly, put it to his mouth and ear, and activated a stud on its side.

He said, "Dunninger? You might as well come on out of there, or we'll have to blow you out and that might wind up plastering you around the walls . . . No, we won't kill you. Not yet. Not if your family ponies up the ransom . . . Don't be a dizzard, Dunninger. Of course we can get you out of there. We're here in the pillbox, aren't we? Stop trying to stall, nobody's coming to your assistance. This house is too far away from any other for the ruckus to have been heard, and we have a scrambler blanketing all communications. So come on out of there before we scrape you out."

He listened for a moment longer and then hung the phone back on the wall. He looked at the steel trap door to the bomb shelter below.

Two more civilian-clad, armed men had crowded into the small compartment. They looked down at the doctor working on Rick Flavelle, who had passed out.

The doctor said, "Here, you two men carry this fellow out to the chopper."

One of the newcomers grumbled, "Why not let him die? Chet is dead and two of the other boys have copped one."

"Because we're not butchers. Now get this man to the aircraft."

While the two were carrying Rick out into the garden patio, the trap door began cautiously to rise. The three remaining gunmen trained their weapons on it. The commander reached down and grasped the steel door and pulled it completely back. On the steel ladder below stood an apprehensive man in his late middle years, white of face, lips trembling. He was clad in swimming trunks.

"Come on, come on," the commander of the terrorists said. The other climbed out fearfully and put his hands high over his head. He saw the two bodies and winced. The commander jerked his head. "Come on, this way."

Harold Dunninger said, doing his best to keep a tremor from his voice, "Where are we going?"

"To a hideout until we collect the ransom. If we collect it."

"Oh, don't worry. Don't worry about that. You'll collect it. Don't worry."

"We're not worrying—either way."

They passed through the garden, into the house, and down the hall toward the front door. Everywhere were signs of the short battle that had been waged so recently, including two bodies in uniforms similar to those of Rick and Alfredo.

Outside, a copter had landed on the extensive lawn. The two gunmen who had carried Rick out were hoisting him up into it. More armed men in prole clothing were streaming from the house, two of them with bandaged wounds. They were in high good humor, calling back and forth to each other banteringly.

The commander said, "One of you boys go back and get some clothes for this character. Cozzini, bandage his eyes. He's got a reputation as a sharpy."

When all had embarked, the craft swept off the ground and reached for altitude. The commander, seated next to the pilot, said evenly, "Get out of here soonest. It won't be long before one of those damned servants gets himself untied. Shouldn't be much more than an hour before the IABI is after us."

"Right," the pilot said.

Still blindfolded, Harold Dunninger, now in better command of himself and making an effort to control his trembling, was pushed down on a hard seat in the copter. At least, thank God, Betty and the children were now safely in Mexico.

And then the chilling thought came to him. He and Betty hadn't been getting along these days—ever since she had found out about that ridiculous little harem he'd been keeping down in the city. The group sex thing. Betty was of the old school, had even insisted on marriage. But now they had been planning divorce, and Betty would have the reins of his fortune when it came to the ransom. What was to prevent her from taking an uncompromising stand against the kidnappers, refusing to meet their demands? On his death, she would inherit the whole fortune, one of the largest on the continent. Damn!

Betty had let him know, in no uncertain terms, that she hated him for what she called her betrayal. The bitch didn't realize that she'd lost what appeal she had possessed as a young woman. Now, though pushing sixty, he still had the sexual drives of a man in his thirties. Those bimbos he kept were only for occasional orgies, nothing important. As for the family, he loved the two boys and had grown used to Betty. He hadn't wanted the divorce; was still arguing with her about it. But she was adamant. Oh, God, Betty! Would she meet the kidnappers' demands? After all, it was only money. There was always more, endlessly more, where it came from.

The aircraft slid into a landing and again he was hauled, pushed, led blindly this point to that. Now he was in some kind of a building, perhaps a dwelling. Nor did his captors utilize an elevator. Instead, he was marched up stairs, down a hall, then pushed into a room. A door slammed behind him.

Harold Dunninger stood there a while, his eyes still bandaged but his hands free. Finally, hesitantly, he reached up and tore the blindfold away.

He was in a small bedroom. It could have been a servant's room in any of his own houses. But no, not even his servants lived in quarters as drab as these. Two chairs, a table, a dresser, a bed, an open door to a small bath. On the bed lay some of his clothes, including shoes. Whoever had snatched up the things had forgotten socks and handkerchiefs. On the table was a plate of sandwiches which looked less than appetizing and a half-liter plastic of beer. The furniture was less than new, the rug on the floor well-worn. There was one window, but what looked like tar paper had been taped over it on the outside so that he couldn't have looked out without breaking the glass, and he assumed that this would bring punishment.

For lack of anything else to do, he donned shirt, slacks, and shoes. They hadn't even brought him underclothing. No Tri-Di set, not even a radio or books. The pockets of his slacks were empty.

There came a gentle knock at the door and Harold Dunninger looked up, apprehensive again. Before he could respond, a stranger entered.

None of the kidnappers he had thus far seen had looked like desperadoes. They had been dressed as proles, but they hadn't been vicious, in spite of the circumstances. But this one was different.

Among other things, he was only about twenty, and one had to look twice to realize that he wasn't younger. He had what only could be described as a hesitant face. Polite, well bred, fresh-faced, as though he hadn't been shaving very long, and far from aggressive. His expression was almost apologetic. He was well-dressed in sports clothing and wouldn't have looked out of place with a tennis racket in his hand.

He said, "Good afternoon, sir."

Harold Dunninger stared at him. "Who the hell are you?"

The other flushed. "My name's Thomas Spaulding, sir." He stood there almost like a waiter or a butler at attention.

Dunninger continued to eye him. He said finally, "Well, what do you want?"

"I've come to . . . to be with you, sir. Do you mind if I sit down?"

"It's your jail," the older man snapped, somehow feeling relief at this development, somehow gaining courage from the appearance of this inoffensive youngster. He himself took one of the chairs at the table.

"I'll do what I can to make you as comfortable as possible under the circumstances."

The tycoon snorted in disgust. "Comfortable! Under these conditions? What could you do to make me comfortable?"

"Anything within reason—something to read, something to eat besides those sandwiches? Perhaps, something to drink beyond the beer there? Writing materials? Or would you just like to talk?"

"Talk about what, goddamn it?"

"Anything you like, sir. I'm here to keep you company."

"Thanks," Dunninger said, even able by now to mount sarcasm.

Thomas Spaulding looked anxious and cleared his throat. "Perhaps you'd like a Bible. Or would you prefer a United Church brother to talk to?"

"Those ignorant bigots? There's never been such a corrupt, stupid religious movement in the history of the race. I'm a Catholic, boy!"

"Yes, sir. I remember now. Would you like a priest?"

The cold went through Harold Dunninger and his face went slack. After a long moment he said, "What do you *mean*, would I like a priest?"

Young Spaulding said, "I am not superstitious myself, sir, but I have no prejudice against those who are. I thought . . . I thought it was the custom of your faith to make peace with your God before . . ." He let the sentence dribble away.

The older man stared at him, cold fingers walking down his spine. Finally, he got out, "You're going to shoot me. That leader of yours, that one who talked me out of the bomb shelter. He said you wouldn't kill me.''

"Comrade Ostrander knew you wouldn't be killed *if* the ransom was paid. But I doubt if he promised anything more. You have twenty-four hours, sir. If the fifty million pseudo-dollars is not forthcoming by that time, I am afraid that . . . that your life is forfeit.''

"Fifty . . . *million* . . . pseudo-dollars.''

"Yes, sir. Comrade Ostrander has already made the initial contact. The ransom is to be paid into a special numbered account in Tangier. And there must be guarantees that no attempt will be made to prosecute anyone. If such attempts are made, you will be, uh, eliminated.''

Harold Dunninger slumped back in his chair, his eyes wide. Betty would never permit such a sum to escape her hands. Yes, it was available. But she would never . . . not Betty. In spite of the fact that she had been born into luxury, and certainly had lived in luxury, Betty was a compulsive pennypincher. She made a point of prowling the kitchen, enraged if the servants opened a bottle of wine for themselves. The allowance she doled out to the boys was a farce. Harold Dunninger augmented it secretly each week. Her pennypinching was proverbial. Fifty million pseudo-dollars? No. Never from Betty, even in the best of times.

Harold Dunninger said shakily, "I'll take that drink.''

"Yes, sir.'' Young Spaulding got up and went to the door, opened it, and stuck his head out, obviously speaking to a guard stationed in the hall.

Dunninger's mind raced. Or tried to. He had to get out of here somehow, within twenty-four hours. Was this kid armed? If so, was there any way to take his gun, and get through the guard which they obviously would have posted? He closed his eyes and groaned. Harold Dunninger was no muscle-bound hero. He'd let himself go to pot over the years. He'd never been much for sports, even as a youngster. And even if he was able to overwhelm Spaulding, there would be more of them beyond, downstairs—Men trained and experienced with guns, while he hardly knew enough to fire one. He closed his eyes in sick dismay, his stomach beginning to roil.

Tom Spaulding returned with a squat bottle and a glass and put them on the table before the captive.

Dunninger shakily took off the bottle's cap and poured. It was a bottle of his own prehistoric whiskey. It would seem that his kidnappers weren't above looting. He knocked back the spirits with a quick motion. He had to make some sort of plans.

The young man had seated himself again and was looking in compassion at the captive.

Dunninger said, "Are you supposed to be seeing that I make no plans for escape?"

The other seemed embarrassed. "Well, no, sir. It was my idea. It goes back to the old British and French army days of the late 18th century. All officers were gentlemen; they came from good families—aristocrats. If one was to be shot in the morning, a fellow officer was assigned to stay with him in his cell and, well, *be* with him. Take messages to his family or sweetheart, help him make out his will, if necessary. Talk with him. Possibly read the Bible with him. That sort of thing. Just, well, keep him company."

Dunninger eyed him, even as he poured another stiff drink. "Why'd they pick you?"

The boy looked embarrassed again. "I suppose it's because I know you, sir. We come from the same background. My father was a close friend of yours."

The older man was staring now. "You're Pete Spaulding's boy? Why, I remember you now. Tommy Spaulding. I haven't seen you since you were about ten or eleven. A thin little fellow, always nervous."

"Yes, sir. I remember you, too, Mr. Dunninger. Very clearly."

"Look, call me Harold," the other said. His voice had an edge of excitement now. "Look, Tommy, I've got to get out of here. My wife'll never pay that ransom—never in a million years. We've got to figure some way of getting me out of here."

The young man blinked and shook his head sadly. "I'm afraid that's impossible."

"But look, these people are killers. They're kidnappers. Mad dogs must be shot down on sight."

Tom Spaulding was still shaking his head in rejection. "No, sir, they're idealists. Don't you know whose hands you're in? We're the Nihilists."

"We?"

"Yes, sir. You must realize, we don't have anything against you as an individual. We're opposed to the socioeconomic system you represent. We are going to change it."

The tycoon closed his eyes once more and tried to wrench his mind into thought. He opened them again and said desperately, "See here, boy. That sum your Comrade Ostrander demanded is ridiculous."

"Yes, sir. It was purposely made so, to attract attention to your case."

"It'll never be paid. But I'll tell you, Tommy, on my word of honor, that if you can get me out of here, I'll give you five million pseudo-dollars, all tax-free. All deposited to your account, no questions asked, say, in Switzerland or Nassau. My word of honor."

"Sir," the other said sadly, "you don't understand. Even if I did need the money—and I don't—it wouldn't interest me. I'm a devoted member of the Nihilists, and though I'm sorry that you are in this position, I'm dedicated to ending this social system. I'm willing to participate in the liquidating of others, if required to accomplish our ends."

Dunninger glowered at him. "You're completely around the bend. You're crazy."

"I don't think so, sir. The world's in need of change. The overwhelming majority of the race is living in misery and degradation."

The tycoon said impatiently, "What the hell do you think you'd replace our system with?"

"We differ on that question. You see, Nihilists don't ever expect to come to power ourselves. We're basically anti-organization, if you can comprehend that. We're against the status quo, but we don't offer a definitive alternative system. We believe production should be democratically owned and we believe in world government, but not of the present systems."

Dunninger groaned in the face of what he thought sheer madness. "But what do you think you're doing? You assassinate people, especially rich or powerful people. You commit arson and sabotage. What's that got to do with reforms? You're nothing but terrorists."

"No, sir. Our basic goal is to spur the people into alternatives to capitalism and communism. Most people never consider the possibility of a basic change in their own system. The system tells them that what prevails has always been and will always be. They fail to realize that nothing changes as steadily as social systems.''

Dunninger was in despair. "You'd prefer what they've got in the Soviet Complex?''

"We're against them both. In the West, production means are owned by a few private individuals. In the East, it is in the hands of the State. To the rank-and-file citizen, it makes comparatively little difference. In short, we're trying to goose the world's population into thinking about change.''

"So you're actually willing to murder me, to gain what you think are desirable ends.''

"Yes, sir, we are,'' the boy said simply.

"It's not fair; I've never killed anybody in my life!''

The boy looked at him and took a deep, unhappy breath. "Haven't you? Maybe you never pulled a trigger, but the blood on the hands of *your* social system is unbelievable. Millions have died due to pollution and disease brought about by your rampaging industry. Millions have died from poisonous foods and drugs that were continued because they made a profit. Why has cancer erupted geometrically over the last century and a half? Mr. Dunninger, you don't even *know* how many deaths you've caused.''

Dunninger tipped up the whiskey bottle once again. The boy was a wild-eyed unthinking fanatic. Given time, he might have been able to get through to him, convince him how wrong he was, how misguided. But he, Harold Dunninger, didn't have time. He had less than twenty-four hours now.

Harold Dunninger upended the bottle, killing it.

"Can you get me another one of these?'' he slurred.

Chapter Thirteen:
Roy Cos

Roy's secretary Mary Ann, publicity man Jet Peters, and writer Ferd Feldmeyer sat in a row on a couch before the Tri-Di screen in the luxurious winter villa of some absent northerner. The variable-image Tri-Di screen was set into the wall of the living room. At the moment, it was just large enough so that the people on lens were life-size. There were some uncanny attributes. Though the trio had been exposed to Tri-Di projections all their lives, the illusion was as though they could have spoken back and forth with Roy Cos and the others being shown.

The face of a well-known commentator was smiling as though earnest, sincere, and oh-so-friendly.

Mary Ann frowned, her plain face impatient. She said, "You've got the wrong station, Ferd. That's Ken Butterworth. I listen to his commentaries every day."

Jet Peters swigged at his highball. Sitting around waiting for the broadcast, he'd already had enough to still the characteristic tremor of his hands. He said, "Ken is Roy's announcer. Forry ponied up fifty thousand to get him for just a few minutes. Nothing but the best for Roy Cos. That Brit shyster in Nassau will be sweating thirty-eight caliber turdlets at the rate Forry goes through that million pseudo-dollars a day. Christ only knows what we're paying for fifteen minutes of prime time on an international hookup."

The life-size figure seated behind the desk said, "Folks, this is Ken Butterworth, yours truly. Tonight, I have a surprise for you. If you follow the news at all, you know that Roy Cos has gained instant fame as the Deathwish Wobbly. Roy Cos, a dedicated idealist, is risking his life—perhaps sacrificing it—to bring you the message of the Industrial Workers of the World—the Wobblies. Mr. Cos is unsusal for a man with a message. He doesn't insist that you subscribe to his admittedly radical view—only that he be granted the opportunity to say it and allow you to make your own decisions.

"Roy Cos's life has been insured for an unbelievable sum. So long as he lives, he has a very large credit line. Unlike others who sign Deathwish Policies, Roy Cos is devoting his credits to spreading his message. His life expectancy might be measured in hours. But tonight he will bring you his program of basic changes to our social system. He plans further broadcasts . . ." the news commentator paused dramatically ". . . if he survives. Folks, I present Mr. Roy Cos, the Deathwish Wobbly."

Ken Butterworth faded out and Roy came on lens, sitting at a similar desk. Flanking him and behind stood Billy Tucker and Ron Ellison, their faces alert, their eyes periodically roaming.

Ferd's plump mouth seemed to pout. "What the hell are *they* doing there?" he said.

Jet Peters laughed. "One of Forry's ideas to emphasize Roy's continual danger. They're in a little studio in one of the smaller Tri-Di stations about fifty miles from here. I don't know where. There's not a chance that anybody knows where they are, and even if they did, they couldn't get into that studio. But it looks authentic. Roy is being guarded every minute."

Mary Ann said, even as Roy started his talk. "He looks awful. His face is too pale."

"Too heavy, too," Ferd said. "Put some of the cosmetic boys to work on him, Mary Ann. He needs to cut a sympathetic figure. Kind of romantic."

Roy was reading his speech somewhat stiffly. He'd never appeared on the airwaves before. The three watching had heard the speech a dozen times before and had all had a hand in its final polishing, so they didn't bother to listen too closely.

Jet said, "He needs coaching. Forry ought to hire a couple of actors to give him some pointers." He looked at Ferd. "Where do we meet the rest of them after the broadcast?"

"Search me," Ferd said. He looked at Mary Ann.

Mary Ann said, "No. That's why I had you pack, ready to go. We're to meet Roy and the others at a prearranged street corner, ditch our car there, and then go on. I don't know where."

"I hope the hell we don't get separated from them," the publicity man growled.

Ferd took a sip from his glass of beer. "Well, from now on, the credits start accumulating," he said in his fat man's voice. "Now we come out from cover and start spending that money. Do you realize we've already made seventy thousand apiece? We've been on the payroll a week and Forry hasn't allowed him to use his credit card at all. Man, when he does—it'll all hit the fan at once."

The secretary put her elbows tight against her sides in feminine rejection. "Don't talk about the money we're making," she said. "It sounds ghoulish."

Jet said to her, "Where are we going to meet them?"

"On a street corner."

He scowled impatiently. "What street corner?"

She was embarrassed. "Forry told me not to tell anyone."

The publicity man didn't get it and said, "You mean he doesn't even trust us?"

"Oh, don't be a cloddy, Jet. It's not just us. He didn't tell anybody where we were to rendezvous, except me. Only one of us needs to know. The fewer people who know, the less chance there is for an accidental leak."

Roy Cos finished his talk and Forry Brown took over, seated in Ken Butterworth's place, lending him a spurious celebrity. The scrawny little newsman was more at home on lens than Roy. He said, squinting his faded gray eyes, "Thanks to all you people for listening. As Ken Butterworth said, Roy will have more to say—if he survives. It's rumored that the contract for his death—his murder—is in the hands of the legendary Graf Lothar von Brandenburg, of Mercenaries, Incorporated. In short, it's just a matter of time now. Roy Cos and his staff are on the run. But I'm going to let you listeners in on something: we are not going to give advance notice of Roy's broadcasts. Instead, we're going to spring them at just about any time, any place. You might even keep your video recorders taping. Tomorrow or the next day, just by chance, you might come onto another Wobbly broadcast. If and when you do, phone three of your friends who might be interested, and tell them that the Deathwish Wobbly is again hurrying through one of his talks before the Graf's killers can catch up to him." A one-beat pause before Forry delivered his clincher: "They just might catch him while he's on camera."

Jet came to his feet and said, "I'll finish packing my bags. Got some things I've got to cram into them." He left the room.

Mary Ann looked after him thoughtfully.

Forry, on the Tri-Di screen, was continuing. "We applied to the Inter-American Bureau of Investigation for protection and were ignored. The only guards Roy has are four friends, fellow Wobblies. They are unarmed. They applied for permits to carry weapons but were denied. I suggest that any listener who is indignant over this get in touch with his congressman and senator. Demand that Roy's guards be allowed weapons! The Graf's gunmen will be armed to the teeth. Of course, most of you do not yet support the Wobbly cause. I, Roy Cos's manager, am not a Wobbly. But we all subscribe to the American tradition of fair play. We all believe that this dedicated man *must* be heard, before his inevitable fate overtakes him. Good night, fellow members of the human race. If you see us again, all of us will have been very, very lucky"

The screen faded.

Suddenly, Mary Ann was on her feet, hurrying from the room. She went down the hall to Jet Peter's bedroom. It was closed but there was no lock.

She pushed through and entered briskly.

The publicity man was standing in the middle of the room, a pocket transceiver held to his mouth. His habitually bleary eyes widened, and for the briefest of split seconds it looked as though he was going to hide what he was doing. But that was nonsense.

Her eyes accused him silently.

He looked at her. "One of my publicity outlets. I thought of one last thing I could plant in a . . ."

Mary Ann said crisply, "No. All evening long you've been trying to find out where Roy is—where we were to meet and where we were going."

"Don't be a mopsy," he said contemptuously, deactivating the transceiver and returning it to a side pocket.

"I want to know to whom you were talking."

"None of your goddam business."

"I want to know, too," a voice said from behind her. Ferd Feldmeyer stepped into the room.

Mary Ann said to him, "I passed his room earlier and saw his bags there on the floor. He was already packed. His excuse for leaving while we were still listening to the broadcast wasn't valid. And now I caught him phoning somebody."

Ferd looked at the publicity man wearily. "What the hell's the matter, Jet? Wasn't ten thousand a day enough to keep you honest?"

Jet Peters stared at him. "Ten thousand a day? Don't be silly. He won't last the next twenty-four hours—especially after that broadcast roasting the contracting corporation and the Graf. You two ought to come in with me. I was offered a quarter of a million pseudo-dollars, tax free, just for fingering him. They'll boost that now, if all three of us cooperate."

"What some assholes will do for money," Feldmeyer said, shaking his head. "I always thought you were a square guy in a sloppy sort of way, Peters. You and Forry and I have known each other for a long time. You shouldn't have sold Forry out. You undoubtedly contacted the Graf's people on your own. They wouldn't have known how to get in touch with you, or even that you were working for Roy."

The other said in a quick rage, "Poor Cos is going to get it anyway! What difference does a few days make? We'll collect our ten thousand a day as long as he lasts and then, when they get to him, we'll get a bonus of maybe another half million from the Graf when they burn him. The Graf never reneges on a deal."

"No," Mary Ann said bitterly. "And neither do I, you cynical gob of snot."

Ferd Feldmeyer held out a hand. "No more reports, Peters. Give me your transceiver."

"Get screwed, you fat jerk."

Ferd's eyebrows went up in his lardy face. "Peters, I'm twice your weight and ten years younger. Do you really wanta try me?"

Jet glared but finally dipped a hand into his side pocket and brought forth the communications device. The speechwriter took it, dropped it to the floor, and ground it under his heel. "You stupid, greedy bastard," he said. "You not only don't get the seventy thousand pseudo-dollars, but you won't get anything from the Graf's outfit, either." He turned to Mary Ann. "Let's go. We don't want to keep them waiting."

Carrying their bags, Mary Ann and Ferd piled into the car parked in the driveway. In actuality, it was Jet Peters's vehicle, which bothered them not at all. Mary Ann drove.

Under way, Ferd Feldmeyer growled, "The idiot. Didn't it ever occur to him that when the Graf's boys finally polished off Roy, some of us might go, too? They might just toss a grenade, getting us all. Then the Graf wouldn't have to renege on the quarter of a million he promised Jet. There wouldn't be any Jet to pay off."

Mary Ann said, "Well, at least we learned one thing."

He looked over at her, still disgusted at the defection of his friend. "What?"

"It's definite that it's the Graf's contract."

"A hell of a lot of good that does us," he said. "The Graf's men are far and away the most efficient in their rotten business."

The corner where they were scheduled to rendezvous wasn't far. The small Tri-Di station couldn't have been many miles away. Forry wasn't telling anything he could withhold.

Mary Ann parked, and within three minutes another car pulled up alongside them. Les Bates was at the wheel, Forry beside him. The rest were in the back.

Forry called over, "Hurry it up. Let's get out of here."

Mary Ann and Ferd brought their luggage over and stuffed it into the large compartment of the limousine. Ferd crowded into the front with Forry and Les; Mary Ann got into the back with Roy and the three other guards, taking a jump seat.

Roy said, "Where the devil's Jet?"

Ferd answered wearily, "He sold out to the Graf. Mary Ann caught him reporting. Evidently, he'd promised to finger you."

Les took off, accelerating rapidly.

"Damn," Forry said angrily. "I didn't expect any of the team to get the gimmes this soon."

They rode in silence for a moment.

Les said to Forry, "Where are we going?"

And Forry said, "I don't know."

They all looked at him blankly.

He said impatiently, "Don't you get it? *None of us knows*
where we're going now. So at least we're sure that the Graf's
gang won't be there waiting for us. Anybody have any ideas?
One thing, from now on we have to be more out in the open.
We've got to have as much security as possible, but with Roy
available to the media. He's got to give interviews, issue
statements, keep in the public eye. We can buy media time,
but that doesn't mean that we can ignore free publicity. So,
any ideas?"

For a time, as they sped across the country, all were blank.

Billy Tucker said hesitantly, "I was thinking in terms of
getting a couple of mobile homes and keeping on the move.
Just turning up from time to time for broadcasts."

Roy objected, "Then we'd be hiding from the news people
as well as the Graf and we'd miss all that free publicity
Forry's talking about."

"And that's going to get your message across even faster
than your own talks," Mary Ann said.

Dick Samuelson said, "I hope the organization is grinding
out our pamphlets fast enough to meet the demand."

"They won't have to," Forry said. "But never fear, profit-
making publishers will get into the act. If there's a market,
before the next week is out, you'll see more material on the
Wobbly program than you ever suspected could exist. But to
get back to it. Where do we go?"

Ron Ellison said hesitantly, "I know a big hotel in Miami
where they've got a king-size penthouse.

"I worked there once," Ron told him. "I know the place.
It wouldn't take much to secure it. There's only one private
elevator, with a steel door. And there's another steel door at
the only stairway. The place was originally built with the idea
of attracting South American politicians who'd taken off with
their country's treasure, or Syndicate men, or maybe Tri-Di
stars who wanted to get away from their fans."

Forry said sourly, "There are quite a few places in southern Florida of that type. Anything special about this one?"

"Well, yes," Ron said. "When I was working there, there
were three or four other Wobblies besides me. Hotels are
automated to hell and gone, these days, but you've always
got to have some staff."

"I get it," Roy said. "Having our own people planted in

the hotel means that much more security. They might be able to spot something offbeat and report it to you."

"That's right," Ron said nodding. "You'd be surprised how fast gossip goes through a big hotel. Suppose one of the Graf's men turned up claiming to be from the phone company and wanting to get into the penthouse for repairs. The hotel electrician, a chum-pal of mine named Larry, would spot him in a minute. Either that or he'd tag along with him, just to be sure, as long as he was in the hotel."

"I'm sold," Forry said. "Ron, get on your transceiver and find out if that penthouse is available. If so, rent it in your name. Don't mention anything about Roy or me. Say you'll pay in advance daily but don't let on that you have endless funds. Say you're coming in tonight."

While Ron was making arrangements, Forry said to Roy, "If I know this type of hotel penthouse arrangement, there'll be a private entrance, probably at the rear of the hotel. Ron will know. We'll go in that way. You and I will have scarves around our heads, on the off chance that somebody who saw the broadcast might spot us. We want to be organized in that place before our coming-out party to the news syndicates."

"Right," Roy said. He took a deep breath. "How long do you think I'll last, Forry?"

The other took time to light a smoke before answering. He said, trying to keep feeling from his voice, "I don't know. Probably longer than anybody thinks. There are some aspects of this one that the Graf's boys haven't run into before. In the past, the suckers who signed the Deathwish Policies to have their fun and spend their credits did it in public—nightclubs, restaurants, bars, shops, theatres. They were sitting ducks. We're going to present them with a whole new set of problems."

They pulled up before the looming beachside resort hotel an hour later and were met at the private entrance by the manager. Monsieur Pierre Boucherer was a product of the best Swiss hotel management school, therefore, a whiz at fawning.

He fawned. He welcomed their party of eight with pure enthusiasm. He saw nothing untoward in the heads of two men swathed in scarves. He saw nothing untoward in the party insisting on taking up their own luggage to their extravagantly expensive skytop rental. He would have seen nothing untoward if they'd all had live coral snakes for neckties. He alone accompanied them to the penthouse.

It took two trips in view of their number, the amount of luggage, and the fact that the elevator was only medium-size. But at last, all of them were gathered in the spacious living room.

"Jesus," Billy Tucker said, looking around, taking it all in. He had obviously never been in a luxury hotel apartment.

Monsieur Boucherer fawned, even as he rubbed his gloved hands together. "And now, how may I serve you?"

Forry, still masked like a Moslem virgin, looked over at the bar. He then sent his eyes around to his companions. "What's your favorite guzzle?" he said.

They looked at him in mild surprise for a moment, but then: "Medium dry sherry," Mary Ann said.

"Whiskey," said Roy, who was also still swathed, but then, "No. Make that Scotch."

"Yeah, Scotch," Ron said.

"Bourbon," Dick said. "Real hundred-proof sour mash."

"Me, too," Bill said.

"I'm a beer man—but none of this synthetic stuff," Les said.

"Brandy," Ferd said, running a small tongue over his fat lips. "French cognac."

"Cognac for me, too," Forry said. And then, to the manager, "Send up two cases each of sherry, Scotch, bourbon, and cognac, and ten cases of Pilsner Urquell. All of the best quality the hotel cellars provide."

The manager gaped at him blankly. He said, "But sir, the bar is automated, either for individual drinks or by the bottle . . ."

"Send up the cases," Forry said. "This penthouse has a kitchen, of course, and a large pantry, deep-freeze and all?"

"Of course, sir."

"I want it completely stocked within a couple of hours, from your stocks on hand, with enough food to last us a month or more. The very best, mind you."

Monsieur Boucherer was too taken aback to remember his fawning. He opened his mouth to protest, to declare the abilities of the hotel's chefs, but then closed it again. "Yes, sir," he fawned. "And what else?"

~Forry said, "This room is going to be converted into, uh, something of an office. We'll want a half dozen desks and the standard equipment to go with them—TV phones, voco-typers, library boosters for the National Data Banks. All of this should be up here in the next couple of hours."

The manager blinked. "Yes, sir."

Forry pressed on. "I understand that there's a stairway, steel-doored at both ends, leading up here. I want the door at the other end kept closed and two hotel security men posted at it twenty-four hours a day. They are to pass no one."

That, evidently, was not an unknown desire on the part of guests registered in the penthouse. Monsieur Boucherer was able to make with a fawn again. "Certainly, sir."

"Two guards are to be stationed at the elevator as well, twenty-four hours a day. No one outside this party is to be allowed to pass without my okay. My name is Brown."

"Very good, Mr. Brown."

"For the moment that's all. I'll see you in the morning about the credit transfer to cover all this. It will be on a Swiss International Numbered Account."

"Of course, sir."

When the manager was gone, the little ex-newsman sighed and unwrapped his scarf; Roy Cos did the same. Forry sent Ron and Dick to double check the doors. Les Bates made a beeline for the bar, calling over his shoulder for orders.

The others slumped into seats, all suddenly weary.

Roy said, "What's the idea of ordering all that guzzle?"

"And all the food, for that matter?" Mary Ann nodded.

Forry said, "Anything we order tonight is probably safe. It's unbelievable that the bogeymen know we're here. But after tomorrow morning, when we let it out where we are, nobody in this team is to drink or eat anything that doesn't come from our private stock. Don't dial for drinks on the autobar, don't have any food sent up from the kitchens. From now on, we're poison-conscious. Also conscious of the fact that a bottle can be gimmicked with explosives. Take off the cap and *wham*."

"Yeah," Roy said in resignation. "From now on, we've got to assume that anything that could possibly kill us, will."

Mary Ann glanced over at him, her eyes sad, but she said nothing.

Roy glanced at his diminutive manager. "What was that about you asking the IABI for protection? And about the guns? I didn't know you'd requested gun permits for the boys."

"I haven't," Forry told him. "But it sounded good over the air. Bring home to the viewers the toughness of the spot you're in. At that stage, it was just as well the IABI didn't know where we were, even if they did want to guard us. They're undoubtedly infiltrated by the Graf's organization, and we'd have put ourselves on the spot. And asking for gun permits for them would have revealed the fact that Ron, Billy, Les, and Rick were lined up with you and that might have led to tracking us down. If the IABI denied we'd asked for protection, nobody would believe them."

"You're quite a Machiavelli, Forry," Ferd wheezed.

Les had served them drinks and they settled back in satisfaction. They all felt the tensions of the past few days.

Forry said, taking out the last pack of cigarettes he had bought in Nassau, "I hope that soapy manager can come up with tobacco as well. I'll have to order that, too, before the night is out. That's all I'd need, some doped cigarettes."

He looked over at Ron. "You know this place better than any of the rest of us. Go around and decide what rooms each of us should have. Give Roy the most strategically located one—you know, the one that's furthest from both of the elevator and staircase."

Dick stood and walked over to the French windows that opened onto the hotel's roof. There was an extensive garden, largely of potted plants, a swimming pool, a sun deck, tables, and folding chairs. He said, "What's to prevent a chopper from settling down out there with a few of the Graf's lads in it?"

"Nothing," Forry growled. "We're going to have to post a full-time guard outside."

Dick turned and looked at him. "There's only four of us."

Forry nodded. "I know." He looked at Roy Cos. "We're going to need another four of your Wobblies. Have you got four more like Ron, Les, Dick, and Billy?"

The Wobbly national organizer sighed. "There aren't as many of us as all that, you know, and we're not all young, unattached, strongarm types. And probably a lot of the membership don't even agree with what I'm doing."

"All right," Forry said sourly. "But we need at least four more guards, preferably familiar with guns."

"Guns? What guns?" Dick said bitterly. "Just one of the Graf's pros with a shooter could blow the asses off us all."

Forry looked at him. "By tomorrow we'll have guns. You can buy anything in this country if you have enough credit, and as of tomorrow, we'll be openly spending Roy's million a day. As an old-time crime reporter, I have a few contacts. Gyrojets all right?"

"Yes," Dick said, happier now. "Both handguns and assault rifles."

Roy said, "I'll get together with the boys and we'll try and pick four more guards." He turned to Mary Ann and Ferd and said, "How'd the broadcast go over?"

Mary Ann said, "Well, good and bad." She glanced over at Forry. "For one thing, his presentation isn't too good. His appearance is, well, poor. A hero can't be pale and dumpy."

Forry ran his eyes over the Wobbly organizer, who was grimacing, and nodded. "I should've thought of that. There're injections these days that can darken his complexion, or we could use a sunlamp. And we can have him massaged and dieted down to the point where he doesn't look so lardy."

"Hey," Roy said in protest.

They ignored him.

"There's another thing," Ferd Feldmeyer said. "That first speech was good enough, perhaps. It summed up the Wobbly program. But we can't just repeat it over and over again. We've got to have fresh material."

"Like what?" Dick asked, in rejection. "I thought it was swell. Gave the movement's stand exactly. That's the point of the whole thing."

The speechwriter shook his head. "You can't just keep hitting the viewers over the head with a flat statement of what you want. You've got to come up with new, exciting stuff; something to keep them coming, wanting to listen in to future programs."

Ron said, "But we've got nothing else to say."

Ferd took another pull at his cognac. "Then we've gotta find some exciting details. Almost anything that's a current issue, something they aren't doing right under this so-called welfare state.

"Take VD—various drugs have been developed up over the years to combat venereal diseases. First the sulfas. They were tremendously effective when first discovered, but in a few years, new strains of gonoccocci had developed that were immune to sulfa. Then the antibiotics like streptomycin came along, but the germs adapted to them and eventually thrived. Well, suppose we put our scientists to work on a whole series of new antibiotics. Then, on D-Day, everybody in the country would take the new antibiotic, whether or not they had ever had any venereal disease. Every man, woman, and child, including the president and Roman Catholic cardinals. Later, one of the other new antibiotics would be given everybody, to nail the germs missed that first time. And from then on, nobody would be allowed into the United States of the Americas until they'd had their antibiotics. This is a half-assed description of an idea some researcher wrote, and I may have some of it wrong. But I know smallpox was eradicated. I bet VD *could* be."

"Great," Roy said, "but it has nothing to do with fundamental social change. It could be done under any system."

"But the thing is," Ferd said patiently, "to get to the people, you've got to *participate*, take a strong stand on everything from pollution and depletion of natural resources to ending war, women's rights, race problems, and all the rest. Your stand should sound more sensible than anybody else's, or else more Godly. And you've got to sound off about it, louder and more insistently than anybody else. If you're ever going to get a following, that'll be how."

The identity screen on the door buzzed. Ron and Billy popped to their feet.

"That'll be the first load of food and guzzle," Forry said. "You boys supervise it. Roy and I'll go into our rooms so that nobody'll recognize us."

"I'm going to bed anyway," Roy said. "I'm bushed to hell and gone and I've got a sneaking suspicion that tomorrow'll be a busy day." He paused and added in deprecation, "I've got a suspicion that the rest of my *life* is going to be a busy day."

It was a half-hour later that a knock came at Roy Cos's

bedroom door. He was lying on his back in bed in his pajamas, hands under his head, staring at the ceiling. Beside him, on the night table, was a drink he had brought from the living room. It was untouched.

He looked at the door and said, "Come on in."

Mary Ann was clad in a simple white nightgown and sturdy bedroom slippers. She carried a half-empty bottle of Scotch. Her hair had been combed out and her face glowed as if freshly washed—or freshly made up.

Roy said, his tired hazel eyes puzzled, "Hello, Mary Ann. Something up?" He came to one elbow.

"That should be *my* question," she smiled, and closed the door behind her. Her face had a flush which, Roy decided to his surprise, brought a wistful beauty to her ordinary plainness. Mary Ann Elwyn would never be thought of as a pretty girl but her femininity was there, now that she had discarded her brisk office efficiency.

She brought her eyes up and to his and the flush deepened. "I thought you might be lonesome," she said, her voice low.

Roy stared at her. Plain, Mary Ann might be, but even the dreary nightclothes she wore couldn't disguise the healthy womanly body. Her breasts were high, her waist taut, her legs surprisingly long. Roy hadn't noticed those legs before. It seldom occurred to men to scrutinize the Mary Ann equipment.

For a moment, he couldn't remember when last he had bedded a woman. It had probably been one of the Wobbly members.

Roy said, after running a hand through his faded brown hair, "Sit down, Mary Ann."

She sat on the edge of the bed and again avoided his eyes.

He said, "Look, there's obviously no future in me. If we happen to get caught up emotionally—well, I won't be *able* to feel grief."

She didn't say anything to that.

He said, an edge in his voice, "I don't want charity, Mary Ann."

She looked up at him. "Then you're a fool. I do, Roy. I'm lonesome, too."

He said quickly, "I'm not exactly the romantic type. I know what I look like, what I am. Those four boys guarding me are more nearly your own age. And they're all good, healthy . . .''

"Oh, shut up," she said. She threw back the bedclothes and squirmed herself in beside him, after tossing her bathrobe to the foot of the bed and kicking off her slippers. "I'm not interested in boys. I'm interested in a loving man." She flicked off the night table light. "And you're the most loving man I've ever met, Roy Cos."

Chapter Fourteen:
Frank Pinell

Frank and Nat Fraser got off the metro at the Odeon Station and started up the street. As in practically all large cities these days, vehicular traffic in Paris was at a minimum though pedestrians and bicycles occupied the streets even at this time of night in Left Bank, still the home of artists and Sorbonne students.

Nat Fraser looked over at his younger companion approvingly. He said, "Cobber, you look like a regular toff in those new duds. A little on the Frenchy side, gawdstrewth."

Frank snorted at the tall, gawky Australian. "They ought to look good, you ponied up enough credits to outfit me."

"Nothing's too good for a cove working for the bloody Graf." Nat looked up at a street sign. "Rue Monsieur Le Prince," he read. "That's it."

Frank said, "Who's this Colonel Boris Rivas?"

"Old-time mercenary. Mostly Africa and Near East. Last time I saw him was in Yemen. He had a contract there with some fifty commandos and a few hundred ragheads. Too bloody-minded by far for my liking, cobber. I was done on the bone but I did a bunk instead of joining up."

Frank frowned. "Now I really need a translation."

"I don't go for finishing off women, kids, and old folks. Fair dinkum, I don't. Rape, killing civilians, looting—old Boris gets his lollies out of it. Bad business. If the situation pickles, you might have to depend on those women and old coves. Hide you, feed you, if they're lucky enough as to have anything to eat. Maybe nurse you, if you've copped one."

He looked up at a sign over the doorway of a dilapidated building that looked a good two centuries or more in age. *Hotel Balcon*.

"This is it, cobber. Just follow me bloody lead. Rivas is

competition to the Graf. This is his last bloody chance. He comes in with the mucking organization, or the barstid's had it, and that's the dinkum oil.''

"You mean we, uh, shoot him?''

The other grinned cheerfully. ''More likely he'd shoot us first, cobber. But we're here under a bloody flag of bloody truce. Let's go.''

The hotel lobby was no more impressive than the outside of the building. It had the odor of long decay. Its lone occupant was a bent old man behind the desk, obviously the concierge.

"What room's Rivas in, cobber?'' the Aussie said.

To Frank's surprise, the old man spoke English. ''Top floor. Room 505.''

"Too right,'' Nat said, and made a gesture with his head. ''Get your arse out of here.'' The old-timer studied the set of Nat's jaw, then scooted out a door behind his desk.

Frank looked at him in surprise.

"He's been paid,'' Nat said, heading for the stairway. There was no elevator.

The building was five stories high and Nat Fraser had obviously been in third-class French hotels before. At each landing he pushed a button in the wall which turned on a low wattage bulb just long enough for them to reach the next landing. The management of the Hotel Balcon did not waste electrical power.

On the fifth floor, the pressing of the light button gave them just enough time to find room 505. Nat Fraser knocked on the door and the hall light flicked off before the portal opened.

A huge black was there, almost as tall as the Australian and, if anything, broader of shoulder, deeper of chest. He was the blackest man Frank Pinell had ever seen—actually ebony in complexion—yet his face was more nearly European than Bantu. He was a beautiful physical specimen and his movements belied his size; he moved like a black leopard.

Nat said, ''The colonel is expecting us.''

The black opened the door wide without change of expression. Room 505 turned out to be a small suite. Since doors were open, it could be seen that there were two bedchambers and a bath. The place was better furnished, more comfortable than would have been expected of the Hotel Balcon.

The room they had entered was filled with chairs, a table, files, piles of papers, maps, and correspondence. Behind an old metal desk sat Colonel Boris Rivas. Rivas sat straight in his chair, his posture military. His face was dark and somewhat oily, so that he looked more like a Greek or Turk than a Frenchman. His black hair was streaked with gray and looked as though it could use a shampoo. He was on the brawny side, and wore his civilian clothing uncomfortably.

His dark eyes gleamed dislike but he said, in passable English, "Sit down, Fraser." He looked at Frank, sent his eyes over to Nat again, but then brought them back to Frank, whom he took in at greater length. "And who is this?" he demanded.

Nat had taken one of the comfort chairs, crossing his long legs. Frank sat down in the other. The big black leaned against the wall and watched them, his face still expressionless.

The Australian pushed his bush hat to the back of his head and said, "The arrangement was that there be two of us and two of you. Fair dinkum. This is Frank Pinell, one of the Graf's newest boys. Frank, our cheeky cove behind the desk is Colonel Boris Rivas. Who bloody well promoted him to colonel, nobody seems to know."

"That's enough provocative talk, Fraser," the colonel snapped. "And this is Sergeant Sengor, long ago of the Senegalese Airborne Commandos, my right-hand man—and bodyguard." The colonel brought his eyes back to Frank and said, "You wouldn't be related to the late Buck Pinell, would you? There is a resemblance."

Frank wrinkled his forehead and said, "My father's name was Willard."

"He was a mercenary?"

Frank said uncomfortably, "Could be. I was very young when he died and I was told very little about him."

"If you're the son of Buck Pinell, I'm surprised to see you in the employ of Brandenburg. Pinell was a man. The Graf is a wolf."

Nat said, "Cooee, who's giving with the mucking provocative talk now?"

Rivas ignored him. "I've always suspected that Graf Lothar von Brandenburg was responsible for Buck Pinell's death."

"Pull your head in," the big Australian growled. "A fine

bloke you are to throw such narky nonsense around. You're
crazy as a kookaburra if you think the Graf did Buck in. They
cobbered up with each other when they were both no older
than joeys.'' He looked over at Frank. ''I never met Buck
Pinell meself; before me time, gawdstrewth. But if he was
your father, he was a wowser, from all they say.''

The colonel hit his desk a double rap in impatience. ''Shall
we get on with it?'' he said. ''You contacted me for a
meeting. Very well, what do you have to say? I warn you, I
will not be intimidated by Brandenburg's cheap threats.''

Nat Fraser grinned at him. ''The Graf wouldn't spend his
bloody time on a cheeky zany like you, Rivas. Peter Windsor
sent us, strewth. The mucking message is simple enough for a
dingo to get it through his block. The mercenary business is
too bloody small for any competition. So Windsor says this is
your last mucking chance. You and your whole bloody outfit
are invited to join up with Mercenaries, Incorporated.''

Boris Rivas's dark face went darker still. He made little
attempt to conceal his rage. ''Or else?''

''Windsor thought you'd know,'' Nat said easily.

''Fraser, you can take this message to that pig Windsor. I
am in control of all contracts in this part of Common Europe.
I shall continue to be. I am not afraid of the Graf. His
organization hasn't handled a sizeable mercenary operation
for years. His contracts these days are almost all individual
hit jobs which, of course, are more in keeping with his
talents. Sergeant, see the gentlemen to the door!'' Boris Rivas
pushed out of his chair and made his way over to his improvised bar where he sloshed a sizeable drink into a highball
glass, adding no mixer to it before knocking it back.

Without speaking further to the French mercenary, Nat
Fraser came to his feet and made a gesture with his head to
Frank. ''Let's do a bunk, cobber. This bloody arse is asking
for it, strike me blind if he isn't.''

The sergeant, his face still empty of expression, opened the
door for them.

When they were gone, the colonel, still in a rage, snarled
to his guard, ''We'll see about Nat Fraser, the lickspittle.
That Windsor scum has his gall sending two of his gunmen to
try and intimidate me. Me! Why, I've seen more combat than
Brandenburg and Windsor put together.''

He sat down again at his desk and angrily dialed on his TV phone.

When the face appeared, he snapped, in French now, "Captain Bois, get over here with as many of your lads as you can assemble within a few minutes, to man my hotel. The Graf has thrown down the gauntlet. We'll have to confer. I'm getting in touch with Major Dupres and Captain Flaubert as well. There's a possibility that we might have some trouble with that Australian swine, Fraser."

The face on the screen was that of a thin man, somewhat bucktoothed and now looking cautiously unhappy. "What did Fraser have to say? Dupres informed me that you were to meet with him."

"Peter Windsor demands that we ally with the Graf. In a subservient position, without doubt."

Captain Bois said, still cautiously, "And what did you tell him?"

"I threw him out, of course—Fraser, that is. But now I'm alone here with Sergeant Sengor. I think we'd better move some of the lads into the hotel, just to be sure. One doesn't know what that murderous Fraser's orders might be."

The thin man shook his head. "Sorry, Boris. You're not big enough to go up against the Graf. He tolerated small organizations such as ours in the past, while recruiting our best men. But now contracts are too few and far between for him to allow competition. He's amalgamating every mercenary group still outside the ranks of Mercenaries, Incorporated."

"Traitor!"

The other shook his head again and his tone was apologetic. "I talked it over with Flaubert. We've both had offers from Windsor to go on the Graf's full-time retainer, with promotions. I'm afraid we're taking the offers, Boris. I suggest that you make your own peace with him. He'd probably promote you to brigadier."

"Brigadier, you ass! He hasn't had a brigade-sized contract since '80."

The other's face was rueful, even as it faded from the screen.

Boris Rivas was livid. He came to his feet again, went back to the liquor, and repeated his performance of a few minutes before. He said to the impassive black, "Get a drink, Sergeant," and returned to the desk.

Sengor went over to the bottles, poured himself a small gin, and returned with it to his place against the wall, near the door.

Rivas flicked on the phone screen again and dialed. When the face appeared, it was that of a coarse, middle-aged man who looked as though he was half drunk. In fact, even as he sat there before the screen, he lifted a glass to his lips.

Rivas snapped, "What's the matter with you?"

"Nothing."

"Well, confound it, get over here with any of the men you have in that bistro with you. We're having a fracas with the Graf and his pigs."

"I know. The word is all about town."

The colonel stared at him. "Spread by whom?"

"By Bois and Flaubert, among others. They said that you're washed up, Boris. They're signing with Brandenburg."

"And what do you think, Henri?" the colonel snarled in a high rage.

The other took another drink. "I've stopped thinking. I can't afford it. Peter Windsor hasn't approached me. If he doesn't by the weekend, I'll offer him my services. If he doesn't want them, it looks as though I'm retired."

The face faded and Rivas slumped back in his chair for a long moment. Finally, he got up and poured himself another drink, a smaller one this time. Carrying the glass with him, he went over to one of the curtained windows. He said to the black, "Turn off those lights."

The sergeant brushed his hand over the switch at the side of the door. Rivas stood to one side of the window and pushed back the curtain a few inches. Across the street, he could make out a figure standing in a doorway. He let the curtain back and for a moment leaned against the wall, breathing deeply. He knocked the drink back and threw the glass across the room, shattering it against the far wall. His hand went beneath his coat to emerge with a small Gyrojet, a silencer attachment on its muzzle.

"Come on, Sergeant," he muttered. "It's you and me now. We'll go to ground and start recruiting for our counterattack. That scum Brandenburg doesn't know what fighting men are. He *hires* lads to do his dirty work; hasn't been in action himself for decades. I just wonder how impregnable that Wolfschloss of his really is.''

The sergeant opened the door, peered up and down the dark corridor, then let the colonel precede him. They hurried down the stairway, the colonel pressing the light button, as had Nat Fraser, at each landing. And at each landing they shot glances up and down the hotel corridor. The lobby was empty.

"This way," Rivas snapped. "Out the back. To the alley."

They went behind the desk and utilized the same door that the concierge had disappeared through on Nat Fraser's orders. They went down a dark, narrow corridor to the portal leading out into the alley. The colonel, gun in right hand, cautiously opened it and peered through.

The alley was dark, very black, and led to the left. It had no lights at all. One end led out onto the street; the other was a cul-de-sac blocked by a high brick wall. On each side, the walls were blank and tall. The only light came from the street, fifty feet away. The door through which they emerged was at pavement level. The alley was cobblestoned, going back to the days of Napoleon the Little. As they emerged into it, two figures entered from the street, cautiously, half crouched.

"Damn!" the colonel snarled. "We can't afford a shoot-out here. The flics would lay it at my door. Back, back the other way!"

But then he slowly, as though with great care, leaned forward and went down onto his knees. He coughed softly, then leaned forward again and put his hands on the cobblestones in front of him. The Gyrojet pistol clanged to the paving. He slowly bowed his head, as though staring in fascination at the cobbles before him. There was a splashing sound. His arms and legs seemed to give way at the same time and he fell forward into the puddle of his own aortic blood.

Nat Fraser and Frank Pinell came up, tucking their guns back into holsters beneath their coats. They stared down at the body. A four-inch combat knife handle protruded upward from the body of Boris Rivas. The Australian looked up at the sergeant and nodded. "Be with you in a meejum minute, Sengor."

He turned and led Frank, who had been staring at the fallen man in dread fascination, twenty feet down the alley.

Nat said, his voice unruffled and unhurried, "You do a bunk back to the hotel and get your things. I'll stay here with the wog and do the necessary. Your orders are to go to Vaduz, in Liechtenstein, and to the Wolfschloss—that's the Graf's stronghold. You're to contact Peter Windsor there. I won't be seeing you again, cobber, not this time." He stuck his right hand out. "It was bonzer getting to know you, Frank."

Frank Pinell ignored the hand and looked into the other's face coldly. He said, his voice even, "I won't shake hands with you, Fraser. You're no friend of mine. You and Panikkar had it all worked out to set me up for that Mahdi job. Anybody with a brain in his head could see that it was a one-way trip. I don't know what happened, or why, but at the last minute this Peter Windsor, or somebody else on the Graf's staff, diverted me to this instead. I played along with you for a while, Fraser, just to see what the hell was going on, but I never would have taken that Mahdi job. It was suicide."

The big Australian nodded. He took off the bush hat, reset the brim, then returned it to his head. "What you say's the dinkum oil, cobber. Sorry. It was out of my mucking hands. I have to take whatever orders they give me. You see, they've got a lock on me."

He turned and went back in the direction of the sergeant, who had the body of Boris Rivas under the arms and was hauling it back into the dark hallway of the hotel.

Frank took the rocket shuttle from Paris to Zurich, then a vacuum tube to Buchs, on the Liechtenstein border. The vacuum tube line crossed the tiny principality on its way to Vienna but didn't stop in Liechtenstein. There was evidently no shuttleport, nor even an airport. Frank began to get the idea of just how small and remote this country was when he had to take a surface bus to complete his journey.

There had been no customs inspection at the border; that was taken care of in Vaduz itself. He didn't spot any police but the bus station had an official look about it and there were several men lounging about clad like those stationed at Colonel Ram Panikkar's fortress-like estate in Tangier—berets, commando-type uniforms, and paratrooper boots. They carried Gyrojet carbines as naturally as though they had been born with them in hand. None of them paid any particular attention to Frank, who was the sole passenger debarking at Vaduz.

There was a desk with a sign reading *Customs and Immigration* and, carrying his own two bags, he made his way to it. The young man there, dressed in civilian garb rather than a uniform, looked up at Frank's approach.

He frowned slightly and said in English, after taking in the newcomer's appearance, "I'm afraid you have made a mistake, sir. Liechtenstein is not a tourist country. There is nothing particular here to attract visitors. If you hurry, you can return to the bus, which makes its next stop in Feldkirch, in Austria. You can take the vacuum tube from there to Innsbruck or . . ."

Frank said, "Thanks for the wholehearted welcome, but I'm here to see Mr. Peter Windsor at the, uh, Wolfschloss, whatever that is."

The other's voice became more brisk. "I see. May I see your identification?"

Frank brought forth his International Credit Card, which had been given him by Colonel Panikkar in Tangier. He had wondered at the time if it was a forgery, but evidently not. He had drawn on it for credit when traveling without any difficulty. He wondered how many pseudo-dollar credits he had to his account.

An International Credit Card, as always, doubled as a passport. The customs man glanced at it and then put it in a slot. In moments, a voice from the desk screen spoke in German. The official nodded and handed it back to Frank. He must have pressed a button with either hand or foot, since one of the uniformed men came up.

The customs man said, "Escort Mr. Pinell to the Wolfschloss. He is to see Mr. Windsor at the donjon."

"Right," the other said, and took Frank in. He lifted one of the two pieces of luggage and said, "This way."

Frank followed him out to a small parking area and to one of the several jeeps there. They put the bags in the back and climbed into the front.

The other looked as though he was probably American and

spoke like it as well. He must have been roughly Frank's own age but had a toughness about him somewhat reminiscent of Nat Fraser.

As he started up, he said, "First trip here?"

"That's right," Frank said.

"Bore you shitless unless you're quartered up in the schloss. Not bad up there."

"What's a schloss?"

"Castle."

Frank said, "American?"

His guide hesitated momentarily before saying, "Canadian."

"I guess that makes you an American these days. Been here long?"

The other looked over at him briefly, then turned his attention back to the road without answering. It would seem that questions weren't good form locally, though the Canadian had asked the first one.

It was an excellent road. They had passed out of Vaduz in moments. Frank said, "I work for the Graf, too. At least, I think I do."

That didn't seem to lower any barriers. They went on.

Frank look up shortly and said, "For Christ's sake."

The driver grinned. "Looks like something out of a fairy story the first time you see it, eh?"

Frank had never seen a castle before, save in historical Tri-Di shows. He had no idea that they could be this large. The Wolfschloss was built atop a small mountain. Even the lower foundations were a thousand feet above the valley floor. It brought to mind an action-filled movie revival of the last century, depicting the good guys storming the Alcazar in Segovia. They had used catapults, small primitive cannon, battering rams, and finally, scaling ladders. It had been on the gruesome side, with the defenders pouring melted lead and boiling oil down on the attacking forces. The good guys had finally taken the castle by storm, but Frank had wondered ever since what sort of soldier would be idiot enough to be first man up one of those scaling ladders.

He had never expected a castle to be as large as the looming Wolfschloss. He wondered if it had ever been captured in the old days. He didn't see how it could have been, before the advent of heavy artillery.

Along the road, since they had left Vaduz, they had passed guard houses and on two occasions concrete pillboxes, heavy automatic weapons projecting from their slots, but they had been stopped only once, and then, briefly. The guards were obviously acquainted with his guide.

Now they pulled up before an ultramodern building with two heavy steel cables extending from its interior up to the schloss. There were ten or twenty other vehicles in the parking area.

They got out, each carrying a bag, and headed for the entry. There were two guards there, armed with the usual Gyrojet automatic carbines, stationed to each side of the metal door, and one who, by his shoulder tabs, was obviously an officer with a sidearm in a quick-draw holster.

When the two approached, the guide gave an easygoing salute to the officer and it was returned just as offhandedly.

The guide said to Frank, "Your identification?"

Frank handed it to the officer, who looked at it briefly, handed it back, and said, "Go on in, Mr. Pinell. You're expected. Welcome to the Wolfschloss."

The metal door slid to one side, into the thickness of the wall, then slid silently shut behind them. They were in a moderately large room, steel of walls, ceiling, and even the floor, which was, however, carpeted. Six armed men studied the newcomer.

One of the seated officers held out his hand without words and Frank handed over his International Credit Card again.

There was a faint buzzing sound, and the officer looked at him coldly. Two of the guards hurried over. The other two covered Frank, less than casually now.

The officer said, "You're carrying a shooter."

"That's right," Frank told him.

The two guards frisked him quickly and came up with his stubby Gyrojet with its attached silencer. It was put on the desk of the examining officer.

That worthy said dangerously, "You mean you've got the gall to try and get in to see Mr. Windsor armed?"

"For Christ's sake," Frank said, mildly impatient. "It was issued to me by Nat Fraser, in Tangier. Nobody told me where to hand it in."

The officer looked at him for a long moment, then down at

the gun. "It's one of our models," he muttered. He flicked on a desk screen and spoke into it in German.

The officer finally looked at Frank's guide and said, "Take him up, Colin."

While this was going on, two of the other guards had taken Frank's luggage, opened both bags, and gone through them. Frank got the feeling that they were being electronically scanned at the same time.

His guide, Colin, said, "This way, Mr. Pinell."

They went through another metal door and into what turned out to be the cable house proper. It looked like the waiting room of a small shuttleport. There were unupholstered benches and chairs, and a small bar at which a pretty young blonde, in a feminine version of the ever-present commando uniform, presided. There were two more guards at their ease here, and three civilian-dressed, bored-looking men, all carrying very ordinary-looking attaché cases.

The ceiling was only partially roofed and the double cables, which were attached by heavy links of chain to the floor, extended through the opening. In only moments, a cable car came sliding into the room and descended into the slot built for it into the floor. One of the guards went forward and unlocked its door. Two passengers emerged, one a tall, well-dressed black carrying a very large briefcase, the other an efficient-looking, middle-aged woman who looked Spanish or Italian. They headed for a door other than the one Frank and Colin had utilized.

The three other men, one an Oriental, entered the cable car. Frank and his guide got in, too. The car was rectangular, with rounded corners and modest windows. By the looks of them, none of the windows could be opened, and Frank suspected that the glass was bulletproof. As Frank took a seat, the guard outside locked the door and they took off with a slight lurch, climbing at a sharp angle though the swaying gondola remained horizontal.

Frank stared out a window in fascination. Beneath them were scrubby, hardy trees and massive, jagged boulders, occasionally with wiry grass. From time to time he could spot a zigzag trail ascending the hill. It looked as though it hadn't been used for years and, from time to time, there were indications that it had once been wider—perhaps a narrow road. In the distance were spectacular snow-topped Alps.

He looked over at Colin and said, scowling puzzlement, "You mean that this cable car is the only access to the, uh, schloss? Surely it can't be supplied from a gondola?"

"Of course not," the other grunted. The guide was slumped back in his seat, not bothering to look out. He had obviously made the trip many a time.

In ten minutes, the cable car swung into an aperture again and settled on its skids into another slot. Frank could see, through the windows, only a small portion of huge castle wall, partially brick, partially massive stone, before they passed into the interior.

A guard unlocked the door and all issued forth. The three other passengers hustled off. They left the waiting room of the terminal by one door, and Colin led Frank through another.

The steel room into which Frank was ushered was similar to that below, but not identical. For one thing, there were ports in one of the walls which evidently overlooked the cable car ascent. Before each of them was mounted heavy weapons of a design Frank had never seen before, even in films. There were six guards on duty here and, once again, two officers. Their shoulder tabs looked more impressive than those the two below had worn.

He went through much the same procedure as before: he was electronically searched, and his credit card was checked out, then handed back to him. "Righto, corporal," the bored officer said. "You're cleared for the donjon."

"Yes, sir," Colin said, saluting in the offhand manner that seemed to apply to these professionals.

This part of the castle had been reconstructed recently. On the other side of the metal door through which they exited was a modern, though militarily barren corridor, which couldn't possibly have dated back to medieval times. It extended only fifty feet or so before they were confronted by another heavy portal, which automatically opened for them onto a vista which made Frank gasp.

Before him lay an immense area, more like a park than the courtyard of a looming fortress—a park devoted largely to sports. From where they entered, Frank could see an enormous swimming pool at the far end, with scores of bathers, both men and women, enjoying the place. Nearer were a dozen tennis courts, also well patronized. And nearer still, a fairly good-sized putting green, largely patronized by older types. There were also practice courts for basketball and jai alai. Between them were pleasant walks, extensive lawns neat as a golf green, fountains and gardens spotted here and there.

To the right, however, was also a copter landing pad, and on it two aircraft, one a heavy cargo carrier, the other a fighter, weapons protruding from apertures. Frank realized then what his guide had meant when he'd answered that the cable car wasn't the only manner of supplying the Wolfschloss.

One had to look about the walls, the battlements, the projecting turrets, the round towers at the corners of the walls with their conical tops, to realize that this was indeed the interior of a castle, centuries old.

"Not bad, eh?" Colin said. "The Graf must have spent a mint doing the enceinte up like this." He led the way.

"Enceinte?" Frank said.

"The ward," the other told him. "The open area inside the walls."

It came to Frank that the Wolfschloss must house the population of a small town. The buildings, snuggled up against the heavy stone walls, were sufficient to provide all the needs of thousands.

The closer Frank looked, the less medieval it seemed. He could make out anti-aircraft guns, missile launchers, mortars, and machine guns. He said with a touch of sarcasm, "One small nuke and that's the end of the whole works."

Colin looked over at him as they walked. "Straight down, about half a mile, are the bomb shelters. You're as safe here as you'd be in the Octagon in Greater Washington."

"I'd hate to dig myself out, afterwards."

"You wouldn't have to. There are tunnels leading off to exits more than a mile away. The Wolfschloss couldn't take a fusion bomb, maybe, but it could take a helluva lot."

"Where are we going?" Frank said.

"To the donjon."

"What's a donjon?"

"The keep."

"That tells me a lot."

"In the old days, it was the final defense. It was where

everybody retreated when the walls were breached. Now the Graf and his staff live there.''

Frank could see the keep, the highest and the largest of the towers. It was a castle within a castle and must have been one hell of a disappointment to come up against in the days when you had nothing more than a crossbow, sword, and battleaxe.

He was apprehensive about what was to come in his confrontation with Peter Windsor, the Graf's front man. One thing was certain: there was no line of retreat for *him*. If something went wrong, there was no possible way for him to get out of the Wolfschloss, even if he had been armed.

Chapter Fifteen:
The Graf

As Frank and his guide drew nearer to the keep, its true size became ever more impressive. By the time they drew up to its sole entrance, he realized that it was as large as some apartment buildings.

Before the entry were stationed four uniformed guards and an officer. Gone was the easygoing air Frank had come to associate with the mercenaries of the Graf. These five were alert and efficient.

Colin came to attention and saluted the officer, who responded just as snappily and then eyed Frank.

"Franklin Pinell, sir," Colin said crisply. "On appointment to see Mr. Windsor."

"Your identification, sir," the officer said, holding out his hand.

Frank gave him his card. At this rate, the thing would be worn out before too long.

The other examined it carefully, returned it, saluted Frank with the same snappiness, and said, "You're expected, sir."

The ancient medieval door had long since been superseded by a massive steel one. Built into one side of it was a smaller door, just wide enough so that two persons could have walked in side by side. It now slid open. Colin said to Frank, "This is as far as I go, Mr. Pinell. I'm not cleared for the donjon. Good luck."

Frank went through the door and was again surprised, as he had been by the parklike effect of the enceinte. The basic medieval aspects of the keep had been retained. The stone walls and narrow apertures were still there. The floors were still flagstone. Otherwise, the ground floor of the keep seemed an ultramodern office building.

There were a score or so office workers in the lobby,

walking briskly here or there, papers in hand. They ranged in age from Frank's early twenties to sixty or more but most, both men and women, were on the youthful side. Some were uniformed, some not. Frank approached the first of the desks, mildly surprised that it wasn't automated. Behind it sat a sharp-looking young blonde who would have done the reception room of the largest multinational corporation in Manhattan proud. She smiled encouragingly.

Frank said, "Franklin Pinell to see Mr. Peter Windsor."

"Your identification, please?"

She took his card, put it into a desk slot, and scanned the screen before her. She returned it to him, and said perkily, "You're expected, sir. Elevator one."

The three elevators were numbered in gold. Number one seemed somewhat more ornate than the others. Frank stepped in. There was no order screen, nor any other manner that he could see of activating the compartment. He shrugged.

The door closed and started upward. And continued upward. It would seem that Mr. Peter Windsor was officed in the higher reaches of the keep. Eventually, it came to a halt, and he emerged into an office containing four desks and four very busy workers. It was quite the swankest office Frank had ever been in, including that of Ram Panikkar in Tangier. It was difficult to realize that he was in the nerve center of a castle going back to the days of Richard the Lion-Hearted.

One of the clerks got up from her swivel chair and came toward him briskly, smiling in the same pert manner as the receptionist below. She was dressed in what Frank thought must be the latest from Paris. She said brightly, "Fräulein Krebs is expecting you, Mr. Pinell. If you'll just come this way."

He said, "I was to see Peter Windsor."

"Yes, sir," she said, leading him across the room to a door which was lettered *Margit Krebs* in gold. Evidently, he was going to see Fräulein Krebs whether he liked it or not.

The identity screen picked them up and the door swung open. The girl said, "Mr. Pinell," and stepped back.

The office inside was luxurious to a point that Frank had never witnessed even in the most lavish Tri-Di shows. Withal, it managed to project a touch of femininity. It could never have been taken for a man's room. Above all, it radiated wealth. Frank was no art expert, but recognized Impressionist paintings when he saw them. There were two on the walls. He had no doubt whatever that they were originals.

Behind one desk sat a serious, studious-looking young man and a woman of, say, thirty-five behind the other. Her strikingly handsome face was difficult to estimate. She had beautifully dark hair, wore tweeds that couldn't disguise a very good figure, and her smile was efficient. But her eyes?

Those eyes had a predatory look as they ran up and down Frank, taking in his face, his frame. He had a feeling new to him. It was usually the man who looked at a woman in such a way as to mentally undress her, estimate her capabilities in bed. Now he felt as though positions were reversed. Did Fräulein Krebs do this to every man she met?

She said, "Franklin Pinell," even as she rounded her desk and came toward him with her hand outstretched. "We've been looking forward to meeting you."

He shook and murmured some amenity, wondering who in the hell *we* could be. Why in the world would a bigshot in Mercenaries, Incorporated want to see him? Surely there wouldn't be anyone in the organization lower on the totem pole than Frank Pinell. He had been astonished at the reception he had been getting all the way from Vaduz to here, the inner reaches of the keep.

Margit Krebs said crisply, "That will be all, Kurt."

The young man at the desk stood, clicked his heels, and said, "Ja, Fräulein Krebs," and left.

When he was gone, Margit said, leaning her buttocks back against her desk, "And what do you think of the Wolfschloss?"

He managed a small grin and said, "Flabbergasted. I had no idea of the size of these European castles, nor the excellent condition some of them are in."

She nodded at that and smiled. "They're not all so large, of course. And Lothar spent a considerable sum in renovating this one."

"Like I said, I'm flabbergasted. How many people live here?"

"It varies from day to day, but right now there are 2,321, counting you. Six left yesterday on assignments, but four others returned."

He blinked at her.

She laughed and said, "I have total recall, which is one of

the reasons I am Lothar's secretary. You see, some items involving Mercenaries, Incorporated can't be written down. With me on hand, Lothar doesn't need written records of such items. The records are in my head.''

"Lothar?"

She cocked her head a bit to one side. "Lothar von Brandenburg . . . the Graf."

"Oh." He cleared his throat. "Actually, Ms. Krebs, I was instructed to see Mr. Windsor. I'm not sure why."

"Margit," she told him. "In the inner circles, we're informal. I'll take you to Peter right now. He's expecting you and is rather on the curious side." She turned and headed for a door opposite the one by which he had entered.

For a moment, he looked at her blankly. *Inner circles? Was the competent, efficient, handsome Fräulein Krebs suggesting that Frank Pinell belonged to the inner circles of Mercenaries, Incorporated? She obviously had made some mistake. But how could anybody as sharp as the secretary of the Graf be that far off? And why should the notorious Peter Windsor be curious about meeting Frank Pinell?*

He shook his head and followed her. They went down a short corridor and, without knocking, she pushed open a door and strode in briskly. More hesitantly, Frank followed.

The office beyond was almost identical to that of Fräulein Krebs in size, but there was only one desk, and the feminine element was missing. The wall decorations were of a military nature, including paintings of war scenes and a flag which was holed in various places by what looked suspiciously like gunfire, and including a submachine gun which was racked in the manner that sportsmen display their shotguns or rifles.

Behind a somewhat battered and littered desk sprawled a lanky man, a report of some kind in his hand. He wore tennis shoes without socks, khaki walking shorts, and a khaki shirt, its sleeves rolled up. Frank's first snap judgment was that the other couldn't be much older than himself, but later realized on seeing the wrinkles at the side of the eyes that Peter Windsor projected an air of youth that wasn't there. He was almost twice Frank's age.

Margit said briskly, "This is Frank, Peter. I'll check with Lothar." She turned and left.

"Sit down, dear boy," Windsor said. And then, as Frank

was doing so, "Yes, I can see the resemblance. You could only be the son of Buck Pinell."

Frank said, "You knew my father?"

"Not too well, really. Saw him off and on for a few months, I'd imagine. I don't think that he really fancied me, if the truth be known."

"I didn't know him much myself. I was too young and he was away most of the time. What was he like?"

The other thought about it, sending his lime-green eyes ceilingward. He murmured finally, slowly, "A sort of dashing chap. He liked combat, I shouldn't wonder. Some men do, you know. They live for the excitement. He liked nothing so much as to find what he considered a just cause and then fight for it. He didn't mind making a profit at the same time, but for him, the enjoyment was in the combat. For myself, and for the Graf, I think, it has always been purely business. Buck fought for causes, we for money. He wasn't really cut out to be a soldier of fortune, you know."

"How do you mean? From what I've come to understand, he was a mercenary."

The Englishman nodded. "He was a soldier but I fancy that the fortune part of it wasn't of uppermost interest."

Frank didn't know if he quite understood that or not.

The other put down the report he'd been perusing, took up another, and rapidly scanned it. He said, "And how did the Boris Rivas affair come off last night?"

"Exactly as you had it set up. Everybody close to the colonel had been bought—even the concierge at his hotel and his long-time bodyguard. Poor bastard never had a chance."

Peter Windsor said coldly, "Never give an opponent a chance if you can avoid it, Pinell. Take every opening you can, every advantage. In that manner you'll live longer. Rivas had his chance. He was a bloody fool for not coming in with us. There was no use mucking around with him when he refused."

Frank said, "I suppose that Senegelese sergeant of his will get a good position with Mercenaries, Incorporated now."

Peter Windsor shook his head at him. "No. He'll be paid the amount promised and sent on his way. If he'd betray Rivas, how can we be sure that he wouldn't betray us, given the opportunity? The Graf never welches on his commitments but, on the other hand, he demands loyalty."

Frank said, very evenly, "How did the ethical code apply to me? I was to be sent on an impossible mission. It's unlikely that I could have escaped."

The Englishman shook his head again. "At the time, dear boy, you weren't actually a member of the organization in the same sense that our exuberant Nat Fraser or Colonel Ram Panikkar are. However, you were offered a sizeable sum, a hundred thousand pseudo-dollars desposited to your account in the Bahamas, before you were to leave for Central Africa. Upon the success of your mission you were to make your escape and enjoy the amount in whatever manner you saw fit. Very well, where was the betrayal? If you accomplished your assignment, your pay was awaiting you."

Frank said softly, "The colonel told me there was to be a chopper available for me to escape in—not that I was to be on my own."

Peter Windsor raised eyebrows and said, "He did? He wasn't authorized to make such a pledge. I've always thought Panikkar a bit of a swine. I'll have to take this up with him. It wouldn't do for the chief's reputation to have such items bandied about."

There was a faint humming at one of the desk screens and Peter swung his feet down to the floor. "That's the Graf now. Come along, Frank."

Frank stood, and as he did so, his eyes came upon the racked submachine gun. "A keepsake from the old days?" he said.

The Englishman said dryly, "I haven't used it for some years, but it's still kept loaded."

He led the way, strolling casually out a rear door and down a short, empty hallway to an elaborate double door. The screen on it picked him up and half the door opened. They entered.

The Graf's informal office was impressive. So was the Graf. He stood at the ceiling-to-floor window which framed the Rhine and its valley, his hands in the coat pockets of his immaculate business suit. He was staring out, his face characteristically expressionless. On their entry, the short-statured Graf turned, and, for a long moment, stared at Frank. Frank, feeling uncomfortable, came to a halt and simply remained on the spot.

The spry old soldier approached and looked him in the face with open candor. The American was taken aback by the smoky gray-flecked irises of the other's eyes and more so when Lothar von Brandenburg put his womanishly small hands on his shoulders.

The Graf sighed and said, "Yes, you could only be Buck's son. You're Buck as I first knew him, many years ago when we were both, ah, callow youngsters." He turned to one of the oversized couches and lowered himself, saying, "Sit down, Franklin."

Peter Windsor cleared his throat and slumped into one of the chairs, crossing long legs nonchalantly. He said, "He does look like Buck, at that. I told him so."

Frank found a place and joined them, still without the vaguest idea what he was doing here.

The Graf said, "We were somewhat surprised when your arrival in Tangier was reported."

There was no point in pussyfooting around. Frank had already decided there was no retreat. He said, "I couldn't have been much of a surprise. It was already set up. I suspect that the two IABI men were in on it, possibly even Judge Worthington back in the States. Certainly the cab driver and the two muggers in the medina in Tangier. First came Nat Fraser, as implausible a knight in armor as ever came down the pike. He took me to your Colonel Panikkar, who lavished good will on me, supposedly putting me deeply into his debt. He gave me strong arguments for taking an assignment for you. I might look young and ah, callow, as you put it, but I'm not as much a fool as all that. It was a suicide project. Actually, I wouldn't have taken it, but Panikkar didn't know that. I played along, just to see what the hell was going on. But it was called off from your end, before I ever turned it down. What's got me wondering is why."

The Graf remained silent through all that. Now he nodded.

Peter Windsor said, "Because we discovered that you were the son of Buck Pinell, dear boy."

Frank hadn't taken his eyes from the Graf. He said, "Boris Rivas claimed you might have been the cause of the death of my father."

The old man nodded again. "Then, for once, Rivas spoke the truth. I was the cause of your father's death, Franklin."

Frank stared at him.

The Graf said, "It was my fault, but I did not kill him, Franklin. Your father died in my arms, after saving my life. He sacrificed himself to rescue me. He was my best friend, and I, his. I have not had many friends in this life, Franklin. His last words were to put your life in my care."

The young American took long moments to assimilate that. Finally, he took a deep breath and said, "You didn't seem to do much in the way of carrying out his request."

The Graf said, "It was taken out of my hands. Your mother was fanatically against me and all I stood for. She had been violently against your father's, ah, profession. When my representative approached her, she absolutely refused to allow me to participate in your raising. She refused to accept any of your father's extensive earnings, as she had always refused while he was still alive. The relationship between your father and mother was not a close one, Franklin. She was contemptuous of him. She only continued to allow him to visit occasionally because he was your father and you loved him. Your mother was a good and compassionate woman with whom Buck Pinell was deeply in love. She refused to marry him, though he wished it. Their affair ended when she discovered your father's way of life."

"But my mother is dead now."

The Graf's usually expressionless face registered surprise. "I didn't know that. I should have kept a closer check on you as the years have gone by. But still, I hadn't wished to interfere with your mother's plans for your education and upbringing. It was the only thing for which she would draw upon your father's accumulated fortune and, even then, frugally. I had planned to make contact with you upon its completion."

"It's completed now," Frank said flatly.

"I see. And the employment computers didn't select you for a position in whatever field you had selected?"

"That's correct. In *any* of the fields I selected."

"Why not?" the Graf said bluntly.

"Because there are jobs in our economy for only about five percent of the population. But the fault is largely mine. I switched subjects too often. I started in aviation, but after a few years, I could see that it was becoming so highly auto-

mated that there were going to be practically no positions
available. So I switched to space and spent a few years
cramming so that I might be chosen to go to Lagrange Five or
the Asteroid Belt. But then the government began cutting
back drastically on new space expenditures, so drastically that
it was all but impossible to get out to the space islands. So
then . . .''

"Very well. I can see your problem. So when you finished
your schooling you were unable to find employment."

"Actually, I've never quite finished it, though it became
more difficult after my mother's death and my source of
income was cut off. She never gave me access to my father's
resources, hating them as she did. I'm not even sure that she
could have. I don't know what the legal arrangements were.
Since then, I've largely been on GAS. However, I've held a
few small jobs out of the ken of the computers. In between I
continued my studies as best I could."

The Graf leaned back in the couch. "You might consider a
position in my organization, Franklin."

Peter Windsor had been listening, his eyebrows a little
high. Obviously, much of this was new to him but he learned
best by listening.

Frank Pinell, who had been gaining confidence over the
past fifteen minutes, shook his head at the old mercenary's
words. He said, "I have certain reservations. Nat Fraser and
Colonel Panikkar gave me a rundown on the position you
assume on the things you do in your, uh, organization. However, I suspect that toward the end, at least, my father might
have had some of the same reservations. What did they call
him? The Lee Christmas of the 21st century. I've read a little
about Lee Christmas. I wonder if he ever went in for outright
political assassination."

"Possibly not. I checked on this early American mercenary
after Fräulein Krebs gave me a bit of his background the other
day. He was an uncouth, uneducated man—a railroad worker,
I understand, before becoming a soldier of fortune. Undoubtedly, he had the usual prejudices of his time and his
upbringing."

The Graf's voice was becoming a bit impatient. "See here,
Franklin, you must realize that mankind accepts the fact of
killing his fellow man under acceptable circumstances. What

are acceptable circumstances is the bone of contention. Even the assassin can become a hero—given circumstances. Let us take a few examples from the history of your own very aggressive nation. Davy Crockett, Jim Bowie, and Colonel Travis, heroes of the Alamo, were not Texans. They were American adventurers; mercenaries. The Alamo was not garrisoned by Texans, it was garrisoned by men of many nations sent to that part of Mexico to seek their fortunes with their guns. The flag that flew over the Alamo was that of a troop of New Orleans volunteers. How many true Texans were there I do not know, but certainly Crockett was not one of them. He had been a Representative in Congress from Tennessee.''

"I didn't know that,'' Frank murmured.

The Graf went on. "A group of American mercenaries during the First World War formed the Lafayette Escadrille, a pursuit squadron in the French Air Force. By American law, this should have deprived them of American citizenship. Instead, as soon as the United States entered the conflict, they became heroes, and their squadron became part of the American forces. The Flying Tigers who fought as mercenaries under Chiang Kai-shek against the Japanese before Pearl Harbor? These men were all highly trained pilots from American army, navy, and air force schools, and they flew the latest in American fighters. They were paid for each plane they shot down, with American money funnelled to China. *But they were mercenaries*, and became American heroes, instead of losing their citizenship.

"So much for mercenaries; let us consider assassins. Suppose that in my own country the General Staff had been successful in assassinating Hitler. Would they not now be heroes?''

The young American was unhappy. He said, "Panikkar and Nat Fraser gave me similar arguments. They didn't convince me.''

Peter Windsor said, "Let's face reality. Man kills his fellow man for profit, don't you know? Take the owner of a colliery. The mine is unsafe because he has ignored expensive safety devices. It caves in and fifty of his miners are buried alive. Indirectly, he has killed them—for profit. Is he ever brought to trial? I fancy not. He is a pillar of the community.''

The Graf said, "But enough of this for now. You must be

tired, Franklin. We'll meet for dinner. No need for you to
make a decision at this time.''

Evidently, he had signalled somehow since Sepp, the liver-
ied butler, materialized. *"Bitte, Herr Graf,"* he said, bowing.

"Sepp," the elderly mercenary said, "this is Mr. Franklin
Pinell. See him to his suite. I suppose his bags have been
delivered by now. And see that he is assigned a valet.''

"Ja, Herr Graf." Sepp turned to Frank. "Mr. Pinell?''

Frank nodded at Peter Windsor, came to his feet, and
followed the stone-faced servant out a side door.

In the medieval stone corridor along which Frank followed
Sepp, the elderly servitor said politely, "If I may say so, sir,
you resemble your father remarkably.''

"So everybody's been telling me. You knew my father?''

"I had the honor to serve with him in two campaigns, sir,''
Sepp said, his voice politely inflectionless. "Before I lost my
leg.''

Involuntarily, Frank glanced down and now noticed that the
servant limped lightly.

Frank said, "I had gathered that the Graf made a policy of
granting suitable compensations for his wounded men. Shouldn't
you be living in comfortable retirement somewhere?''

"Well, yes, sir. But you see, I am wanted by both Interpol
and the American IABI. I am safe here.''

"That you are,'' Frank smiled. "From what I've seen of it,
this castle has many attributes of a resort. Shouldn't you be
able to retire right here?''

They had reached a heavy wooden door and, for a moment,
the servant stood with his hand on the knob. For the first time
Frank saw a slight expression on the other's usually immobile
face. It was ruefulness. He said, "I suppose so, sir. However, the Herr Graf is used to my service. And . . . besides, it
is of interest to be here in the center of things.''

He opened the door and they stepped inside. Frank's luggage lay in the living room's center. The suite was spacious—an
extensive living room with ornate wooden furniture, a bedroom with an enormous canopied bed, a large bath, and what
Frank assumed was a small study. He was again surprised at
the art of whatever interior decorater had redesigned the
donjon of the Wolfschloss. The man had been a genius in
merging the old and new. That the rooms were those of a

Dark Ages castle was obvious, but they were modern in the best sense of comfort. That they had once been cold, damp, and grim could easily be imagined, but not with the modern conveniences added. The suite was absolutely palatial.

"It is satisfactory, sir?" Sepp said with polite anxiety.

At this height in the keep, it had undoubtedly never been necessary to continue the narrow bowmen's apertures that prevailed on the lower levels. The windows were spacious and looked out on a picturesque setting of Alps, glaciers, streams, and the upper reaches of the Rhine.

Frank shook his head. "It's a beautiful suite, Sepp. What was this about a valet?"

"I'll assign you Helmut, sir. A very reliable servant."

"What do I need him for?"

The old soldier-turned-butler seemed a touch surprised. "Why, sir, he'll do for you. Something like a batman, an orderly, sir."

Frank sighed. It would be an advantage to have somebody who could show him the ropes. He didn't even know his way around the corridors. He said, "All right, but tell him the less I see of him, the better."

"Sir, Helmut will never intrude unless summoned. Is there anything else, sir?"

Frank looked around. There was even a heavy wooden bar, which looked handcarved, set up against one wall. "I suppose not," he said. "Thanks, Sepp."

"Not at all, sir. I was always a great admirer of your father, sir. In the fracas in which I lost my leg, he carried me over a kilometer through enemy fire to the nearest field hospital." He coughed before adding, "Although he was wounded himself."

Frank couldn't think of anything to say to that, and the ramrod-erect old man turned to leave.

When he reached the door and was about to open it, he hesitated momentarily, then half turned and said, "Don't trust any of them, Mr. Pinell."

Chapter Sixteen:
Frank Pinell

In the Graf's informal office, Lothar von Brandenburg was saying to his aide, "What do you think of him, Peter?"

Peter said slowly, "Frank seems a straight-speaking young man. Adequate education, all that sort of thing."

The Graf looked at him. "You seem to have reservations."

"Well, not really. But you seem to accept him rather wholeheartedly. He is frightfully young to be taken into our inner circles."

The older man gave one of his rare, gray smiles without humor. "He is older than you were when I first met you, Peter."

The Englishman waggled a hand in rejection. "Perhaps we went to different schools."

"We shall sound him out further at dinner, but meanwhile, I am quite impressed," the Graf told him. "Ram Panikkar and that Australian fellow didn't hoodwink him for a moment. Meanwhile, let us be about the day's developments. Where is Margit?"

It wasn't a question that needed an answer. Margit entered immediately, obviously having been summoned.

She said briskly, "Lothar, Peter," and took her chair.

Peter said, "There's one item, Chief, on which we should get cracking. This Roy Cos, who signed a standard Deathwish Policy in Nassau."

"The Wobbly organizer? Yes, of course. I thought we notified Cellini, in New York, to put a couple of top men on him."

"Jolly well," Windsor said in disgust, "but our Mr. Cos is still with us and Brett-James, who sold the contract, is screaming like a chap with the blue spiders. Cos and his business manager, a Forrest Brown, are spending money like autumn leaves on the wind. Ordinarily, the poor bloody clods who sign these contracts have neither the imagination to spend a fraction of their million pseudo-dollars a day available, nor to avoid our people. They usually go on a drunken, woman-chasing binge in some expensive resort. They take the most posh suites and they buy—dear God, do they buy!''

The Graf eyed him in incomprehension. ''But what does this Cos fellow do?''

''He's spending, right up to the hilt each day, on prime Tri-Di time for his lectures. He's also renting huge auditoriums for his rallies, and hiring a large staff of bodyguards and aides, such as publicity men and speech writers.''

Margit said, ''Can't he be reached through bodyguards or other employees?''

Windsor shook his head. ''Not so far. We had a publicity man lined up but he was discovered. The bodyguards are all trusted Wobblies and the attempts to bribe them into defecting have all met with violence. But that's not the only difficulty. His message is beginning to get over. For a century and a half the few radicals of the United States have been a laughingstock. Nobody bothered to listen to their demands for fundamental changes, don't you know? But now the proles, caught up in the emotion of his plight, are beginning to consider his program. I've heard from two members of the Central Committee of the World Club. This man is a potential danger to the overall program. They demand that he be liquidated posthaste.''

The Graf said, ''Notify Cellini to drop all else and concentrate on this man. Why can't he be picked off by a sniper from a distance?''

''Because wherever he goes there are mobs around him. Not just bodyguards—there are eight of them now—but his staff and thousands of gawking curiosity seekers, most of them at least partially in his favor. A hit man can't get near him without running into considerable danger, and from a distance, there are so many people about him that a man with a rifle can't get a clear bead on the sod.''

The Graf said impatiently, ''That is for Cellini to solve, Peter. And that brings up the matter of the World Club. How did the operation against Harold Dunninger work out?''

"Completely as planned. A really good show. Nils Ostrander deserves a bit of a bonus."

The mercenary head looked at his secretary. "Refresh me on the details, Fräulein."

Margit's eyes went vague. She recited, "Harold Dunninger, international tycoon. Candidate member of the Central Committee of the World Club and, until his recent death, considered most likely to be admitted to the Central Committee upon the retirement of Grace Cabot-Hudson. He belonged to the so-called liberal element in the Central Committee, which includes such people as Jeremiah Auburn, Fong Hui, and Mendel Amschel, who wish to see the forming of a world state based on more democratic principles than most. The liberal element is opposed by such members as Harrington Chase, John Warfield Moyer, and the Committee's secretary, Sheila Duff-Roberts. Also, of course, by such candidate members as the Prophet of the United Church and yourself. It became necessary that Harold Dunninger be eliminated to increase your chances of being nominated a full member of the Committee. Obviously, it could not be handled in the usual manner or suspicion would immediately fall upon Mercenaries, Incorporated. So our mole in the Nihilists was instructed to kidnap Dunninger and hold him for a ransom of fifty million pseudo-dollars, with his life forfeit if the ransom was not paid."

The Graf interrupted, speaking to Peter Windsor. "Suppose he had paid the ransom. Then the Nihilists would have had no escuse to execute him."

Peter yawned and said, "We looked into it thoroughly. He was on the outs with his wife, don't you know? And she was in control of his interests in his absence. We were quite certain that she would never pay such a sum. She didn't. He's dead and the killing laid at the doorstep of the Nihilists."

The Graf thought about it and finally nodded in agreement. "Very well, I understand that the Central Committee is in session in Rome. You will go there as my deputy, Peter, and exert what pressure you can to have me entered as a full member into the Committee. I assume that your strongest competitor for the honor will be the Prophet."

Windsor said thoughtfully, "Don't you think it would be better, Chief, if you went yourself? You've been a Candidate

Member for years but none of the Committee have ever met you. You'd throw more weight if you attended, I shouldn't wonder.''

The Graf grunted contempt of that opinion. "Peter, I have not left the Wolfschloss for twenty years. The last time I did, three separate attempts were made on my life. The last nearly succeeded. No, I'll stay here. Keep in mind that the Prophet will also be represented by a deputy. He has no intention of permitting a rumor that he is so worldly as to belong to the World Club. Is there anything else?''

Peter said, "One other item that ordinarily I wouldn't bother you with. A black named Horace Hampton, who seems, ah, an enigma. He is an active member of the Anti-Racist League in America and indications are that he will soon be raised to membership in their National Executive Committee. This Anti-Racist League has come under the scrutiny of the World Club. So long as they were confined to North America alone they could be largely ignored. But with the Central Committee about to take steps to expand the United States of the Americas, these militant anti-racists take on a new posture.''

"How do you mean?'' the Graf said impatiently.

"The next step in the erecting of a World State is to invite Australia and New Zealand to join the United States of the Americas. The computers conclude that, if invited, they will join. Perhaps Great Britain and Ireland will be next. In all four countries there are few minorities, so the anti-racists are no difficulty. However, offering membership to still other nations poses a problem. Suppose India is approached. If the Anti-Racist League were to infiltrate and influence India, her votes would swamp the new United States of the World.''

"What has all this got to do with Horace Hampton?''

"He is one of the more intelligent and aggressive members of the League. Sheila Duff-Roberts has given us a contract on this mystery man. I strongly suspect that the National Data Banks have been corrupted to the point of his dossier being a fake.''

Margit said musingly, "It isn't the easiest thing in the world to infiltrate the American National Data Banks.''

"No, it bloody well isn't,'' Peter said. "And it seems

unlikely that an organization as short of funds as this League could do it.''

The Graf said, ''So we have a contract on the man. Very well, have it executed.''

Peter looked at him. ''Chief, it occurs to me that we might send young Pinell to deal with this beggar.''

The older man's eyes narrowed. ''Why?''

''Because the boy's inexperienced. You've obviously got plans for him. Very well, he handled himself well on the Rivas assignment, to the extent that he was needed at all. But it would seem to me that he needs a bit more blooding. No particular hurry, but it will give him an opportunity to learn something about the organization. He'd have to work through our local representatives in the States, of course.''

''I'll consider the matter,'' said the Graf. ''Very well, if that's all, I'll see you tonight at dinner.''

Dismissed, Margit Krebs and Peter Windsor came to their feet and headed for the door.

In the corridor, as they headed for their own offices, Margit looked up at the rangy Englishman. She said, softly, ''You didn't mention to Lothar that this Horace Hampton is considered the most efficient field man in the Anti-Racist League and very dangerous as compared to our Frank.''

He said, ''If you thought so, why didn't you say something to the Chief to that effect?''

''Possibly, just to find out what you're up to, Peter, dear.'' She eyed him mockingly. ''You couldn't be getting second thoughts about Buck Pinell's son, could you, Peter? For years now, you've been second man in Mercenaries, Incorporated. Undoubtedly, you've expected to take over when the Graf either retires or dies.''

''Who's better suited to take over the reins? But Lothar's in a position to turn over the whole organization to this stripling. If he did, an outfit that has taken half a century to build could go down the spout overnight. Then where would you and I be, Margit, old thing?''

She reached the door of her office and stood there for a moment, considering it.

''How do you stand?'' he demanded.

''I don't know,'' she said evasively. ''Perhaps you're over-estimating Lothar's acceptance of Frank.''

"Perhaps," he grunted and went on.

She looked after him and thought to herself, *Peter is beginning to wonder if the Graf isn't getting too old for the job. Perhaps a touch of senility. I'd hate to be in the crossfire if it came to a showdown. Margit, my girl, you'd better start considering on what side of your own bread the butter is on.*

Dinner that night was another revelation to Frank Pinell, in a day that had been full of them. The baronial hall in which it was held was one flight up in the keep from the offices and suites. The whole floor was evidently devoted to the Graf's living quarters.

Frank had entered the palatial living room attired in the dark suit which Helmut, his newly appointed valet, had laid out for him. There hadn't been much of a choice. He had bought two suits in Paris, on Nat Fraser's suggestion, and several pairs of shoes. All the clothing he had brought with him from America he had discarded, also at Fraser's suggestion. But now he realized that he had made a mistake. The Graf, Peter Windsor, and Margit Krebs were all in evening wear. Margit looked stunning and ten years younger in a simple black silk affair that brought out the pale perfection of her Scandinavian skin. She wore but one item of jewelry, a matched string of pearls whose deep pink luster was obvious from across the room.

The three were seated about a cocktail table, sipping drinks and chatting, as Frank came in. The Graf looked up and frowned but then said, "Please give us the pleasure of your company, Franklin. Sit down." The Graf added smoothly, "We always dress for dinner, Franklin, but I assume your travel clothing is limited."

Frank said, "I've never worn so much as a tuxedo, not to speak of tails. You don't when you're on GAS, you know."

"Forgive me. It skipped my mind that you didn't inherit your father's fortune. Yes, Sepp?"

The butler leaned forward slightly and spoke to his master in German.

"Ah," the mercenary grunted. "Dinner is served. Margit?"

With his secretary on his arm, followed by Peter Windsor and Frank, he passed through the double doors into the dining room.

Compared to the refurbishing of the rest of the keep, the

dining hall had hardly been touched by the genius of an interior decorator. Frank could well imagine the old days when some long-dead duke, princeling, or archbishop had held forth here. His closest henchmen would be present with their women, wassailing about a huge round table, while minstrels and clowns provided medieval entertainment, as scurrying servants brought on heaping platters of food, and huge mugs with foaming beer, mulled wine, or subtle mead.

The table, however, was considerably smaller than that which must have prevailed in the old days. It would have seated eight at most. The setting was on the awesome side, so far as Frank was concerned. He had never eaten with more cutlery than knife, fork, and spoon, never eaten by candle-light, and most certainly had never eaten off gold.

The Graf sat at one end of the table, Margit at the other, and Peter and Frank across from each other. It came to Frank that Peter Windsor was a changed man in evening dress, after his informal sports garb of the day. Now he looked as though he had been born to wear formal evening attire; a matinee idol couldn't have been more at ease in it.

Sepp presided with two footmen, also in livery, behind each chair. No more than two sips were taken from a wine glass before it was instantly refilled. It was all on the thick side so far as Frank Pinell was concerned.

It got thicker as the meal progressed. He recognized exactly two of the dishes presented, or at least the ingredients. One was a potato dish which would have been hard to miss, and one a delightful scallop-based fish course. He made the mistake of commenting on the scallops.

"Ah," the Graf said, pleased. "You mean the Coquilles Saint Jacques Parisienne? It is one of Albert's specialities. He will be overjoyed to know you approve."

Peter said, after sipping at his Chablis, "Albert is one of the three best chefs in Common Europe, Frank. It's a privilege to eat from his kitchen, I should think."

Frank said, "You mean to tell me that one of the best three cooks in Europe works here for just the three of you? I'd think he could get a job in any restaurant in the world."

"The four of us now," his host said magnanimously. "Fortunately, Albert is in no position to tender his resignation."

Margit said dryly, "Liechtenstein is somewhat like Tang-

ier, in that there are no extradition laws; and since Albert
made the mistake of killing his wife, he sees fit to remain as
Lothar's chef.''

"Poisoned her, to be exact," Peter said blandly.

Frank looked down at the morsel of scallop on his fork and
closed his eyes in sorrow.

There were eight courses in all, with eight wines, winding
up with a dessert which Margit told him was Nesselrode
Pudding with Sabayon Fruit, served with a slightly chilled
sauterne.

Largely, the dinner conversation consisted of the Graf ex-
pounding on his dreams and turning on what small charm he
boasted in order to win the younger man over. Both Margit
and Peter seemed surprised at the extent to which he revealed
top secrets of the innermost circle of Mercenaries, Incorporated. It would seem that Lothar von Brandenburg was most
certainly now considering Frank to be a member of that
circle, in which case, it was the most rapid promotion the
organization had ever seen.

All of the servants save Sepp spoke nothing but German,
and the table conversation was in English.

The Graf had said, "You are acquainted with the World
Club, Franklin," while still on the oxtail soup.

"Just slightly," Frank said. "Isn't it an organization of
economists, philanthropists, and international do-gooders seeking solutions to worldwide problems?"

"That is the facade we present to the man in the street,"
the other said, satisfaction in his voice.

"We?" Frank said.

"Mercenaries, Incorporated is represented in the highest
echelons of the World Club."

"That surprises me. I pictured the organization as a group
of old-timers with more credits than they know what to do
with, supporting a lot of foundations."

Peter Windsor gave a snort of amusement.

The Graf said, "I expect within a short time to be nominated to the Central Committee, which consists of but ten
members and has the ultimate say in all of the World Club's
policies."

"I didn't even know they had a Central Committee,"
Frank admitted.

"You're not supposed to, dear boy," Peter said.

The Graf shot him an impatient look before turning back to Frank. He said, "The real goal of the World Club, Franklin, is world government—a world that has become one under the aegis of the Club. Obviously, such a united world will no longer have wars and . . ."

Frank interrupted, "But then what would happen to Mercenaries, Incorporated? It seems to me that your organization depends upon a multitude of antagonistic nations. You should be supporting nationalism, not trying to do away with it."

The Graf smiled his gray smile. "It's a far-seeing man who is able to accommodate inevitable changes, Franklin. Sooner or later there will be world government. When it comes about, I wish to be part of its direction, not a leftover from the past. This new world government will still have police, still have armed forces . . ."

Frank interrupted again. "Why armed forces?"

The old mercenary nodded at the question. "To *keep* the peace. Contrary to popular belief, the first need a state has for an armed force is not to fight foreign enemies but the potential enemy within. As an example, take Latin America before it amalgamated with the United States. They spent billions annually building up their armed forces though there hadn't been a major war in South America for a century and a half. Those arms were to keep their own people in subjection. So in the future, armed forces will still exist. I will be at their head."

Frank looked at him in open skepticism.

Margit said, "The first steps have already been taken, Frank—the formation of the United States of the Americas. The World Club is already secretly agitating in Australia and New Zealand for them to apply for admission into the United States. For a long time now, those countries have been closer to America than to England and the rest of Common Europe."

Frank looked over at her. Candlelight did nothing to detract from the charms of Margit Krebs. She flashed sloe eyes at him, aware of their impact.

He made a mental note of her obvious availability, then turned back to his host. "If the United States of the Americas eventually becomes a United States of the World, wouldn't the IABI become the international police force?"

The Graf waved that aside, saying, "It's true that John Warfield Moyer, a member of the Central Committee, foresees a united world in which his IABI will be the sole police force; but his organization has been a farce since before the FBI and the CIA were joined together. An organization of clowns, headed by clowns, compared to my own. Moyer will be taken care of, in good time."

Frank thought about it. He said slowly, "Then you're in the process of phasing out your mercenary activities in expectation of becoming legal under this new world regime."

"That's one way of putting it," Peter said.

Lothar von Brandenburg said, "You are beginning to have second thoughts about my organization, Frank?"

"Perhaps. What about these assassinations, though?"

"Such as the Mahdi? The only thing that will make sense under a world government is a state religion. The United Church, under the Prophet, backs the World Club. The fanatic who calls himself the Mahdi stands in the way of the amalgamation into one of all the world's religions. I'm afraid he must go. Others, too, of course. Always remember, Franklin, that a comparatively few key figures can change history. The example of Somerset Maugham comes to mind. In his earlier years, while working for British espionage, he was sent to Petrograd to sabotage the Bolshevik revolution. He wrote later that if he had been sent two weeks earlier he might have accomplished his task and the revolution would never have taken place. How would he have done this? He probably had in mind the assassinations of Lenin and Trotsky and perhaps of a few others of the old Bolsheviks."

The American said grudgingly, "I suppose in some respects you've made your point. Under some circumstances, assassination can be called for. But what happens when someone approaches you with a proposal to kill someone who doesn't deserve killing?"

The Graf raised his eyebrows. He put down his glass of wine. "My dear Franklin, we are pragmatists, not mad dogs. Our interests are not *only* money. Suppose, for instance, that Mercenaries, Incorporated was approached by an enemy of the Prophet. As I told you, we support the United Church in its efforts to join all organized religions into a single worldwide state church, ending once and for all conflicts between

faiths. Very well, not only would we refuse the contract, but
we would inform Ezra Hawkins, the Prophet, about this foe
of his, so that he could take steps to protect himself.''

"By hiring Mercenaries, Incorporated to eliminate the enemy?'' Frank said.

Peter Windsor chuckled. "You're catching on, dear boy.''

Following dinner, they sat for a time in the living room
over coffee and cognac. The talk drifted, in deference to
Frank, to stories involving his father. The Graf carried most
of the conversation, since his relationship with Buck Pinell
had extended over years, but Peter Windsor was also able to
contribute a few anecdotes. Most of the stories were of a
humorous nature and it came to Frank that combat veterans
seldom talked much about actual combat itself. When it was
shop talk, yes; something involving business at hand. But not
as light conversation. Perhaps amateurs might brag of their
exploits under fire, but professionals, no. And you couldn't
get much more professional than Lothar von Brandenburg and
Peter Windsor.

When the party broke up, Margit offered to conduct Frank
back to his suite. The winding corridors and stone stairways
of the keep took some learning, and under the influence of the
wines during the meal and the generous brandies following it,
Frank wasn't sure he could find his way unaided. The Graf
looked tolerant, Peter amused, as they said their goodnights.
On the morrow, Frank was to be assigned a guide to show
him the Wolfschloss in detail.

As they strolled along the stone corridor, Frank decided
that nicety wasn't called for.

He said, "Your rooms, or mine?''

She looked up at him from the side of her eyes. "I thought
you'd never ask. Yours. You might never find your way bck
to your own suite in the morning.''

And that was the full extent of their courting, their preliminary love play. Margit was a businesslike woman, in her sex
life as well as her secretarial work.

In fact, she was as straightforward a woman as he had ever
bedded, and at his age, Frank had seldom gone without
horizontal refreshments when he had desired them.

In his bedroom, she had stripped with flattering haste, and
had pirouetted exactly once, to show off the woman's body,

saying, "Like me?" before sliding into the emperor-sized canopied bed.

His voice was on the thick side as he told her, "Yes," climbing out of his own clothes.

"Good heavens," she said, teasing him, "is that for me?"

"Yes," he said hoarsely, already rampant.

Not for Margit Krebs were new variations of the world's oldest theme. She took her sex straight and lustily, somewhat surprising Frank, who had expected unique desires on the part of this sophisticated wanton. Perhaps that would come later, he decided as he performed for her. For the present, his lady wanted immediate basic action.

And wanted it again, within minutes after they had both reached rapturous climax. He began to wonder if he had known what he was getting into, so to speak.

Later, as they rested, both staring up at the rich cream-colored canopy above, he said, only partly in humor, "And what is a nice girl like you doing in this kind of work?"

She followed along. "What's the classic answer to that? Just lucky, I guess."

"Come on, come on. On the face of it you're the junior member of the staff that runs the toughest organization on Earth. Why would a woman like you want to hold down such a job? With your obvious ability you could get top positions anywhere. So why be the notorious Graf's secretary?"

She looked at him strangely. "It's where the power is."

"I don't understand."

"The Graf is the single most powerful man in the world, darling. Not the wealthiest, not the one with the most political clout, but the most powerful. Others may not always realize that, but he is."

"Why?"

"Because he holds the life of every other living person in the palm of his hand."

He thought about that for a long moment, before saying, "But that's him, not you."

"The Graf doesn't operate in a vacuum," she told him patiently. "There is no such thing as a one-man dictatorship. Hitler, Stalin, Mussolini, Mao were the heads of teams. Without the team around them, they wouldn't have been able to cope. The same with Napoleon and Alexander the Great.

Alexander would have been nothing but a headstrong, alcoholic youth had it not been for Nearchus, Parmenion, and other leaders trained by his father Philip. True enough, the Empire broke up upon his death, when the team started fighting among themselves. But while they were still a team, with him at the head, they were invincible. So it is with the Graf. He does not stand alone, making all decisions. He has a team. I'm part of the team. You might be, too.''

That quieted him.

She said, a quirk of amusement there, ''I should warn you about Lothar. I think perhaps he's getting a bit tired of Peter, who isn't quite as young and pink-cheeks as he used to be.''

That came as a surprise. ''You mean he's gay?''

She laughed. ''What is your old American expression? He's as queer as chicken shit.''

''Not my cup of tea,'' he said gruffly.

''You've already proven that, darling, though I do hope that you're up to proving it again.'' She reached over to stroke him intimately.

Frank said, ''Wizard, but hold it for just a little, eh?''

''You mean that literally?'' she said, wickedness in her voice.

''You're a sexpot. Did anyone ever tell you that?''

''Yes.''

He frowned again and said, ''What ever happened to my father's estate? From what you people say, he must have been a partner for something like twenty years. When he died my mother refused to take anything except enough to educate me on. What happened to the rest?''

''Why, I don't know, darling.'' She frowned as well. ''And I should know. I'm supposed to know everything connected with Mercenaries, Incorporated.''

Chapter Seventeen:
Lee Garrett

When Lee Garrett reported to the office of Sheila Duff-Roberts early in the morning of the day after she had arrived, it was to find the Amazon-like secretary of the Central Committee of the World Club already deep in work. A cigarette, half an ash, dangled from the side of her mouth, and the smoke from it spiraled upward.

Sheila looked up, did her sparse smile, and said, "Good morning, darling. I rather expected you to return here after your lunch with Jerry Auburn yesterday. Do sit down."

Lee took the indicated chair and said apologetically, "We ran into some difficulty. By the time it was ironed out I felt exhausted and Mr. Auburn took me back to my suite."

"Difficulty?"

"He was attacked in the restaurant by a waiter, apparently a Nihilist. I've read about them, of course. But . . ." she shook her blond head ". . . good heavens, I didn't know it had gotten to the point where they were attacking prominent people right in the open."

The other at last noticed the length of her cigarette ash and tapped it off into her improvised ash tray. Her eyes narrowed. "Nihilists! The bastards are really getting out of hand. Just recently they kidnapped one of our candidate members of the Central Committee and shot him when his wife couldn't pay a fifty million pseudo-dollar ransom. Something simply will have to be done. What happened?"

"It was terrible. The man was about to shoot Jerry—Mr. Auburn—from behind. But something made him turn and, well, Jerry knows savate and . . ."

"What the hell's savate?"

"A method of fighting with the feet; an old French sport with some aspects of karate. Jerry disarmed the man and had kicked him unconscious before the others arrived. The manager, of course, was extremely upset. He said that the waiter was a new man who had only been there for a few days. He called the police, of course.''

Sheila shook her head. ''Trust Jerry to come up with something like that, fighting with his feet. Undoubtedly, he'll report on it later. With almost all of the Central Committee in Rome, we can't afford to run chances of assassination. Which reminds me: we're to have a party tonight. All of the Central Committee members and candidate members will be present. It will give you an opportunity to meet them and for them, of course, to get an impression of you. In the ballroom, beginning at nine.''

Lee frowned. ''Candidate member?'' she said.

''Yes. You see, there are but ten members of the Central Committee, plus myself as secretary. Most of them are rather elderly. So, at any given time, there are as many as a score or so candidate members, waiting to be made full members upon the death or retirement of any of the present incumbents. One of the matters to be handled at this session is such a promotion. Grace Cabot-Hudson hasn't been active for some time, so she is being asked to retire to the position of Central Committee Member *Emeritus* and a new member will be appointed.''

In an angry movement of a well-manicured hand, she took up another cigarette and lit it, before going on. ''And it's ten to one that it won't be another woman. Male dominance still prevails in the Central Committee. You'd think that at least half the members should be female, but no. The male ego we still have with us.'' She snorted. Then, ''Well, be that as it may, dear, I'll see you at the party tonight. Have you met any of the other members, besides Jerry?''

''I haven't had the opportunity.''

''I mentioned you to Fong Hui, who has just rocketed in from Hong Kong. He'd like to meet you. Fong is the only Oriental Central Committee member, though there are candidates from Japan, India, and Indonesia.''

''When did he wish to see me?''

''This morning.'' Sheila Duff-Roberts touched a button on her TV phone.

Almost immediately, a door leading to the back opened and

a girl bustled through. She was a tiny thing, smaller than Lee Garrett and absolutely dwarfed by the Junoesque Sheila. She was a bit on the plump side, which didn't detract from her vivacity.

Sheila said, "Lily Palermo, Lee Garrett. Lee is to be my new secretary, Lily darling, to replace Pamela. But you girls can get to know each other later. Right now, I'd like you to take Lee to Fong Hui's apartment. The old fuddy-duddy's expecting her."

"Right away," Lily said. And to Lee, "My, you must have spent a fortune on that hair."

Lee came to her feet and said to Sheila, "See you at the party, then."

"Good-O, darling," Sheila said, already back at her work.

As they started down the corridor, redundant with art as everywhere in the Palazzo Colonna, Lee said, touching her hair, "Believe it if you will but it's my own and I do it myself."

"It's lovely," Lily told her and giggled. "You should have been at the *partous* last night. You would have been the hit."

Lee made a moue. "Group sex turns me off," she said.

The other looked at her from the side of her eyes. "I'm surprised that Sheila is taking you for her secretary then."

Lee shrugged. "It was rather thrown at me, without my having much to say about it, though frankly, this whole World Club thing has its fascinating aspects."

"Oh, it's the most wizard job you can imagine. You're right in the middle of the most important goings on in the world. You're really on the *inside*."

Lee said idly, "Whatever happened to Pamela, the girl I'm taking over from?"

"I don't know. She was awfully nice. Kind of a little serious, even more dedicated than most. Irish, and she still talked with that soft brogue they have."

"What was her last name?"

"McGivern. She wouldn't take anything from anybody, not even Sheila. They'd argue hammer and tongs."

"Maybe that's why Sheila let her go."

The little girl was silent for a moment, as they rounded a turn in the wide corridor. Then she said quietly, "Sheila never fires you from any of these jobs. She might transfer you to some other position, somewhere else. But she'll never fire you."

"Why not?"

The other wasn't quite happy at the question. "Well, I suppose if the computers selected you in the first place, you have more than usual ability, and the Central Committee doesn't want to waste it. Besides . . ." she hesitated for a moment ". . . you're in on so many top-secret matters that they wouldn't like you to blab them around." She rolled her eyes. "I can just see somebody who once worked for the Central Committee sitting down and writing a book about it."

Lee thought about that. She already had several new things to think about this morning. For one, she had gotten the damnedest impression that Sheila had already known about the attack on Jerry Auburn before she had told her. But then, it was Sheila's job to know everything that happened pertaining to the Central Committee members.

Lily brought them up to an imposing door, similar to that which opened into Sheila Duff-Roberts's salon. Once again, there was no identity screen. She knocked briskly, then reached down for the bright brass knob.

She smiled brightly at Lee, said, "See you later, dear," turned and tripped briskly away.

Lee entered, closing the door behind her. She blinked in surprise at the large room's decor. She had stepped from a Roman Renaissance corridor into a chamber which should have been eight thousand miles away, in a Chinese palace or mansion of the Ming dynasty. One had no doubts whatsoever that all of the exquisite furnishings, all of the art, and even the rugs, were genuine antiques. The whole room belonged in a Chinese museum.

There were two occupants—an old man behind an intricately carved ebony desk, and a girl, certainly not over twenty, wearing a sleek, long, yellow, high-collared cheongsam. She was kneeling upon a dais, plucking a thin Mandarin melody from a jong resting on the floor before her. Her slim fingers played over the instrument as though caressing a lover.

The old man was frail with a wisp of a white beard and a bald head poised forward on his long neck with great natural dignity and grace. He wore the red-tasseled, crystal-topped cap and the navy-blue gown of the scholar.

Lee said formally, after bowing, "May I trouble your chariot? My name is Lee Garrett."

His aged eyes took her in for a moment, then the slightest of smiles appeared on his yellowish parchment face. "My chariot is untroubled. Pray take an honored chair."

"I am totally unworthy."

"The unworthiness is mine," he told her. "My office is favored by your visit."

Lee sat across the desk from him and said, "It is a poor woman's delight."

"The office shrinks in humble shame before your footsteps."

Fong Hui shook hands with himself, keeping his delicately tapered fingers well within his long loose sleeves.

The Chinese girl who had been playing the jong stood and trotted toward a rear door. She turned without speaking, bobbed several bows, and left.

Fong took Lee in again, the faint smile still in his eyes. "I suspect that you would have been capable of going through the formal greeting of years past in the original Mandarin."

Lee Garrett acknowledged the compliment. "Only awkwardly, Mr. Fong. My father was a diplomat. When I was a young girl he was stationed for two years in the People's Republic in Peking. He was an ardent linguist and always insisted that the family study the language of the nation to which we were posted."

"Such talents will be welcome in the position Ms. Duff-Roberts tells me you are to occupy." He smiled faintly again and let his eyes go about the room. "Undoubtedly, you are surprised at both my office and my attire."

"I have always been a great admirer of the art and culture of the Celestial Empire, Mr. Fong."

His thin voice held a touch of exasperation. "And I have long been displeased by the increasing domination of the Western culture. But I wage a losing battle. The culture of the West sweeps everything before it—its modes of dress, its food, its manners and mores. An accident of history gave the European and North American powers domination over the world for at least the present, so that the habits of the West have prevailed to the detriment of other cultures, not necessarily inferior. As to dress, without doubt the Chinese cheong-sam and the Indian sari are far more flattering to the feminine figure than the awkward garb of Europe. And throughout the world now, all cities are beginning to look like Cleveland, Ohio, while such architectural gems as Angkor Wat in Cambodia and Kyoto in Japan are now no longer anything but museums on a grand scale.''

Lee said, "I agree with you, Mr. Fong. Even Rome now has its seven hills surrounded by sky-high condominiums and high-rise apartment buildings for the antlike existence of the proles, the slums of the welfare state."

He was obviously enjoying her company. "My dear," he said, "you seem wise beyond your years. Perhaps some evening, after adjusting to your new atmosphere, you will honor me with your presence at dinner. My chef is from Shanghai."

"I am overwhelmed, Mr. Fong. I consider Chinese cuisine the world's finest."

The old man touched his wisp of white beard and said, "And now, my dear, tell me: what are your impressions of the World Club?"

She said hesitantly, "I am somewhat overwhelmed. Its scope is much greater than I had thought. I am inclined to wonder whether it has bitten off more than it can chew. The problems seem insoluble to me."

He nodded. "When I was a boy, confronted with my youthful unsolvable problems and in despair, my father once said, 'What were you worrying about last year at this date?' And I saw on reflection that all my unsolvable problems of that time had, indeed, been solved or lost relevancy. The same might be said to apply to the long-range troubles of man. This is the year 2086. What were our difficulties one century ago in 1986? In those days, savants were aghast at the world's problems; surely they would never be solved. But let us ask the question again. Suppose that an American in the year 1986 was to look back a century to 1886 and consider the problems of that time. The Indian Wars were not quite over; Custer's forces had been destroyed only ten years before and Geronimo had kept the Southwest in a state of siege. Labor troubles were paramount, the anarchists at their peak. The Haymarket bombing killed seven, wounded sixty. The

American Federation of Labor was not yet strong. America was in an unprecedented state of growing pains. The robber barons of industry were taking over the country wholesale. Immigrants were swarming in to the point where nearly half of New York City couldn't speak English, to the dismay of the earlier-arrived Anglo-Saxons.''

Lee laughed softly. "I see what you mean. By 1986, the problems of 1886 had all been solved, or disappeared. And so, is your suggestion, will be the problems of our time by 2186.''

He smiled in return but then became more serious. "Tell me, my dear, what do you think of our Sheila Duff-Roberts?''

She said carefully, "I don't know her very well as yet. She seems very capable.''

The old man nodded. "I am afraid that she is too prone to take on authority which should remain in the hands of the Central Committee, with the assistance of its candidate members, though I defer to the majority in retaining her as secretary.'' He hesitated. "Nor do I think that she should participate in the sometimes differing currents of the World Club.''

He must have caught the puzzlement in her eyes and said in amusement, "Did you think that all was accord in the Central Committee, my dear? Happily, it is not. If it were, I myself would withdraw. A frozen program is seldom a valid one, certainly not over a period of time. It was one of the prime weaknesses of the Marxists back in the 19th and 20th centuries. Marx and Engels did their work as early as the first part of the 19th century. Their *Communist Manifesto*, written in 1848, predicted an imminent breakdown of capitalism and a proletarian victory. A century later, the capitalist system had changed and was stronger than ever. Marx and Engels had died, but most of the so-called Marxists continued to follow them as though no changes in political economy had taken place; as though such developments as fascism and the state capitalism of the Soviet Union had never raised their ugly heads. At any rate, there are conflicting opinions in the Central Committee of the World Club and I, to a degree, welcome them. When two minds meet, both learn something. An Einstein cannot meet with a moron and exchange opinions without both learning something—however little.''

The American girl said, "But what are these differences in

opinion? I had gathered from Sheila and Jerry Auburn that the goal of the World Club is world government.''

He smiled his little smile again. ''It is, but there can be varied types of world government. So you have met our debonair Jeremiah Auburn. He is a young man with depths not immediately perceived by some. Indeed, there was considerable difficulty in nominating him to the Central Committee. However, his father before him was a member and such, ah, old-timers as myself and Grace Cabot-Hudson were adamant in vouching for him. The three of us have similar views pertaining to the nature of the world state to come. We had hopes that Candidate Harold Dunninger, who also had somewhat similar views, would replace her upon her retirement. Unfortunately, he was recently murdered by the Nihilists. Opposed to our view are John Moyer of the American IABI who, I suspect, sees the future government as a police state, and Harrington Chase, with his strong racist beliefs, who undoubtedly sees it as a government of whites over the rest of humanity. Some of the candidates, such as Lothar von Brandenburg, I am sure, see the future government as a dictatorship, while Ezra Hawkins, of the United Church, probably desires a theocracy. Ah yes, my dear, I am afraid that there are conflicting currents within the ranks of the World Club.''

Lee said thoughtfully, ''I can see that there must be ramifications that never occurred to me.''

The faint sound of a muted gong came from the inner depths of the apartment and the old man smiled ruefully. ''I am afraid that my physician reminds me that it is time for my nap.''

The American girl stood immediately. ''I must thank you for wasting so much of your valuable time on one who is so ignorant of the great problems resting upon your honorable shoulders.''

''The pleasure, my dear, is mine. You are to fill an important post, privy to the innermost developments of the World Club. One cannot know the future, but perhaps one day you may even succeed to the position now occupied by Ms. Sheila Duff-Roberts.''

Lee bowed formally, said, ''With your permission, Mr. Fong,'' and turned and left.

Behind her, Fong Hui sighed softly. Old his clay might be, but he still had an eye for a superlatively pretty girl.

Lee Garrett puzzled out the route to her own suite, only twice losing her way through the rambling, twisting corridors of the Palazzo Colonna.

Inside it, she carefully locked the door before going into her small office. She checked the time on her wrist chronometer, then put her shoulder bag on the desk top. She activated a secret compartment in the leather purse and brought forth from it a device like a ballpoint stylo. She pressed a stud on its side and began moving slowly about the room, pointing the gadget here, there, and particularly in the vicinity of electronic devices such as the TV phone.

After thoroughly going over the office, she returned to the living room and resumed her activities. As she approached the apartment's second TV phone, sitting on a small table against a wall, her device began to buzz faintly. Her eyes widened in suspicion and she approached closer. The buzzing increased. She nodded to herself and then continued about the room. She finished the living room and continued her task in both the bedroom and the bath, but she found no more electronic bugs. She deactivated her device, returned to her office, and replaced it in her shoulder bag, extracting from the same secret compartment another device. She also took up her pocket transceiver.

She went back to the living room on her way, pulling a thin antenna from its place in the flat metallic box of her device, which looked something like a small cigarette case. She placed it next to the TV phone and pressed a stud. It began to hum faintly.

She sat down on the couch, turned on her transceiver, flicked the scrambler button, and dialed.

The answering voice came almost immediately.

Lee said hurriedly, "I'll have to make this quick. There's a bug in my suite. I have the muffler on but heaven knows what would happen if some monitor was checking manually. So, briefly, everything is going better than we could have dreamed of. I am the Secretary of Sheila Duff-Roberts, the secretary of the Central Committee. I am meeting the ten members, one by one by one. So far, I have found more division among them than we had known. Grace Cabot-Hudson is to be replaced; the Graf and the Prophet are top contenders for her position. Both will add to the extremist element in the Committee.''

A thin, faraway voice spoke from the transceiver.

Then she said hurriedly, ''I must go. There is to be a party tonight which I'll attend. Meanwhile, check this, if you can. A Pamela McGivern, an Irish girl, was the former holder of my job. I don't know what happened to her but I was indirectly informed today that once one takes a job this close to the Central Committee one doesn't quit. Obvious question: where is the McGivern girl?''

The voice spoke again.

And Lee said, ''I'll be *very* careful. I'm a little afraid.''

She switched off the transceiver, hurried over to the muffler and deactivated it as well, then took it back into the office and hid it again.

Chapter Eighteen:
Jeremiah Auburn

It soon came to Lee Garrett, when she attended the party in the ballroom of the Palazzo Colonna, why Sheila Duff-Roberts's position was so important. The Committee itself was undoubtedly the most informal presiding body of a large and influential organization of which she had never heard. Sheila's office held it all together. Present at the get-together were nine of the ten Central Committee members, about a score of candidate members, and another score or so of prominent supporters and employees of the World Club who had not as yet attained Central Committee rank, but were knowledgeable of its secret nature and headed various of the foundations, research groups, pressure groups, and lobbies. All were in formal dress but that was as near as Lee could see to it being a formal affair. She would have called it a cocktail party, at most. The buffet was one of the most elaborate she had ever seen, and Lee Garrett had attended many an embassy affair. There were tobacco fumes in the air as well as those of cannabis.

Men predominated by far. She noticed a dozen other women, most in their middle years, and most gave the impression of being the wives of male members. One wore a golden Indian sari but otherwise all were gowned most expensively in the latest styles. Two of the men wore Arab garb, but all the rest were in European dress, though at least half were of dark complexion, including one very black man who, unlike the others, didn't seem at ease in his black tie and tails. For a moment, as she surveyed them, she wondered about the conservatism in men's dress. Formal attire had changed precious little since the days of Abraham Lincoln. Sports and daily wear, yes; evening wear, no. A guest at a reception given by

Woodrow Wilson probably wouldn't have looked out of place here tonight.

When she first entered there were as many servants present as guests, tending bar and the buffet, carrying drinks and canapes, running the errands waiters run. But very shortly after she arrived they seemed magically to disappear, to her surprise. Then the realization came: those present were not in a position to be overheard. For the balance of the evening, the guests helped themselves to the buffet and the abundant drinks at the two bars.

She recognized only a few people—Sheila Duff-Roberts, of course, and Jerry Auburn, and Fong Hui, who inclined his bald head in salutation when their eyes met. Across the room was Nils Norden, an unconventionally jovial Swede who had been pointed out to her though thus far they hadn't met.

No, this was no formal party; merely a get-together of the bigwigs of the World Club. They stood or sat about the ballroom of the renaissance palace chatting, arguing, debating; sometimes friendly, sometimes in heat, and in groups of anywhere from two to eight. Most seemed to make a policy of circulating around, joining one conversation for a time, then drifting on to another individual or group.

Sheila had suggested Lee's presence as an opportunity to meet not only other members of the Central Committee but the other influentials of the World Club as well. For the moment, she didn't quite know where or how to begin. But then, from across the room, Jerry Auburn waved to her. He was standing with Sheila Duff-Roberts, who was dressed in a stunning, bright-blue evening gown which surely must have been designed with only her in mind. With them was a stranger who bore a fragile handkerchief with which he daintily touched his lips after each sip at the champagne he carried.

Lee approached hesitantly, wondering if the wave had meant she was to join them, and Jerry beamed at her. He held a highball glass in hand and, by the darkness of its contents, it was either straight spirits or nearly so. His shining eyes and flushed face indicated that the drink probably wasn't his first.

When she came up to the others, Jerry waved his glass in a gesture of welcome and said, "Honey, meet Carlo Brentanto.

Carlo, this is Lee Garrett, Sheila's new secretary. A knockout, which you wouldn't recognize, though Sheila does."

Sheila, who had a brandy glass in hand, murmured throatily, "You look stunning in that gown, darling."

Carlo Brentanto said, in almost a lisp, *"Incantato,"* and bowed over Lee's hand gallantly.

Jerry said, "Carlo's been explaining that the gays should inherit the Earth."

"Certainly, they should have a greater say in its governing," the Italian told him coolly. "After all, my dears, they have been outstanding throughout history. It is ridiculous that there isn't a single homosexual in the Central Committee."

Jerry took a pull at his drink and said, "Well, we have our imposing Sheila."

Sheila snorted.

"Over and over, the homosexual has proven himself down through history," Carlo argued, after daintily sipping. "Can you think of anyone more outstanding in the military and in government than Alexander the Great, Caesar, Frederick the Great, and many more prominent than Plato? Man has reached his heights when the homosexual was most widely understood—The Golden Age of Athens; the Renaissance here in Italy."

"Tolerated, but not exactly in power," Jerry said. "Off hand, the only governments I can think of that were ruled by the gays were Sodom and Gomorrah—and they came to a fiery end."

"I've always wondered what it was they did in Gomorrah," Lee murmured.

"You name it, they did it," said Jerry.

Sheila gave her curt little laugh and said, "I'm gratified to see you have a sense of humor, darling."

The Italian fluttered the hand bearing his handkerchief and said, "Oh, all of you are quite hopeless. I think I shall go over and join the admiral."

"I have no doubt you'll try," Sheila purred.

He left and the three of them looked after him for a moment.

Jerry said, "How in the hell did he ever get into the candidate class?"

"Actually, he's quite brilliant and the Brentantos are the wealthiest family in Italy," Sheila told him. "What was it you wanted to talk to me about, Jerry, before he interrupted us?''

He finished his drink and said, "Oh, yes. When I asked you yesterday what had happened to Pamela McGivern you said that I'd undoubtedly hear later. I haven't. In fact, I've asked a couple of the Committee and none of them seem to know, though Chase managed to mutter that it was good riddance. I don't believe that our Pamela was capable of hiding what she thought about his racist leanings."

Sheila said, "She was becoming quite impossible. It's one thing my being somewhat of a minister without portfolio in the Central Committee, but, after all, she was only my secretary, and there was no reason for their putting up with her opinions."

Jerry cocked his eye at her. "Minister without portfolio, eh? I didn't know that was how you regarded yourself, Sheila. I thought you were more like a Man Friday. You're sure that you're not beginning to take on responsibilities beyond those the Committee had in mind?"

Sheila's silent irritation was only partially concealed.

He said, "Now, what happened to Pamela? I, for one, liked the girl, and so did Fong Hui, among others."

"I dismissed her, giving her a bonus of fifty thousand psuedo-dollars."

"Without consulting anyone, eh?"

"I didn't think it necessary. After all, she was *my* secretary. I originally employed her on my own, without consulting anyone."

"What happened to her? Where is she now?"

Sheila frowned slightly. "I wouldn't know. Perhaps she returned to Ireland."

"Perhaps," he said. He looked at Lee. "Neither of us has a drink. Should we go on over to the bar and remedy that situation?"

"Thank you," Lee said, and turned her eyes questioningly to her superior.

Sheila did her bleak smile and said, "Run along, dear, and do meet as many of those present as you can. You'll be working with all of them later."

Jerry took Lee by the arm and led her to one of the bars

which had been set up in the ballroom, immediately across from the buffet tables. For the moment, it was unoccupied.

He dropped the curt air he had assumed with Sheila Duff-Roberts and said, "What will it be—champagne? One of the candidates has his own vineyard near Rheims. He provides us with the best vintages."

"That will be fine, Mr. Auburn."

"Jerry," he told her. "I'll stick to cognac."

There was a long row of ice buckets, each with a bottle of sparkling wine. He selected one which had already been opened, took up a clean glass and poured for her, then took up a half-empty bottle of impressive-looking brandy and renewed his own glass with a generous charge. She had been right. Save for two ice cubes, he was drinking his spirits straight. Lee winced at the idea of putting ice in good cognac.

She said, "Cheers," and sipped at her wine. It was certainly as good as any she had ever tasted.

A small, thin, slightly hawk-nosed, dignified elderly man came up and poured himself a glass of sherry. He nodded at Jerry and looked questioningly at Lee.

Jerry said, "Mendel, this is Lee Garrett, Sheila's new secretary. She's a bit bewildered, undoubtedly because she didn't know the Central Committee was composed of such far-out folk. Lee, this is Mendel Amschel, a Committee member and once my father's closest friend."

"I'm charmed, my dear," the newcomer said, taking her hand. "I don't know why, but one never expects surpassing beauty in a girl who must also be surpassingly intelligent and competent."

"Why, you old goat," Jerry protested. "I saw her first."

Lee was fully aware of the identity of Mendel Amschel, reputedly the head of the richest bank in Common Europe, although his name seldom appeared in the news.

"You flatter me, Jerry," the older man said, smiling gently at the girl. "However, if I were twenty years younger . . ."

"You'd still be sixty," Jerry said. "You dreamer."

"Gentlemen, gentlemen," Lee protested. "Isn't the Code Duello still legal in Italy? If you must fight over me . . ."

"Right," Jerry said. "The *bois* at dawn. I'll get Peter Windsor to second for me. I see him over there, talking to the Archbishop. Competent man in a fight, I understand, but don't turn your back on him. You might get a knife in it, even though you thought he was on your side.''

The banker raised his eyebrows at the younger man. ''I suspect when it comes to a vote to replace our Grace Cabot-Hudson, you are not likely to opt for the Graf.''

Jerry said testily, ''I doubt if the original founders of the World Club ever expected professional killers to be represented in the Central Committee.''

''I discussed it with Harrington,'' the other said. ''He pointed out that most of the former mercenary activities of Lothar von Brandenburg are now becoming phased out, but that there will always be a need for espionage and, ah, strong men even in a World State.''

Jerry dismissed that opinion. ''It's true mercenaries are on the wane, Wizard. But the Graf is expanding into other lines. Personal assassination hasn't been so prevalent since the days of the Borgias. He's simply computerized it.''

The Viennese banker scowled at him questioningly. ''Isn't that largely a matter of gossip and rumor? Every homicide in the world is being laid at the door of the mysterious Graf.''

''Yes.'' Jerry looked thoughtful. ''And that reminds me. I wanted to see Peter Windsor and ask about the death of Harold Dunninger. He's the one I would have voted for to take over Grace's seat on the Committee, rather than either the Prophet or the Graf.''

''So would I have, my boy,'' Amschel said. ''But the Nihilists, who seem daily to become more bold, got through his defenses.''

''I wonder,'' Jerry said. ''At any rate, I want to talk with Windsor. You two get to know each other; see you later.''

When the younger man had gone, Amschel sighed and said, ''Our Jerry Auburn is considerably different than I remember his father.'' He smiled slightly. ''Perhaps it is the generation gap, after all. I was Fredric Auburn's contemporary. Jerry seems a bit precipitous. I wince at his confrontation with the Graf's representative.'' He turned his eyes from the retreating Jerry and brought them back to Lee. ''I imagine everyone is asking you what you think of the World Club.''

''Well, yes,'' she told him carefully. ''My first reaction is that the Central Committee's plans seem to be somewhat premature, though I support them. Is the world ready for a universal government?"

"Ready or not," he said with a touch of resignation in his voice, "it is the only answer. Today, the world is on the precipice of disaster. What is the old Britishism? The chickens have come home to roost. The slowly developing problems of the past three centuries have now reached a head."

Lee demurred. "Oh, come now, the world is comparatively dormant at present. There are no real immediate crises. We haven't known a major war within the lives of anyone now living."

He shook a thin finger at her. "My dear, it is astonishing how quickly matters can develop when conditions are ripe. Consider the spring of 1914 when everything seemed stable. The Kaiser was securely on his throne, Franz Joseph of the Austro-Hungarian Empire on his, the Sultan ruled the powerful Ottoman Empire, and the Czar of all the Russias had recently celebrated the 300th anniversary of Romanoff rule. Five years later, there was no major monarchy in Europe save England, and capitalism itself had collapsed in Russia, the largest nation of the world. No, my dear, comparatively overnight, world institutions can radically alter, given the right, or perhaps I should say the wrong, conditions."

She took a full lower lip between perfect white teeth. Then, "And you think such conditions exist today?"

"Yes." He looked about. "Come, my dear, let us find a place to sit down. My friend Fong Hui tells me you are an interesting young woman. Frankly, I was sorry to see Pamela McGivern leave, but if it was necessary at least we seem to have found a competent replacement. Would you like me to fill your glass?"

"No," she said. "No, I have plenty." She followed him to a fifteenth-century couch set against one of the large chamber's walls. When they were seated she said, "And what do you foresee in the nature of this new World State? What kind of government will it be? I get the impression that there is considerable difference on this among Central Committee members."

He conceded the validity of that. "Yes, there is. Some of us wish to continue the type of democracy that now prevails in the United States of the Americas."

She sipped again at her wine, frowning slightly. "You advocate a two-party democracy with both of the parties controlled by a power elite?"

He smiled his little dry smile again. "Yes. I am a product of my class and my age. My class owns the so-called Western world. I believe that they should govern it. Benevolently, of course, and maintaining all the liberties that man has achieved. Perhaps half of the Central Committee and even more of the candidate members concur."

"And the ordinary citizens, including the proles: they are still to have the vote?"

"Yes, of course, my dear. Why not? It keeps them happy to think that they have the ultimate say. Every four years we put up two candidates and let them take their pick. What could be more democratic than that? You must realize that even at the height of the Empire, the Roman proletariat had the vote. They usually sold it to the highest bidder, of course, but they had it. The proles, my dear, we shall always have with us. They are the masses who labor at the undesirable jobs when labor is needed, or fight as common soldiers in times of war. They are the nonentities. The world has passed them by. A typical example is the peons of Latin America, now assimilated into the United States of the Americas. Uneducated, untrained, they were pushed from a burro society into one of electronic computers. They won't adjust, nor will their children. Like the Roman proletariat, they must simply be fed and otherwise taken care of by the state, as cheaply and efficiently as possible, and forgotten about."

"But there are exceptions among them. There surely are many exceptions."

"Of course, and they must be found and encouraged. Thomas Edison was born in poverty and had only about three years of grammar school. But he was a genius. Andrew Carnegie came to America as an immigrant and fought his way upward into the highest ranks of the powerful. Oh yes, there are many exceptions. The ancestor of Harrington Chase who founded the Chase fortune was an oilfield worker in Texas."

Lee shook her head and put her empty glass down on a small table beside the couch. "I had always thought the

World Club to be composed largely of economists whose research was supported by wealthy philanthropists."

The international banker was obviously amused. "Don't exaggerate the contributions of economists, my dear. They are highly overrated compared to us, the pragmatic. If there was ever a group to which the question, 'If you're so smart, why aren't you rich?' applies, it is the economists. Economics aren't as complicated as all that but the economists mythologize the subject. There are exceptions, but most of them go through life as second-raters—teaching, writing books that few read and even fewer understand, or selling their services to governments or the powerful. They make their way with gobbledy-gook terminology, but practically never do they get rich. Even a five-percent advantage on knowing what way the stock market was going to go would make them wealthy, but they simply don't know. Karl Marx himself, that analyzer of the capitalist system, lived and died in poverty. Did you ever hear of a Rockefeller, a Dupont, a Getty, or any other founder of the great American fortunes, who was an economist?"

Lee's smile was inverted. "I am afraid that you are making a cynic of me, Mr. Amschel."

The smile he returned was thin. "I hope not, my dear. You are far too charming to succumb to cynicism. However, take as an example the monetary crisis of the last century. Every economist in the world was working on the problem of the collapse of international money. There was not enough gold or any other precious metal in the world to back the needed mediums of exchange. All nations, particularly your United States, simply began printing paper money, which had no value since it represented nothing. Inflation was rampant. Inflation, of course, is not a matter of prices going up, but of the value of money going down. The United States, with a two trillion dollar a year economy, faced disaster because it had issued perhaps four hundred billion dollars' worth of paper without backing. Did the economists solve the problem? No. It was solved by an obscure speculative writer."

"I didn't know that!"

"Oh, yes. He proposed that the government, in taxing the two hundred top corporations of the United States, take ten percent of the taxes in the form of their common stock. This was amalgamated into what was called United States Basic

Common, a sort of gigantic mutual fund. Its shares, of course, paid dividends based on the combined dividends of the corporations. The stock was placed on every stock exchange of the world to seek its level. Each year, the government added its new common stock, taken in the form of taxes, to its U. S. Basic Common. Anyone who had dollars could turn them in for Basic Common. In short, the money of the United States, now called pseudo-dollars since there was no gold behind them, was now backed by the American economy.'' The banker made a little snort. ''It wasn't long before all other developed nations followed the lead. The world now has valid currencies.''

Halfway across the room, Jerry Auburn was interrupted on his way to seeing Peter Windsor.

Harrington Chase, his inevitable glass of bourbon and branch water in hand, waved him down. The American tycoon was a stereotype of the cattleman or oil entrepreneur who had flourished in the old Southwest. He differed little if at all from his progenitors. A Henry Ford or a Joe Kennedy might have come from rough-and-ready, tough-and-tight-eyed schools, but in two generations their descendants were attending Ivy League universities and had become ladies and gentlemen who conducted themselves as aristocrats—America's new nobility. But not the Chases! Harrington Chase's fief was a ranch enveloping two large counties overlapping in Texas and Oklahoma, larger than the areas of several northeastern states. Big and ruddy of face, his bulk no longer called for his riding his famed Palominos, but he usually still affected riding boots. And a king-sized cigar, even when police were in the vicinity, was always in his mouth. He also, Jerry knew, invariably ordered steak and potatoes, in the most celebrated restaurants, with apple pie and ice cream for dessert.

With Chase, as usual at a Central Committee session, was his closest associate, John Warfield Moyer, for some twenty years Director of the IABI. A square-cut man in his late fifties, Moyer, with his bulldog face, shaggy brows, and cold, accusing eyes, looked every inch what he was: a high-ranking police officer. In his case, the highest ranking in the world.

Chase said, with an overriding joviality, "Hold on, Jerry, old-timer."

Jerry Auburn came to a halt, albeit reluctantly. "Something up, Harry?" He knew perfectly well the other hated that name. He nodded at Moyer. "Hi, Fuzzy," he said, inwardly pleased at the director's wince.

Harrington Chase hefted his glass up and down a couple of times pontifically. "We've been mulling over the replacement of Grace Cabot-Hudson, now that she's let it be known she's resigning."

Jerry said, "I had been inclined to Dunninger . . . until somebody got to him."

"Never cottoned much to Harold myself," Chase said pompously. "Kind of a goddamned liberal. Show me a liberal and I'll show you a man on the verge of a coyote Euro-communist. But at least he was a white American, just like us three."

Moyer looked at Jerry: a policeman's look. "What do you mean, somebody got to him? Those Nihilist subversives shot him when his people wouldn't pay the ransom. His wife must have thought they were bluffing."

"So they say," Jerry nodded. "Which leaves the field more or less left to Ezra Hawkins and Lothar von Brandenburg, two of the most unlikely candidates for a seat in the Central Committee I could imagine."

Harrington Chase puffed out his cheeks. "At least the Prophet is a God-fearing Christian, a white man, and an American. We Americans ought to stick together. We wouldn't want to see a slant-eye like Iyeyasu Suzuki, or a nigger like Sri Saraswate, on the Committee."

Jerry took him in. "It's never been proven that the Prohpet can read or write. Supposedly, the top echelons of the World Club are composed of highly intelligent, well-educated men and women, not superstition-spouting demagogues."

"Look, boy, us Americans have a manifest destiny to run this world. It's in the cards. But unless we hold the cards, we'll wind up with the wogs taking the pot."

The younger man regarded him, doing little to disguise his contempt. "Harry," he said, "do you realize that half the United States population is below average in intelligence?"

The billionaire's eyes all but popped in indignation. "That's a damn lie!" he rumbled.

Jerry shook his head in pretended despair. "Your American chauvinism does you little credit, Harry. Of course, half of *every* population is below average, and the other half above average. What do you think average means?"

The oilman sputtered, then took a heavy slug of his bourbon.

Moyer said, obviously getting it before his colleague did, "What's that got to do with the Prophet being elevated to the Central Committee, Auburn? It seems to me that having a man of God in our number makes good sense. The fact that the majority of us are among the world's wealthiest rubs some people the wrong way, especially the liberal intellectuals. The Prophet heads the biggest church in the world, and every day it gets larger."

Jerry turned his gaze to the IABI head. "And did it ever occur to you, as a fuzzy, that the number of crimes in a city each year is proportional to the number of churches there?"

The other stared at him. "You must be around the corner, Auburn. The more churches, the less crime."

Jerry shook his head in sorrow. "On the face of it, fuzzy, the larger the town is, the more churches there are. And the larger a town is, the more crime there is."

Harrington Chase said angrily, "You're getting away from the point, Jerry. The point is, we don't want any more kikes like Meyer Amschel in the Central Committee, and no more chinks like Fong Hui."

Jerry said, "We'll see about that when it comes to the vote, Harry. In my opinion, Amschel and Fong may be on the oldish side, and overly conservative, but they're two of the best we've got. And now, excuse me; I want to have a few words with Windsor. Has it ever occurred to either of you that the Graf is so afraid of leaving that castle fortress of his that he always sends a deputy to represent him? What kind of a Committee member would he make if he never bothered to attend sessions?"

Before the arrival of Jerry Auburn, Archbishop Willy Beck and Peter Windsor had been hitting it off jolly well, as the Englishman might have put it. The Graf's right-hand man, now in impeccable evening wear, was a far cry from the languid, easygoing young man of the Wolfschloss. Now, in

the view of his peers, he presented himself as the British
aristocrat—straight of posture, clipped of voice. His companion was dressed in black and wore the reversed collar of
clerical tradition. They were approximately the same age,
approximately the same height, but there the resemblance
ended, save for goals. Willy Beck, a lifelong evangelist who
had first taken the stump at revival meetings in the American
Bible Belt at the age of fourteen, had the sanctimonious face
of his trade—long, expressionless, save for a sadness which
tugged at the heartstrings of his feminine followers. Indeed,
his face had been compared to that of Lincoln before the
beard. His voice was soft, with a depth of sorrow similar to
that of an undertaker. His railings against the evils of drink
and tobacco were his trademark, which would undoubtedly
have led the faithful to goggle at the Manila cigar he now
held in one hand and the glass of that most delicate though
strong of spirits, Hungarian barack, in the other.

The Archbishop was saying, "Yes, you are quite correct.
The Prophet foresees, once the World State has come to
power, the reestablishment of the Holy Office, the Inquisition—
under a more inspiring name, of course. Heretics must be
rooted out. At this point it is quite impossible, but once the
United Church has become the State Church of the World
Government, matters will be different. Since the days of
Socrates the organized religions have found that to be the
ultimate truth. But now, at this point, we must rely on other
means to confound our Godless opponents, and that is why
the Prophet sees the need for greater cooperation between our
two organizations."

Peter Windsor said, sipping at his Scotch, "You put it
most interestingly, Your Excellency. In what manner do you
think the United Church could be of use to us?"

"In most of the present-day branches of the United Church,
my son, we follow the rite of confession. Perhaps a judicious
leader might be reluctant to reveal his secrets, but often the
same restraint does not apply to his more devout wife. It is
astonishing, the information that is revealed in the confes-
sional booth, especially if encouraged by a trained confessor—
information that would be priceless to an organization involved
in espionage."

"Bloody marvelous," Peter Windsor said, lost in admiration of the possibilities. "And in return?"

The Archbishop's face was sad. "Alas, my son, in this sin-ridden world the true faith often has what would seem insurmountable obstacles raised by the followers of the Adversary. Such enemies of the United Church would feel the wrath of the heavens. Who knows what might befall a strong official of some false faith who exhorts his fellows to refrain from cooperation with our Holy cause . . ."

"Chaps such as the Mahdi, I wouldn't wonder," Peter said.

"Indeed. Our sainted leader, Ezra Hawkins, spent long hours in prayer before coming to the reluctant decision to remove this limb of Satan from the scene, so that his deluded followers might at long last see the true path to salvation."

"Long hours in prayer?" Peter said musingly. "I say, do you chaps really find time for that sort of drill?"

Willy Beck sighed. "Peter, sometimes I am inclined to think that Ezra takes himself a bit too literally in his role of Prophet. It does not do for a religious man, or a politician, to believe too much in his own propaganda. The more one knows his religion the less he believes, if he is a pragmatic man."

Peter accepted that, pursing his lips. "However, the Prophet is, shall we say, no longer young. And history tells us that it is often a devoted follower of a great prophet who finally witnesses the flowering of the new religion. It was not Jesus who founded Christianity as we know it, but Paul. And Mohammed never saw Islam spread beyond Arabia. It was the second-generation Moslems who conquered half the known world."

"A point well taken, my son. And who can tell what the good Lord has planned for the future. But tell me, how is the health of the Graf these days?"

The Englishman shook his head regretfully. "I am afraid that Lothar is aging rather rapidly, don't you know? Sometimes he seems to make rather ill-considered decisions."

Archbishop Beck shook his head, also in sorrow. "Not long for this world, then. However, undoubtedly, when he goes to his reward there will be more youthful hands to take the reins of his worthy organization."

Peter Windsor fixed his green eyes on the other man's face for a long calculating moment before he said, "Perhaps we should talk this over in more detail in the near future. I suspect that matters are coming to a head faster than some of us realize."

It was then that Jerry Auburn came up, recently refilled glass in hand, dark blue eyes with a faint glaze. He said, not quite slurring, "Hi, Peter. Done in any poor cloddies of recent date? Hi, Willy, saved any good souls lately?"

"All souls are good, my son," the Archbishop said unctuously.

"You ought to know; you must get a wide variety of them. The United Church will take anything into its ranks, down to and including animists."

The Archbishop was sadly forgiving. He said softly, "In my Father's house there are many mansions. We are all one in the loving eyes of God, be he called Jehovah, Allah, Brahma, Maya, or The Great Spirit."

Jerry said, taking another healthy pull at his drink, "Or Artemis and Pan, for the sake of the various witch cults. You'll adapt to anything to suck another faith into the United Church. If the Aztec religion was still in existence, you'd allow them to cut out the hearts of a few thousand victims each year. If the Canaanites were still with us, they could throw their firstborn into the flaming bronze maw of Ba'al."

"Surely, my son, this is not a subject upon which to jest." There was sorrow in the voice of the Prophet's right-hand man, but his eyes were narrow and cold.

"I wasn't kidding," Jerry said. "The archives don't record what long-dead con man first dreamed up religion and put nine-tenths of the human race on the sucker list, but he must have been a genius."

The Archbishop said, his long face expressionless, "I am neglecting my duties as the representative of a candidate member of the Central Committee. I must pay my respects to Harrington Chase. His devotion to the United Church is well known; only last week he contributed a million pseudo-dollars. If you'll forgive me."

When he was gone, Jerry said to Peter Windsor, "I hate to see you two getting together."

Peter said, "Oh, Willy's all right. I assume that most of us in the World Club are either agnostics or atheists, but we'll always have religion with us, and I'd rather see the United Church on our side than have it oppose us.''

"Sometimes I wonder what our side is," Jerry said. He fixed his eyes on the tall Britisher. "Have you heard about the attack on me yesterday?"

The other looked worried. "Yes, I did, Jerry. Jolly good that you were able to thwart the beggar."

"Yeah, wasn't it? What I've been wondering about was who fingered me."

"What do you mean, dear boy?"

"I mean that it seems unlikely that cloddy went to all the trouble to get a job at the *Hostaria dell'Orso* just to take a crack at the first wealthy customer to come along. If he had, he would have polished someone else off long before I arrived on the scene. It's the most expensive restaurant in town and there's a fistful of millionaires and top politicians there every day. No, he was waiting for me. Somebody had tipped the Nihilists off that it was my favorite eating spot. I'd just got in to Rome the same day. And he was waiting."

Peter looked distressed. "What's your point, old chap?"

"All of a sudden, the Nihilists seem to be taking an extraordinary interest in members and candidate members of the Central Committee. It was only a few days ago that Harry Dunninger was knocked off by them, back in the States. If he hadn't been, sure as hell the Central Committee would have nominated him to full membership. With him eliminated, it looks as though either the Graf or the Prophet has a much better chance. If I'd been knocked off, both of them would have the chance."

"I don't follow you."

"I think you'd better try." Jerry Auburn's eyes had lost their alcohol sheen and were now very level.

The Englishman shook his head. "Really, old boy, I don't know what you're talking about."

"Your people had the contract to guard Dunninger. When the Nihilists raided his estate, four of the guards had been pulled off, weakening resistance so that overwhelming the defense was a cinch. Now, what I want to know is what contracts you people have with the Neo-Nihilists."

Peter Windsor flushed in indignation. He said strongly, "Really, Auburn, your suggestion is inadmissible."

Jerry's voice was winter cold. "I'm asking you if you have contacts with the Nihilists. If you tell me no, and through my people I later find out that you have, your organization is mud in the World Club, chum-pal. Remember that I'm a member of the Central Committee. All by myself I can blackball the Graf from ever becoming a full member. I think I could throw enough weight to have him tossed out of the World Club entirely. And that would hardly fit in with your plans, would it, Windsor?"

"Now, see here, Jerry," Peter Windsor said hurriedly. "You're getting off onto the wrong foot. Of course, the Graf has infiltrated the Nihilists, along with all other subversive organizations. A great deal of our work is espionage. We infiltrate everywhere, especially into organizations having any sort of political connotations."

"So, who's your head mole in the Nihilists?"

The other stared at him. "We haven't one. We have several plants among them but they're not of enough importance for us to go to any great extent to infiltrate them. It's just a matter of keeping the sods under observation. Had we gotten news that poor Harold Dunninger was to be kidnapped, we would have immediately informed him. The Graf, after all, is a loyal candidate member of the Central Committee."

Jerry Auburn took him in for a long, cold moment. "We'll see about that," he said. He finished his drink with the stiff-wristed motion of the practiced drinker, turned on his heel, and headed for the bar, leaving the Englishman staring after him, boiling anger in his pale killer eyes.

Lee Garrett gave up at about one o'clock in the morning. She had done her best to make acquaintances, as ordered by Shelia Duff-Roberts, and had met perhaps a dozen of the members and candidates. She had spent the last half hour in the company of Nils Norden. From what she had gathered, the Scandinavian tycoon was on the fence so far as the divisions within the organization were concerned. If Chase and his colleagues were the right wing of the Committee, and Jerry Auburn was on the left wing, then Nils Norden must be thought of as the center. Not that she'd discussed the World

Club with him to any extent. Largely, he seemed interested in conducting her back to her suite—and to bed.

By this time, she had learned the layout of this part of the Palazzo well enough that she had no trouble finding her way to her quarters. She sighed her weariness, kicked off her shoes, picked them up, and headed for the suite's interior, her bedroom in mind. To get to it, she had to pass through the living room. She was surprised to find the lights were on.

Then she spotted Jerry Auburn sprawled on the fifteenth-century couch, his feet, shoes and all, up on one arm of the priceless antique. His inevitable glass was on a low table, within easy reach. He looked up at her.

"What is the meaning of this, Mr. Auburn?"

"Jerry," he said. "If we're to become lovers we must forget formalities."

"Lovers!" She dropped her shoes onto the floor and slipped her feet into them. "If you came here to . . ."

He held up a weary hand. "Please. No indignation. I never rape girls. I've never had to. In fact, sometimes they rape me."

She snorted and ran her eyes over his sturdy athlete's body. "It'd take quite a mopsy to rape you, my friend."

"I rape easily—a flaw in my character," he explained, swinging his feet around and to the floor. "Sit down, Lee. I have something to ask you."

"I'm tired," she said. "I want to go to bed." But she sat, taking one of the antique chairs, which was more comfortable than it looked. It would have to be.

"So do I," he told her earnestly. "But we'll get to do that later." He pointed at the phone, the one she knew was bugged. Her eyes widened when she saw, sitting next to it, a muffler similar to the one she had utilized.

"Nobody's listening in," he said, reaching over and picking up his glass.

"I don't know what you're talking about," she got out.

He took back some of his drink. "You know, everybody's been telling me that this evening," he told her. "Peter Windsor, for instance. However, you're reporting to someone. Whom? Don't bother to deny it, honey. We often monitor the quarters of new employees, on the off chance that they're an attempt to infiltrate the World Club. You'd be surprised how many elements would like to know its inner workings. By chance, the monitor in this case is an old family friend, indebted to my late father. He reports to me first—and sometimes I'm the only one he reports to. At any rate, honey, he tells me that your bug was muffled for a time. Obviously he couldn't tell me whom you called, nor what you said, but he was aware of the muffler. So what is a nice girl like you doing with a sophisticated piece of electronic equipment and who were you calling, to report what?''

She glared at him angrily, even while her mind raced. "My mother!'' she got out finally.

He closed his eyes in pain and pushed his left hand over his mouth. "Oh, *come on* now, honey.''

She said challengingly, "My mother is Rosamond Brice.''

He cocked an eye at her. "I know Rosamond Brice. Or did. She doesn't look old enough to be your mother. And, what's more, she doesn't act like a mother. She's been in more beds than I've been in automobiles. And when she comes to town the local distilleries put on an extra shift.''

Lee went to the bar and poured herself a drink from the first bottle that came to hand. She took down a quick snort and made a face. Absinthe. She poured some water into it and returned to her chair.

She said defiantly, "My mother and father weren't married, but for a time they evidently had a somewhat hectic love affair. For some reason, she agreed to have a baby. By the time I came, the affair was waning. Mother couldn't bother with me; I interfered with her good times. But father wanted me and raised me. We loved each other very much. After he died, I became friends with Rosamond although we're worlds apart as a rule. When I told her I was to work for the World Club, she told me that they'd probably bug my rooms and gave me a muffler so that we could talk without being overheard. She knew about mufflers because she always uses one. She's afraid of jealous wives, sweethearts, or whoever, listening in on her calls to lovers.''

He looked at her for a long disbelieving moment.

She came to her feet and said, "Oh, hell; come on. I suppose this was inevitable.''

"Come on where?'' he said.

"To the bedroom. I'm going to rape you a little.''

Chapter Nineteen:
Roy Cos

Roy dreaded getting up, but that feeling of dread was now a daily occurrence. He couldn't bring himself to face the coming day. How long had it been now—a couple of weeks? More than that. At least he was giving the bastards a run for their money. One of the newsmen had told them that Oliver Brett-James, in Nassau, had been fired by the outfit issuing the Deathwish Policy Roy had signed up for. Evidently, the cosmo-corp's executives blamed the Englishman for not spotting potential trouble in the offbeat Roy Cos and his manager. Long before this, they had begun losing money on the deal. Not only were the premiums eating them up, but the so-called Deathwish Wobbly was spending his million pseudo-dollars per day at an unprecedented rate. How many people did he have on his payroll now? Over twenty, Roy supposed, counting the stenographers down in the offices on the floor below—a payroll of more than two hundred thousand pseudo-dollars a day! If he wasn't feeling so damned depressed, he might have laughed. Imagine Roy Cos spending over a million a week on his staff.

Mary Ann, on the pillow next to him, said, doing her best to keep the anxiety from her voice, "Something wrong, darling?"

He looked over at her. Mousy of face, Mary Ann Elwyn might be, but a mouse of very special attractions. It was the first time in his life that he'd had a deep involvement that went beyond mere sex.

"No, not really," he told her.

She looked at her wrist chronometer. "You're supposed to hear that Tri-Di singer this morning for the United Church broadcast."

"Yeah," he said, staring up at the ceiling. "What was his name again?"

"Stevie Summers. He's the current big thing in nostalgia folk song revivals."

Roy sighed and said, "How's Forry getting along with the hotel manager?"

She laughed shortly. "He's reversed the flow of crap, you might say. The first few days, guests were moving out wholesale when it was learned that the Deathwish Wobbly was staying here. Evidently, they expected the whole New Tropical Hotel to be bombed flat or something. But that didn't last. Thrill seekers zeroed in wholesale. One of Ron's friends who works in the lobby says the manager is turning down bribes that run up to a thousand pseudo-dollars for reservations. Same old story—thousands of silly dizzards would give their right arms to be on hand when the Graf's men get to you. I mean if," she added contritely. "Sorry."

He ran a weary hand back through his shaggy, faded brown hair. "Nothing to be sorry about," he told her. He dug around for something else to postpone getting out of bed. "How'd that girl check out?"

"The one who got in with the reporters yesterday? She's evidently what she said she was, a celebrity hound. She wanted to see you in person, wanted to try to get your autograph. The guards shook her down just like everybody else and she had nothing remotely resembling a weapon, so they let her through. Supposedly, she was a reporter."

"If she could get past all of our security, so could somebody else," he said bitterly.

"We'd better go and check out this Stevie Summers, darling."

"All right." He swung his legs out over the side of the bed. Ignoring his bedroom slippers, he went over to the chair where he had thrown his clothes the night before and began to dress. Mary Ann got up too and went to the closet. The prole clothes she brought forth were as similar to his own as possible.

She looked over at him. Roy Cos had lost the extra ten pounds or so of weight and now looked drawn rather than pasty of face. The sunbaths on the roof, which Forry Brown had insisted upon, had wiped away the pallor. It came to her that Roy must have been quite good-looking as a young man. Twenty-five years of inadequate diet and exercise hadn't done him any good, nor had the long hours of sitting around small, drab rooms arguing political economy, night after night.

Forry Brown and Ferd Feldmeyer were in the living room with three of the guards who bore short, stocky Gyrojet automatic carbines. Dick Samuelson, in particular, carried his with a practiced ease. It had turned out, when the weapons were first procured, that Dick had spent a hitch in the Skyborne Commandos, and he'd taken over the duty of instructing his less knowledgeable Wobbly colleagues in their use.

Also present was a rather vague-looking young man, somewhere in his early twenties. He bore a guitar and was looking both impatient and bored. His fans might have swooned over him, Roy decided, but he looked like nothing more than a gangly kid.

Forry, dressed identically to Roy, and looking somewhat ludicrous in prole attire, squinted through tobacco smoke at his employer. He said, "This is Stevie Summers. I promised him five thousand to sing one song as a preliminary to you roasting the Prophet."

"It ain't the money," the singer said. "I hate that sapsucker."

Roy nodded, went over to his desk, and took up a little red pamphlet, thumbed through it to the page he sought, found it, and handed it to the boy.

"This is a book of old IWW songs," he said. "This is the one I wanted you to sing. It was written by one of the early Wobblies, Joe Hill, who was executed in Utah for a crime he didn't commit because he was a radical. You sing it to the tune for the old hymn, *In the Sweet Bye and Bye.*"

"Gotcha," the boy said. He looked over the lyrics for a moment, then began to strum and sing. To Roy's surprise, the singer's voice, though soft, grasped with appeal.

> *Long-haired preachers come out every night,*
> *Try to tell you what's wrong and what's right;*
> *But when asked how 'bout something to eat*
> *They will answer with voices so sweet:*
> *You will eat, bye and bye,*
> *In that glorious land above the sky;*

Work and pray, live on hay,
You'll get pie in the sky when you die.
And the starvation army they play,
And they sing and they clap and they pray,
Till they get all your coin on the drum,
Then they tell you when you're on the bum:
You will eat, bye and bye,
In that glorious land above the sky;
Work and pray, live on hay,
You'll get pie in the sky when you die.
Workingmen of all countries unite,
Side by side we for freedom will fight;
When the world and its wealth we have gained
To the grafters we'll sing this refrain:
You will eat, bye and bye,
When you've learned how to cook and to fry
Chop some wood, 'twill do you good,
And you'll eat in the sweet bye and bye.

The boy ended with a bang on the strings, looked up and grinned. "After that, the Prophet'll want to crucify you."

"That's the idea," Roy said. "He's lined up with the other side. We want to make that clear." He looked at the folk singer. "That old radical song is kind of primitive as propaganda goes but it won't put you on anybody's shitlist, will it? The Prophet throws a lot of weight. With me, it doesn't make any difference. He'll have to stand in line if he wants to take a crack at me."

Stevie Summers shook his head, "The kids I sing for don't go for this holy-roller fling. So far as we're concerned, he can bugger himself with a wood auger. By the way, my old man's a Libertarian. I've heard a couple of your bleats on Tri-Di. Your two organizations oughta get together."

"There's been some talk about it," Roy nodded.

Forry said, "We better get ready for that press interview." He took young Summers by the arm and led him to the door, going over details about the broadcast.

Roy sat down at his desk and looked unhappily at the pile of mail before him. He thumbed quickly through it. There was nothing from anyone he knew. All strangers.

He said to Mary Ann, "You want to go through this and

spread it around to the girls for the standard answers? By the way, how come I haven't met any of the stenographers?''

Mary Ann came over from her own desk, carrying a letter. She said, ''Forry doesn't want them on this floor. Two of them are Wobblies, but the others are outsiders. For all we know, the Graf might be able to get next to one of them. It's just as easy for a woman to take a crack at you as a man.''

Roy shook his head but said, ''I guess you're right. What's that?''

She put the letter down before him. ''It's from Wobbly headquarters in Chicago.''

Billy Tucker, who was also dressed identically to Roy Cos, said, ''Oh, oh. I was beginning to wonder when we'd get a kick from the Agitation Committee. Some of those speeches Ferd has been writing for you aren't exactly the standard message the Wobblies have been making for the last century or so.''

Roy ripped open the envelope and quickly scanned the letter.

''I'll be damned,'' he said. ''I've been promoted from national organizer to a member of the Agitation Committee.'' He looked up at Mary Ann. ''That's our executive committee, headed by the national secretary. He wants me to attend a meeting being organized by Synthesis.''

''What in the hell's Synthesis?'' Dick Samuelson said. He was lounging against the wall, next to the door to the corridor, his carbine under his right arm.

Roy grunted and said, ''A new outfit that's trying to get all the radicals together. The whole shebang: Libertarians, Nihilists, Wobblies, the Anti-Racist League—everybody but those Eurocommunist slobs.''

The door buzzed. Samuelson readied his gun and checked the identity screen. It was Forry Brown.

The newsman came in followed by Ferd Feldmeyer, who was carrying a sheaf of papers. The speechwriter, like all the others of the team, was in prole dress identical to that worn by Roy. It had been one of Forry's ideas. The whole team dressed exactly alike. As they invariably moved in a tight group whenever they were in public, a hit man, at any distance at all, would have his work cut out telling which one was Roy. Roy had protested, particularly in the case of Mary

Ann, but she had overruled him. As with the grossly fat Ferd and the king-sized Billy Tucker, there was small chance that even a myopic assassin would confuse her with his target, but the whole crew of them being dressed alike wouldn't help him any.

Forry, noticing the letter in Roy's hand, said, "What spins?"

"I've been made a member of the Agitation Committee. They want me to attend a special meeting that's being held in an attempt to amalgamate all radical groups."

"That's out. No more public appearances," Forry told him sourly. "From now on, I've made arrangements for your broadcasts to be made from right here. The fuzzies stationed at your last rally picked up two armed men before they even got near enough to you for our boys to be needed. Next meeting, there'd be more than two, and it's just a matter of time before one or more of them gets within firing range. From now on, you don't leave the New Tropical Hotel. You don't even leave this floor."

Roy said, "I'll have to attend that Synthesis meeting, if the national secretary wants me to."

"Screw the national secretary. Let him represent the Wobblies. He's expendable; you're not. You're the Deathwish Wobbly and you've put your message over more widely than all the rest of your outfit put together since it was first started."

Roy shook his head, feeling tired all over again. "I appreciate what you're trying to do, Forry, but I'm a member of an organization, not just a one-man agitator. I take orders from our elected officials just like Billy and Dick here do."

The little newsman shrugged angrily but gave up and fished a cigarette pack from a jumper pocket.

Ferd Feldmeyer tossed his sheaf of papers on the desk before his employer "Here's the United Church broadcast. I played it the way you said, stressing the fact that the Wobblies have nothing against religion per se since a man's relationship with his God is his personal business. But when organized religion intrudes on politics, it's no longer a matter of religion. They're as vulnerable as any other political organization."

Roy Cos was quickly scanning the speech. He said, "You used some concrete examples—the Roman Catholic Church, during the Middle Ages in particular, Islam, Shintoism in

Japan, and all other religions that have supported class-divided society down through the ages?''

''Sure, sure,'' Feldmeyer said, running his obscenely obese hand back through thinning blond hair. ''Practically every large church—once it got big—has supportd the status quo. And the Prophet's United Church is no exception.''

Dick, at the door, reported, ''The rest of the boys have finished shaking down the reporters.''

''Okay, let them in,'' Forry said.

There were a score or so of reporters and photographers. They were followed by three more of Roy's Wobbly guards, who stationed themselves alertly about the walls of the room, while the newsmen found places.

Most of the reporters had been here before. Roy's press interviews were daily affairs, as were his sessions with freelancers doing special articles. The senior of the newsmen, a wrinkled veteran, who was moist of eye from prolonged battles with the bottle, said, ''What spins, Roy?''

Roy Cos, seated behind his desk, said, ''I'm still here, Don. What're my odds today?''

''The bookies are giving even-steven that you get it today. Two to one that the Graf's boys get you by tomorrow. Four to one the next day, eight to one by the next,'' Don told him.

Mary Ann winced; her face looked sick.

''Jesus,'' Forry said. ''What're the odds that he lasts the week out?''

Don said, flatly, ''A hundred to one against. The word is out that the Graf's getting uptight about this. He likes to operate on the q.t. Publicity isn't his forte. The insurance companies are probably giving him the prod, too. All this publicity about the Deathwish Policies is giving them a black eye. People all over, not just in the States, are getting indignant. It pretty well shows that anything goes in this profit-oriented world. The multinationals are completely without morals. A man is put in a position where he can't make a real living and then coerced into giving up his life in return for a few days of hedonism. Yeah, the pressure is increasing on the multinational insurance companies, on the Swiss banks, on Lloyd's of London—any outfit that's got a finger in the pie.''

Roy said, his smile working the usual wonder on his stoic face, ''We'll make a Wobbly out of you yet, Don.''

The old reporter looked at some of the photographers and said, "Why don't you guys wait until the interview's over before getting your pix? You just get in the way when we're trying to tape for Tri-Di."

"Elitist," one charged amiably, and sought a chair.

Forry said, "No special releases today, chum-pals. Fire away if you've got any questions for the Deathwish Wobbly."

One of them called out, "Roy, what's your stand on world government? It's in the air these days. You've probably heard that the Congress has invited Australia and New Zealand to join the United States. And it looks as though England and Ireland will get the same invitation."

Roy said, "We Wobblies are in favor of world government but can't see much advantage to it, so far as the proles are concerned, so long as class-divided society is retained. We'd just continue to be in the same undesirable spot, subsisting on GAS. World government under an industrial democracy would be desirable, but under the status quo it would merely give the powers that be better control of us. Instead of having dozens of countries, each with its own special conditions, its own rules and regulations, they'd have all of us under the same thumb."

Another reporter held up a hand and said, "After you've taken over, are you Wobblies going to continue to use the computers to decide who's going to work at what jobs?"

Roy Cos touched the end of his nose and frowned. He said slowly, "What you've got to understand is that Wobblies are advocating an industrial democracy. It'll be up to the people to decide such questions as that. We might come up with *our* ideas on how it should be handled, and then when the new order has taken over, the people might say, screw that, and vote in something else."

The questioner laughed and said, "Well, what is your personal opinion? How would you vote?"

Roy said, "Yes, I'd be in favor of continuing to use the computers to select who should have what job. However, there are some angles. We don't expect to put all of the population back to work at *production*. They're not needed to produce all the products and services necessary for society. That's where we differ from the Luddites. They want to destroy technology so that the whole work force can go back

to production. That's ridiculous. After a million years or so
man has finally solved the problem of producing all the
articles we need. Now we can settle back and enjoy our
longing for leisure. True leisure is not wasted. It's not only an
opportunity to loaf. Man must spend this leisure intelligently,
not sitting before Tri-Di screens sucking on trank pills or
drinking syntho-beer.''

Another reporter called, ''Sure, but you'd be up against the
same trouble we are now. There simply aren't enough jobs to
go around. The computers can't find jobs where there aren't
any.''

Roy said, a bit impatiently, ''What I just said was that we
don't expect to put everybody back to work at production and
services. But such jobs aren't the only kind of employment.
Everybody physically and mentally capable of working, studying, or participating in the arts and sciences can be found a
place. Be you ever so humble, the computers should be able
to find *something* for you to do, the biggest consideration
being that it's what you like to do. If you've got a leaning
toward one of the arts, then they won't have you cleaning up
the environment.''

While Roy continued to field questions, one of the still-
photographers sitting on the sidelines waiting his turn yawned
and said to his neighbor, ''That's an interesting box you've
got there. An old-timer. What is it, a holo or lite?''

''Holo,'' the other said.

The first one yawned again and said, ''I don't believe I've
ever seen you here before. Who are you working for?''

The other ran his tongue over his lower lip. ''International.
The editor sent me over for a few shots for . . .''

The first photographer's face had frozen. His voice was
louder. ''Like *shit* you are! I'm representing International and
I've never seen you before.''

Billy Tucker dropped his gun and lunged across the room,
sent Roy Cos sprawling from his chair and landed atop him
behind the desk, his arms spread, his huge wrestler's body
completely covering the smaller man.

One of the Tri-Di cameramen brought his rig crashing
down on the head of the false photographer, who reeled,
dropping his camera. Ron Ellison came charging up from

where he had stationed himself against a wall, reversed his stubby carbine, and clubbed the man.

Another one of the reporters, in advance of his fellows, stepped in close and drove his fist into the interloper's solar plexus. The others came up, largely getting in each other's way.

"Son of a bitch," one of them snarled.

Don, the veteran, looked at his Tri-Di photographer, who had sacrificed his camera in the initial attack. "You stupid cloddy," he said. "That's ten thousand pseudo-dollars worth of box. How're we going to explain it to the office?"

Forry Brown, rubbing his thin fist over his scraggly mustache while staring down at the fallen man, said absently, "The Deathwish Wobbly will pick up the tab, plus a bonus of five thousand." He then looked at Ron. "How did this bastard get by you?"

Ron said defensively, "He's not armed. We shook him down like everybody else, real thoroughly. He hasn't got so much as a pocket knife."

The photographers were all recording the scene, particularly of the fallen man, the shattered camera beside him, and of Billy Tucker and Roy, now emerging from their place on the floor behind the desk. The hulking Billy looked shamefacedly at the shambles.

Mary Ann said, "Possibly he's like that girl yesterday. Wanted to see Roy in person. Talk to him. Get his autograph."

The reporter who had originally started the ruckus by denouncing the now-unconscious intruder said, "Yeah, possibly. Let me take a look at that damned camera of his. He said it was a holo. He doesn't know his ass from a holo in the ground."

"I'll pretend I didn't hear that," Don said as the other scooped up the camera under discussion from the floor.

While all watched, he fiddled with it. The back came away. Whatever the complicated jury-rigged device inside was, it had nothing to do with holo cameras.

"For Crissakes, let me see that," Forry rasped, taking it from the other's hands. He stared at the insides, turned the instrument over to check the lens.

He said in wonder, "This isn't a camera. It's a dart gun.

The dart's fired by springs and comes out through the opening where the lens is supposed to be.''

"I'll be damned," Don said. "You gotta admit, the Graf's tricky. When all these boys were firing away at Roy, flashing lights and all, this bastard could have fired his dart without anybody noticing it. It might feel like nothing more than an itch, and Roy'd scratch it. And, sure as hell, the poison wouldn't work until our phony photographer, here, was already on his way out of the building, safe as a pig in shit.''

Roy shook his head wearily, sighed, and said to Ron, "Couple of you boys get him out of here and turn him over to the fuzzies down in the lobby.''

Forry said, "Tell them that our lawyers will prefer charges. If we can get him to admit he was hired by the Graf, we'll sue Lothar von Brandenburg through the World Court. Not that it'll do any good directly, but it'll be one more bit of damning evidence against the whole establishment.''

Don said, "We'll do up the releases from that angle, Forry. Come on chum-pals, let's get out of here. This is news!''

When they were gone, Dick said, "Roy, the party's getting rough—two people in two days penetrating our security. Maybe we ought to go to ground again; hide out somewhere.''

Roy shook his head again. "In the first place, there's no place to hide. They'd find us, sooner or later. In the second place, there'd be no more broadcasts, no more publicity. We're just beginning to get the message over. We can't stop now.''

Ron said, "Did you see how those news boys lit into him? They got to him before we could. That slob'll spend a week in the prison hospital, if he's lucky.''

Forry squinted his eyes through the dribbling smoke of his inevitable cigarette. "It's a good sign," he said. "The press has been sympathetic from the first. Hell, it's been first-rate copy since we first made our news releases. But now they're really rallying around.'' He chopped out a cynical laugh. "Can you imagine some of those tough bastards beginning to accept what Roy's saying?''

"It's early in the day for it," Roy said, "but how about a drink? I could use one. That dizzard almost accomplished what he came for.''

Mary Ann looked at him in alarm. "You don't mean that he fired a dart at you!"

"No. But I was nearly squashed to death under Billy, here."

As Ron went over to the bar to take orders, there came the *blat-blat-blat* of a copter outside.

Dick Samuelson took up his automatic carbine and went out through the French windows to threaten it off. It wasn't anything new. Since the word had gotten out that the Deathwish Wobbly was stationed in the New Tropical Hotel penthouse, aircraft, undoubtedly hired by rubberneckers, had circled almost daily. Roy's team had decided that the threat of a commando raid on the part of the Graf's men wasn't very likely. The invaders would have been at a considerable disadvantage, now that Roy had augmented his guard to eight well-armed men. They would have been mowed down as they attempted to disembark. Besides, in the shootout, Roy would have been able to escape, along with Mary Ann and the other noncombatants of the team.

Taking their drinks, they paid little attention to the guard who had gone out on the roof and was shaking his weapon at the aircraft, until Ron blurted, "Jesus Christ! Dick's down!"

The three guards in the living room dropped their drinks to the floor, grabbed up their guns, and headed for the roof garden on the double.

Dick was sprawled out on the terrace in agony. He called weakly, "Sniper! On the roof opposite!" His face contorted and he passed out.

Billy and Les ran for him, grabbed him by the arms, and pulled him back toward the penthouse, bending double to present as small a target as possible. Ron upended a heavy wrought-iron patio table and knelt behind it, steadying his Gyrojet on its edge. He traversed the roof opposite with rapid fire, emptying the clip with one burst. He slapped the side of the gun so that the magazine fell away and fumbled in a pocket of his prole jacket for another.

Dick's two rescuers hauled him into the living room, where the others were standing to each side of the windows out of the line of fire. Billy and Les dragged their fallen companion to a couch and got him onto it.

Billy, his face pale, snapped, "He's hit bad! Doctor!"

Mary Ann, her usual prim efficiency slipping, squealed and dashed for the phone on her desk. She banged the activating stud and screamed, "Doctor! Doctor! Immediately in the penthouse. Emergency, emergency!"

Ron, bending double as his companions had, came hurrying back from the rooftop garden. "He's gone, I think," he blurted. Breathing deeply, he stared at Dick, sprawled on the couch. Roy, Forry, Billy, and Les were all hovering above him, trying to get his jacket off, trying to staunch the flow of blood. He said, "It must've all been a put-up. That chopper came over to draw us out. The guy on the roof was waiting. Dick's about the same size as Roy and, of course, we all dress the same."

"Where the hell's that doctor!" Forry grated.

One of the new guards opened the door and stuck his head in. "What the hell's going on?" he said, his eyes bugging when he saw Dick. "There's a doctor out here."

"Let him in, for Christ's sake," Roy said. "Dick's been hit. He's bleeding all over the place."

The doctor came hurrying in. He was in a white jacket and carrying the standard physician's black bag. He was a dignified-looking type, gray of hair, weary of face.

As he headed for the fallen man, those gathered around Dick Samuelson made way for him. Even as he crossed the room, he snapped his bag open and began to fish in it. Billy roared, "He's no damned doctor," and made a flying tackle.

The newcomer dropped his bag and smashed into the floor, hitting full on his face. The wrestler swarmed onto him, expertly, snagged an arm and pressed it behind and up the back.

Ron scooped up the bag and stared down into it. He reached inside and brought out a small Gyrojet hideaway gun. "Holy smog," he said, "a shooter."

The other guards came pressing in from the corridor, guns at the ready.

Billy hauled the fake doctor to his feet and slugged him mercilessly in the face, shattering his glasses and bringing blood.

"Another doctor," Forry blurted at Mary Ann, who had abandoned her phone and was standing, both fists to her mouth, her eyes popping in distress. "Have the manager come, accompanying the regular hotel doctor. Goddammit, Dick's still pumping his life out.''

She got back on the phone.

Forry said to Billy, in disgust, "How in the hell did you know he wasn't a doctor?''

Billy Tucker, who was still manhandling his victim, aided now by Les, who was no gentler, looked slightly embarrassed. "I don't know,'' he admitted. "Just instinct, I guess.''

They all looked at him. The wrestler said uncomfortably, "He got here too soon. Besides, he looked too much like a doctor.''

Forry closed his eyes in weariness. "Give me strength,'' he muttered.

Roy, who had settled down in his chair behind his desk, said emptily, "Take him down to the lobby, Billy. You go too, Les. Turn him over to the fuzzies. Same story as that photographer.''

Ferd Feldmeyer was over at the bar, pouring himself a fresh drink. He said, "We'd better call the press boys back. This makes a bigger story.''

"To hell with publicity,'' Roy snapped. "Take care of poor Dick first.''

A half hour later, the place was reasonably cleaned up. The faithful guard, Dick, had taken a side wound. Happily, the slug hadn't been explosive, as was so usual these days, and had gone completely through. According to the hotel doctor, there was little fear for his life—only a protracted stay in the hospital.

Forry said, "He'll continue on the payroll like everybody else.''

Ron looked at him. "You're damn right he will.''

Ron was the only guard in the room for the time. Billy was out on the roof, on the off chance that either the copter or the sniper might make a return performance. The others were in the corridors or stationed at the entries. Everybody was uptight.

Feldmeyer shook his head until his lardy jowls wobbled. He said, "What motivates a cloddy like that? Suppose he'd got his gun out and shot Roy? We'd all have been on him like a ton of bricks. He didn't have a chance of making a getaway.''

Forry grunted. "When the Graf can't find anybody else to

take a chance, there's always the John Wilkes Booth type kicking around that you can steam up to do the job. Think of all the international fame that would accrue to anybody who finishes the Deathwish Wobbly. Besides, one way or the other, the Graf will probably have that fake photographer and the phony doctor loose within six months. With his kind of money and muscle, you can do almost anything in this world.''

In spite of all the excitement, Roy hadn't dispelled his earlier despondency. He took a pull at his third drink, though they hadn't had lunch yet.

He said, his voice reflecting his inner despair, ''Dick might have been killed.''

The others were seated around, quiet in their own inner thoughts.

Ron looked over at his chief quickly. He said, rejection there of the other's obvious thoughts, ''Dick knew that. We all knew we were taking a chance when we signed up. You're the only one not taking a chance.'' He hesitated, before adding, ''You don't have a chance, Roy, but you're in here pitching. What would you expect us to do? We're just as avid Wobblies as you are.''

Roy Cos shrugged that off. ''It was a mistake,'' he said, deep weariness in his voice. ''What good's it done? I don't see the multitudes swarming in to join the Wobblies.''

''There are some,'' Mary Ann said, trying to keep obvious compassion for her lover from her voice.

Roy looked at Forry, rather than her. ''Yes,'' he said. ''Most of 'em are crackpots trying to get in on the act. We don't need crackpots. We need devoted militants.''

''They're not all crackpots,'' Ron said. ''And it takes time to make a good Wobbly. A lot of study. A lot of background.''

''No, they're not all crackpots,'' Roy said. ''Some are undoubtedly IABI men ordered to infiltrate us and act as agents provocateurs. Some are probably in the pay of the Graf, getting in where they can do the most damage. What's the old Russian adage? When four men sit down to talk revolution, three are police spies and the other a damn fool.'' He was still looking at Forry Brown. ''You and your story about Sacco and Vanzetti.''

Forry lit another cigarette from the butt of his old one. ''They wanted to get over their message. By being idealists.

The American people heard their message but rejected it, which is undoubtedly what they should have done. Anarchy didn't fit the country's needs. All right, you wanted to have the chance of getting over the Wobbly program. You're doing it. Now it's up to the program. If the majority of the people think it's good, they'll support it. If they don't, they won't. What's your beef, Roy?" His tone was sour.

Roy nodded, tired still. "They haven't accepted it."

Ron said, "They haven't had time, Roy! For Chrissakes, it's only been a couple of weeks or so."

His chief ignored that, saying, "You know what the trouble is? Always in the past when there was a fundamental change in the working, the people were driven to it, usually by hunger and despair—the French Revolution, the Russian Revolution, the Chinese before that, all the way back to the slave revolts in Rome led by Spartacus. But we don't have any hunger now, in the Welfare State. GAS takes care of everybody. Not on a very high level, but nobody starves, nobody goes unsheltered or unclothed, and medical care is free. The proles today are largely what Marx used to call the lumpen proletariat. He expected them to side with the enemy when the chips were down. And our lumpen proles are lumpen indeed. Go into any autobar in the slummiest part of town and say anything against the government and you'll have a fight on your hands. One of the platitudes they have is their slogan, *it was good enough for Daddy and it's good enough for me*.

Ron said uncomfortably, not at his ease in arguing with the older man he admired so much, "You knew all that before we ever started, Roy. It's admittedly a long road, but if we're right, sooner or later we'll win."

"So far as I'm concerned, and maybe Dick, it'll be later," the Deathwish Wobbly said bitterly.

Chapter Twenty:
Jeremiah Auburn

When Jerry Auburn awakened, it was to find Lee Garrett next to him, up on one elbow. She was frowning puzzlement.

He grinned, his eyes glinting amusement, and said, "Did I put up a valiant enough battle for my honor? I wouldn't want the word to get out that I was an easy lay."

"What?"

He said, "When you raped me last night."

She was frowning still, ignoring his sally of humor. "I'm still wondering where I've met you before. At first I thought it was just your voice, but now I seem to find facial resemblances to someone I've met somewhere. Have we?"

He laughed. "Yes, for a short time. But not under such circumstances that I ever expected to wind up in your bed, honey. In fact, I lied to you. Told you I didn't think blondes were . . ." He chuckled again. "Someday, maybe, I'll tell you about it. Right now, you wouldn't believe me anyway."

"Don't be cryptic, Jerry."

But he dropped it and his voice became serious. He said, "I'm going to be leaving today, Lee. I've got some things to do in the States. Besides that, I don't think I'd win high marks in a Roman popularity contest right now. After that attempt in the restaurant, I'd rather be on my own turf."

She nodded at that. "I heard a few rumors last night that you haven't been exactly ingratiating yourself among some elements in the World Club but then, of course, you were a little drenched."

"No," he told her definitely. "I knew what I was doing and I was doing it deliberately. I don't like the present drift of the World Club and I want to bring certain things to a decision. At any rate, I want you to get in touch with Mendel Amschel and Fong Hui and let them know that if it comes to a vote on a new Central Committee member to get in touch with me, through you. I'm going to give you the number of my tight beam transceiver. You're not to tell Sheila, or anyone else, about this."

"But I work for Sheila Duff-Roberts. I can't . . ."

He interrupted her. "And she works for the Central Committee, and Amschel and Fong and I are members of that committee, so you work for us, above and beyond your obligations to Sheila."

"I suppose you're right." She hesitated, then said, "Jerry, what happened to Pamela McGivern, the girl who preceded me?"

"I don't know," he said grimly. "It's one of the things I intend to find out."

He got out of bed and went to where he had so hastily disrobed the night before. He gathered up his clothes and headed for the bathroom, Lee looking after him thoughtfully. It occurred to her that though she'd had several brief affairs, she'd never before met a man with whom she might have considered a more permanent relationship. But then she snorted in self-amusement. He was Jeremiah Auburn, for years the leading igniter of the Rocket Set. Obviously, if he'd gotten to his age without more prolonged alliances, he wasn't interested in one. She wondered, all over again, where she could possibly have met him before—as he had now admitted.

His decision made to return to the States, Jerry Auburn faded out of Rome as inconspicuously as he had appeared. He didn't even bother to pack a small bag. All his requirements could be met on his personal air yacht.

He drove out the Appian Way to the International Shuttleport and directly to his king-size airliner. On the way, he had alerted the captain of his arrival and the fact that he wanted to be airborne immediately. A skeleton crew was always aboard, so that ordinarily he could have taken off immediately. However, the balance of the crew of eighteen, including the stewards, was undoubtedly quartered at the shuttleport's International Hotel and would be aboard as soon as he was.

The flight was uneventful. He sat in the main lounge, staring unseeingly out one of the larger ports at the sea, far beneath. What he had told Lee wasn't exactly correct. It wasn't just a matter of wanting to bring things to a decision. They were coming to very basic decisions, and Jeremiah Auburn was a high-survival type. He wished to be out in front directing matters along the path he favored.

He had a steward call ahead and have one of his limousines available when they landed, and to alert customs to pass him through without the necessity of his going to the administration building. It was his standard procedure. VIPs such as Jeremiah Auburn could be met on their private aircraft and not be bothered with the inconveniences suffered by the common herd. In such respects the 21st century differed not at all from the centuries before it; wealth and power had their privileges.

The limousine sped him to Manhattan and through its deserted streets, arrogantly remaining on the surface rather than taking the underground highway. They pulled up before the minor entrance on the side street behind the towering office building which was his destination. He entered the building, fishing in his pockets for his key ring and the small silver key for his private elevator.

The elevator sped him up to the high-level floor he used for his personal offices and living quarters while he was in residence. He emerged into the reception room and nodded at the dazzlingly smiling girl at the desk.

"Oh, good afternoon, Mr. Auburn," she gushed, rising. "We've been expecting you, sir."

"Wizard," he told her brusquely. "Tell Barry Wimple I'll see him in my quarters in five minutes."

"Yes, Mr. Auburn," she simpered.

For Christ's sake, he thought inwardly, *let's not be too damned effervescent,* as he pushed his way through to the office behind. It was staffed with two neatly suited accountant types and two gorgeous, efficient-looking women who could have landed Tri-Di parts portraying brisk secretaries of upper-echelon corporation executives. They were all deftly at work when he entered; whether make-work or not, he didn't know. They all stood and chorused smiled greetings, and he nodded back while striding across the room.

He had a suspicion that if he'd said, "Miss Jones, come into my apartments, I want to lay you," not one of the four would have blinked an eye and Miss Jones would have trotted after him. He had a dozen such staffs in half a dozen countries throughout the globe.

Simmons was waiting for him in the living room, ramrod-stiff, subservient just to the correct point, not sickeningly so.

"Welcome home, Mr. Auburn," he said.

Jerry looked around the lush room. "Did you think this was home?" he growled. He headed for the bar, adding over his shoulder, "I came without luggage. Check to see if all my needs are available. Tell the chef—what's his name here, Henri?—that I'll probably dine in the apartment tonight. Alone."

"Yes, sir, of course. Yes, it's Henri, sir. He's anxious that you taste his new dish based on shad roe."

"Wizard," Jerry said, taking up a cognac bottle from the bar and pouring into a glass generously. The butler faded. Jerry sat down on a couch, put his feet up on a cocktail table, and took a pull at the drink.

Barry Wimple entered from the door that led to the offices. He was the epitome of the senior executive. Jerry Auburn sometimes wondered if they took courses in grooming at New Harvard Business College. He had never seen a senior executive who wasn't groomed to his teeth. He suspected that the other's clothing bill was greater than his own.

"Welcome back, Mr. Auburn," Wimple said. "Was your trip to Europe satisfactory?"

Jerry regarded him coolly. "How did you know I went to Europe?"

The other looked at him in distress. "Why, Mr. Auburn, Captain Wayland of your air yacht recorded it in his report."

Jerry made a note to do something about that. He didn't like anybody at all to know where he was at any given time. But obviously Wayland had to make reports on his expenditures, costs of fuel, landing fees, and so on.

He said, "Barry, I want you to get a few heavies in here when I'm in residence."

"Heavies, Mr. Auburn?"

"Hard types; guards. And I don't want you to hire them from Mercenaries, Incorporated. I've got reason to believe there might be a contract out on me. Get them from some competitor of the Graf."

His New York office head blinked at him. "A contract?

You mean . . . but, sir, that's ridiculous. Who could possibly want you . . .''

"Not everybody loves me like you do, Barry. So, six guards. I want them here this afternoon, inconspicuously, and I want them to shake down anybody who comes to see me."

"This afternoon?"

"Yes, preferably. But especially tonight. Is Lester here?"

"Yes, Mr. Auburn. And Ted Meer as well, as you instructed."

Lester was a carbon copy of Barry Wimple, fifteen years younger. One glance marked him as an efficient, supercilious WASP who would wind up a millionaire by middle age almost without trying.

Jerry nodded at his greeting and said, "Lester, I want you to find out who is the head of Mercenaries, Incorporated in North America. Have him here this evening. Tell him that the meeting is confidential. I'm assuming that New York is his base of operations."

Lester stared at him blankly, a touch of dismay there. "Mercenaries, Incorporated, sir?"

"You heard me. If they're here, and they should be, there must be some manner of contacting them. Start earning your pay, damn it. Don't you know any upper slot news people, or someone in the IABI? Either should know."

Wimple cleared his throat. "I have a niece who is married to a captain of detectives in the Inter-American Bureau of Investigation, Mr. Auburn."

"That ought to do it. Anything else pressing on the agenda, Barry?"

His senior aide said, "There's a representative from the Lagrangists waiting to see you, sir. When the order came for your limousine, I took the liberty of informing him that you were to be here this afternoon and that you might work him into your schedule. He's on his way. Of course, if you haven't the time . . .''

"Lagrangists?" Jerry said. "You mean from Lagrange Five? What does he want?"

"He wouldn't say, sir. He wanted to discuss it with you face to face. He was upset when I told him that you had retired and seldom devoted time to business matters anymore."

Jerry grunted. "Send him into my office when he arrives. I

don't believe I've ever met a real space colonist before. Brief me, Barry. How much have we currently got invested in Lagrange Five and the Asteroid Belt Islands?''

"Two hundred and twelve million and, ah, some change, Mr. Auburn. Largely in the Satellite Solar Power Plants.''

Jerry grunted again. ''That much? All right, you two, get going. I'll see the Lagrangist in my office and the Mercenaries, Incorporated bastard here in my quarters, both as soon as they've arrived. And remember, Barry, I want the new guards to frisk them before they see me.''

The two left. As they crossed the outer office, Lester said to his higher-up, ''He's a tough sonofabitch.''

Wimple looked at him from the side of his eyes. ''I'd probably be the same if I had inherited a few billion.''

Jerry Auburn was idly looking at some reports he wouldn't ordinarily have bothered with when the man from Lagrange Five was announced. He hadn't known what he had expected; among other things, possibly an older man than this, if the other was an official representative from the space islands.

Ian Venner was disgustingly healthy looking. He must have been exactly the height and weight that the insurance statistics averaged out on a man of his age. He was a sun-faded blond, sharp blue of eye, with a good mouth on the wide and dry humorous side, and a strong chin. He looked as though he either owned the place or didn't give a damn who did.

''Sit down, Mr. Venner,'' Jerry said, even while sizing the other up.

''Just Venner,'' the newcomer said crisply. ''We don't use the term Mister in Lagrangia.''

Jerry said, ''Why not?''

''It is derived from the word master and I don't wish to be anyone's master any more than I want someone else to be mine.''

Jerry refrained from twisting his mouth in amusement. ''What can I do for you, Venner?''

''The Space Federation is desirous of buying out your holdings in space, Auburn. I've been sent to make initial contact.''

''Man, you don't waste words. What federation? I don't usually handle this sort of thing. I have aides who make business decisions in which I seldom involve myself. I didn't even know there was a federation in Lagrangia.''

The other nodded, not as though he approved of Jerry Auburn's divorcing himself from the details of his enterprises, but as though he had already heard of the fact. He said, ''Recently, a loose-knit organization has been formed to represent the united needs of Lagrangia and the Belt Islands.''

Jerry scowled. ''United States of the Americas? Common Europe? The Soviet Complex? The Reunited Nations? Or a combination of two or more, or all of them?''

''No. The federation represents only space colonists actually living in space. We have no other affiliations.''

''Don't be ridiculous,'' Jerry growled. ''Every island in space is controlled by either some Earthside nation, the Reunited Nations, or by consortiums of multinational corporations.''

His visitor was shaking his head. ''Times are changing. One by one, we're buying out private interests in Lagrangia and the Asteroids, and most of the new islands are colonized from the older islands but have no political ties to them, or to the original nations which first founded them.''

Jerry was staring at him now. This was absolutely new. There wasn't much news about the space projects any more; they were being played down drastically, as budgets were being cut on the space program. Still, he should have heard of this.

He said, ''You mean to tell me that up in space you people get together and build a new island that has no affiliation whatsoever to Earthside private enterprise or to any specific nation?''

''That's correct. We're tired of misguidance from, ah, Earthworms.''

''Earthworms!''

The Lagrangist wasn't without humor. He laughed lightly and said, ''An old joke.''

Jerry said, ''But buying out my interests in solar power and such. Where the hell would you get the credits? One of my executives just informed me I have over two hundred million in investments in space.''

The other agreed to that. ''From the first, pay in space has been astronomical, compared to that Earthside. And, frankly, there is comparatively little to spend it on. We don't particularly go for ostentatious living, conspicuous consumption. We have no desire to keep up with the Joneses, or have a larger house, or boat—in those islands large enough to have suitable bodies of water—than our neighbors. I don't mean that there are any rules against it, but we simply don't do it. We pile up the credits. Some of the more energetic among us began to put scientific and industrial space developments to work for exports—artificial diamonds, for instance. Now we have enough money to buy out Earthside interests and, uh, I believe the term you use down here is to nationalize them."

"Why?" Jerry said blankly.

His visitor sighed. "For one thing, you Earthworms are usually unable to identify with our problems. You send instructions that are ridiculous considering the situations that apply. Often you send directives to expand in some direction in which expansion is pure nonsense, or refuse to divert funds to some effort which is absolutely necessary. It's something like England running the Thirteen Colonies from three thousand miles away. The British had no conception of the problems that faced American colonists."

Jerry Auburn was astonished. He came to his feet and made his way over to his office bar, his face in thought. "Drink?" he said.

The Lagrangist said, "You wouldn't have any Reman Riesling, would you? Top Earthside wines are one of the few things we haven't been able to duplicate in Lagrangia. We're working on it," he added quickly.

"I have some," Jerry murmured, still in his other thoughts. He filled glasses and returned to his desk, extending his visitor the dry white wine.

After settling back into his chair and swallowing some of his brandy, he said, "So: the space colonists are attempting to cut ties with Mother Earth."

"Some mother," the other said wryly. "More like a stepmother."

"How do you mean?"

"Earth has, from the beginning, only exploited Lagrangia and the Belt Islands. Almost all the profits are funneled back to Earth, rather than being used for continued expansion of the space program. A corporation wants immediate dividends;

not, uh, pie in the sky a century from now. We have a different view. We've got a different dream."

Jerry was becoming increasingly intrigued. "So you're having trouble with Earth. Such as?"

The other took another sip of his wine, appreciatively. He looked at the multibillionaire and said, "Almost all funds for the space programs have been cut to ribbons. It's practically impossible for a top scientist or technician from whatever country to get permission to migrate to the space islands. Even ordinary folk are highly discouraged from leaving for Lagrangia or the Asteroids. Whenever we make a scientific breakthrough in the islands we immediately rush the details Earthside, but of recent years the Earth nations do not reciprocate. They keep their discoveries to themselves."

"Why should we do that?"

Venner shrugged and frowned before answering. "We're not sure. Maybe we're going too fast in the islands; the Earthside powers are afraid we'll upset the boat, come up with changes that will threaten the status quo. We're contributing to future shock with a vengeance. Sooner or later, almost every Earth institution will be threatened with change as a result of developments in space."

"Probably true." Jerry thought about it before saying, "These new developments of yours. What kind of political system have you dreamed up?"

"We're experimenting with a half-dozen alternatives." The other flashed a grin of deprecation. "None of them very similar to anything now prevailing Earthside."

"I'll be damned," Jerry said. Then, "Look, with emigration being deliberately discouraged, how are you populating these new islands of the Federation?"

The other looked him straight in the eye. "Partially from natural increase. We still like kids in the space colonies. But even more so from the original islands."

Jerry looked at him quizzically. "Wouldn't the original islands take a dim view of losing their inhabitants in that manner?"

Ian Venner wasn't fazed. "Some of them do, especially in the Belt."

"I'd think the Soviet Complex would send the KGB up en masse."

"They do. And *they* defect. For that matter, so do the IABI men, and those from the Common Europe Interpol, while chasing felons who've run to Lagrangia. My own—never mind," he finished, smiling to himself.

"Jesus," Jerry muttered. "I'll have to have my people do me a brief on this. I had no idea . . ." He scrutinized the Lagrangist again. "How are racial problems in Lagrangia and the Asteroids?"

"What race problems?"

Jerry was impatient. "You know: conflict between the races. Blacks, whites, yellows . . ."

The man from Lagrangia was just as impatient. "Auburn," he interrupted, "when you're out in deep space and something happens to your suit, you don't give a good goddamn whether the person next to you is black, yellow, or green. Death only comes in one color. In space, all humans cooperate, or they die. We pay no more attention to a person's race than his religion, if he has any—which he most likely doesn't."

Jerry said, "Come again?"

Venner was still impatient. "That's one of the reasons we're on the shit list. The Prophet has been pulling out all the stops when it comes to space colonization. He found out about twenty years ago that there wasn't a single church in Lagrange Five and demanded that he be allowed to build a United Church mission in our Island One. Obviously, we couldn't care less, so he built it and manned it."

"But nobody came, eh?" Jerry Auburn was amused.

"Oh, we all came. Once. In fact, some came back again for the second time . . . for laughs. Good grief, Auburn, any emigrants to the space colonies are screened to hell and gone, not for just competence in their line of work, but for intelligence, education, Ability Quotient. How many of them do you think can believe in the religious mythologies of the Jews, the Christians, the Moslems, the Buddhists, the Shintoists, or any of the rest? And if we tried to teach the Genesis account, Noah's Ark and the rest, do you think any of them would swallow it? Sorry."

Jerry got up and went over to the bar to refresh their drinks. He returned with them and said, "I begin to see why you people are getting uptight. So you've been rather quietly acquiring all private investments in space that you can get your hands on, as fast as you can finance it. But why approach me directly? Why not resort to various stock exchanges and buy up a controlling interest in Auburn Space Development, Incorporated?''

Ian Venner said, "It's a question we debated. However, your grandfather was one of the first to invest in Lagrange Five, and he did it with no strings attached. He didn't make quick initial profits and keep them Earthside. For two decades, he reinvested all income from space back into the projects. When he died, your father continued the policy. And he didn't use Earthworm directors. He was the first to have sense enough to appoint experienced Lagrangists, usually second-generation colonists. Nor have we had any interference from you since you have inherited the Auburn interests. So we decided, in all fairness, that we should consult you without the bullshit."

"You did it, that's a fact," Jerry Auburn said. He thought about it for long moments during which time the other held his peace. He sipped at his brandy until the glass was empty, then put it down and turned to one of the screens on his desk. He flicked it on, and when a face faded in, said, "Barry, make arrangements to sell all our interests in Auburn Space Development to the Space Federation. I have a gentleman here in my office named Ian Venner, from Lagrangia. Go over the details with him. You'll have to relay this to Central and to Sillitoe in London and Flaker in Berlin. But first, buy what common shares you can and add them to our holdings you turn over."

Barry Wimple gaped, but Jerry flicked the switch again and turned back to the equally gaping Lagrangist.

Venner said, "But look. We make a policy of paying cash, when we've accumulated enough credits to swing our latest acquisition. This was to be the largest thus far. We don't want to be saddled with paying interest for . . ."

"No interest," Jerry said flatly. "I'm turning my space properties over to your Federation." He stood and extended a hand. "Perhaps, someday, you'll be able to do a favor for me. Meanwhile, you can use those credits you've accumulated the hard way to buy up some other properties. The move is on, Venner, to create a world government. If such elements as the United Church are in control of that world state, you people are going to be in the soup. You'd better make your-selves as independent as possible, as soon as possible."

The Lagrangist, still in something of a daze, shook hands. He said hesitantly, which was out of character for him, "I don't know what motivates you, Auburn, but I assume that you've thought this out. And I can assure you that the Federa-tion is most anxious to grant that favor."

Jerry smiled suddenly. "No racism in space, eh?"

The other was mystified. "That's right. There hasn't been from the beginning."

When Ian Venner was gone, Jerry went back to his living room, got a double brandy from the bar, and spread himself out on a couch. He remained there for a couple of hours, staring unseeingly out the huge window which overlooked Manhattan. From time to time he got up to replenish the glass.

At one time he said aloud, "What in hell am I doing in this position?"

And ten minutes later he answered himself. "I was born into it."

It had grown dark outside by the time the identity screen buzzed on the door leading to the offices. He sat erect and looked over. It was Lester.

Jerry said, "Yeah?" a slight slur in his voice.

"Mr. Luca Cellini is here, sir."

"Send him in."

The door opened and an alert-looking stranger entered. In his late thirties, he could have been one of Jerry's staff, so far as appearance was concerned. He was dark of complexion in the Sicilian tradition, clean and handsome of features, sharp of eye. He took the room in completely in one quick sweep, then turned to its occupant.

Jerry got up and went over to the bar for still another drink, saying over his shoulder, "Sit down, Cellini. You're the Graf's local man?"

The newcomer seated himself in a comfort chair and crossed his legs, adjusting his beautifully tailored trousers.

He said, "That's right, Mr. Auburn, and for both hemi-spheres of the Americas. What can I do for you?"

Jerry came back, reseated himself on the couch, and viewed

the other. He said finally, "What would you take to sell out the Graf?"

Luca Cellini stared at him for a long moment. Then he said, "First of all, nine lives, like a cat."

Jerry said nothing, took a sip of his drink.

Cellini leaned forward a bit. "Mr. Auburn," he said "I don't want to antagonize you. I know who you are, and I know how much weight you can throw. Even the Graf wouldn't want to antagonize you. However, I've been working for Lothar Von Brandenburg for over twenty years. One of his scouts brought me off the streets when I was a kid. I've been with him ever since. He even sent me to school. Now I'm settled in the organization. The pay's good, more than I could ever have expected with my background. In short, Mr. Auburn, I owe the Graf. He's been more than a father to me."

Jerry took another pull at the drink, without removing his eyes from the other. He said slowly, "The Graf's a has-been. Mercenaries are rapidly becoming a thing of the past, and so is selling arms to would-be revolutionists. Already Latin America, once a lucrative field of operation for you, is now part of the United States and sealed off from your operations. And that's just the beginning. World government is on the way. When it comes, there will be little use, anywhere, for mercenaries and illicit arms sales. Hit men for the Deathwish policies will be gone, since such policies will be illegal with a World State. There'll be a great fall-off in bodyguarding and assassinations, since most of them are international and there won't be any nations. The Graf is hedging his bets, trying to get into the upper hierarchy of the World Club so *he'll* have a place in the new scheme of things. You rank-and-file employees will largely be dropped. So, looking out for your own interests, you'd better get out while you can."

Luca Cellini had not worked his way up to his present standing in the Graf's organization by being slow.

He said, "Mind if I smoke?"

Jerry shook his head.

The New Yorker took out a gold cigar case and from it drew a panatela. The end had already been pierced. He brought forth a gold lighter and lit the long cigar carefully. He said, "I couldn't sell out the Graf. He'd get me no matter where I tried to hide. Just as easily as he gets those Deathwish policy suckers. Few of them last a week."

Jerry nodded, taking back more of the drink that he didn't need. His eyes were already shining in the characteristic way they did after a half-liter of spirits.

He said, "Try this. We'd arrange a shootout in which you were involved. You'd supposedly take a couple of hits and the ambulance would haul you off to a clinic owned by a doctor on my payroll. He'd operate on you, making a few impressive-looking scars and possibly taking a half inch or so out of one of your shin bones, so you'd be left with a noticeable limp. When you were released from the clinic, the doctor's report would read that you were ninety percent disabled, possibly one of your kidneys shot away, or something. My people know how to do it. You'd report to the Graf or Peter Windsor or whoever you report to, that you have to retire. So you go to some island paradise like Samoa, and settle down living the good life in retirement on whatever pension the Graf settles on you, and especially the sum I give you. You stay there at least until Mercenaries, Incorporated is gone from the scene—possibly Lothar von Brandenburg as well. Possibly you spend the rest of your life where you're not apt to run into any of your present associates. So, the question is still, what would you want to sell out the Graf?"

Luca Cellini was staring again and breathing deeper now. He said, "Could I have a drink?"

His host motioned with his head toward the bar. Cellini went over to it and poured himself a triple from the same bottle his host had used, He swallowed part of it and returned to his chair.

He said, "One million pseudo-dollars, tax-free and untraceable."

Jerry nodded in agreement. "Very well. As you leave, Lester will make arrangements with you to deposit that amount to whatever account you prefer. I assume that you have at least one secret account in Nassau, Tangier, or wherever."

Cellini nodded. "I know you don't welch, Mr. Auburn. I trust you. What did you want from me?"

"What happened to Harold Dunninger?"

"He was kidnapped by the Nihilists. When his wife wouldn't pony up the ransom, they hit him."

"I know what was in the news. How did you set it up?"

The otber moistened his lips. "I was supplying his body-guards. There were twelve of them, four on a shift. I pulled four of them off at the crucial time, supposedly rotating them. The orders came from Windsor. The Nihilist who pulled off the kidnapping was one of ours. We've had him planted with them for years. He placed the ransom amount so high that there wasn't a chance Dunninger's wife would pay it. We'd checked her out to make sure."

"What's the name of your mole in the Nihilists?"

"Nils Ostrander."

"New subject: What happened to Pamela McGivern?"

Cellini shook his head. "Never heard of her."

Jerry thought about it for a moment, then accepted that and said, "What else has been going on under your jurisdiction?"

"We've diverted all our best men to hitting the Deathwish Wobbly."

"Who?" Jerry scowled.

"Roy Cos, a screwball radical who took out a Deathwish Policy. Instead of blowing the credits coming to him like all the rest, he's devoted it to buying prime time so he can sound off against the system. He's surrounded himself with a flock of guards, all devoted to him, and we haven't been able to get through. He's scheduled to show in a couple of days. All the screwball outfits are getting together in Chicago for what they call a synthesis meeting. He's supposed to represent the Wobblies."

"I guess I have heard about him," Jerry said, his voice deeper in its slur now, his eyes brighter. He was obviously at least half drenched in booze. "What else?"

"Nothing much. They sent over a new man from the Wolfschloss." Cellini looked up. "That's the . . ."

"I know," Jerry said. "The Graf's fortress in Liechtenstein. Go on "

"Kid named Franklin Pinell," Cellini growled. "It's not the way the organization usually operates. Windsor said to cooperate with him one hundred percent. Handle him with kid gloves. Graf's orders."

Jerry eyed him. "What's he supposed to do?"

"Hit a spade named Horace Hampton, evidently. Never heard of Hampton."

Jerry Auburn's face froze. All of a sudden, he didn't seem quite so influenced by the drink he'd been putting down. "Why?" he got out.

"Damned if I know. There's a contract on him. Why we couldn't have handled it is a mystery to me. Routine stuff."

After a moment, Jerry said, "Anything else?"

"Can't think of anything."

"Wizard. Go out to Lester. He'll cover you with all that we've agreed on."

The executive came to his feet, looked at the man who had just bought him, then, without further words, turned and headed for the door.

Jerry finished his drink, went over to the living room's small desk, and sat down before the screen there. He flicked it on and said, "Ted Meer."

When the face of his aide appeared, he said, "Check as deeply as you can on these men. First, a Franklin Pinell. All I know about him is that he's young, has recently been in Europe, including Liechtenstein, and is connected with Mercenaries, Incorporated, evidently on a high level. Second, Roy Cos, the so-called Deathwish Wobbly. Third, a Nils Ostrander of the Nihilists, evidently one of their more militant members; possibly connected with some of their more flagrant operations. And, oh yes, who are we currently using for our private investigations in Common Europe?"

His aide said, "We're still using Pinkerton International, Mr. Auburn."

"Very well. Get them to put all-out effort into checking a Pamela McGivern, an Irish girl, recently employed as a secretary by the World Club, at their headquarters in the Palazzo Colonna in Rome. She disappeared about a week or so ago. This is crash priority, Meer. I want results immediately."

"Yes, sir."

Jerry Auburn flicked the screen off, sighed, and went back to the bar.

In the morning, he had a raging hangover. He went into the bathroom and got a bottle of Sober-Ups from the medicine cabinet, shuddered, and took one. Still in pajamas, he went into the living room and stretched out on the couch, after touching a button set into its armrest.

Simmons entered, immaculately correct. He took one look at his employer and said sadly, "Yes, sir."

"Wipe that goddamned superior, long-suffering look off your face and bring me about a gallon of Italian Expresso."

"Yes, sir." The butler left.

Jerry Auburn went through the agony of the stepped-up recuperation from overindulgence. When he at last felt semi-healthy, he groaned, took himself over to the desk, and flicked on the screen.

Ted Meer appeared, looking weary as though he hadn't been to bed the night before.

Jerry said nastily, "Why in the hell don't you take pep pills when you've got a siege before you?" He knew that his aide had an aversion to stimulants but was in no mood to sympathize.

"Yes, sir," the other said.

"Well, what have you found out?"

"We have the Dossier Complete of Roy Cos, as well as his activities of the last weeks since he has broken into the news. The material is on your desk. We have drawn a blank on Nils Ostrander. It is obviously an assumed name. The IABI is on the verge of arresting him in connection with the kidnapping and death of Harold Dunninger but thus far has insufficient evidence with which to operate. There is a vague hint that higher ups are protecting him, though that would seem impossible."

"Shit it is," Jerry muttered. "Go on."

"Franklin Pinell was recently deported from the United States after four felony sentences, the last of which was a homicide, He was sent to Tangier but he never reported to the Moroccan police. He is the son of the late Willard Pinell, known in mercenary circles as Buck Pinell. The elder Pinell, in partnership with Lothar von Brandenburg, founded Mercenaries, Incorporated over twenty years ago. Present location of Franklin Pinell is unknown."

Jerry said, "He's here in the States. If he's a deportee, undoubtedly under an alias and with false papers. Put the Pinkertons on his trail. What about Pamela McGivern?"

"There hasn't been sufficient time for much of a report, save that she has not returned to Ireland. Her family lives in Dublin. They haven't heard from her for a month."

Jerry thought over what he had been told for a few moments, then said, "Keep at it. If anything important breaks, get in touch with me immediately. Keep digging on this Franklin Pinell and get some background on his father, Buck. Find out everything you can about him, especially his relationship with Lothar von Brandenburg." He hesitated, then went on. "I also want to check out a Lee Garrett, including all the dope you can get on her father and mother, who evidently weren't married. She's currently in residence at the Palazzo Colonna in Rome and has the job formerly held by Pamela McGivern. Check for any hanky-panky there might have been in her being selected by the computers for her job there. I don't want a cursory report on this. I want deep digging. It's extremely difficult, but not impossible, to jimmy the computers or the data banks."

"Yes, sir," Ted Meer said. "Anything else, Mr. Auburn?"

"No. I'll get in touch, Ted." Jerry turned off the screen and ran his hand over his facial stubble.

He thought some more, then reached for the screen again, touching the stud that would deactivate the video. He dialed slowly, remembering the digits. Max Finklestein's face appeared, frowning at the fact that his own screen was blank.

"Who is it?" he said, rubbing the end of his Armenian nose in irritation.

"Hamp," Jerry said. "Horace Hampton."

"How the hell do I know it's Hamp?" Max said irritably.

"The last time I saw you we had our faces buried in the leaves behind the *We Shall Overcome* Motel, with Tom Horse and Joe Zavalla. Something's wrong with my damn transceiver."

"All right," the other said. "What spins, Hamp?"

"I'm tired of being on leave. What do you want me to do?"

"You'll have to check with National Headquarters, Hamp. I'm not running you anymore. I've been promoted to the National Executive Committee. I'm being sent up to Chicago to represent the Anti-Racist League at the Synthesis meeting."

Jerry blinked. This was better than he could have expected. His mind racing, he said, "I've heard a little about that meeting, Max, some of it disquieting. I want in."

Max Finklestein said, "Why?" puzzlement in his voice.

"As muscle. Among others, Roy Cos is going to be there and so is Nils Ostrander."

"I know about Cos, but who's Nils Ostrander?"

"The Nihilist who engineered the kidnap killing of that multimillionaire, Harold Dunninger. There's an off chance that the IABI might try to pick him up at the meeting."

Max said suspiciously, "How in the name of Christ do you know?"

"Sticking my ears out. Ever since this Roy Cos character has been sounding off, everybody and his cousin have been talking about the different radical organizations. Not just the Wobblies, but all radicals. The idea of fundamental change is in the air."

Max considered it. He finally nodded and said, "All right. I'll check it out with the Executive Committee but they'll undoubtedly okay it. Each organization is allowed two delegates. You might as well be my partner. Suppose we meet there."

"Wizard," Jerry said. "See you, Max."

He cut the screen, then flicked on the video again and the switch for his harassed aide. Ted Meer's face came on.

Jerry said, "One more thing, Ted. Plant a news story, and I mean really plant it, so that nobody who listens to the news at all could possibly miss it. The story is that Horace Hampton, an alleged suspect in the recent attack on Governor Teeter, will be present representing the Anti-Racist League at the Synthesis meeting to be held by radical groups in Chicago."

His aide said, "Yes, Mr. Auburn. That name again?"

"Horace Hampton, damn it. Take some pep pills!"

He flicked off, then immediately back on again. He dialed and almost immediately his own face was there on the screen. He said, "Hi, Jim. What spins?"

His double grinned at him. "I still think I've got the best goddamn job in the world."

Jerry laughed. "You probably have at that, you chronic hedonist. I do all the work, you have all the fun, and between us we're Jeremiah Auburn. Okay, Jim. You're to surface again, immediately. This time, drop the recluse bit. Go to one of the gambling resorts—Monte Carlo or Nice. Drop a hundred thousand or so at roulette, or whatever. Enough so that it'll be picked up by the news people and have society commentators asking whether Jerry Auburn is coming out of seclusion to rejoin the Rocket Set.''

"Got it," Jim said. "Great. Back to the high life. Do I need to know what it's all about?''

"No. Not necessary." Jerry's face broke into another fond grin. "Just be sure to remember the names of people you meet and what you did with them, especially the mopsies you might lay, you damned screwing machine. We'll have to get together again one of these days, Jim, and bend a few elbows. It's been a long time since we've sat across a table from each other and tossed back a few. There's something weird about getting drenched and sitting across from you . . . yourself.''

"Tell me about it," Jim said. "The last time I didn't recover for days. And it wasn't just because I was looking at my own face.''

Jerry laughed and flicked the screen off, touched another switch. This time, Barry Wimple's face came on.

Jerry said, "I'll be leaving town again, Barry. Dismiss the staff. You and Ted and Lester check into Central, of course. I don't know how long it'll be before I'm back this time.''

His senior executive was aghast. "But, Mr. Auburn, I've got a dozen top-priority matters . . .''

"That's what I pay you for, Barry," Jerry said, brushing aside the other's complaint. "The decisions are up to you and the rest of your boys. When you start making bad ones, it's your ass. Meanwhile, I want the staff cleared out of here before noon.''

"Yes, sir," the old man said unhappily.

Jerry turned him off, then slumped in his chair for a moment and took a deep breath before heading for the master bedroom. He passed through it into the dressing room, went into the bath, and to the medical cabinet, which he opened with a small key to bring forth a hypodermic needle. Minutes later he returned to the dressing room. He sat down before the mirror, pulled out a drawer, and took up the small box containing his colored contact lenses.

"Doc Jekyll, meet Comrade Hyde," he muttered.

Chapter Twenty-One:
Horace Hampton

Horace Hampton looked up at the lanky, stoop-shouldered man who hovered over his table in the automated bar, grinning down at him.

"Thought I'd find you here," Max Finklestein said. "It's the nearest bar to Assembly Halls."

"Hi, Max," Hamp said. "Have some of this syntho-beer. How did Shakespeare put it? 'Weaker than woman's tears,' or something. They ought to stick it back in the horse."

"Not up to your usual standards, eh?" the older man said, even as he slid into a chair opposite the black. He put his credit card in the table's payment slot and dialed for a mug of the brew.

Hamp looked at him. "What's that supposed to mean, old chum-pal?"

The center of the table sank down to return with the beer. Max took a drink of it, then wiped the coarse foam from his lips. "It means that usually you drink more expensive stuff than the proles have to put up with."

The other's look turned quizzical. "How do you know?"

"I've been checking up on you."

"Wizard, and what've you found?"

"That you're not exactly a down-and-out nigger subsisting on GAS." Max grinned at him in deprecation.

"That's the trouble with you kikes," Hamp said. "Nosy."

Max Finklestein said, "I was sitting around one day, minding my own business, when the thought came to me that the Anti-Racist League was in better funds than it should be. Most of the membership consists of minority elements who'd contribute a lot to the cause if they could, but they can't—they're largely on GAS. Somehow the organization never seems to lack sufficient funds, though. So purely out of

272

curiosity, I began checking on the source of the larger donations that come through. And guess what I found?''

"I know what you found," Hamp said. He finished his beer and dialed another.

Max said, "Why all the secrecy? Why not just openly donate it, in one lump sum, instead of here and there in dribbles?''

Hamp sighed and said, "Because I'm of the opinion that a race, a nationality, or a social class should finance its own emancipation. You mustn't hand somebody freedom on a platter. Suppose I came out and gave a million pseudo-dollars to the Anti-Racist League in a flat sum. Then the membership as a whole would stop their pathetically small donations, as meaningless. But it's not meaningless for a man to give up his guzzle, his sometime extravagance, or his occasional splurge, for a cause he believes in. It's not meaningless for him to sacrifice. It's part of his fight for freedom."

"Quite a speech," Max said. "Where'd you get all this money, Hamp? Or is it a secret? Are you a big-time crook? That's all the organization needs in the way of publicity—one of its most active members turning out to be a crook.''

Hamp sighed. "Come off it, Max. It's according to what you mean by crook, I suppose. Yesterday, I tuned in on this Deathwish Wobbly, who we're supposed to get together with tonight. According to him, the whole upper class is composed of crooks. Their wealth has been stolen from the useful workers.''

"So you're upper class."

"I suppose so. It's a long story, Max."

The other looked at his wrist chronometer. "We've got time."

Hamp sighed again. "It starts with a slave down in South Carolina—Pod Hampton. I haven't a violin to play so I'll skip the details of the hard time he had. When he finally lit out, he took old massa's silver with him. In fact, the kind old massa was on the rich side and some of the so-called silver was gold. Pod managed to get it, and himself, up to Boston. And there he swore a great oath, understand? He wasn't going to spend any of his, ah, ill-gotten gains on himself. Instead, he was going to invest it and use the proceeds to fight for freeing his people.

"At that time there was no valid organization putting up such a fight. He thought the Abolitionists were a bunch of impractical do-gooders, a bunch of starry-eyed whiteys who, beneath it all, believed that blacks really were inferior, and should be pampered like children by those who were good of heart, rather than being exploited as slaves. He continued to invest the money; railroads, mainly. When he died, both the securities and the dream went to his oldest son who, if anything, was even more solidly anti-racist than the old man. He managed the investments—some land in the so-called Great American Desert really paid off—but didn't spend much of it on himself. During his lifetime the Civil War took place, but it didn't take any genius to see that the freed blacks weren't much better off than they had been as slaves. And there was still no organization that seemed fit to turn the money over to. Those were the boom times of industrialization, and the money was still largely in railroads. It grew. It grew still more under *his* son. And along here somewhere, it became obvious that not spending any of it no longer made sense. The fortune needed full-time management—office employees and so forth. The next son dropped railroads and went into automobiles."

Max whistled softly.

Hamp went on, after dialing still another syntho-beer. "These sons all continued the dream. They were devoted to ending racism. They'd progressed beyond the point of fighting for black rights alone. They were also smart enough not to throw the fortune away on lost causes. They were hanging onto it until the right time and the right organization came along. The fortune was kept as secret as possible and they led very simple lives while managing it. Remember, they were smart. One by one, as new developments such as radio, the airplane, and later, electronics, came along, they got in on the ground floor. For instance, one of them helped launch IBM back in the 1920s."

"That would explain it, without the other stuff," said Max.

"And along in here came a new development. It wasn't practical to live like misers while hoarding a fortune that would one day be used to end world racism. To manage a modern fortune, you've got to be educated in top schools, you've got to have the correct social and financial contacts, which are often the same people. In short, you've got to move in the right circles. It's all part of the great fortunes game. A Rockefeller, a Mellon, a Rothschild, can't operate out of a sleazy flat in Harlem. At any rate, Max, I'm the current holder of the purse strings and the Anti-Racist League is being doled out all the funds I feel it can handle at this point.''

Max was eyeing him. "I'll be damned," he said. "That fortune must be king-size by now."

"It is," Hamp said dryly. "And the present descendant of Pod Hampton still has the dream."

Max said, "But for Christ's sake, you shouldn't be risking yourself carrying out extreme assignments for the organization."

Hamp looked at him flatly. "I refuse to finance activities that I'm not willing to take on myself. If Indians like Tom Horse and Chicanos like Jose Zavalla are willing to take the risks they do, so is Horace Hampton."

Max nodded acceptance of that stand. "Right," he said. "I assume you want me to keep this to myself."

"If I thought you couldn't, I wouldn't have told you," Hamp said.

Max looked at his wrist chronometer again. "I suppose we ought to get going. The Synthesis committee has rented a small hall for the meeting. Only delegates are to be admitted— and their bodyguards."

As they stood, Hamp looked over at him questioningly.

Max laughed. "I assume nobody'll have bodyguards besides Roy Cos. That rule was made with him in mind. From what I hear, they average two attempts on his life a day, the poor bastard."

They headed for the door. "Yeah," Hamp growled. "Every hit man in Mercenaries, Incorporated has zeroed in on him."

They went out onto the street and headed for the Assembly Halls, a commercial building devoted to a score of rentable halls ranging from a large auditorium to small lecture rooms that would hold audiences of fifty or so.

Max was eyeing his companion strangely. "How do you know?" he said.

Hamp covered. "Just guessing. It makes sense. It's not just

that insurance conglomerate that wrote the Deathwish Policy now. Poor Cos has everybody and his nephew down on him—the United Church, the government of every country in the world that fears revolutionary change, the World Club, God knows who else. He's the sorest thumb to show up for many a year.''

Max said, frowning, "Why the World Club?"

The black shrugged. "They want a World State, but under their wing—not the kind he's agitating for.''

As they got nearer to the building in which the meeting was to be held, the crowd began to manifest itself. There were several police cars, lights flickering above them, a police ambulance, and a contingent of uniformed police stationed across the street from the entrance to the halls. There was also one Tri-Di unit mounted atop a truck, and a couple of hundred curiosity seekers, gawking. Among them were twenty-five or so teenagers of both sexes, each carrying a child's baseball bat. These latter were dressed identically in prole clothing—sweaters and denim shorts.

Hamp said, "Not much of a turnout when you consider Cos is exposing himself. I'd think there'd be thousands.''

Max said cynically, "The news media has been given orders to play down the Deathwish Wobbly. They can't ignore him entirely, news being news, and the fact that he might get burned any minute. But they're trying to ease coverage on him and especially this meeting. Every radical organization going, no matter how zany, is on Roy Cos's bandwagon, whether he wants them or not. Everybody's beginning to have second thoughts about whether basic changes ought to be made in the world's socioeconomic systems, even in the Soviet Complex and the People's Republic of China.''

They came up to the entry to the halls, just as two heavy limousines slid quickly to the curb immediately before them.

"Cos,'' Max grunted.

Four men, Gyrojets swinging from their hips in quick-draw holsters, sprang from the first vehicle and immediately dashed back to surround the second one, each of them at a corner. Their hands rested on their guns and their eyes were never still as they scanned the crowd, not excluding the police or the Tri-Di crew. Two of the doors of the second limo opened and three more guards erupted. They immediately stationed themselves between the car and the entry, and they too had their hands on pistol butts. The teenagers with the baseball bats pressed closer, between the guards and the building entrance.

Two more men got out of the second limo and looked up and down the street, one apprehensively, the other as though resigned.

Max said, "Jesus, is that the Deathwish Wobbly? Colorless looking little guy, isn't he?"

Forry Brown was saying, "Inside. Let's get inside, damn it. I don't like to be out in the open like this."

Roy Cos grunted and they headed for the door, the guards crowding around them now.

Roy Cos's manager hesitated and looked at one of the kids with the baseball bats. "Who the hell are you?" he said.

The boy saluted with his bat. "We're the Junior Wobblies, sir. Come to help protect Comrade Cos." He wielded the bat as though it was a field marshal's baton.

Roy Cos looked at him. "Junior Wobblies?" he said. "There is no such organization. If there was, I would have heard of it."

The boy wasn't fazed. He looked to be about seventeen— man sized, but with a teenager's awkwardness. "We've organized on our own, Comrade Cos. We haven't had time to get in touch with the national organization for their approval. There's fifty of us here surrounding the building. If any of these professional mercenaries show up, we'll give 'em hell."

Ron grunted in disbelief and his hand tightened on his Gyrojet.

But Forry shook his head. "Let them alone," he said. "The Graf doesn't have any teenagers in his outfit. His need is for experienced professionals." He clapped the boy on the shoulder. "Carry on, kid."

"Yes, sir."

Hamp and Max had joined the Wobbly contingent as they entered the building, three of the guards going ahead.

Max said to Roy Cos, "We're the delegates from the Anti-Racist League."

Roy shook hands. "I suppose you know my name," he said. "And this is Forrest Brown, my business manager."

"Max Finklestein and Horace Hampton," Max introduced them.

"The meeting's on the third floor," Forry said nervously. "Let's get going." '

Ron and Les got into the elevator alone and rode up, to check out the way. The other guards packed around Roy and Forry, waiting.

Roy looked over at Hamp wanly and said, "A helluva way to live."

The black nodded. The other was right. The elevator returned.

On the third floor, Ron and Les were waiting. The whole group proceeded to a hall down the corridor from which sounds were emanating. They were evidently a bit late.

Two members of the Synthesis committee were at the door checking credentials. Roy Cos, on the face of it, hardly needed them, but he went through the motions of proving himself a delegate from the Wobblies. Max presented a letter identifying himself and Horace Hampton.

The meeting was a bore, doomed to failure from its inception. The Synthesis group, which had proposed it, was obviously sincere in its desire to unite all the radical elements but, as Hamp whispered to Max Finklestein, sincerity alone was dull as dishwater.

There were perhaps thirty-five present, including the Synthesis committee, the bodyguards, and various delegates. The leading representatives were those from the Wobblies, the Nihilists, the Luddites, and the Libertarians, in addition to the Anti-Racists. The other delegates were from splinter groups and some, splinters from splinters. There was even one representative from an organization evidently unknown to the others, called Technocracy, Incorporated. Going at least a century and a half back, the Technocrats opted for a world government dominated by scientists, engineers, and technicians. He wasn't quite booed down.

A table in front of the hall acted as a rostrum and each delegation was called upon to give the program of its organization. Roy spoke for the Wobblies, Max Finklestein for the Anti-Racist League, a Nils Ostrander for the Nihilists, and a blowsy woman named Bertha Holtz held forth for the Libertarians, who evidently carried high the banner of the new women's lib and that of the gays as well. After these four stars, the splinter groups each had their turn, turns that dealt almost exclusively with hair-splitting.

Hamp and Max had seated themselves next to Roy Cos and Forry Brown, the guards being strategically placed about the room, all standing with their backs to the walls. Hamp spotted Nils Ostrander, who sat next to a younger, very earnest-looking man whose suit was by far the best of any of those present. He also spotted the other person he was looking for, an athletic-looking young fellow in his early twenties. The chairman had introduced him as the sole delegate from one of the smaller organizations back East, of which Hamp had never heard, and suspected that no one else present had either.

By the time each organization had had its say, the chairman was looking distressed; indeed, downright unhappy. He said, "Did anyone else wish to speak?"

Hamp stood and said, "I wouldn't mind doing a little summing up."

He was invited to the table and stood in front of it, rather than behind.

He looked over them, sighed, and said, "This meeting is a farce and I suspect that by this time most of us realize it. It's been a farce because its purpose is unobtainable. The organizations here can't get together because they don't stand for the same things. I can't figure out what some of you *do* stand for. Everybody here is against something, but damn few are *for* anything. Cos's Wobblies at least have a program, whether or not it's valid, but the Nihilists proudly announce that they haven't. All they want to do is tear down the present social system without having anything definite to replace it. The Libertarians want to reform the present Welfare State by granting more GAS for all proles, by pushing through still further rights for women and gays. They aren't interested in complete change, just reform. The Luddites want to turn the wheels of progress backwards. They want to destroy modern technology and return to the days before automation and computerization, when all of the labor force was needed in production, distribution, and services. The trouble is that you can't uninvent things any more than you can unscramble eggs. We of the Anti-Racist League have only one thing in common with the Luddites: our interest isn't in overthrowing

People's Capitalism and neither is theirs. Neither is it the interest of the Libertarians. In fact, in the ranks of anti-racists are some who are wealthy and have an interest in maintaining the status quo, save on the racial question. You see, none of us stands for the same thing. We can't unite.''

The audience stirred, some muttering among themselves.

Nils Ostrander, the delegate from the Nihilists, was on his feet angrily. ''That's defeatism! Quite a few of us stand for the complete dismemberment of the welfare state. We ought to get together to pull this rotten system down.''

More mutterings and still more agitation. The saturnine Max Finklestein was looking at his companion in amusement.

Hamp said deliberately, ''I've done a lot of wondering about the Nihilists. You are a continuation of the terrorists of the late 20th century, such as the Symbiosis Army here in the States, and the Sekigun, the so-called Red Army of Japan, and similar groups in Germany and Italy. Anti-establishment, but pro-what? And, given the viewpoint of those who opt for the status quo, you serve a very definite need. Whether you want to be or not, you serve as agents provocateurs. The assassinations and kidnappings laid at your door serve to turn sincere people of good will away from any movement that proclaims the need for fundamental change. People are repelled by what you do in the name of radicalism, which puts a chip on their shoulders about all revolutionary groups— including the Wobblies, who foreswear force and violence and want to make their changes through legal means. In short, you're the kiss of death to all the movements represented here tonight. If there was no such organization as the Nihilists, it would be to the interest of such outfits as the United Church, the IABI, the World Club and, for that matter, Mercenaries, Incorporated, to start one. They use you to louse up the image of anybody advocating change.''

''That's a lie!'' Ostrander yelled in indignation.

''Is it?'' the black said emptily. ''Let me give an example. Recently, the multimillionaire World Club man, Harold Dunninger, managed to get himself on the shitlist of the United Church, as well as in the bad graces of some of the higher-echelon members of the World Club. Names? Harrington Chase, Moyer of the IABI, and Lothar von Brandenburg, the Graf, who was anxious to take the place scheduled for

Dunninger in the top ranks of the World Club. Obviously it wouldn't do for Dunninger to be eliminated by one of the Graf's men. So the job was delegated to the Nihilists and the blame put on them."

"That's a lie, you bastard!"

"No, it isn't, Ostrander. You engineered it yourself. You're a mole in the Nihilists, an agent of the Graf."

The Nihilist delegate was gaping at him, his face white, only partially in anger. His younger companion seated next to him was eyeing him strangely.

Hamp shrugged in contempt. "You pretended it was a kidnapping to raise funds for your organization but you put the ransom so high there was no chance of it being met. Then you killed him, per orders of the Graf. I don't have the proof with me here tonight, but now that I've made the charge, I have no doubt that your fellow Nihilists will look into the matter."

The black flicked a hand at the chairman to indicate that he was through and returned to his chair.

Forry Brown looked at him, amusement on his wizened face. "You really throw the shit in the fan, don't you?"

Roy Cos was looking thoughtful. "You know," he said, "I think you're right, Hamp. I've often wondered about what motivates those Nihilists. They're just too far around the bend to be true."

Hamp's talk had been the finish of the meeting. It broke up into squabbles, everybody standing as they argued.

Max said mildly, "What happened to our friend, Nils Ostrander?"

Billy Tucker had come up, worried about the way the gathering was now milling around. He said, "I just saw him light out, arguing with that kid with him. Shouldn't we get out of here?"

Hamp said to Roy, "I'd like to talk to you a little more. Could it be arranged?"

Roy Cos said, "We're staying in a suite at the Drake, just for the night. Why don't you come over with us?"

"Right," Hamp told him. "But just a minute. I want to say something to someone here."

"Hurry it up," Forry Brown told him, scowling. "I don't like Roy to be exposed to so many people for so long, and we've still got to run the gauntlet in the street. By this time the word's probably gotten around that the Deathwish Wobbly is inside this building and there might be a few thousand rubberneckers out there, with a few of the Graf's men sprinkled among them."

Hamp made his way across the room and confronted one of the delegates, who looked as though he was preparing to leave.

Hamp said, looking directly into the man's eyes, "Hello, Pinell. I understand you're looking for me."

The other was too young to be very adept at covering but he tried. He said, "The name's Merson and I represent . . ."

"Your name's Franklin Pinell," Jerry interrupted flatly, "and you were sent by the Graf and Peter Windsor to hit me. You're the son of the late Buck Pinell, co-founder of Mercenaries, Incorporated, who has an account amounting to some forty-five million pseudo-dollars in a bank in Berne."

Frank Pinell's eyebrows went up in shock. He said, "How the hell would you know a thing like that?"

"I own the bank," Hamp said. "Now, look, I want to talk to you but I have something else on the fire right now. Where are you staying?"

"At the Drake, but . . ."

"Wizard. That's where I'm going right now. In fact, maybe I'll register myself. I'll see you later tonight. What name did you say you were going under?"

"Merson," Frank said weakly.

"See you later," Hamp returned to where Roy and Forry and the bodyguards were waiting.

Forry, ever suspicious, said, "Who the hell was that?"

Hamp grunted amusement. "A guy the Graf sent to finish me off. Maybe I'll tell you about it someday."

Some of the delegates were still arguing out in the hall as the group of them headed for the elevator. Max said to Hamp, "I've got some things to do tonight, including a report to the Executive Committee. I'll meet you in the morning."

"Great," Hamp told him. "I'll register at the Drake."

The guards took over again at the elevator. Billy and Ron went down first to check out the lobby. When the elevator returned the five remaining guards, plus Roy, Forry, Hamp, and Max, all crowded in. So did several of the other delegates, two of them still arguing. Forry began to remonstrate about their coming along in this elevator load, but Roy shook his head wearily and the little ex-newsman shrugged it off.

Halfway down, Roy's business manager gave a startled cough. Max darted a look at him. "For Christ's sake," he blurted. "What's wrong?"

The small man's face was wet and shiny and gray of color. He had both of his fists clamped tight against his chest. His jaw was going up and down as if he was trying to say something that wouldn't come.

Les blurted, "He's having a heart attack!"

Two of the guards grabbed the stricken man by the arms, supporting him. The elevator came to a halt at the ground floor and the group emerged, hauling Forry Brown with them. They headed for a chair.

Hamp yelled at the top of his voice, "A doctor! Get a doctor from that police ambulance across the street!"

Forry Brown's eyebrows were high, his eyes bulging as though in surprise. His jaw continued to move, soundlessly. And even as they lowered him into the chair, he passed out.

Two white-jacketed young men, Red Cross bands around their arms, came hurrying in with a stretcher. They expertly snaked the stricken man onto it and trotted from the lobby with him.

Ron said, "I'll go along," and followed after.

Les was the first to recover from surprised confusion. He said to Roy, "Let's get out of here. They'll take him to the hospital. There's nothing we can do and meanwhile, for all we know, there are a couple of the Graf's boys waiting outside."

Roy nodded dumbly.

Hamp said, "Under the circumstances, we'll have to call off our get-together."

But the Wobbly organizer shook his head. "No, if we've got anything to say to each other, we might as well do it. There's no guarantee I'll last the night."

The six remaining guards stationed themselves around Hamp and their charge as the body of them moved out the door and made a beeline for the limousines. Roy, Hamp, and Billy got into the rear of one, two of the guards into the front. Then the three remaining got into the lead car. Hamp looked out the window. The crowd had grown considerably larger and the teenage kids with their baseball bats held it back, very businesslike. A half-drunk prole waved one hand high and yelled, " 'Ray for Deathwish Wobbly!"

"Yeah," Roy muttered as they took off.

The bodyguards of the Wobbly national organizer had their parts down pat by this time. They moved with precision and cool efficiency. The limousines smoothed up to an entry in the area of the Drake Hotel. The three in the lead vehicle popped out and scouted the vicinity, two of them going into the hotel. Then the three returned to the second limousine and stood alert while its occupants emerged. Then all moved into the hotel and took the service elevator.

All of Cos's basic crew were accommodated in one large suite, Hamp was introduced to Mary Ann Elwyn and Ferd Feldmeyer, and Roy went over to the bar while Les told the secretary and speech writer what had happened.

"Damn," Feldmeyer said, his plump little mouth looking petulant. "Those cigarettes. How bad did it look?"

"Bad," Billy said in disgust. "He passed out. But the medics were there immediately. Nowadays they ought to be able to do something. A man no older than Forry usually doesn't die from his first heart attack."

Roy had knocked back a first drink. He said, looking at Ferd, "Had he ever had one before?"

"Not as far as I know. I've known him for years and he never mentioned any heart trouble."

When the drinks had been distributed, Roy Cos looked over at the black. He said, "Well, we should hear about Forry within the hour. Meanwhile, what did you have in mind, Hampton?"

Hamp half emptied his glass. He said, "As you know, I'm from the Anti-Racist League. That's my prime interest. I wondered what you thought of the World Club. The story is beginning to surface that they're in favor of establishing a World State. They're behind bringing all of Latin America into the United States, and now Australia and New Zealand. I suspect that the Common Europe countries will be next and I also suspect that such nations as Spain, Portugal, and Italy will line up overnight, and the rest soon after. Hell, even commie countries, beginning with Cuba and Yugoslavia, wouldn't be far behind.''

Roy said, ''And?''

The black regarded him questioningly. ''It would seem to me that under a World State racism would disappear.''

Roy shook his head very emphatically. ''Why? Suppose we *had* a United States of the World. Why would that end racism? It hasn't been ended in the United States, so far. Sure, if it was a world government under the Wobbly program, there'd be no reason for racism. But under the status quo? Suppose the World Club took over and made the United Church the state religion. The Prophet does precious little to hide his anti-semitism. That reactionary Harrington Chase is hand in glove with him. The Jews aren't about to join up with the United Church, like so many other smaller religions are. Most of them, these days, are agnostics or atheists and won't support any organized religion. Those who are still Orthodox cling to the faith that's held them together for three thousand years. So the Prophet's down on them, and if his outfit ever becomes the state religion, Jews will be in trouble.''

Hamp didn't like that but he accepted it. He said, ''That's only the Jews.''

Roy made a gesture of contempt. ''It'd be a lot of others, too. Racism isn't an accident, it's deliberately fostered in a class society. When there aren't enough good jobs to go around, then it's handy for a ruling class to have the proles fight among themselves. Supposedly the reason the blacks can't get decent jobs is because the whites take them all, and whites say they can't get jobs because the blacks are moving in on them, or the Chicanos, or the Orientals, or whoever. Divide and rule. Keep the proles at each other's throats so they'll never sit down and figure out that they have a common enemy.''

Hamp said in disgust, ''You people have one-track minds. Whatever's wrong, you blame it on the socioeconomic system.''

''That's where the blame usually is,'' Roy said, obviously too soulweary to want to argue. ''The proles go out to fight their war, division by division. One division carries a banner inscribed *Pacifism*, another *Women's Lib*, another *All Power to the Worker's Councils*, another *Down with Racism*, another *Clean Up the Environment, End Pollution*, and on and on.

None of them seem to see that basically it's the same war and that if they unite their divisions they'd have an army, instead of going out separately—and down to defeat."

Hamp said, "Probably a good simile. But now we get to the real reason I came up here tonight. That Deathwish Policy of yours. Are there any provisions restricting your travel?"

Roy looked at him and shook his head. "None at all. I can go anywhere in the world that I want."

"I wasn't thinking about the world. I was thinking about Lagrange Five, or, better still, the Asteroid Belt Islands."

All of them were gaping at him now.

Hamp said to Roy, "Look, basically you've done what you started out to do. You've brought to the attention of the whole world the program of the Wobblies. People are digesting it. Whether or not they'll buy it is another thing. I'm inclined to doubt it. As it stands now, your time is probably limited to hours. The Graf's hit men are the most experienced on Earth and now, I believe, they're all concentrated on you—all of them in this country, at least. So you take off from the Space Shuttleport in New Mexico for Space Station *Goddard*. There you transfer to a shuttle headed for Island One of the Lagrange Five Project. From there you take the next ore freighter to the Asteroid Belt, select an Island most suited to your needs, and spend the rest of your life there, probably bankrupting whatever damned company signed that Deathwish Policy of yours."

Billy said doubtfully, though liking it, "Okay. But then he doesn't get the message over."

Hamp glowered at him. "Damn it, he's already got the message over. But he can continue spouting his propaganda from the Belt! All he has to do is tape his talks and beam them back Earthside for broadcasting. Besides that, he'd have lots of time on his hands. He wouldn't be leading the life of a hunted animal. He could write a book about the Wobbly program. He could turn out a raft of pamphlets and articles."

"Good grief," Mary Ann said, her eyes wide. She looked at her lover, who was still staring at the black man. There was hope in her face.

Hamp said, urgency in his voice, "Don't you see? You'd be safe out there. Among other things, there are no hit men flitting around on the Islands. It takes all the clearance in the world to get into space at all. And it takes a full year for a spacecraft to get from Lagrange Five to the Asteroid Belt, which is halfway to Jupiter. If one of the Graf's men tried to get through to you, they'd have him spotted months before he ever arrived. And he'd be well aware of the fact that even if he did get through and did you in, there'd be no way he could get safely back. Lagrangists are a rough and ready lot.''

Billy said, "If Roy goes, Les and I go too, and probably Ron, just to be sure.''

Mary Ann nodded. "And so do I.''

Roy took a deep, tired breath and said, "None of us goes.'' He turned his eyes to Hamp. "Thanks for the good intentions but the restrictions on going into space are endless. You've got to have some ability that they need out there. You've got to be a scientist, or some kind of technician or highly experienced worker in construction, or electronics, or whatever. I don't have any such ability, and I doubt if any of the rest of us here do. One of their strictest requirements is that you have an I.Q. of at least 130. I don't. You have to have a far above average Ability Quotient. I don't. I'd be a parasite out there, even if they'd let me come, which they wouldn't.''

All eyes went back to Hamp. Mary Ann's were sick, as though he had overfed a false hope.

"That's where I come in,'' Hamp said. He brought forth his pocket transceiver, activated it, and said, "Information? Put me through to Ian Venner of the Lagrangia Asteroid Belt Federation. He is now in New York as their representative.''

He waited long moments for the connection to be put through. Silence permeated the suite's living room.

There came a tiny voice from the transceiver and Hamp said, "Venner? This is Auburn. I'm calling you about that favor sooner than I had expected.''

He paused, then said, "Good. I am in the company of Roy Cos. Perhaps you have heard of the Deathwish Wobbly. Yes, that's him. I want him, and several of his friends, to become space colonists in the Belt. They won't meet your usual requirements. They will undoubtedly remain for the rest of their lives, unless some very basic changes take place here Earthside.''

He listened for long moments, then said, "Wizard. Oh, Venner? I consider your obligation to me now terminated. Thanks and goodbye."

He switched off the communicator and looked back at Roy. He said softly, "If you can make it to the Shuttleport, Venner's people will take over there."

The Wobbly organizer's lips were pale.

It was then the phone screen buzzed. Mary Ann, in a daze, went to it. She said blankly, "It's Ron, at the hospital."

Billy got it out first. "How's Forry?"

But Mary Ann was listening, shaking her head as though in disbelief. Finally, she switched the screen off.

She turned back to them and said simply, "He—didn't make it. And then, "It wasn't a heart attack. It was murder."

"It couldn't have been," Roy blurted. "I was right there!"

Mary Ann said emptily, "Something long, very thin, very sharp. Something like an antique woman's hatpin. Stuck up through the diaphragm, perforating the heart and flooding it with blood."

"He would have yelled," Les said in utter disbelief.

She said, "Maybe. But from what the doctors told Ron, at first he'd only feel mild discomfort, and especially if he had any lung or stomach or digestive disorders, he wouldn't particularly have noticed the pain. But then the pressure would slow the heart down until it stopped. He'd feel faint, breathless, dizzy, as though he'd had a small aortal attack. He'd be dead in five minutes."

Roy said emptily, "It was meant for me."

Hamp stood up and looked at the Wobbly organizer. "No. It was meant for Forrest Brown. The guards were too tight around you. It's gotten to the point where the Graf's men are out to get anybody associated with you, anybody helping you." He looked at Roy Cos's secretary. "Including Ms. Elwyn. That's why you'd better make a beeline for that shuttleport in New Mexico, Cos."

Roy Cos stood too, and said, "What's all this to you, Hampton? I don't even know you. Certainly, you're no Wobbly. But you've gone far out of your way to extend a life I'd given up."

Hamp tossed his head, brushing it off. "You're a man, Cos, and I believe in a man having a chance to have his say.

What was the quote of Voltaire? 'I disagree with what you say but will defend with my life your right to say it.' A lot of your program doesn't come through to me. For one thing, I think you're out of the times. Maybe, up there in the Belt, you'll learn some things and update what you stand for. And maybe—just maybe—they'll learn some things from you.''

Chapter Twenty-Two: Jeremiah Auburn

Hamp stood before the identity screen on the hotel door and looked at it sardonically. The door buzzed open and he entered. The room was on the small, austere side considering that this was the age-old prestigious Drake.

Frank Pinell was seated, watching a news commentator. Now he took in the chocolate features of the newcomer without expression. Without waiting for an invitation, Hamp went over to the autobar and dialed himself a double brandy. He brought the snifter glass back and settled himself into the room's second chair.

Frank reached over to click the screen off but Hamp said, "No, just a minute. What's he saying?"

The commentator was saying, ". . . and if the victim's identification is genuine, the notorious Luca Cellini, long suspected by the IABI to be Lothar von Brandenburg's top representative in the Americas, has been shot to death on the streets of New York."

"I'll be damned," Hamp said. "Peter Windsor is even more efficient than I thought."

The younger man had been staring bug-eyed at the commentator. Now he shakily reached out and turned down the audio. He sucked in air before saying to the black, "You know Peter Windsor?"

"Yes. One of the most competent snakes this side of the Garden of Eden. How he learned that Cellini had sold out, I'll probably never know."

"Sold out?" Frank said. "I . . . I was just talking to him a few days ago."

"Yes, I know," Hamp said, taking an appreciative sip of his cognac. "He was how I found out that Windsor and the Graf had sent you to finish me off."

Frank said, a touch of irritation in his voice, "If you knew that, why in the devil have you come here? Aren't you afraid I'll carry out the assignment?"

"No," Hamp said. "Why did they send you?"

"I'm not too clear about the details. Evidently, it was more or less a standard assignment. Somebody in the World Club wanted you eliminated."

Hamp stared at him. "The World Club! Wanted Horace Hampton eliminated?"

"Yes. If I understand correctly, they're becoming increasingly conscious of the part the Anti-Racist League might play when the World State begins to embrace third-world countries."

"But why *me*? I'm not even a member of the Executive Committee. Just a field worker."

"If I have it right, there are some strange angles to your Dossier Complete. You're kind of a mystery figure. You're also said to be the Anti-Racist League's most efficient man. Somebody figured that if half a dozen of your key members were eliminated, it would be considerably easier to control the organization."

"I'll be damned," Hamp said thoughtfully. He finished his brandy, went back to the autobar and dialed another. He looked at his reluctant host. "Want a drink? It's a pleasure for me to be knocking back guzzle that the Graf will eventually pay for."

"Beer," Frank said.

Hamp dialed the brew, brought it over, and resumed his own place.

Frank said cautiously, "Why did you think I wasn't a danger to you?"

"Because you're a fake. When I told you I own the bank your father used in Berne, I wasn't joking. I own controlling interests in various other banks as well. When Cellini told me you'd been sent to hit me, I had you checked out and then your father as well."

"All right, great. But why do you say I'm a fake?"

"You were deported, picking Tangier. Tangier is the biggest base of Mercenaries, Incorporated outside Liechtenstein. Anybody wanting to make contact with the organization couldn't do better than to go there. You were deported because you had supposedly committed four felonies and the legal computers automatically ordered your deportation."

"What do you mean supposedly?" Frank said, his voice flat.

"The first two felonies, well, they were probably genuine. Certainly the first one, back when you were a kid. Kind of a kid's prank which turned sour. But the third one and the fourth? Nope; you faked them. The murder, the crime that made it definite that you'd be deported, you didn't commit. You confessed to it, but you didn't do it. The way my agents reconstructed the thing, you hung around in the most rugged area of Detroit, possibly the toughest big city in the country, during the most dangerous time of night, for a period of weeks. Eventually, you found what you were looking for, a fresh corpse. You set the stage for getting the blame and you got it, guaranteeing deportation." Hamp took another pull at his brandy. "You're no killer, Pinell. It was all a scheme to get next to the Graf and it evidently worked out even better than you must have hoped."

Frank glared at him. "Why would I do that?"

Hamp shrugged. "It would seem obvious that you want to get your hands on that money your father left. Forty-five million pseudo-dollars isn't chicken feed—not a poultry sum, as the expression goes."

The younger man ignored the pun and said sullenly, "I had no idea it was that much."

"It wasn't originally, but it's been sitting there in Berne for almost twenty years, invested in Swiss gilt-edged securities."

"It's my money," Frank said. "I didn't even know about it until my mother told me on her deathbed. She hated the very thought of the stuff but she hated the Graf even more and didn't want him to get his hands on it. I'm my father's only living relative. My mother suspected, but had no proof, that my father was killed by the Graf. The last time she saw him, he hinted that they were on the outs with each other. My father, it would seem, didn't like some of the new fields into which Brandenburg was expanding. My father was a soldier of fortune, not a hit man."

The black eyed him questioningly. "Why didn't you just go to Switzerland and demand your inheritance?"

"It's tied up in some complicated way I don't understand.

Evidently, my father was on the way to change that when he was killed. I'm not sure about the details but I suspect that the Graf is part of the complication.''

"If Lothar von Brandenburg could get his hands on that money, he would. The sonofabitch is just about bankrupt now. His overhead is astronomical. With your father's money he could retire, or do just about anything else he wanted to do."

"That's what I've suspected, damn it. I think there must be some kind of requirement that both of us must appear, or sign something, before either can get his hands on the amount.''

"So what the hell are you doing tailing *me* around? By the way, didn't Windsor tell you I'm supposed to be a little on the dangerous side? You're a bit inexperienced when it comes to taking me on."

"I don't think Peter Windsor is in on it. I don't think the Graf has told anybody about it, not even Margit Krebs, his secretarial thinking machine." Frank finished his beer and put the glass down. "The Graf put on a big show of friendship. Welcomed me with open arms as the son of his best friend. The implication is that I'm now one of the inner circle and they're breaking me in to the workings of the organization."

"And this is your first, uh, assignment, eh?"

"Not exactly. They sent me along with one of their top operatives to see a competitor named Rivas in Paris. He was invited to join up, or else. He turned down the offer, mentioning in passing that he thought the Graf was responsible for my father's death."

"What happened?"

"It would seem that Windsor, or somebody, had bribed all of Rivas's people out from under him. His bodyguard knifed him to death."

Hamp looked at him in surprise. "And you participated in a thing like that?" His tone turned sardonic. "A nice clean-cut boy like you?"

Frank flushed. "Listen," he said. "I'm not as much of a milksop as you seem to think. As far as I'm concerned, Rivas was no better than Nat Fraser, the hit man who arranged his death. Nor Peter Windsor, the Graf, nor any of the others. I didn't mind seeing him killed at all. Not at all! He was a professional dealer in death. He was the type of man that I would have no moral reserves about seeing killed—or given the circumstances, doing it myself.''

Hamp pursed his lips and chuckled before getting up and heading for the bar again. "Another beer?" he said.

"No thanks," Frank said nastily. "And you act as though you're half drenched already."

"The complaint has been made before," Hamp told him, dialing another double brandy. "But I can still operate."

"And I've heard that story before," the younger man told him in sarcasm. "Sometimes from drivers who explain that they can drive better when they have a couple of drinks in them. Famous last words before they plow into a tree. You're on the death list of the most dangerous people in the world and here you are getting drenched. Hell, even I could take you and, as you so nicely explained, I'm inexperienced."

"Don't try it," Hamp said mildly, taking a pull at the double brandy. "But now we get to the nitty-gritty. What were you doing at the Synthesis meeting if you're not really interested in doing chores for the Graf?"

"I had to go through the motions," Frank said, all fed up with the conversation. "I had to *look* as though I was trying to get to you. For all I know, some of Peter Windsor's other people were there."

"They were," Hamp told him. "What the hell did you think you were going to do to put over your act?"

"I don't know," the other said. "I was trying to play it by ear, hoping something would come up that would enable me to report back, admitting failure but for some good reason. I have to stay in the game, supposedly in the Graf's good graces, until I can find out what's going on. I haven't the vaguest idea, so far, what kind of hold he has on my father's fortune."

Hamp thought about it some more. He said finally, "The reason the Graf was willing to send you after me was that he wanted to get something to hold over you. Some lever that would help him persuade you to do whatever has to be done to get his hands on your father's fortune. If you'd killed me, as ordered, then he'd have had his lever." He knocked back the remaining brandy in one gulp and added, "I just dropped in to let you know I was onto you and to warn you to stay off my back. So now I'll . . . what the hell was that?"

"What was what?"

"That news commentator. What did he say?"

"I haven't been listening."

"Play it back. The last couple of minutes."

"All right." Frank shrugged, pressed the replay buttons, and turned up the volume.

He missed the first sentence or so. The commentator was saying, ". . . the famous rocket-set leader, of recent years turned recluse. Indications are, his sports car left the road, either forced off as suggested by the French authorities, or out of control as a result of overindulgence in alcohol or narcotics at a party he had just left. Executives of the far-flung Auburn empire have thus far issued no statement. Wall Street in the City, London, and the Common Europe Bourse are expected to react heavily in the morning."

Horace Hampton, staring unseeingly, staggered to his feet and headed for the autobar. He demanded of the other, "Play that back again, from the beginning."

Frank Pinell, his expression denoting complete lack of comprehension, obeyed.

The commentator said, "Flash from the French Riviera. The multibillionaire playboy of this century, Jeremiah Auburn, died today in a car accident near Nice when . . ."

"Switch it off," Hamp yelled.

Frank obeyed, staring blankly.

The black sank back into his chair. He swallowed the drink in one gulp. "Jim," he said, meaninglessly, so far as the other was concerned.

"What the hell's the matter?" Frank said.

"Shut up." The black sat there, staring unseeingly. "Jim," he muttered. "Oh, hell, Jim. Why was I such an asshole? I laid you wide open to that murderous bastard Windsor."

"What the devil are you talking about?" Frank said.

"Shut up."

Frank Pinell twisted his mouth in resignation and got up to get himself another beer. He hadn't the vaguest idea what had floored his visitor. Evidently, some bigshot playboy had a traffic accident in southern France. So what? He didn't follow the social news by any means but he had vaguely heard of Jeremiah Auburn, one of those upper-class characters who would spend five thousand on a bottle of wine laid down during the time of DeGaulle. Frank had never paid more than five dollars in his life for a bottle of wine, and then he was splurging.

At long last Hamp shook his head, as though in despair, and got up and went over to the room's small desk. He sat down in front of the phone screen and deactivated the video before dialing.

The face that faded in on the screen looked as though it had recently received a great shock.

Hamp said, "Barry, this is Auburn."

The eyes widened in absolute disbelief. "But . . . but . . . on the news I just . . ."

"I know, I know. So did I. A case of mistaken identity, undoubtedly. Now, this is what I want you to do: refuse any comment to the news media whatsoever. For the time being, above all, don't let it get out that I am still alive. To *nobody*, understand?"

"Well, yes sir." And then, a touch of suspicion there. "How do I know this is really you?"

"Damn it, you know my voice. Besides, who else has access to this phone number?"

"I . . . yes, sir." There was relief in the tone now.

"Wizard. Now, I want you to send Captain Wayland and the plane to pick up two men here at the Chicago North Side Airport. He is to fly them to Europe and the crew is to take their orders as though they were my own. The men's names are Horace Hampton and Franklin Pinell. They will make only one stop, in New York. Mr. Hampton will leave the aircraft just long enough to go into the city and acquire some, uh, equipment at my headquarters there. Have a limousine waiting for him at the airport. Is that clear?"

"Yes, sir. A Mr. Hampton and a Mr. Pinell."

"That's all, Barry. I'll get in touch with you shortly. Meanwhile, mum's the word." He flicked off the phone and turned back to Frank. "Pack your luggage," he said.

The other had been completely flabbergasted by the phone talk. He hadn't any idea whatever of what had gone on. He said, "Why?"

Hamp went back to the bar and dialed another drink. He said, "We're going to Liechtenstein to see the Graf and my old chum-pal Peter Windsor."

The younger man ogled him. "Are you out of your mind?"

"Probably, but your orders were to get Horace Hampton. Wizard; you've got him. He's going back to the Wolfschloss with you." The autobar delivered a full liter of French cognac. Hamp took the top off and applied the bottle directly to his mouth. He then retopped it and handed it to Frank. "Put this in your bag. I won't be taking any luggage."

Frank was still gaping at him. "Bringing you back to the Wolfschloss! Now I know you're completely around the bend, Hampton. That place is a fort. You can't get in carrying any kind of a weapon and once in there's no way of getting out. The Graf will have you by the balls. And probably me as well."

Hamp shook his head. "No. Your story is that I had something interesting to tell you and wanted to relay it to Brandenburg himself. And I'll have the most powerful weapon in the world to take into that fort."

"What? I tell you, they search you all ways from Tuesday, both electronically and physically."

"My weapon comes in a checkbook. Come on, let's get out of here. Wayland will be at the airport by the time we arrive."

The pilot checked their identities with care, obviously somewhat taken aback by this assignment. However, there was nothing to fault them. He handed back the International Credit Cards, saying with a frown to Hamp, "Haven't I seen you somewhere before?"

"I doubt it," Hamp said laconically. "I've never been there."

"Yes, sir," Wayland said, touching the visor of his cap in an informal salute. "What are your orders, aside from the stop-over in New York?"

"Fly to the airport nearest to Vaduz, in Liechtenstein."

"Yes, sir. That'll probably be in Austria."

"And while we're on the way, call ahead and have a vehicle waiting for us, with any clearance that might be required to enter Liechtenstein."

"Yes, sir. I'll check that out. Gentlemen, shall we go aboard?"

To Frank Pinell's absolute surprise, the black seemed to

drink himself sober on the flight across the Atlantic. The bar on the huge aircraft was more elaborate than any Frank had seen anywhere and was presided over by a uniformed bartender and two stewards to serve. Hamp kept them earning their pay.

Frank found himself a stateroom and slept almost all of the way to Austria. He had a suspicion that he was going to need all the rest he could get. He didn't like the prospects for the morrow. When he rejoined his companion, it was to find him sitting in the same chair in the main lounge. Whether or not he had gotten any sleep at all, Frank couldn't tell. If anything, he looked less under the influence of the liquor he had been drinking than he had back in the room at the Drake. There was a new shift of bartender and waiters waiting on him.

Even as Frank seated himself, the chief steward entered and said respectfully, "We shall be landing within the hour, gentlemen."

Hamp looked down at himself. "I suppose I ought to have a change of clothing," he said. He was dressed in a cheap suit, just above prole quality.

The chief steward said, "But, sir, we didn't pick up any luggage for you. The other gentleman, yes. But you came aboard without any bags at all."

The black came to his feet. He said sourly, "I suspect that Mr. Auburn's things will fit me."

The steward goggled. "Mr. Auburn's things?"

Hamp eyed him. "Weren't your orders to take my instructions as though they were those of your employer himself?"

"Why . . . yes, sir."

"Wizard. I'll go and check out his clothes." Hamp started for the corridor which led down to the aircraft's staterooms.

The chief steward, still looking distressed, called after him, "The master suite is at the far end of . . ."

"Yeah, yeah," Hamp muttered.

At Feldkirch it was found that there were no difficulties involved in driving the sports hover-car that was waiting to take them into the tiny principality. They took off, Frank driving, Hamp next to him with brandy bottle in hand, taking an occasional nip from it.

When they reached Vaduz and began driving out the road

to the Wolfschloss which loomed before them on the mountain top, Hamp said, "You'd better call ahead and tell them we're coming. From what I've heard about this place, you run a chance of getting your ass shot off if you approach unannounced."

"Don't you know it," Frank told him, bringing out his transceiver. He went through the routine of dialing the special number Peter Windsor had given him.

When the Englishman's easygoing face appeared on the tiny screen, it was to express surprise. "Frank!" he said. "I say, this isn't an overseas call. Where are you?"

"Coming up on the schloss," Frank told him.

"Then . . . well, you completed your mission?"

"In a way," Frank said. "I've got Hampton with me."

That made Peter Windsor blink.

Frank redirected the transceiver so that the face of Hamp was shown to Windsor. He said dryly, "Peter Windsor, meet Horace Hampton." And then, before either of the others could speak, "I'm coming down the road toward the cable car terminal, Peter. Do you want to clear me through?"

"Of course, dear boy. Come immediately to my office in the keep. Be seeing you, old chap. Cheers." His face faded, still expressing bewilderment.

"First hurdle," Hamp muttered. He put the half-empty bottle in the glove compartment. "Reserve supply," he said. "We might need it later."

"If there is a later," Frank said glumly. They were approaching the first roadblock, a concrete pillbox with three armed men before it. Frank began to pull up but they smiled and waved him on.

Hamp said, "This inner circle you mentioned that you're now being admitted to: who's in it besides the Graf and Windsor?"

"The only one I've met, if there are any others, is Margit Krebs, the Graf's secretary and data bank."

Hamp looked over at him.

Frank said, "She's got complete recall and keeps most of his secrets in her head."

"Nobody else is in this inner circle?"

"Not that I know of. When they're having a conference, the butler, Sepp, is sometimes around and they don't seem to care. He told me my father once saved his life—and warned me about all three of them.''

''Sounds like quite a chummy crew,'' Hamp said. ''How long before we start talking to the Graf?''

''If they see us right on through, possibly twenty minutes or so.''

''Wizard,'' the black said and reached into his jacket. He brought forth a container which looked something like a cigarette case, opened it, and took out a hypodermic while Frank looked at him in dismay. Wordlessly, Hamp rolled up his left sleeve and expertly took the contents of the hypodermic into his arm. He then threw the syringe out the window.

Frank said bitterly, ''Fer chrissakes, Hampton, isn't all that guzzle enough?''

''Thanks for reminding me,'' the other told him and opened the glove compartment for a pull at the bottle there.

They pulled up before the cable car terminal and got out of the vehicle, met immediately by a smiling officer.

He saluted and said, ''Welcome back to the Wolfschloss, Mr. Pinell. I'm Lieutenant Lugos. Mr. Windsor has instructed me to see you to the donjon.'' He looked Hamp up and down.

Frank said, ''This is Mr. Hampton. My luggage is in the back. There's a gun in it.''

''Yes, sir. We'll take care of it.'' The lieutenant turned and led the way.

Horace Hampton seemed only mildly interested in the routine of being admitted to the Wolfschloss, the identity checks, the searches, the cable car ride. And didn't even seem particularly interested when they entered the enceinte in the direction of the towering keep.

Lieutenant Lugos was walking ahead and Frank said, from the side of his mouth, ''You act as though you've been here before.''

The other shook his head. ''No, but I had some of my agents check it out once. They got good video sequences.''

''Even inside the keep?''

''On the lower floors. Not up in the living quarters of the Graf. One tried and didn't make it.''

The younger man stared, ''What happened to him?''

''Peter Windsor happened to him. He was caught, tortured, put under scopolamine and, of course, spilled his guts.''

"How do you know?"

"Windsor dropped a hint to me the next time I saw him. Happily, the others had gotten away before the captured one could inform on them. Our chum-pal, Peter, evidently was more amused by my curiosity than anything else. I suppose the Wolfschloss has been infiltrated before."

They had no more difficulty in entering the donjon than they'd had at the cable car terminal. Five minutes after Lieutenant Lugos surrendered them to the guard at the keep's massive door, they had entered the office of Peter Windsor.

The Graf's right-hand man was, characteristically, lounging in well-worn sports clothes behind his desk, his feet up on its surface. He grinned affably and said as he stood, "I say, Pinell, you're full of surprises." He looked at Hamp and frowned slightly. "Haven't I seen you before, somewhere?"

"People keep asking me that," Hamp said. "I must look like some celebrity."

Peter Windsor shrugged. "No point in mucking around, Hampton. What was your idea in coming here? Doesn't make much sense, really."

"I thought I'd explain that directly to the Graf," Hamp told him. His eyes went around the room, in curiosity, not missing the submachine gun on the wall.

"I dare say that's a good idea," Windsor said, lazily coming to his feet. "Come along, you chaps, Lothar is expecting us."

He led the way down the winding corridor to the Graf's office.

When they entered the spacious office of Lothar von Brandenburg, it was to find the Graf and Margit Krebs seated in the same chairs as during Frank's original interview. To top it, after offhanded introductions, during which no one made any pretense of desire to shake hands, Peter Windsor slumped into the chair he had utilized on the first occasion Frank had met the inner circle. Frank and Hamp sat too, on the same couch but at opposite ends.

For a few moments all was silent as Hamp took in the three of them and they returned the compliment.

The Graf said finally, "To be candid, this confrontation surprises me. I haven't the vaguest idea what you had in mind, Franklin." He turned smoky, expressionless eyes to

the black. "Nor you, sir. Will one of you explain?" He looked
back at Frank and added, "Not, of course, that I distrust your
judgment and discretion, my boy."

"Of course not," Peter said dryly.

Hamp said, "I came to make a deal."

The gray-flecked, uncanny irises turned back to him. "Indeed? Please develop it. I am always interested in deals."

"Wizard," Hamp said. His dark eyes took in the short
elderly mercenary and they were almost as unreadable as the
old man's. "Brandenburg," he went on finally, "you've got
a tiger by the tail. You've built up an empire and now you
can't abdicate. You're just on the verge of being dead broke
and you can't get out from under. The upkeep on this pile of
rock alone must be astronomical and that's not counting your
other establishments scattered around the world, and it doesn't
count the compensations and pensions you're under obligation
to keep up. One of these days, you're going to miss a payroll.
When you do—well, the people on your payroll are the most
dangerous killers in the world."

"What rot," Peter drawled.

"Silence, Peter," the Graf told him without looking in his
direction. He said to Hamp, "Since nothing that is said in this
room this morning will ever go beyond its walls, we might as
well be completely free. What has given you cause to believe
me less than—ah, solvent? My interests are widespread."

"So are mine," Hamp said flatly. "I have sources and I
have my common sense besides. Mercenary use has been
declining for decades. So have clandestine sales of arms. The
citizens of smaller nations are in revolt against their governments so far as military purchases are concerned. They've
had a bellyful of it for a century or so. They're also getting a
bellyful of assassinations and terrorism. All sorts of inquiries
are going out about you and your activities. And this Roy Cos
affair is almost sure to wind up with Deathwish Policies
declared illegal on a worldwide basis, especially if and when
the United States becomes the United States of the World. To
sum it up, your business is melting away, Brandenburg."

"I see," the Graf nodded agreeably. "I am amazed at your
interest in my affairs. But let us delve into it a bit further.
Would it surprise you to learn that my plans include joining
the upper echelons of the World Club and participating, along

with my organization, in the World State?" The Graf's emotionless voice held a touch of smugness.

Hamp shook his head definitely. "No. Not after last night. And not on top of Harold Dunninger."

The old man's voice was now ice. "What about Harold Dunninger?"

"It's come out that you were behind his kidnapping and death. That you wished this candidate eliminated so that you would be able to assume Central Committee membership. But last night you went too far."

The Graf looked over at Margit Krebs, scowling. "What happened last night?"

Peter said quickly, "I was going to bring that up at our morning meeting, Lothar." He cleared his throat. "I fancied that you'd be surprised. Jeremiah Auburn has been reported killed in a vehicle crackup on the French Riviera. An accident, I imagine."

"No accident," Hamp said. "And the Central Committee isn't going to stand for one of its members being coldly murdered for opposing you. Your name will be mud in the World Club, Brandenburg."

The old man hadn't taken his eyes from his top aide. "Why wasn't I informed about this?" he demanded.

"I told you, Chief. I was going to bring it up this morning, don't you know? A bit of bad luck, wasn't it?" Windsor's eyes went from his employer to Hamp and then quickly back again. "You're not taking this bloody fool's word against mine, are you? He's obviously up to something, but the silly ass has put himself into our hands. We'll show him what the drill is around here. A bit of scopolamine and we'll find out what he's all about."

"You must think me a dolt, Peter," the Graf said coldly.

All his languid pretenses were gone. Peter Windsor shot to his feet, his face in a fury. He turned red and stalked from the room.

The Graf said to Margit, who had been sitting quietly through all of this, "Our Peter seems a bit impetuous these days, Fräulein."

"I'd noticed it," she said without inflection.

The Graf turned back to Hamp. "You mentioned a deal. I

confess I haven't the vaguest idea of what you might have in mind."

Hamp said, "Frank, here, was left a sizeable estate by his father. It's in the hands of a Berne bank, almost forty-five million pseudo-dollars in the form of immediately convertible securities. First, you will cooperate in securing the inheritance for him."

The Graf gave one of his humorless chuckles. "I have never heard of such a thing." He turned to Margit. "Have you, Fräulein?"

But Margit failed to take the cue. "Yes," she said deliberately. Her eyes seemed to glaze slightly. "Its provisions are that the fortune be turned over to Franklin Pinell when he reaches the age of thirty. Until that time, he would be able to acquire it only with your permission. Both of you would have to appear in Berne to testify. If he should die before reaching thirty, the fortune goes to various American charities. If you should die before he reaches thirty, then the fortune reverts to him, as soon as he has reached twenty-one—which, of course, he already has done."

For once, the Graf lost his aplomb. He glared at her, started to speak, and then stopped himself. He turned back to Hamp and said firmly, "That doesn't sound like a deal to me, Herr Hampton."

Hamp said, "That's just the beginning. Is there a drink around here?"

Frank groaned low protest but continued to hold his peace. He was almost completely at sea.

Somehow, the Graf must have signalled, since Sepp materialized at a door leading to the back. He bowed and said, "*Bitte, Herr Graf?*"

The mercenary head looked at Hamp, who said, "Cognac, preferably."

Frank sucked breath in and groaned again.

The Graf said, "A bottle of the *Grand Champagne* cognac, the V.V.S.O.P., Sepp, and a glass."

"*Bitte.*" The servant bowed and turned, his limp barely perceptible.

"He won't need the goddamn glass," Frank muttered.

While Sepp was gone, Margit looked at Hamp strangely.

She said, "For some reason, I get the impression that your complexion is lighter than I had at first thought."

Hamp said, offhandedly, "Few American blacks are full-blooded. We have been interbreeding for centuries. One of my grandmothers was a Scot. Before that, I have no idea how many of my ancestors were at least partly white."

"But—your skin," she said, frowning.

"That will be all, Fräulein," the Graf growled.

Sepp entered with an ancient squat bottle and a glass centered on a gold tray. He set the tray on the end table next to the couch on which Hamp sat. The cork had already been removed. Hamp poured with satisfaction. Sepp bowed and withdrew.

Hamp sampled the aged cognac with his nose and sighed. "Damn good brandy," he said, sipping.

Frank rolled his eyes upward in appeal to greater powers.

Lothar von Brandenburg said coldly, "And now, sir, we come to the balance of your deal."

It was then that Peter Windsor re-entered the room. He carried his submachine gun. With all eyes upon him, he took a chair, one that dominated the room.

"That would hardly seem necessary, Peter," the Graf said.

"I jolly well hope not, Chief, but I don't like these two."

The Graf shrugged it off and looked back at Hamp. "Well, sir?"

Hamp said, "When Frank receives his inheritance, I will turn over to you fifty million pseudo-dollars. With it, you can settle down in Switzerland, or wherever else you choose, and announce the, ah, bankruptcy of Mercenaries, Incorporated and your retirement. I would suggest that you take along a dozen or so of your best men, although in Switzerland you should be quite safe. For centuries, avidly sought politicians and others have retired there in high-security villas and lived their lives out in safety."

"Fifty million pseudo-dollars!"

"Take it or leave it," Hamp said, pouring more brandy.

The mercenary head scoffed. "I have never even heard of a black, anywhere in the world, who commanded that amount of credit."

Peter looked at Hamp and said, "You look paler," as though unbelieving. "And I still think you look like somebody I've met before. And your voice, too . . ." He let the sentence dribble away.

The Graf said, "Please, Peter, do be quiet. Well, sir?" This last to Hamp.

Hamp reached into his pocket, brought forth a folder, and tossed it to Margit's lap. "A numbered account in the Grundsbank, in Geneva. Check the balance."

Margit, her face unrevealing as usual while on duty, went to a set of drawers against the wall and opened one of the top ones. Her back was to them. There seemed to be no question but that the Graf was in a position to check the balance of even a numbered account.

After a few minutes of pregnant silence, she turned and said, "The account is considerably higher than the amount mentioned."

The Graf, much of his commanding presence erased, said, breathing deeply, "What else? Confound it, I know there is something else!"

"Oh, yes," Hamp told him, putting down his glass. He bent forward and removed his contact lenses. His eyes, which he directed at Peter Windsor, were a dark blue. "Surprise, surprise," he said. "Show me a bathroom and I'll get the black out of this hair. It looks even prettier, reddish."

The Englishman goggled. "Jeremiah Auburn!" he croaked.

They were all staring now. His complexion was that of a tanned southern European. He fished up into his nose with the nails of his little fingers and brought forth two oval spreaders of metal, his nose losing its broadness.

"But . . . the news broadcasts and the reports from my operatives . . ." Windsor got out.

The Graf roared, "What in the name of God is going on!"

Jerry looked at him with all the emptiness of death in his eyes. He took up the brandy bottle as though to pour again, but before he did he said, "The man who was murdered on the Riviera last night was my brother, James Auburn. You asked me what else; this is what else. I want the man who ordered the death of my twin."

Peter Windsor was on his feet. He sneered, "Are you out of your bloody mind?" He flicked the safety stud on the gun and held it at the ready, but now he turned to his employer of many years. "You would have taken him up, wouldn't you?

You would have sold us all out for his fifty million! Well, thank you very much, but I'm taking over. You'll be washed up with the World Club, but that won't reflect on me. There's still Chase and Moyer who'll back me. And Sheila Duff-Roberts, who has more say about what goes on in the Central Committee than anyone else. It was she who got together with Harrington Chase and suggested the elimination of that McGivern girl and then Auburn, here. She's with me. If I finished you off now, Lothar, I can blame it on Auburn and Pinell and the organization won't question it."

His eyes left the red face of the enraged Graf and went to Margit, who had been sitting through it all, her face noncommittal. "Where do you stand, Fräulein? With me, or with this has-been sod? I can use you in taking over."

Margit cleared her throat softly. "Very dramatic, Peter, and ordinarily I'd have to think about it, perhaps. But as things stand that gun is inoperative."

He chopped out a vicious laugh. "An old trick, Margit old thing, but it won't work. It's loaded, all right. I check that out every day or two. I checked again just before I came back in here. You've taken your stand, you bloody fool."

Margit said mildly, "I didn't say it wasn't loaded. I said it wasn't operative. I didn't like to see the thing around, so I had Sepp take out the firing pin, some time ago."

Peter Windsor swore and pulled the trigger. And then stared down in dismay at the unresponding weapon.

The Graf was on his feet, spry for his age. He turned and dashed for a small cabinet set up against the huge window which dominated the whole side of the room. He grabbed for the top drawer.

But Peter, tennis-trim, bounded after him and, even as he went, reversed the gun. The Graf spun, a small Gyro-jet pistol in hand. Too late. Windsor crashed the gun butt into his solar plexus, sending him reeling backward and into the window and, screaming shrilly, through it in a shower of shards. His thin screams, unbecoming to one of the Graf's image, continued as he plunged downward.

Sepp came into the room quietly, an antique 9mm Luger in his right hand. He took in the scene, his Germanic face politely questioning, still playing the obsequious butler.

Peter snapped, "Sepp, cover these two!" He waved his disabled submachine gun at Frank and Jerry.

Sepp turned to Margit Krebs and his eyebrows went up. "Fräulein?" he said.

"Shoot him," she said flatly. "He just killed the Graf. He'll do the same to us, given the chance."

Peter Windsor yelled, "No!" even as Sepp brought up the automatic and shot him exactly once in the middle of the chest.

Frank, walking like a robot, went over to the window through which Lothar von Brandenburg had plunged. For the briefest of moments he looked out over the superb view of mountain peaks and river. Then his eyes went down.

He shook his head in nausea, pulled in air deeply, and said, "He's splattered all over the side of the swimming pool. Five feet farther out and he would have landed in the water."

Jerry Auburn still bore the brandy bottle in his right hand.

Margit Krebs, efficient as always, went to a wall and pushed back a curtain. Behind it was a microphone. She reached up and touched a switch.

She said, very crisply, "Now hear this. Now hear this. Margit Krebs speaking. The Graf is dead. Those of you near the swimming pool can see his body. Peter Windsor is also dead. They killed each other. Now hear this. Now hear this. The Graf, for reasons of his own, has had the Wolfschloss mined. Within the hour, the schloss will go up. He has thrown the switch. Time is short, but with discipline and complete following of my instructions, we can all be saved. The cable car is totally inadequate for evacuation in such short order. It will be utilized only by the guards and crew who have been in control of it. All others will descend into the bomb shelters and then through the tunnels to the countryside. Women and the more elderly will use the elevators to the bomb shelters. All in good physical trim will use the stairs. The hospital will be evacuated; all patients and medical staff will use the freight chopper to escape. The small jet will be reserved for the senior staff. That is all. Remember, cooperation and discipline will enable us to evacuate completely. Any deviation from my instructions will mean disaster. We will rendezvous in Vaduz for final severance pay and distribution of other funds coming to you. Carry on!'' She turned back to the others.

Jerry looked at her thoughtfully. ''Are there such bombs?''

''No. But I had to clear them out of here before they got the idea of looting.''

''Will they believe you?''

''Yes,'' she said. ''I've been in this job for ten years and I have never lied to any member. I've built up an impeccable record of confidence. Now I'm calling on it. They'll be shocked when I don't turn up at that rendezvous in Vaduz.'' She looked at Sepp. ''You'd better start packing our, ah, luggage; we're heading for Tangier. No extradition there and Interpol will be after us by tomorrow. We should be able to take eight large bags. We four can carry two apiece down to the jet. We're not in too much of a hurry. We want everyone else cleared out of the schloss before we cross the enceinte carrying those bags. You might start with that gold tray with the brandy, Sepp. For God's sake, don't forget any of the paintings small enough to go into the bags; forget the others, no matter how valuable. I'll go to the Graf's private rooms and to the wall safe. I know the combination.''

The impassive Sepp stuck his gun back into his clothing and, taking up the gold tray, left the room.

Jerry said to her, ''How do you know that any of us can fly a jet?''

She was unperturbed. ''Frank, here, told us that he had studied to be a pilot.''

Jerry was looking at her in puzzlement. He said, ''Why did you make the choices you did?''

She shrugged. ''It was all falling apart. You were right, the Graf was all but bankrupt. I found out very early in my relationship with Lothar that in this organization one looks out for oneself. Very well, I have looked out for myself. Had your offer gone through, I might have gone along. The Graf would probably have taken me into retirement with him. As it turned out, when Peter went berserk, I had to play it by ear.''

She turned and left.

Frank glared at Jerry Auburn. ''You damn fool, suppose that gun hadn't been jimmied? We'd all be dead.''

The other grinned at him, a glint in his blue eyes. ''Sometimes you have to take chances. When I saw that gun on his wall, I decided that it was useless. Sooner or later, here in the sanctum sanctorum of the Graf, somebody would have done something to it. Besides, in narrow quarters like this, you can often take a man with a gun before he can finish you off. Why did you think I asked for this bottle of guzzle?'' He grinned again. "I'm a crack shot throwing a bottle."

Frank Pinell took a deep breath. "All right," he said. "How did you pull off that skin-color change?"

The other shrugged. "For a long time we've had chemicals that can change complexion, either lighter or darker. I've known blacks who passed that way, and I once knew a white news reporter who circulated among blacks getting inside information hard for a white man to acquire. He turned himself darker. No big thing."

Frank said, "All right," again. Then, "Windsor got what was coming to him. So did the Graf. I get my inheritance. Margit and Sepp get to loot this place, which should enable them to retire, I suppose. What is there for you, Jerry?"

The other shrugged it off. "For me, there's always the brandy bottle," he said, reaching down for it.

Aftermath

When Jerry Auburn stopped off at Lee Garrett's suite in the Palazzo Colonna, she was gathering her things preparatory to a Central Committee meeting.

She flashed him a smile and said, "Hello, darling. So you're back. Sheila was afraid you wouldn't make it. Where have you been?"

He smiled back at her, which would have been difficult not to do. Lee Garrett, as always, was radiant. He said, "I was just checking out a few things. A few things like the American National Data Banks. Honey, you still make a lousy agent provocateur, spy, or whatever."

She stiffened and then stared at him, at first uncomprehendingly, then slowly it dawned. "Why . . . why, you're that . . . what was his name? Hamp. Hamp, something or other, of the Anti-Racist League. But he was a black and you're white!" She was completely confused.

He grinned at her. "Actually, I'm kind of gray," he said. "Over the generations, I've become so racially mixed I don't know what I am, except that I'm rabidly anti-racist. But to get back to the National Data Banks. It seems that you had a boyfriend. A pretty close boyfriend, which makes me a little jealous of course, since I've been planning on a permanent relationship with you, Lee. And it seems that he had a ranking job in the data banks."

"Why, I don't know what you're talking about."

"Like hell you don't, girl of my dreams. The fact is that you've got a nicely high I.Q. and Ability Quotient but not quite *that* high."

She stared at him, dismayed.

He said, "Your boyfriend jollied around with the equipment so that you were a cinch to be sent here to Rome for a

311

job with the World Club. I doubt if even you expected it to be
quite as good a job as this, though. Now, come on, honey,
what are you really doing here and who was it that you were
really reporting to? And don't tell me your mother.''

She was defiant. "It *was* my mother. She's as opposed to
the World Club's meddling as I am, and as strongly as my
father was. He fought it all of his life and neither my mother
nor I am satisfied about the way he died.''

That took the smile from his face. "They were at it that far
back, eh? So what was his case against us?''

"He wasn't entirely against eventual world government but
he was opposed to it being under control of a handful of Western billionaires, plus a high-ranking police bureaucrat, and a
religious fakir. He was of the opinion that such a government
would stifle healthy competition, which is the source of much
progress. He was absolutely appalled that a State Church was
being considered, not to speak of Mercenaries, Incorporated as
a possible world police. At any rate, mother and I schemed to
have me infiltrated into the World Club to keep an eye on
developments and possibly help expose them.''

Jerry ran the back of a hand over his mouth ruefully.
"Maybe we're not as far apart as all that," he said.

She was still confused. "But you were a member of the
Anti-Racist League.''

"Still am, honey. However, some time ago it seemed to
me that the World Club might offer a quicker way to end
racism, so I got into it, too. As a matter of fact, I belong to
various other outfits. One of them is African-based. They're
fighting racism there—against whites. There's quite a bit of
anti-white bullshit going on in parts of Africa.'' Then he
murmured something that made no sense to her. "Pod Hampton, I wonder if you ever dreamed what the hell you started
when you ripped off that silver.'' He looked at his wrist
chronometer. "But we'd better go to the meeting.''

As they walked the corridor to the conference room, he
looked over at her and said, "How was the news of my
supposed accident on the Riviera received?''

"At first, we were upset," she told him. "We were all
aghast—'' she hesitated—''except possibly Sheila, Chase,
and Moyer. But then, of course, your announcement came
through that it was all a case of mistaken identity.''

He grunted. They reached the Central Committee's conference chamber and a page opened the door for them.

Inside, all the rest were already seated around the heavy oaken table. They were chattering among themselves, two or three more heatedly.

Sheila Duff-Roberts looked up from her papers and said tartly, "Well, Jerry, late as usual, I see."

Jerry Auburn slid into his chair, while Lee took her place next to the committee's secretary. He said, "This will be the last time that will irritate you, Ms. Duff-Roberts."

The majestically proportioned woman looked at him, frowning. "What do you mean by that?"

The buzz about the table fell off as the committee members turned their attention to the two.

Jerry said evenly, "The body of Pamela McGivern has been discovered. After you fired her she began motoring home to Dublin. She was overtaken by a car driven by professional assassins, and run over a mountainside. This type of killing seems to be the latest thing among the pros these days. At any rate, the corpse was hidden, but inadequately."

"That's terrible," Sheila said, seemingly shocked.

"It certainly is," Jerry told her. "It looks as though our Pamela knew too much, so she was turned over to the mercies of Peter Windsor and his boss, the Graf."

All eyes were on him now, a beginning of alarm in those of Harrington Chase and John Warfield Moyer.

Jerry said, "Both Windsor and the Graf are now dead, and Mercenaries, Incorporated dissolved. I was present and heard their last words."

The amazon secretary's face was ashen.

Jerry Auburn went on. "By Central Committee rules, any three members of the committee can remove a secretary. Members Mendel Amschel and Fong Hui got together with me before this meeting and we duly removed Sheila Duff-Roberts."

She was on her feet in fury. She turned blazing eyes to Chase and Moyer, who sat side by side. "Are you going to put up with this?" she demanded.

The big Southwesterner was glaring at Jerry. "It seems precipitous! The rest of us have not been consulted."

Jerry said, completely at ease, "The case of Pamela McGivern is not unique. Harold Dunninger's kidnap death was also engineered by Peter Windsor's men, and that attempt on me which resulted in the death of my brother. In short, ladies and gentlemen, we have narrowly missed imposing on Mother Earth a World Police State, a state more ruthless than any in history, if only because of its universal scope."

Mendel Amschel said quietly to Sheila Duff-Roberts, "And now, if you will leave? If any changes are made in our actions involving you, you will immediately be informed."

She stormed from the room.

The international banker turned his eyes back to Jerry Auburn. "And now, if you will go into the various matters you discussed with Mr. Fong and me earlier today?"

Jerry made himself still more comfortable in his chair. He looked around at the committee members one by one. "If you will excuse the youngest member of this body taking so much time, I will excuse myself by pointing out my recent escape from planned assassination, because I was opposed to certain tendencies recently developing in the World Club. I was also, ah, active in removing the late Lothar von Brandenburg, and it was my agents who discovered what happened to Pamela McGivern."

"Go on," Nils Norden, the Swedish industrialist, said impatiently.

Jerry said, "It has been pointed out that the Central Committee is composed almost exclusively of males, of whites, of westerners, especially Americans, and totally of the wealthy."

"That's as it should be!" Chase boomed, his voice belligerent.

"Is it?" Jerry looked at him. "We meet today to elect a new member to replace Grace Cabot-Hudson. I suggest that we replace not one but four of our membership. I am of the opinion that our goals have shifted from the founding days of our organization and that we should return to them. A world state I think desirable, but not under the domination of the World Club. We should return to investigating the possibilities of the future and even making recommendations, but forswear any attempt to come to power ourselves."

"That's nonsense," the usually taciturn Moyer blurted.

"Who could be more capable than ourselves to govern a world state?"

"Who are we to say?" the Chinese murmured softly.

"I propose," Jerry said, "that we invite a representative of the Space Federation of Lagrangia and the Asteroid Belt Islands to join the Central Committee. It is ridiculous to divorce them from Earthside affairs. Secondly, I suggest that we invite a member of the Wobblies, preferably a woman, since we are so short of female members."

"The Wobblies," Chase boomed. "Those subversives! Those half-assed radicals! They're against everything we stand for."

"That's why we ought to invite them in—to get opinions other than our usual conservatism. Thirdly, I think we should have a representative from the Anti-Racist League. We are talking about a world social order, and surely the so-called colored races are in the overwhelming majority."

"Now I know you've blown a fuse, Auburn," Chase shouted. "A representative from the Anti-Racist League! He'd undoubtedly be a black. We've already got a kike and a chink on this committee and that's too much! Now you'd invite a nigger!"

That ran across the grain with even the usually conservative Nils Norden. "You can be repulsive when you really try, Chase," said Norden.

"Fourth," Jerry pressed on, "we should have another woman representing women's rights. There's still a great deal to be done in that direction, especially in the more backward countries that will eventually be part of the new world society."

The chunky Moyer said, his voice reasonable, "Central Committee rules allow for only ten members on the Central Committee so that it doesn't become unwieldy. Only one is resigning—our respected Grace Cabot-Hudson. Where is the space for all these nominees of yours, Auburn?"

"I propose that three of us resign."

"Who?" Chase blurted, still red of face. "I suppose you are thinking of me! Well, think again!"

Jerry was cool. "I propose that the three be Harrington Chase, John Moyer, and myself. If such resignations are not immediately forthcoming, I shall go further into the details of the deaths of Harold Dunninger, Pamela McGivern, and the attempt to assassinate me."

Silence fell. And continued for long moments.

Finally, the heavyset Chase pushed himself to his feet. He growled to Moyer, "Done! Come on, John, let's get the hell out of this madhouse. They've gone completely around the bend."

When they were gone, there was still long silence.

But then, "Why you, Jeremiah?" It was Fong Hui, his voice typically gentle. "I have always thought of you as a dependable younger member of the committee. Too many of us are elderly."

Jerry looked over at the aged Chinese. "Because, my honorable friend, had I not offered my own resignation, then undoubtedly Chase and Moyer would have fought, and then everything would have broken into the open and possibly the new World Club would never have seen the light of day. Indeed, the old one would have probably gone under." He looked off into an unseen distance and added, his voice low, "Frankly, I'm a mixed-up sonofabitch. And you want to know something else? I suspect so is everybody else. That is, everybody who's trying to make rhyme or reason out of this world we've got on our hands today."

Meyer Amschel said, "It is with regret that I accept your resignation, Jeremiah. However, it occurs to me that perhaps you have some suggestions on those replacements for our suddenly depleted members."

Jerry nodded at that and came to his feet. "I strongly suggest that Ms. Lee Garrett, though with us for such a short time, be appointed secretary to replace Duff-Roberts. She seems to have the qualifications."

Lee sucked in breath in surprise.

"Further," Jerry went on, "to represent the Space Federation, Ian Venner, who is at present in New York. I have no suggestion for the representative from the Wobblies, since I am not very well acquainted with their organization. And, of course, I can hardly recommend a representative for women's rights, though I suggest she be an Oriental."

Fong said, "And the representative of the Anti-Racist League?"

Jerry Auburn said, "From them I would strongly suggest a certain Horace Hampton."